PATH
OF
PERIL

PATH
OF
PERIL

Marlie Parker Wasserman

First published by Level Best Books/Historia 2023

First edition

ISBN: 978-1-68512-240-9

Cover art by Level Best Designs

This book was professionally typeset on Reedsy.
Find out more at reedsy.com

To my family—all of you—with love and appreciation.

"The trip to Panama to see the canal was one of those small, luminous events that light up an era."

— DAVID MCCULLOUGH, THE PATH BETWEEN THE SEAS

Praise for Path of Peril

"Nothing better than settling down with a good, crisp, detail-rich assassination thriller. Someone is after Theodore Roosevelt, and author Marlie Wasserman tightens the screws, ratchets the tension, and twists the plot again and again. Read it."—William Martin, *New York Times* Bestselling Author of *The Lincoln Letter* and *December '41*

"A feast of characters, scenery and history, Wasserman sets the table for a tremendous read. *Path of Peril* is a privileged walk with TR, his wife, his staff and dozens of characters struggling to create one of the "greatest engineering feats of the century."—Chris Keefer, author of *No comfort for the Undertaker,* a Carrie Lisbon Mystery

"Wasserman's new novel, set around President Teddy Roosevelt's visit to the Panama Canal in 1906, is more than just a historical crime novel. Her wonderful style of writing and her painstaking research into how assassins behave makes this book a must for readers. . . . In her profiles of the assassins, she does an excellent job of humanizing them but not excusing their actions or making them out to be heroes. *Path of Peril* is enjoyable and engaging and places the reader at the center of a fast, explosive and intriguing plot—making this new book one that should not be missed."—Mel Ayton, author of *Plotting to Kill the President*

"Wasserman's *Path of Peril* gives readers an exciting leap back in time, to Teddy Roosevelt's 1906 visit to Panama to drum up support for continued work on the canal. The plot focuses on potential threats to the president's life, but the multiple narrators depict fascinating changes in Panama itself

i

set off by separation from Colombia, construction of the largest engineering work to that time, influxes of foreigners to the canal, and U.S. accession to great power status due to its commercial and industrial development. These themes intertwine mysteriously with real and fictitious scenes right out of old-timey albums and stereographs. The book keeps us in suspense until the end, although we know that TR ultimately survives. And we grow to care about some of the actors, a mélange of immigrants from all corners of the planet. Buy this book—you'll love it!"—Michael Conniff, historian of Panama

Cast of Characters

In the list below I include most of the characters in *Path of Peril*, except for well-known people such as John Wilkes Booth and William Howard Taft. I use boldface type for actual historical figures. The names in standard type are products of my imagination. The abbreviation ICC stands for Isthmus Canal Commission, the Panama Canal Zone's governing body, and TR is short for President Theodore Roosevelt.

- Alberto Agresti, anarchist from Paterson, New Jersey, husband of Ernesta Agresti
- Ernesta Agresti, wife of Alberto Agresti
- Caterina Alcalde, wife of Roland Caldwell
- **Manual Amador Guerrero, President of Panama**
- **Maria de la Ossa de Amador, first lady of Panama**
- **James Amos, valet to TR**
- Milton Anderson, former Pinkerton detective, on payroll of John D. Rockefeller
- Arenas, Valeria, matriarch of a leading family of Panama, and wife of Tomas
- Tomas Arenas, patriarch of a leading family of Panama and husband of Valeria
- Harvey Bell, railroad ticket agent
- **Sturges Bennett, manufacturer in nineteenth-century Connecticut**
- **Alexander Berkman, anarchist, lover of Emma Goldman**
- **William Bierd, General Manager of the Panama Railroad**
- **Poultney Bigelow, American journalist**

- **Joseph Bishop, ICC Secretary**
- Aaron Blake, carpenter at Ancon Hospital
- **Charles Bonaparte, U.S. Attorney General, 1906-1909**
- Steven Bonner, policeman in Panama, born in Texas
- Menora Bradford, ICC teacher
- **Gaetano Bresci, assassin of King Umberto I of Italy**
- **S.E. Brewster, ICC recruiting agent**
- **William Broadhead, union leader in Sheffield, England**
- Emily Byrne, immigrant to Panama, of Irish descent, sex worker
- George Caldwell, brother of Roland, owner of Northern Vermont Lumber
- Roland Caldwell, brother of George, real estate agent, husband of Caterina Alcalde
- Alejandro Calvo, immigrant from Spain, leader of work gang
- **Gilbert Carter, Governor of Barbados**
- Bonnie Clifford, Edith Roosevelt's maid
- Henry Coleman, ICC teacher
- John Connell, ICC Assistant Chairman
- **William Craig, bodyguard for TR, died 1902**
- Marjorie Hunter, one-time girlfriend of Roland Caldwell
- **Stephen Crane, American novelist**
- John Cunningham, ICC foreman
- **Anton Czolgosz, assassin, killed President McKinley**
- **Florence Dauchy, wife of Walter Dauchy**
- **Walter Dauchy, ICC division engineer, wife of Florence Dauchy**
- **Ferdinand de Lesseps, entrepreneur behind French attempt to build canal**
- **Herbert de Lisser, Editor in Chief of the *Jamaican Gleaner***
- **Jules Dingler, Director General of the canal under the French**
- **⌐rancis Drake, lawyer and politician living in Iowa**
- **⌐x Ehrman, American Vice-Consul General to Panama**
- **⌐s Warren Fairbanks, U.S. Vice President, 1905-1909**
- wler, owner of Troy Building Supply, uncle to Jeffrey Fowler

- Gregory Fowler, son of Jeffrey and Liza Fowler
- Jeffrey Fowler, ICC division engineer, husband of Liza, nephew of Daniel
- Liza Fowler, wife of Jeffrey Fowler
- **William Gerig, ICC division officer**
- **Benjamin Gilbert, manufacturer in nineteenth-century Connecticut**
- **Emma Goldman, American activist**
- Señora Gomez, hotel proprietor
- Tom Gordon, meat peddler, roommate of Godfrey Moody
- **Dr. William Crawford Gorgas, ICC Chief Sanitary Officer**
- Stefano Grandi, silk weaver and anarchist, brother-in-law of Salvatore Scarpetta
- **Julia Grant, daughter of mayor of Troy, New York, wife of New York City mayor**
- **A.H. Grey, Bucyrus steam shovel operator**
- Magnus Gustafsson, pseudonym for Arthur Sitwell
- **Ernest "Red" Hallen, photographer**
- **William Stewart Halsted, physician who trained Robert Peterson**
- Adelle Hart, one-time girlfriend of Robert Peterson
- Elsa Hunter, boarding house owner
- **William Karner, ICC engineer and recruiter**
- **Jerome Kehl, disturbed Chilean**
- Knox family, sugar plantation owners in Barbados
- **Clara Latta, wife of Maurice Latta**
- **Maurice Latta, Assistant Secretary to TR, husband of Clara Latta**
- Bruce Lighter, foreman in Jeffrey Fowler's crew
- **Francis B. Loomis, Assistant Secretary of State**
- **William Loeb, Secretary to TR**
- **Joe Lonardo, gang leader in Cleveland, becomes crime boss**
- **Alice Roosevelt Longworth, daughter of TR and Alice Lee Roosevelt**
- Maureen McGowan, nurse at Ancon Hospital

- **Claude Coventry Mallet, British Consul to Panama**
- Elliott Marsh, son of Katy Marsh and Elliott Bulloch Roosevelt
- Katy Marsh, seamstress in New York City, maid to Elliott Bulloch Roosevelt
- John Marston, manager at Gilbert & Bennett
- Sally Miller, brothel owner, mother of Sean Miller
- Sean Miller, son of Sally Miller
- **Ignacio Molina, owner of boardinghouse shelled by battleship**
- Godfrey Moody, laborer, roommate of Tom Gordon
- Sarah Murphy, foremother of Emily Byrne
- John O'Malley, ICC security manager for commissaries
- **Frederick Palmer, foreign correspondent**
- Paul Pearson, Lincoln, Illinois station master
- Robert Peterson, doctor at Ancon Hospital
- **Ernest Ransome, engineer and innovator with concrete**
- **Walter Reed, physician and medical researcher**
- **Larry Richey, Secret Service agent, aka Larry Ricci**
- **Presley Marion Rixey, Surgeon General**
- **Maria Roda, anarchist and activist in New Jersey**
- **Alice Lee Roosevelt, first wife of TR**
- **Archibald Roosevelt, son of TR and Edith Roosevelt**
- **Edith Kermit Carow Roosevelt, second wife of TR**
- **Eleanor Roosevelt, daughter of Elliott Bulloch Roosevelt, niece of TR**
- **Elliott Bulloch Roosevelt, brother of TR, father of** Elliott Marsh and **Eleanor**
- **Ethel Roosevelt, daughter of TR and Edith Roosevelt**
- **Kermit Roosevelt, son of TR and Edith Roosevelt**
- **Quentin Roosevelt, son of TR and Edith Roosevelt**
- **Theodore Roosevelt, President**
- **Theodore Roosevelt, Jr., son of TR and Edith Roosevelt**
- **David Ross, ICC purchasing agent**
- Anthony Santelli, Chicago horse groomer, anarchist, brother of Emilio

- J.C. Virden, miner, labor organizer
- **John Findley Wallace, Chief Engineer of the canal, preceded John Stevens**
- James Walsh, forefather of Emily Byrne
- Edgar Winston, British diplomat, assistant to Claude Coventry Mallet
- Shing Wong, store proprietor, son of Wong Kong Yee, accomplice to Arthur Sitwell
- **Wong Kong Yee, shop owner, killed by Colombian shell, father of Shing Wong**
- Lorenzo Zampa, American businessman who traveled to Panama
- Characters with no surnames: Mei and Madeleine, sex workers at La Boheme

Maurice Latta

For forty-one years I honored my oath to President Theodore Roosevelt and his bodyguard to conceal the events of November 15th and November 17th, 1906. On each of those days I agreed to a conspiracy of silence. Last year, that bodyguard died, and TR is long dead. Before I follow them to the grave, I will disclose the perils we faced during the President's historic trip to Panama, to clarify the record and to unburden myself.

My tale begins in the White House clerk's office, where I served as a stenographer during the McKinley administration and where I serve now, with a higher title, fifty years later. At first, I felt no connection with the other fifteen fellows in the clerk's office. I suppose I looked the part, with my regular features and unremarkable bearing. If my appearance fit in, my background did not. Most men working for the President, even at the turn of the century, were college boys. Some had taken the grand tour of Europe. A few had gone to universities in New England. Three, fancying themselves adventurers, had traveled to the West with President Roosevelt, that is, President Theodore Roosevelt. Two of the older gentlemen had been heroes in battles in the South during the Civil War. Most of the White House office workers had nothing to prove, to the President or to themselves.

I followed a different path to Washington. After an unmemorable youth on a Pennsylvania farm, I moved to Oklahoma, where I took my first job

1

as a junior clerk. I filled in paperwork for the more memorable 1893 land rush. Over time my responsibilities and the commands of the head clerk grew distasteful. A friend back in Pennsylvania recommended me for a position as a clerk for a state senator in Harrisburg. I worked for that state senator for one year and two months. Forgive the precision—I like to be accurate with details. Then the legislator was elected to Congress and took me to Washington. Three years later, almost to the day, word spread across town that President William McKinley's office needed a stenographer. By that time I had married Clara Hays Bullen and had two sons. I aimed to improve my lowly position and my meager salary.

I moved down Pennsylvania Avenue from the Capitol to the White House. My official duties, those that were known, started on August 8, 1898. Three years and one month after I started, all hell broke loose in the office. Of course I wouldn't have used such language then. Leon Czolgosz, an anarchist, assassinated President McKinley. Like other Americans, I felt sorrowful. I had seen McKinley pass down the hall daily, but I had never been introduced to him and he never spoke to me.

My clerk's job continued. Theodore Roosevelt became President. Little changed in the routines of our office, except now the President knew me by my first and last name. Maurice Latta. To be precise, Maurice Cooper Latta.

When the President's Secretary, William Loeb, promoted me from Stenographic Clerk to Assistant Secretary on June 4, 1906, I hoped I might have the opportunity to travel, at least up and down the East Coast. Two months later, I heard rumors that TR wanted to assess progress on his canal. Oh, let me interrupt myself for a moment. While conducting my official capacities, I called the President President Roosevelt. Informally I called him TR. By the way, he was the first president to be known by his initials. And some called him Teddy, though I never did so. I am told his relatives called him Teedie. You will hear all these names in my tale.

This trip would be the first time a president, while in office, had ever left the United States. Many Americans thought a president should not travel to foreign soil. That seems odd to us now, after Versailles and Yalta. But in 1906 most Americans didn't give much thought to the rest of the world, not until TR changed that.

I assumed Secretary Loeb, always interested in the press, would accompany the President to the canal. Mr. Loeb would want to shape the stories in the dailies and weeklies. Reporters called him Stonewall Loeb because of the way he controlled their access to the President. To my shock, Mr. Loeb asked me to go in his place.

Today, even after working in the executive offices of nine administrations, now for President Truman (no, I never call him Give 'Em Hell Harry), and managing a staff of 204 clerks, my title, a rather misleading title, is only Executive Clerk. I am proud, though, that the *New York Times* has acknowledged my worth. Four years ago, in a Christmas day article my family framed, the reporter wrote, "The actual 'assistant president'. . . is an official who has been in the White House since 1898 and knows more about its procedure than anyone else. He is Maurice C. Latta, now seventy-four and known as 'Judge' Latta to the White House staff." In truth I know more about what is happening, and what did happen, than most of the presidents I served. That statement is for this memoir only.

I won't dwell on my years in the White House after Panama, but rather on four days in 1906, in and around the Canal Zone. For the public, I want to add to the historical record, which is silent on certain momentous events. For me and my family, I want to remember the turning point, when I came to realize both my limitations and my strengths. I am writing the tale of what I know, what I saw myself. If you wish, you can fill in gaps with stories you gather from the others present that November, the stories I couldn't see.

William Loeb

"I'm tired, Maurice. I followed that wild man to Yellowstone and Yosemite three years ago. Still haven't recovered. None of us could keep up with him." Mr. Loeb, Secretary to the President, was talking to me about Theodore Roosevelt's two-month-long trip to the West. "Now he's sailing to Panama. He'll itch for another frenzied schedule. I can't do it this time. Here's the question. Are you ready for that kind of a trip? Interested in going in my place? I'm forty, you're thirty-six. Those four extra years make a difference, right?

William Loeb sat three feet away from my face at his desk in the White House. When he questioned me, he leaned forward, putting his square jaw one foot from my weaker jaw. What answer did he expect? Modesty? Confidence?

"You surprise me, sir. I have never traveled beyond Oklahoma. I have never sailed, and I've never been responsible for a presidential trip. But I have watched you. I assisted you from afar when you traveled with the President. I will be honest, it would be a big step for me. I wouldn't want to disappoint."

Mr. Loeb sat back, slouched. I had disappointed him already.

"Sir, if you will walk me through the responsibilities, I would be honored to accompany the President."

I will never know if Mr. Loeb truly believed I could handle the job, or if he had no one else in reserve. He shook my hand, sealing the arrangement. A day later, he called me back to his office for instructions.

"Above all, Maurice, keep to the schedule. I'll help you prepare it. We start with essential meetings. Officials of Panama and representatives from other countries. Then we fill in as needed." Mr. Loeb was in his element, flaunting his expertise. "Second, control the access of journalists. Give priority to Frederick Palmer, he's a favorite of Teddy's. And I've been asked to add in a local journalist named Herbert de Lisser. Limit access to those two. Manage the press like I do. Third, names. Keep on you, in your pocket, the identities of the people Teddy is to meet. Whisper him reminders. He's smart, but that makes him seem even smarter. Fourth, keep notes. You'll need them later for Teddy's reports. Last, prioritize telegrams. The pundits are worried that the President, abroad for the first time, won't be in charge of the business of the country. I've reminded them that telegrams will reach his ship and will reach Panama. Sort through dispatches when they arrive and make sure he deals with them."

I feared Mr. Loeb would notice my twitching right leg. Instead, he looked down and hesitated. For more than a second.

"I need to be frank with you about another matter. There could be danger. Jimmy Sloan, the Secret Service agent who heads Teddy's protection detail, he tells me he hears rumors of anarchist plots against the President. He has people checking ships arriving in Panama, looking for suspicious travelers. May not matter. Hunting for an assassin is like finding a needle in a haystack. And there's more. Mrs. R. is frantic. Jimmy—fine to call him Jimmy—won't talk to her. Teddy tells him not to. She tries to get information from me, and I won't talk to her either. She'll see you as easy prey and try you too. A word to the wise—be wary of that elegant lady. She's lived through three assassinations, and she's no fool."

I could think of nothing to say. I was so anxious about my coming secretarial duties that I had forgotten about the President's safety.

"Enough of the serious stuff," Mr. Loeb said. Get yourself new clothing for the trip. Two suits and evening wear. Can't have you looking like a farmer." He must have seen me widen my eyes in a question.

"No extra allowance for that. Hope your Assistant Secretary's salary will stretch."

Edith Roosevelt

November 1906

Edith Kermit Carow Roosevelt married late, at age twenty-five, pleased to be Theodore's second wife. His first, empty-headed Alice Lee, had been prettier, but only her memory was competition. Society column reporters called Edith an elegant, good-looking woman. Even the carpers acknowledged that her sharp nose and chin didn't mar the impression. Those reporters never called her intelligent, but she knew she was that, and Theodore knew too. At age forty-five, after five children and two miscarriages, the last just three years earlier, she remained slender and attractive.

In the White House, Edith stayed busy, watching over sons Ted, Kermit, Archibald, and Quentin, her daughter Ethel, and her rambunctious stepdaughter Alice. Thank goodness Alice had just married, even if it was to Nicholas Longworth III, a bald politician, much older than Alice, with a reputation as a playboy. The wedding nine months earlier had been the social event of the season in Washington. With that extravaganza over, Edith's burdens did not disappear, but she could begin to reorder them. The stepdaughter now moved from second place to third. Worries about Quentin, her youngest, and his mischievous antics rose to second.

Fear for Theodore remained first in Edith's list of worries. The year before, she convinced her husband to buy a rustic house known as Pine Knot in the Blue Ridge Mountains of Virginia. A private retreat. Almost private. Always watchful, she arranged for two Secret Service agents to protect the house every evening without the President's knowledge.

Sounds. They drove her crazy. The pulsating wind and the rattle of cedar shingles at Pine Knot. The scraping sounds of old window frames and squeaky plumbing at the White House. With each sound, Edith heard an alarm. She had trusted Theodore's first bodyguard, "Big Bill" Craig. In a carriage accident four years earlier, Bill died, and Theodore was injured. Now Jimmy Sloan oversaw protection. Jimmy was a good agent. Could even a good agent handle the task ahead? The trip to Panama would attract an international cast of cranks. Edith hoped they were cranks, not trained assassins. After each attempt on Theodore's life, a reporter invariably mentioned the statistics. Three of the last ten presidents had been assassinated, three in about forty years, all in her lifetime. She imagined these numbers branded on her forehead.

Edith needed to identify a member of the trip's entourage who might keep her informed about threats. Jimmy Sloan and his agents had pledged secrecy. Or they dismissed a woman's worries. Thought her hysterical. They would be no help. And Theodore refused to acknowledge her fears, refused to listen. Thought she didn't notice he carried a pistol in his pocket when he mingled with crowds. She would think creatively. She would curry favor with someone else on the trip, someone with knowledge. Maybe that Assistant Secretary who was taking the place of Secretary Loeb. Maurice Latta. He might know, and he might share. She would keep an eye out for him aboard ship.

Maurice Latta

I n the three weeks between Secretary Loeb's invitation and my departure for Panama, I worked during the week on the President's schedule and during the weekend on my wardrobe. Clara helped me select new finery, which took a large chunk out of our savings. We bought two of everything for daytime, one set to wear and a second set to pack in my equally new valise. And one tailcoat, with pants and a matching vest for evening wear. All our purchases except the valise would prove to be wrong for the sweltering weather to come.

On November 8th, I donned a wool suit with a matching single-breasted vest, new black boots that went over my ankles, and a shirt with a stiff, detachable collar. Clara and my sons walked me to the White House, admiring my appearance and wishing me bon voyage. I took leave of my beloved family, then climbed into the designated carriage, trailing the President's carriage to the Washington Navy Yard. I sat next to Surgeon General Rixey, the President's physician. He had attended President McKinley on his deathbed, unsuccessfully. Once in the Navy Yard, Dr. Rixey and I boarded the President's yacht, the luxurious 273-foot *Mayflower*. The Navy gave TR a twenty-one-gun salute and a chorus sang The Star-Spangled Banner. Early in my career, the sort of pomp and circumstance that surrounded our departure impressed me. It still does.

The *Washington Times* commemorated the day, printing on the front page four photographs clustered together—TR, Mrs. Edith Roosevelt, who I would come to know, Dr. Rixey, and me. Clara saved that page in a scrapbook, which we have to this day.

The *Mayflower* sailed down the Potomac to Piney Point, Maryland, then past Wolf Trap Light into Chesapeake Bay. We boarded the USS *Louisiana*, the largest battleship in the fleet, 16,000 tons, carrying 827 crew and officers (I had counted). I hid my excitement. I had never been on any vessel larger than a rowboat. Peeking into every deck and battery, I saw new life rafts and emergency provisions for six days. I worried about those preparations. I need not have worried about an ocean disaster.

Frederick Palmer

Tuesday, November 13, 1906, to Wednesday, November 14, 1906

F rederick Palmer breakfasted at his hotel, Panama City's respectable Gomez House. He sipped the last of his morning coffee at the table set with chipped Royal Copenhagen China, atop a clean, if slightly frayed, lace cloth. He flicked a few crumbs off his beard and full mustache. The other hotel guests at the table pattered about the hot and humid weather, which was perennially the case, and President Roosevelt's visit, which was unprecedented. Señora Gomez, the hotel's proprietor, stood stiffly in attendance in her ruffled blue dress, participating in the discussion only as needed. She or the simply dressed young Jamaican maid she employed would be ready with more toast and hot tea and strong coffee, as important to the Gomez's reputation as its comfortable and reasonably priced rooms.

Palmer fidgeted. He went over the checklist in his mind, half listening to the guests' voices. The things he had to do today and in the next three days. He couldn't relax. He knew he would begin with an exploratory walk, his common practice on any new assignment. He waited until talk around the table subsided. "Señora, thank you for breakfast. I have a question. How far is the cathedral, the one in the central plaza?"

He felt relieved when she answered his predictable question in English, though he might have managed to struggle through Spanish directions. "Just a few blocks to the right, Señor."

11

The balder and portlier of the two gentlemen remaining at the breakfast table nodded in assent. "Don't expect St. Peter's," he said. Palmer detected the drawn-out sounds of the American South.

Palmer noticed Señora Gomez frown. The central plaza was the spiritual and social heart of Panama City, so the proprietress may have taken the disagreeable guest's comment personally. Or perhaps she observed, as Palmer had, that this guest had kept his eye a little too long on the maid. Palmer noticed, too, that the second man at the table, slimmer, fairer, much taller, and more serious than the wisecracker, appeared uninterested in the discussion and only somewhat interested in the maid. When the tall guest asked for more tea, Palmer detected a British accent, not posh, maybe from Yorkshire. Waving goodbyes, Palmer walked out the door into the blinding sunshine of a warm Panama City morning. The smell of toast yielded immediately to the smell of rotting fruit that littered the sidewalks. He could manage the smell now since it was less intense than in Colón, where he had arrived the day before.

As a war correspondent, or what would come to be known too as a foreign correspondent, Frederick Palmer had always looked for the next big overseas assignment. His employers had sent him to the Klondike, to Greece, China, Korea, Japan, the Philippines, but he had missed out on Cuba and didn't want to let go of any of the other great stories of his day. Now TR was about to visit the isthmus—a word even Palmer had to look up in *Webster's* before leaving New York—for what the newspapers were billing as the first time a president while in office had ever stepped out of the forty-five states. Palmer would be there with TR and knew how to write quickly and to scamper to the telegraph to file his dispatches. Scampering might not even be necessary on this trip, because now he was working for a weekly, and his story was not scheduled to run until December 8th. He could take the time to go about his job methodically. His weekly magazine had agreed with his plan to arrive in Panama on November 13th, giving him almost two days to explore the country before the hoopla of TR's scheduled arrival mid-day on November 15th.

All had gone according to plan. On the 13th, Palmer had arrived in Colon, one of two port cities in Panama. He had sailed on the *Advance*, an aging steamer. The quarters on the *Advance* were crowded, dirty, and the food despicable, but he was used to such conditions, and at least the sea was calm. The steamship stopped in Bridgetown to board thirty Negros who had labor contracts to build the canal. Since they were confined to below decks, Palmer saw little of them. He did hear them. Their chants persisted in his memory, in an unfamiliar lingo. The melody had stayed in his head, not the words. He remembered only the refrain. *Somebody's dying every day*.

After disembarking from the *Advance* and overcoming his sea legs, Palmer explored Colon. He watched the activity on the wharf. Young and old Negro women, some balancing trays of fruit and some standing and staring intently at arriving ships, waited for passengers hungry for food. Foremen driving rickety wagons came to pick up new recruits. Drivers of coaches loitered, eager to take passengers to the town's mostly shabby boarding houses. Palmer experimented to see if shallow breaths lessened the stench, but soon he gave up and filled his lungs. The mass of people on the wharf seemed unaware of the smell. He turned away from the wharf toward the town.

The stories he had heard from others about the filth were understated. Keeping to the raised wooden platforms that served as sidewalks, Palmer could avoid the mud, but barely. One of his talky shipmates told him that the platforms were new, in honor of the President's coming visit, and they were an improvement over the previous swamp-like conditions. Hard to imagine. He would need to find a tactful way of describing Colon's filth for his news magazine. But there would be no polite way to describe the smells of overripe fruit, sweating bodies, and the animal excrement that littered the mud beside the dirty wooden boardwalks. Palmer did not think of himself as fastidious, especially not after reporting from the Klondike and China. At times he couldn't bathe for weeks. But this month, he would be in the company of officials, not of other unwashed journalists. He readjusted his straw hat to achieve the more stylish angle he saw on others. He forced himself to concentrate on what he saw, not what he smelled.

Palmer had left Colon at noon the previous day, riding on the Panama

Railroad southeast to the other port, Panama City, where he walked this morning. He had arranged this side trip to see the landscape in advance of the President's arrival. The railroad car wasn't bad, with its prickly straw seats and separate cars for different classes. Most of the passengers sat quietly, aside from a few men rambling on about the President's visit. The three-hour, forty-seven-mile trip across the isthmus went quickly and served its purpose. Out the smudged window, covered with dead and dying insects of species he didn't recognize, he stared at the jungle and the mountains in the distance.

With a little effort, Palmer opened the window near his seat, letting in flies and muggy air. Still no breeze. He could hear low-pitched growls, almost constant. He must have looked puzzled. A friendly passenger sitting across the aisle explained. The angry chants came from howler monkeys. Palmer could make out groups of them in the nearby trees. Farther along, he heard the shrill cries of macaws, probably the scarlet macaws in the fauna books he had consulted in New York but were too heavy to pack. He strained to listen as he felt sweat beading down his back.

Worried he couldn't remember all these oddities, Palmer grabbed his worn leather notebook with its crushed corners. The pages of the notebook stuck together just as his shirt clung to his damp neck. He jotted down "palm trees," writing next to those words, "corozo variety?" He had read about those. "Different from palms in the Philippines?" Those he had seen the previous year.

At points, the jungle cleared for a mile or so. Then Palmer saw the rusting metal equipment the French left behind when they abandoned their own efforts at digging a canal. Train cars lying on their sides, steam shovels covered with grime and twisting vines, sheds leaning at a precarious angle. Hulking monuments to defeat. Palmer stuck his head out the window, into the muggy air, thinking he might see Compagnie Universelle du Canal Interoceanique painted on the equipment. If those words had ever been there, they were long gone.

After each patch of ruined equipment, he saw a different scene—a bigger patch of shiny new equipment and buildings announcing the American

14

presence. Some war correspondents called it triumphal presence. The sounds changed when the new equipment came into view. He heard the deafening noise of drilling. Palmer watched as the passenger who identified the howlers closed his window to muffle the noise. Palmer followed suit. In future years, when Palmer thought back over his days in Panama, he would forget the howling and the drilling, but would remember the mugginess, the lush vegetation, and the rolling of the train. These would register in his mind as a single sensation, melded with reflections on the course of events.

By dinner time, Palmer arrived in Panama City. Stifling air, just like in Colon, but this city looked cleaner, and its colonial-style buildings appeared substantial and impressive. After a short walk, he found the Gomez, a pleasant boarding house recommended by the same shipmate who had warned him about Colón's mud.

This morning, November 14th, with the help of Señora Gomez's directions, his first stop would be the cathedral. From Mr. Loeb's confidential memorandum, which had arrived in New York from the White House two weeks earlier, Palmer knew that the cathedral—or at least the front of it, opening onto the plaza—would be the principal stop on the President's itinerary, where he would be welcomed and could offer greetings in return. The *Catedral Basílica Santa Maria la Antigua.* Unlike many of his fellow journalists, Palmer thoroughly researched his assigned locations—flora, fauna, and physical settings. If he could observe the plaza's architecture and sight lines now, then later, he could concentrate on TR's speech.

Finding the cathedral easily, Palmer stopped to admire the colonial plaza at the foot of Ancon Hill. On three sides, the square was surrounded by offices, along with multi-story masonry houses and apartment buildings. Ornamental wrought-iron balconies decorated the second and third stories. Many of the buildings had French doors with louvers on all levels, reminding him of New Orleans. The cobblestone and brick streets leading into the plaza followed the grid pattern he had seen in Spanish colonial towns. At the edge of the plaza, two purple jacaranda trees struggled for light in the square, where the buildings on the eastern side blocked the sun. This is where TR would give his address on Thursday, Palmer thought, with no premonition.

On the west side of the plaza, along Calle 7a Este, he saw the gray stone cathedral with mother-of-pearl decorations inlaid on its two white towers. As the crotchety boarder warned at breakfast, the cathedral appeared less imposing than the ones Palmer had visited in Europe. It rose over the plaza, but without a commanding presence. Palmer was only thirty-three, but he had seen more of the grand cathedrals of the world than anyone he knew.

The few men and women walking in the plaza appeared well-dressed. Not the latest of fashions, but more than respectable. In a corner of the plaza, a group of Negro workers unloaded bunting and banners from wagons, speaking to each other in what Palmer thought was English, or something close to English. Similar to the dialect he heard a few days earlier from laborers on the *Advance*? Another group of workers sorted through versions of the country's new flag—a rectangle divided into four quarters, two white, one red, one blue. Workers' voices rang across the plaza as they shouted hello to each other. Palmer imagined that even in black and white, the bunting and flags would show well in any photographs Red Hallen would take that week. The two men knew each other. Palmer, through his connections, had recommended Hallen to photograph the President's trip.

For the next two hours, Palmer wandered, memorizing the layout of streets and dodging puddles. At least here, in Panama City, he had a chance of keeping his cuffs clean, unlike in Colón. Sweating under his straw hat, eager to escape the noon sun, Palmer entered a Chinaman's shop two short blocks off the plaza. Brightly colored silk kimonos hanging in the shop's window tempted passersby. Inside, Palmer thought he smelled incense, or the scent of herbs used for healing. He surveyed the tobacco, spices, silks, pots and pans, trying to cool down for a few minutes.

On a table covered with knickknacks, Palmer glimpsed a used map for sale, folded in a fan shape. He spread it out. The map was larger and more detailed than the small map in the atlas he had brought with him from New York. The long shape of Panama went from the top left of the map, near the Caribbean, diagonally across to the bottom right, near the Pacific. He could see lines with cross hatches for the railroad he had traveled on the previous day, spanning the full diagonal of the isthmus. Two dot-and-dash lines ran parallel to the railroad, on each side of it, indicating the ten-mile-wide Canal Zone administered by Americans. Colon and Panama City, oddly, were outside the Zone. He could see the names of the towns spread out along the spine of the railroad—first Colón in the northwest, then Cristobal, Silver City, Gatun, Gorgona, Matachin, Las Cascadas, Empire, Culebra Cut, Paraiso, Red Tank, La Boca, and finally Ancon and Panama City, where he stood now, at the southeast, on the bottom of the map. With mild curiosity, he noted that someone had scribbled the words "gold town" in pencil next to Cristobal and the words "silver town" next to Empire, Las Cascadas, Paraiso, Red Tank, and of course, Silver City. If he thought about the use of the words silver and gold at all, he might have guessed that the Spanish had hunted for those minerals when they grabbed Panama. He would learn the uses of those words later.

Speaking clearly and slowly, Palmer asked the surprisingly young Chinaman behind the counter, "What can you tell me about this map?"

"It was owned by an engineer from Alabama. He was only in the Canal Zone for six months. Then he got scared by Yellow Fever and left." The Chinaman sniggered. "I don't think he wanted anything to remind him of this place. Hmmm, you don't seem as frightened of Yellow Fever as most people who hear that story. I always add, don't worry, that was before Dr. Gorgas did the cure." Palmer nodded. He knew Gorgas had eradicated the disease. The Chinaman paused. "I can sell the map to you for three dollars, U.S."

Palmer wasn't sure that the magazine he was writing for would cover that cost, but he needed the detailed map to make sense of the place. He pulled bills out of his wallet. As he did so, he noted that the Chinaman was unusually talkative. Palmer recognized an opportunity for news. "Your English is good," he said, with the question implied.

"My new customers are surprised. I grew up in Panama and went to school here, with an American teacher.

"Ah, now I understand. How long has your family lived here?

"My father came from China, but I never knew China."

17

"Well, as strange as this may seem, I have been to China. In 1900 I reported on the Boxer Rebellion. I went to Shanghai on the East Coast and Tianjin in the North."

The Chinaman's face showed surprise.

"Let me introduce myself. I'm Frederick Palmer. As I said, I'm a reporter, a foreign correspondent. I've been sent here for a magazine in New York, *Collier's*—have you heard of it?—they've never sent a reporter here before—to wire them stories about the President's visit. Your map might help me understand the landscape of the isthmus."

"You have been to China, and I have not." The shopkeeper's expression continued to show surprise. "My name is Shing Wong. Now I own this store." He drew out the word own longer than necessary. Palmer knew to look impressed, as he was.

"Are you here to help build the canal?"

"Oh, no," Palmer said. "I doubt I could build much of anything. But I observe what the others build. That's what the President plans to do too. Observe. Right?"

Shing Wong hesitated. Took a few seconds to talk this time.

"I heard that Teddy landed in Colón already, a day ahead of schedule," Shing Wong said with a self-important grin. "You might want to hurry there to see all the hoopla."

Shing Wong must have noticed Palmer's puzzled look. "I'm certain."

"Damn. How did you find out he's already here?" Just a smirk from the Chinaman, no answer. Now Palmer would need to retrace, in the other direction, the trip he had just made, a day sooner than expected. To get the story and get it soon enough to please his New York editor, Palmer would have to rush back to Colón.

"Apologies. I'm usually more polite. You've given me a good update." He folded his map and pocketed it in his jacket, turning to leave.

"I keep my ears to the ground," Shing Wong said as he watched the journalist exit his store. Palmer had a remarkable memory, but he would forget the end of this conversation.

Maurice Latta, Edith Roosevelt

Saturday, November 10, 1906, to Wednesday, November 14, 1906

Aboard the USS *Louisiana*, I spent the voyage to Panama assuring myself I could fill in admirably for Secretary Loeb, assuring myself that the entourage wouldn't dismiss me because I was merely TR's Assistant Secretary, assuring myself that I would act efficiently and responsibly for our country. I also spent a few minutes each day thanking the Lord I did not suffer from seasickness on my first ocean voyage. The bottle of Lyon's ginger extract that Clara slipped into my valise remained unopened.

While aboard, I made the acquaintance of other members of the entourage, including the three Secret Service agents who guard the President. Jimmy Sloan headed the protection detail. Despite Jimmy's informal nickname and Santa Claus-like full cheeks, he spoke and acted with authority. Next in line of seniority came stocky Frank Tyree. The junior man was Larry Richey. Their names were familiar to me because back in the White House, Mr. Loeb referred to them often, calling them the three muscleteers, his private pun. All three looked as though they could tackle an enemy, especially Larry. He was average height, nice-looking, and above all, powerfully built. I noticed his good looks and from ship gossip, so did Mrs. Roosevelt's maid, a young woman who comes into my tale later, as a forgotten witness to events. Incidentally, it became a matter for speculation whether the maid's observation about Larry's looks—and I should add, his about hers—ever turned into something more. The maid understood her mistress's standards. No hanky panky, a phrase I did not know back then. And Agent Larry Richey could have no doubt about TR's standards for behavior. Manly but loyal.

Larry and I became steadfast friends while on board, despite the sixteen-year difference in our ages. Most days, he seemed older than twenty-one, or else I interpreted bravery as maturity. He was smart too, sharper than many of the men back in my White House office, though Larry had less schooling. By the end of the voyage, I learned that the surname Richey once had been Ricci. I didn't immediately recognize the import of his original name. Now I suspect we befriended each other because we both had backgrounds that others might have considered unsuited to our current responsibilities.

The USS *Louisiana* had been outfitted with the latest in ship-to-shore telegraphy. The day after we set sail, the operator handed Agent Jimmy Sloan a confidential telegram from the police chief of Panama. Jimmy shared the telegram with his men. The key sentence, which Larry memorized, seemed momentous at the time. "My men have arrested Jerome Kehl, who disembarked from a ship landing in Colón today." The police chief had no need to identify the prisoner further for Jimmy. Jerome Kehl, a Chilean on the list of names the White House shared with Panamanian officials, tried to gain entry to the White House three years earlier and threatened to kill the President.

Shortly before we landed in Colón, Panama's Caribbean port, Larry confided in me with tales about Jerome Kehl. Larry said that in my role as Assistant Secretary, I warranted such information. The agents would need to interrogate Kehl promptly, to confirm their belief that he traveled to Colón alone. I suspect Larry feared he would not live up to expectations, a fear that echoed my own fear, and he talked more than he should have simply as a means of comfort. We each needed a friend on the *Louisiana*. Larry asked me not to disclose what he had said, not to anyone. As he must have anticipated, that came easily to me, then.

I remember the voyage not only for Larry's good company, but also for the discouraging news about what became known as the Brownsville affair. 1906 had been a difficult year for relations between Whites and Negroes.

On August 13ᵗʰ, three months in advance of our Panama trip, news came over the wires about a riot between Whites and Negroes in Brownsville, at the southernmost tip of Texas. Few Americans remember Brownsville now, but it almost tore the country apart. A mob of twenty Negro soldiers stationed there—part of the 25ᵗʰ Infantry—shot up the town. Or that was the story printed in many newspapers. The soldiers killed a White bartender and seriously wounded a town policeman. TR assumed the evidence against the soldiers was legitimate and stated his annoyance that not one of them would reveal the identity of the primary culprits. He issued a contentious order requiring that the entire regiment, 167 Negro soldiers, be dismissed without honor and without a trial. A predictable uproar followed. While Americans continued to argue over the justice of that affair, a race riot broke out in Atlanta in September. Over twenty-five Negroes were killed, more were injured, and two White citizens died. The controversy following the riot did not center on what TR did, but on what he didn't do. He stayed silent.

The Brownsville and Atlanta turmoil continued as the President set off for the canal. TR insisted he had been unbiased by race and implied that his decision on dismissal was firm. Aboard the *Louisiana*, the crew whispered about the President's position. Some sailors pointed out, either with praise or disgust, that TR had invited Booker T. Washington to dine at the White House. Others pointed to TR's less open-minded positions, again with either praise or disgust. In public, the few times anyone aboard ship asked my opinion, I maintained my standard loyalty to the President. Only to Larry Richey, over a game of checkers, did I express reservations. He listened, keeping his thoughts to himself.

A day earlier than expected, we arrived in Limon Bay, near Colón. While we were at anchor, I welcomed a group of stuffy officials, including the President and first lady of Panama, and the two journalists who were on Secretary Loeb's approved list. I was surprised to see that one of the two was a Negro and hoped this would not present a problem. Aside from greetings and introductions and escorting the group to the wardroom for the dinner to which I was not invited, I had no further duties. I used my free time to write a dispatch to Secretary Loeb, detailing our arrival.

When I handed my dispatch to the telegraph operator, I encountered Mrs. Roosevelt sending a message to her children. She asked me to join her for a nightcap, not of alcohol but of tea, more to my liking and to hers. Though the invitation surprised me, I readily agreed and followed her to the sitting area of the presidential stateroom. As we walked, I smelled a flowery scent, perfume, unusual on a battleship. The lady stood almost as tall as her husband, with a sharp nose that did not in the least mar her pretty face. I wondered if she was lonely, with her husband tied up with journalists, but the way she sat at first, elbows close to her body and hands folded over her lap, I sensed something other than loneliness. "Mr. Latta," she said, after dismissing the steward who brought the tea service, "do you hear any news from Mr. Loeb, or from Mr. Sloan?" She poured tea slowly, trying to control a slight tremor despite the calm waters of the bay.

"News?" I said. "About the Brownsville affair in Texas? Those. . . Negro soldiers?" I caught myself before saying, "mistreated."

"No, Mr. Latta." She took a long pause. "I mean news about threats. Threats to my husband."

I confess that my first reaction was pride—pride that Mrs. Roosevelt thought me important enough to have such news. William Loeb, the man I was filling in for, belonged to TR's inner circle and would know about threats. Jimmy Sloan, head of TR's protective detail, would manage threats. Now, here in Colón's Limon Bay, Mrs. R. expected me to be alert to peril. My pride lasted a second, then I realized my awkward position.

"Mrs. Roosevelt, I know nothing new. Of course, we have always heard threats, and Mr. Sloan usually tackles them well." I looked at her, doing my best to unclench the muscles around my jaw. The poor woman's hand still trembled.

Mrs. R. saw she caused me worry too and changed the subject. "Do we expect more rain?" And then, "I enjoyed meeting the wife of the President of Panama at dinner. Mrs. Amador. Oh, do remind me of her full name."

"Maria Ossa de Amador," I said, relieved I had committed that name to memory.

"Good to have a lady on board," Mrs. R. said. Then she winced. "Of course, I have the company of my maid, but I could talk to Mrs., I'll call her Maria right now, about other topics—the formalities of the trip." Even then, I wondered if Edith Roosevelt would have caught herself for forgetting her maid if I had been one of her husband's aristocratic cronies. And as I noted, this maid, nearly forgotten by Mrs. R., also has been forgotten by history.

We moved to other topics, with no pause suggesting it was time for me to leave. Mrs. R. may have sought a conversation partner that night as well as a source of information. She unfolded her arms and began to relax. She shared her thoughts on the Brownsville affair, supporting her husband's decision to discharge the Negro soldiers without honor. To this day I recall thinking that although her position was wrong—I am certain evidence was planted against those poor men—she understood the complex arguments on the matter. I also recall deciding to learn from Larry and to keep my thoughts on Brownsville to myself.

As we finished our tea, I knew I should not leave until I said something comforting. "Mrs. Roosevelt, if Agent Sloan has news of an impending threat, I will share that information with you." She angled her head, assessing the timber of my voice, the weight of my assurance. I offered a silly, small bow as I left, not knowing what else to do.

* * *

Edith Roosevelt tried to relax aboard the USS *Louisiana* as the ship sailed through calm Caribbean waters. She succeeded, until the ship arrived in Colón and set anchor. The three Secret Service agents intensified their watch, put their heads together. She looked for Mr. Latta, expecting him to divulge the latest particulars. He made the next step easy. She spotted him near the telegraph operator. Ordinary looking man, except for his high forehead. Asked him for tea and talk. The poor fellow could barely swallow. She hadn't raised four sons for nothing. She knew his assurances about security were lies. As he walked away, with a phony promise to keep her informed, her chest constricted as her mind wandered to thoughts of Mary

23

Lincoln, Lucretia Garfield, and Ida McKinley.

Frederick Palmer

Wednesday, November 14, 1906

F rederick Palmer left the Chinaman's shop in Panama City, dashing back to his room at the Gomez to claim his rucksack and settle his bill. Then another dash to the all too familiar train station. Weeks earlier, when Palmer received Secretary Loeb's memorandum, it included a note that Assistant Secretary Maurice Latta would be the staff member accompanying TR. Loeb instructed Palmer to present himself to Latta on the morning of the 15th, at Colón. Rereading the memorandum, Palmer wondered why Loeb thought the President would arrive on the 15th while the Chinaman insisted TR had arrived already, a day early. Who was this Latta fellow, Palmer wondered? A younger version of William Loeb, TR's affable, square-jawed secretary who could ease or block a journalist's path to the President? Palmer knew that path had been greased for him for what might be the best story of the year, but he needed to make sure his privileges would last.

Hurrying along the platform at the train station, Palmer spotted a cluster of five men outfitted in well-pressed and formal business attire and one woman dressed in finery that stood out at the simple station. Palmer recognized Joseph Bishop, the shortest of the men, authoritative looking with his bald pate and clipped beard. They became friends in New York, where Bishop had served as a renowned newspaper editor. Roosevelt, looking for a man who could shape reporters' stories, appointed Bishop to be Secretary of the Isthmian Canal Commission. Palmer realized that the contingent ahead of him must be heading to see TR too. Three of the men peered into the distance for an arriving train, squinting in the sunlight, shrugging. Didn't they know that at midday, when the laborers had already traveled to their worksites in second-class cars and their supervisors in first-class cars, the Panama Railroad had a limited schedule?

Palmer walked up to the group and smiled at his old friend.

"Ah, Frederick, I thought I might see you here," Bishop said. He turned to his colleagues. "Gentlemen, meet Frederick Palmer of *Collier's Magazine*, assigned to be the President's official news correspondent this week."

That morning when Shing Wong, the shop owner, mentioned Roosevelt, Palmer had not said that he knew the President. Few reporters outside Washington had advised TR, but Palmer had, many times. The President's interests included foreign events and intrigue as well as American politics. Previous presidents who sought news of unrest had to rely on biased communications from war ministries. This President preferred eye-witness accounts. Reading that Palmer had traveled to foreign wars for his reporting, TR summoned him to the White House. First, they talked about Japan. Then more summons to discuss other sites of unrest. On visits to the White House, Palmer always stopped to meet with Secretary Loeb, to exchange rumors and gossip about the press. Mr. Loeb had assured *Collier's Magazine* that Palmer would be welcome on the Panama trip, in an official capacity.

"Pleased to meet you," bellowed one of the flock of officials on the platform, a tall, stout man with graying hair and a trim moustache. "I'm Theodore Shonts, Chairman of the Isthmian Canal Commission. Around here we call that the ICC, or just the Commission." Then John Stevens, the Chief Engineer with a reputation as a fearless railroad man, and Dr. William Gorgas, the white-haired Chief Sanitary Officer, introduced themselves. TR admired Stevens and everyone knew that Gorgas had purged the isthmus of Yellow Fever. Shonts, Bishop, Stevens, Gorgas—all familiar names to Palmer. But who was the fifth man, old and ramrod straight?

"Pleased to meet you," he said, with barely a trace of an accent. "I am Manual Amador Guerrero, the President of Panama. And the beautiful lady by my side is my wife, first lady of Panama, Maria de la Ossa de Amador."

Palmer had heard from TR during their talks that Amador was a cautious leader, while his wife took center stage. A year before, Maria Amador had stolen the show by dancing with Secretary of War William Howard Taft in the ballroom of Panama's Presidential Palace. Despite Taft's hefty weight, newspapers reported that the two partnered well together. By the end of the week, Palmer would realize that with Amador's decorum and his wife's *joie de vivre*, the Panamanian presidential couple was a mirror image of America's presidential couple.

The introductions concluded, Joseph Bishop addressed himself to the others. "Fred and I have known each other for years. You might say we are both members of the fourth estate. We've shared a beer or two in New Amsterdam, though I've been at it—that is both the writing and the drinking—a bit longer than this whippersnapper here. Don't let Fred's years mislead you. He's covered more battlefields and reported from more countries than anyone I know. And Teddy likes him almost as much as he likes me." Bishop turned to Palmer again. "Fred, you probably know that Teddy appointed me Secretary of the ICC." Palmer nodded in acknowledgment. "I handle newspapers and journalists. Ted Shonts over here, we call him The Other Teddy. He handles all the other ICC business."

Palmer realized that to anyone on the platform observing the group, he would appear odd man out. Of average height, with a nondescript brown moustache and beard, he looked decades younger than the others. Youth was not the only difference. Palmer dressed more for the jungle than for diplomacy. Yet the officials welcomed him. Perhaps the mention of *Collier's,* with its wide circulation and articles by Jack London and Upton Sinclair, made an impression.

Or maybe Chairman Theodore Shonts had already heard Joseph Bishop's endorsement of the reporter or knew of Mr. Loeb's seal of approval. "Happy to meet you," Shonts said. The ICC chief official did not hesitate to speak for the others. "I'm afraid we're in a hurry. The President landed a day earlier than expected. We had big plans for his reception tomorrow, but now, with such short notice to travel, we've managed to gather just a few of us. Mrs. Amador has graciously rushed to our side too. We will have a social hour with the President, and Mrs. Roosevelt will have some company. That is if this damn, sorry Maria, train ever gets here." Maria offered a small, expected, forgiving smile.

"Mind if I ride in the same car with you?" Palmer asked, addressing himself to Shonts. Clearly, this pompous man considered himself in charge of the informal delegation as well as the ICC. Palmer knew to be polite, even obsequious. He said the cliché to himself, whatever it took to get the story.

For the remaining ten minutes, as the group waited impatiently for the train to Colón, and for the next two hours in the private car—Shonts had ordered the train engineer to speed up by rolling past most stations—Frederick Palmer asked questions. The schedule for completion? The eradication of disease? The availability of labor? The officials packaged their answers. Already familiar with the sights and howls out the window, Palmer could concentrate on news about the canal. He suspected the officials added a rosy slant and could almost envision them patting each other's backs. ICC Chairman Shonts, slouching in his seat, spoke about the progress Chief Engineer Stevens had made on the dig. Next to Palmer sat Dr. Gorgas, a pleasant smile etched on his face, remarking how Shonts had wisely given the Sanitary Department resources to eradicate disease. Gorgas showed no signs of pride, though his actions had saved the lives of thousands. President Amador, who insisted Maria take the window seat, made sure to say that he was thankful for U.S. support for Panama's Conservative Party, which he led. John Stevens, the quiet man of the group, scowled in the corner, grumbling whenever the train slowed that he needed to get back to his office. Palmer had heard of Stevens's exploits when he served as engineer and then general manager on the Great Northern Railroad, exploring one western pass and discovering another. In the Canal Zone Stevens was spared wolf attacks and blizzards, but he still faced a daunting task. Palmer scribbled his observations in his notebook as the train rumbled northwest toward Colón.

The man Palmer wanted to talk to the most was his old friend Joseph

Bishop. The arrogant ICC Chairman, Theodore Shonts, managed the Commission day-to-day, but Palmer knew that Roosevelt cared only about Bishop. As ICC Secretary, Bishop shaped the press in the Canal Zone, aiming for the positive picture TR needed to convince Congress to continue to fund the canal.

About an hour into the trip, the train stopped at the Culebra Cut, known simply as the Cut, the iconic place where the canal linking the oceans would be most visible and most dramatic. Palmer had done his homework, but he still wasn't sure if the word Culebra referred to snake, its meaning in Spanish, or to the mountain ridge the engineers were cutting through, or both. This was the one stop Shonts had allowed in his hurry to get to Colón. At the bustling Culebra station, dozens of men got off from other cars, some because they had reached their destination, others because they wanted to buy food from the women selling fruit and fish on the platform. Through the window, Palmer watched haggling over prices, mostly in English.

Palmer stood up. "Can I get you anything?" he asked his seatmate, the doctor. Turning around to the officials nearby, he added, "or anyone else?" No interest. Palmer was the only passenger to step down from the private car. He hadn't eaten since breakfast at the Gomez and trusted the food the local women were hawking. He guessed that this stop would give him a chance to change seats as well as to eat. Returning with a banana, he sat in the empty space next to Bishop.

"Do you think our Teddy will be happy with what he sees here?" Bishop shook his head while pointing to one ear. The noise near the Culebra Cut was deafening. Palmer asked a second time, louder. This time Bishop nodded.

"Do you know about those stories that circulated," Bishop said, "the ones Poultney Bigelow, I'm sorry to admit that we call him the chicken when a few of us are alone at the bar, wrote about corruption here and delays?" Palmer smiled. Yes, he knew.

Mr. Loeb's memorandum to Palmer included not only a timetable and an introduction to Maurice Latta, but also a bit of history, to serve as a warning. Ten months earlier, another American journalist, Poultney Bigelow, had published a scathing article. He wrote about delays and scandals on the canal, embarrassing and angering ICC Chairman Shonts and Chief Engineer Stevens, the very men on this train. Though these officials were too proper to make jokes about Poultney Bigelow's name in public, they smirked in private. Shonts and Stevens still harbored a distrust of journalists.

"Poultney Bigelow's stories were trash," Bishop said. "This here out the window, all this energy, activity, what you're going to see and report on, this is what Teddy hopes for. We're raising the flag and controlling the seas. The canal, well, it's hard to exaggerate its importance to him. You know how Teddy feels about the Navy. Sea power is everything. He never fails to remind me that in the War of 1898, it took sixty-eight days for a battleship to get from Seattle to Cuba. Teddy won't let that happen again. And now that we don't have much frontier left to conquer, Teddy sees the canal as the new frontier. He'll be happy here. When he looks around, he'll delight in the progress. I'm sure."

Bishop paused to glance around. The other men were deep in conversation and the racket from the Cut died down a bit. Lowering his voice and leaning in toward Palmer, Bishop whispered. "But we don't need another Buffalo. Jimmy Sloan and I go way back—you know Jimmy, right?" Palmer, mystified, shook his head. "Teddy's protective detail guy. His bodyguard. Well, Jimmy's nervous. That's off the record. As long as there's no trouble, you know the kind I mean, this will be a grand trip."

Had Bishop really whispered "another Buffalo?" The name of that city awakened memories of the assassination of William McKinley, five years before. Palmer fixed his eyes on Bishop. The sound of talk rose up again, incorporating the full group, making it impossible for Palmer to question Bishop further. The conversation went back to everyday topics. ICC Chairman Shonts harangued about the condition of the tracks. President Amador quietly suggested that the Americans had greatly improved the route. At last, the train pulled into the Colón station, just as the rain arrived.

"The rain will drive down the heat, right? Palmer asked as the men lined up to leave the train.

"Ha, you'll see," Bishop said as the others chuckled.

30

The men walked from the station toward the wharf into a throng of men raising umbrellas over their heads. Palmer lost sight of Bishop, his best source for more information. Palmer would have to focus on the setting to set the stage for his reporting. The port city of Colón looked nothing like it had the previous day. He saw clean streets and smelled no rotting fruit, only fresh paint. Rain began to drench the bunting stretched across porches and the unfurled flags of two countries, but even the sodden decorations didn't diminish the festive atmosphere. Reaching Front Street, Palmer, at last, spotted Bishop and joined him in the crowd. The men—and Maria Amador, along with a few more plainly dressed women—gazed into the distance. At the edge of the crowd, Palmer saw several men with children on their shoulders, eager to witness the historic event. No one paid attention to the rain, as umbrellas, hats, and newspapers failed at protection.

Spectators stared in wonder at the imposing USS *Louisiana*, the battleship that had carried TR along with his small entourage, now anchored in the bay. Two armored cruisers, the *Tennessee* and the *Washington*, anchored too, had provided escort. This armada was a formidable sight, even for Palmer, who had observed the European blockade of Crete a decade earlier.

After ten more minutes of rain, the crowd thinned. Palmer saw Bishop turn to the side. "Someone I know," Bishop said. "Another journalist." He motioned to a dark-skinned man.

"Herbert, let me introduce you. Herbert de Lisser, meet Frederick Palmer, here for *Collier's*. Fred, Herbert is editor-in-chief of the *Jamaican Gleaner*. Even younger than you, just twenty-eight. And one of the journalists I trust. You are both here for the story of the decade."

De Lisser piped up to justify his presence, not to greet Palmer. "Mr. Latta, I am sure you know him, the Assistant Secretary. He wired me President Roosevelt's invitation to board tonight for a visit since the *Louisiana* arrived early. The President said he had questions for me." Palmer registered only a faint accent while straining to hide his dismay. Mr. Loeb had written nothing in his memorandum about a second journalist. De Lisser had received an invitation for that night? De Lisser alone? Palmer had rushed back to Colón, assuming he would be the first and only reporter on the scene.

His instructions in Loeb's memorandum were clear. Meet the President's train at the Colón station at 7:30 on the morning of November 15th. From the time of the war in the Balkans, at the start of his career, Palmer had competed with other journalists to file his story first. He had led the pack and expected to do the same in the calmer environment of Panama.

Later Palmer would hear de Lisser's story from Bishop. Rumor was that one of de Lisser's parents was Jamaican and the other a European Jew. Bishop couldn't remember which parent was which. He wasn't sure he believed the story since de Lisser, a handsome, well-dressed man of average height, was darker than the café au lait he would have expected. But Bishop did remember that de Lisser had an excellent education and considered himself a man of letters. That education had been on display for Bishop in the year they had known each other.

Shit, the President invited de Lisser aboard, Palmer groused to himself. Not what Palmer's colleagues at *Collier's* in New York would have expected. Those journalists talked incessantly about charges that Roosevelt disliked Negroes, the conclusion many came to when reading about the Brownsville Affair, where TR blamed a mob of marauding Negro soldiers for killing a white man. TR's actions and words led many to conclude that the President had no love for the colored man. Palmer had stood up for TR, believing him to be fair-minded. Here was more evidence on the side of fair. Maybe too fair.

The rain continued, but the downpour ended. Shonts, now soaked like all the others, approached the three newspaper men—Bishop, Palmer, and de Lisser. "I can just see the ship's tender. That's the skiff coming to take us to the *Louisiana*," Shonts said, addressing himself only to Bishop.

"Good, Theodore," Bishop said, using Shonts's first name. "This fine reporter—meet Mr. Herbert de Lisser from the *Jamaican Gleaner*—has been invited and can come along with us." Bishop left no room for Shonts to question the color of his skiff mate.

"And Theodore, I'm sure TR would like to see Fred too. Probably would have wired him about the ship's early arrival and invited him aboard if he'd known where to reach him. We'll have a full skiff."

Palmer took a breath, gave Bishop a smile of gratitude.

Waiting to board the rocking tender with the others, Palmer stared at the back of de Lisser's neck, visible between his neat linen jacket and his hat. Palmer had seen one or two dark-skinned journalists on his travels, but it was a rare sight. It wasn't de Lisser's color that bothered Palmer, but his profession. The Jamaican would provide local knowledge and could publish his story in a day or two, ahead of Palmer's in *Collier's Weekly*. But de Lisser's newspaper, probably headquartered in Kingston, was invisible in the States, and perhaps of questionable reputation. Palmer could provide national context. *Collier's* would get the full story. Or so he thought as he boarded the tender.

Herbert de Lisser, Frederick Palmer

Wednesday, November 14, 1906

So far, the day had gone very well indeed for Herbert de Lisser. The President had welcomed him aboard the anchored USS *Louisiana*, not with the same bear hug he bestowed upon that other journalist, Mr. Frederick Palmer from *Collier's*, but warmly enough. A marine had ushered the officials and reporters—all of them—into the *Louisiana*'s elegant, wood-paneled private dining room. The President explained that the Navy had retrofitted the room for the voyage to Panama. De Lisser withstood the stares of that stout man seated across from him, the one they called Chairman Shonts. He would see that de Lisser knew how to eat with silverware. He even knew which fork to use first. And which wine glass was for the Cabernet. He would eat slowly and deliberately. When dinner ended, the President wished most of the diners goodnight, while inviting de Lisser and Mr. Palmer to stay for a chat. The journalists moved their chairs, to sit closer to the President at the head of the table.

De Lisser did most of the talking, steering the conversation as he pleased. "Yes, you are correct, Mr. President. These workers earn more money than they made in Jamaica and Barbados, but their expenses are higher than they were on those islands. They write home complaining about the quality and the cost of the food. They complain too about the hard labor, but they expect that. I want to write about conditions they face, for the *Jamaican Gleaner*, and what measures you might take to help. I hope you want change

34

as well." The President thrust his barrel chest forward and continued to listen to de Lisser's bill of particulars.

Occasionally Palmer interrupted. "I understand conditions for the American workers have improved," he said. De Lisser would give Palmer the benefit of the doubt—he probably intended to report accurately. But from the man's question, de Lisser could tell that the *Collier's* reporter wished to present an encouraging picture. He would focus on White workers, on machinery, on progress moving earth. De Lisser turned the talk back to the diggers and their food.

* * *

Frederick Palmer tried to push aside his envy. *This talkative Negro journalist just wants the President's ear, like everyone else.* He would be no threat to the access Mr. Loeb had promised. Except this access was no longer precisely exclusive if readers counted de Lisser's newspaper as credible.

As de Lisser droned on about conditions for the laborers, Palmer began to look around the room to admire the carved walnut furnishings. He saw a young man with dark hair and a muscular build sitting stiffly outside the *Louisiana's* dining room, just within view. Two other men, both tall, one clean-shaven with a round face and one stocky, came to speak with the young man. Palmer guessed the two new arrivals were in their early thirties, at least a decade older than the youngest. None of the three men wore the uniforms of the marines who manned the *Louisiana*. Palmer could not hear the conversation between the men, but he had a hunch that the clean-shaven, round face belonged to Jimmy Sloan, the Secret Service agent Bishop had mentioned a few hours earlier. The three men may have carried weapons hidden under their suit jackets. From where Palmer sat, he could not be sure. His eyes darted back and forth between watching the President's reactions to de Lisser in the dining room and watching the men in the hall. Palmer mused to himself that *Collier's* readers would be interested in improving conditions along the canal, but they might be more interested in

35

the President's protective detail.

When the interview with TR ended, a marine escorted the journalists off the ship, onto the tender, and back to Colón's wharf. Before Palmer could say good night, De Lisser offered a quick good night of his own and walked off. Palmer headed to Colón's only decent hotel, the Linton. He did not know where de Lisser was headed.

Maurice Latta

Thursday, November 15, 1906

Very early on our first morning docked in Colón, still in the miniature but private berth I merited as Assistant Secretary, I heard scrambling feet. Through the porthole, I saw that the sun had not yet risen. It was Thursday, the official landing day in Panama. My leisurely time aboard the USS *Louisiana* was coming to an end. If I strained my neck to the left, I could see activity on the side of the ship. The sailors, with the ship's captain watching, lowered the big man seventy-five feet down into the USS *Louisiana*'s tender. TR was not tall, but we were all aware that he had gained twenty-one pounds since his unanticipated transition from vice president to president. Fortunately, I was not expected to accompany him in his pre-dawn perambulations along the shore. I could wait to take a tender at 7:30.

I had my official assignments for that day and for the following days. I carried the President's itinerary and crammed schedule in my portfolio with the names and titles of the 117 people he was expected to meet. Seventy-six of the names were English, forty-one were Spanish. I would unobtrusively coach TR on those names, doing my best with pronunciation. I would take notes the few times he stood still enough to dictate. And reach out, I was told in confidence, to a Mrs. Katy Marsh, in care of John Connell in Chairman Theodore Shonts's office. I knew that Shonts chaired the Isthmian Canal Commission. I had met the arrogant official when he and his colleagues boarded the ship to greet TR, but I had never met John Connell, the assistant chairman. I handled the Katy Marsh task before leaving the *Louisiana*, giving a Marine messenger a letter in a sealed envelope the President had put in my hands the previous night. Not for several days would I have any idea of the astonishing content of the letter addressed to Mrs. Marsh, and then only because of highly irregular circumstances.

Mrs. Roosevelt breakfasted alone in the presidential cabin while the rest of us, ranging from Surgeon General Rixey to TR's valet Amos and Mrs. R.'s maid Bonnie, ate as usual in the dining room. I sat next to my friend Larry Richey, and he sat across from Bonnie. I had noticed that Larry seemed increasingly more interested in talking to Bonnie than to me, but I didn't mind that morning because I was obsessing about my duties for the first day on the isthmus. I read and reread the schedule, brushing toast crumbs off the crucial piece of paper.

At 7:30, I left the ship for the first time in six days to board a tender along with Mrs. R. and Dr. Rixey. Since we each weighed far less than the President, the transfer to the tender was undramatic. Mrs. R. looked lovely in a white dress with a wide-brimmed hat and tulle veil and of course, long gloves. As we came ashore, both a little wobbly, she saw me and smiled through her veil. I sensed she remembered and appreciated our conversation the previous evening. I steadied my eyes on her for a long second, trying to signal that I had no news of threats.

Standing on the Colón pier, I saw the President in his white linen suit, pulled tight across his middle. He paced up and back along the waterfront, waiting for his entourage. At first, there was no large welcoming party, just Walter Tubby, who was the canal's Chief of Division and Supplies, and a few of his henchmen. The poor man was stuck with that name, but he was by no means a depiction of its meaning and presented himself well. I learned the previous night that Chairman Shonts, thinking he and his colleagues could not be at the pier as early as TR, enlisted Tubby for 7:30 welcoming duty. Shonts and the rest of the party that had rushed aboard ship to see TR had slept over at the Linton Hotel, Colón's finest. (Only later did I realize that Mr. de Lisser would not have been allowed at the Linton and must have slept elsewhere.) After a while, the small welcoming party swelled, with the arrival of officials and their wives and a full contingent of major and minor dignitaries, all dressed to the nines. My own suit, which seemed appropriate when Clara and I packed the previous week, paled by comparison. I tried to ignore the fact that I alone wore wool.

We left the wharf, walking a block to the railroad station. Off to one side, I spotted the three muscleteers, scanning the crowd. Off to the other side, I saw a man of average height and ordinary appearance, except dressed informally, almost like an explorer. I recognized Frederick Palmer from the night before. Later, I would become increasingly familiar with his broad mustache and close-set eyes. He approached me, holding out his hand.

"Mr. Latta, you are Mr. Loeb's assistant, right? We met for a moment on the *Louisiana* last night, just before dinner. I think you are expecting me today."

"Yes. Good to see you again."

Mr. Palmer addressed me respectfully, despite the assistant in my title. He shook hands firmly. I assured him that he was welcome and that I would honor Mr. Loeb's offer of full access to the President. He smiled and seemed satisfied. We stood together, watching a group of schoolchildren surround the platform and begin to sing. I wondered to myself, as I would many times that week, how well the West Indies' dark-skinned children grasped the lyrics they were singing. "Land of the free," "sweet land of liberty," "land where my fathers died, land of the Pilgrims' pride." Did these words fit the setting? I glanced at Mr. Palmer to judge his reaction. He was looking down, jotting notes to himself.

Waiting on the platform for us were four open-air train cars, covered with thatched roofs and festooned with flags and bunting. They were Decauville trains, made in France—one thing the French did right. The train engineer greeted us with a nervous smile. He would drive that train expertly for the next few days, wearing his uniform and a proud grin. He told the President that this particular train had been ordered in 1885 by Ferdinand de Lesseps, the entrepreneur behind the French attempt to build the canal, and that it was known by the name La France. That was not necessarily a good omen—after all, the French had failed at digging the canal, many had died, and de Lesseps had given up in disgrace. If others listening to the gabby engineer recognized the awkwardness of the train's name, they were too polite to either frown or smirk.

Boarding the train was a memorable experience. Agents Jimmy Sloan and Frank Tyree climbed on early and quietly. (There was no sign at that point of Larry Richey.) The President and Mrs. R. followed, along with Surgeon General Rixey. Then the ever-so-proper dignitaries scrambled, almost falling over each other, to sit near the President. Perhaps as Assistant Secretary I should have anticipated the melee and provided a seating plan in advance. I focused instead on a smaller problem. I had to ensure a sensible seating arrangement for the reporters, Mr. Palmer and Mr. de Lisser. The night before, I sought out Mr. Bishop, the shortest of the gaggle of officials who had boarded the USS *Louisiana*. As Secretary of the ICC, he shaped press coverage and knew the reporters. (I tried to avoid saying the whole name—Isthmian Canal Commission—which made me sound like a stuffy outsider.) Mr. Bishop proved himself both amiable and insightful. I asked if there would be objections to Mr. de Lisser sitting in the second car, just behind the President's car. I knew that some officials who would be in the second car were southerners. The Brownsville Affair, with news and complaints still coming over the *Louisiana's* wires, haunted me. Against this backdrop, I had to think about seating arrangements.

I am sure Mr. Bishop was aware of this backdrop too. He told me that the reporters should ride in the second car, but in the back, and that I should seat Palmer next to de Lisser to make it seem as though the back was for the reporters. He said he did not think Mr. Palmer would feel insulted. When I saw the second car filling up, I gently ushered the reporters to the rear seats there. Knowing my place, I, too, sat in the second car.

That car may have been second in line, but not in class. It was quite comfortable, no worse than the Baltimore, Chesapeake & Atlantic, or the Baltimore & Ohio railroads. I had almost as good a view as the officials in the first car, though the rain that began as we boarded turned to a downpour and splattered us. I was determined to observe everything I could, to paint a picture of the country later for Clara and the boys. The train rolled past jungles with groves of bananas and what I later learned were plantains. That's what I saw with my eyes, but there was also a lot for my ears. Every few minutes, we heard a strange howling, which Mr. Palmer (I eventually called him Fred) explained was the sound of monkeys. When that sound died, another sound rose—the ear-splitting noise of machinery used for drilling and digging. A man in our car explained that because of Chief Engineer Steven's tight timetable, certain machines ran even in the rain. Besides seeing and hearing, there was what we all felt, the constant mugginess as the downpour became torrents. Every time we have a humid day in Washington, and there are many of them, I am reminded of my first train ride in Panama. I feared the tracks would slide in the mud.

The train engineer slowed us down often to stop at stations in towns and hamlets along the way. At most of them, more schoolchildren gathered despite the rain, singing anthems and waving wet flags, trying to get the President's attention. TR and Mrs. R. responded to every group with waves and smiles. Mrs. R.'s right glove must have been soaked.

When we started moving again, we saw work trains full of earth and rock, steam shovels, and precariously placed cranes. My knowledge of engineering and dredging was non-existent, but here is what I learned on the fly. When Mr. John Stevens took over as Chief Engineer, he figured he needed to improve the railroad to make serious progress. The only way to get the dirt out of the canal was to take it out by train. He added tracks, improved existing tracks, and stockpiled dynamite. West Indian laborers drilled holes in the mountainside and filled them with explosives that they detonated to loosen the rock. Then amazing steam shovels grabbed the dirt and stones and transferred all that into open trains called spoil cars. Special machines packed the dirt tightly. Then those spoil cars discarded the dirt. The French had moved it into nearby ravines. The Americans had to look for more distant solutions, like landfills or dam sites. The administrative town of Balboa, built from spoil, had once been a swamp.

Each area along the path of the canal had parallel tracks, allowing trains to go in two directions at once, at different grades. The loaded spoil cars would travel to landfills on downhill tracks, almost coasting, and the empty ones would return to the job site on uphill tracks—the Chief Engineer thought of everything. Machines called dirt spreaders evened out the remaining soil. Looking up the mountains on either side of the railroad, we saw horizontal terraces of what appeared to be miniature toy tracks, with hundreds of laborers tending to them, layered up the slopes. We learned that trains ran 800 times a day.

Like all the passengers on the President's train, I was awestruck. I had never seen that many men working that hard. Five days later, TR would write an ill-advised letter to his teenage son Kermit. "With intense energy, men and machines do their task, the white men supervising matters and handling the machines, while the tens of thousands of black men do the rough manual labor where it is not worthwhile to have the machines do it." I did not know about that letter until after TR's death.

As we passed these excavation sites, the shovel operators blew their whistles in salute. I don't remember all the stops we made, except for one, Matachin. I learned that name referred to dead Chinese, which I should have realized if I had thought it through. Chinese workers had been brought over by the French to dig the canal. Hundreds died in large numbers from overwork and disease. First La France, then Matachin—too many reminders of failure. This President would push on until he could claim success.

Two Sweatshop Workers

September 1901, over the course of several days

Sally Miller and Katy Marsh sat at machines side-by-side on the eighth floor of New York City's Asch building, sewing dresses. Ten years later, this would be the scene of the infamous Triangle Shirtwaist Factory fire, but in September of 1901, it was simply an ice-cold sweatshop that employed women who could sew, and sew quickly, and sew for long hours, and sew without breaks, regardless of where they came from or what they had done before. Sally and Katy shared a before problem. Both had ten-year-old sons. Neither had a husband. Sally, an attractive woman with brown hair, a shapely figure, and a non-stop mouth, had been in a temporary romance with an Irish mobster, a card-carrying member of the Five Points gang. The cad was talented at stealing and pimping. Sally welcomed the extra dollars. She knew what he did day and night, even when it excluded her.

Katy, who would be considered similarly attractive if admirers could see past her fatigue, had a different story. After leaving Germany and emigrating through Ellis Island, she worked as a maid in a townhouse at 29 E. 38th Street, where she fell for the married gentleman owner, Elliott. But Elliott proved to be less than a gentleman. Ignoring his children, Eleanor and little Elliott Jr., and ignoring his wife, who was pregnant with their third child, Elliott plunged into alcohol. He plunged into Katy as well. Elliott was a good-looking man, much liked by all. Katy may have tried to fight him off.

Or maybe she welcomed his attentions. We will never know. Five months later, the mistress of the household dismissed Katy, with no references.

As Sally and Katy toiled together in the frigid workshop, both dressed in garb more frayed than the frocks they were fashioning, they talked, quietly, their conversation muffled by the hum of hundreds of sewing machines. Most of their talk centered on the foreman's attitude, especially if the girls sewed too slowly. After time, their talk turned in a different direction. Sally was the first to share her story.

"I told that lout I was in the family way, with his babe. He never believed me," she whispered. "He didn't think Sean was his son. Wouldn't give me a blasted cent. I begged the Five Points gang boss to help, to put in a good word or a good kick, but he didn't believe me either."

Katy smiled at Sally's story. Sally glanced over, her turned eyes serving as an invitation. But Katy kept her own story to herself for a few days. If she was going to share with her new friend, she needed to talk when the sounds of the machines were just right, quiet enough for Sally to hear, not so quiet that the whole room of girls could hear. Waiting for a break was pointless—the foreman allowed only seven minutes. Waiting for lunch was pointless as well—the girls gobbled their food quickly in a crowded room. But mid-week the foreman told half the girls in Katy's section of the sweatshop to go home because orders had slowed that week. Katy and Sally could stay. Katy found her opportunity and moved her chair inches closer to Sally's.

"You told me about your boy Sean," Katy said, lowering her voice. "I can do you one better, about my boy Elliott." With a slight German accent, in fits and starts when she became agitated, Katy told of her employer's promises, gifts, entreaties, desires, assignations. "When the missus saw my belly, she never asked who done it. Just threw me out. She knew. She vas mad. I never heard that little lady yell 'til then." Katy looked over her shoulder to make sure no one listened. She wasn't through. She raced on.

"I named my son Elliott after his father. He vasn't going to help me, denied it vas his." Katy saw Sally wince at her accent. She tried harder. Just like your man. Doesn't matter if they're rich or poor. I hired myself a lawyer. He

44

said Teedie, that was Elliott's brother—he wasn't vice president then, he was on some commission, but he was still part of that upper class of swells—his brother wouldn't want anyone to know Elliott was such a scoundrel."

As Sally listened, she reminded herself to work on her own accent, to push it upstairs a bit, away from Five Points. Then she heard the words "vice president." She gasped. She had never imagined that Katy's lover—or defiler—was a Roosevelt, brother to Theodore.

The women shushed as the high-handed, nosy foreman walked the aisle, checking to make sure the pile of garments to be sewed on the left of each machine was getting lower and the pile of finished garments on the right was getting higher. Even when orders slowed, the women were expected to hustle.

Katy knew she had triggered Sally's interest, always good for friendships. The next day, between the foreman's rounds, Katy found a minute to share more. "And there's another thing I want to tell you. Elliott, I mean the rich Elliott, not my son. He had three children with his wife. He named one Elliott, like I named my Elliott, but that son died of scarlet fever. And there was another son, too, born three months after my son. Elliott, he went shagging from bed to bed, even soused. But the oldest child, Eleanor, she's the special one. The Vice President loves Eleanor almost as much as his own children. He wouldn't want his friends to know that Eleanor had a half-brother whose ma—me—was a maid. And the vice president's wife, that stuck-up Edith. She wouldn't want anyone to know that her rich family wasn't perfect. My lawyer said I could make a heap of money if I threatened a scandal. But in the beginning, the Vice President—he was stupid about this—didn't believe his brother was the father. Mr. Bigwig Vice President hired a detective to sort it out. The detective knocked at my door. Said he wanted to look at the baby. He had a photograph of Elliott in his hand. He took one look at my little Elliott and then scurried out as fast as he come in. He must have told Mr. Vice President that little Elliott really did look like his pa Elliott. My lawyer said that Teddy agreed to pay. But just $4000, not the $10,000 I wanted. I said I'd take it. When would I ever earn that much? But that's the last time I heard from that bastard lawyer. He never sent me

45

a penny."

Katy and Sally eyed the foreman rounding the corner. All talk stopped. But Sally remained curious. Later that afternoon, she pressed Katy for more.

"You mean the lawyer cheated you?"

"I rang the bell at his office a hundred times. He never answered. And Elliott, he was either a drunk or insane or both. And my friends from his house tell me he had other women friends after me. Ahhh. He died seven years ago. He never even saw little Elliott. Now I have no money, and my son has no pa."

One day after the last of these confidences, Leon Czolgosz shot President McKinley. A week later, McKinley died. The vice president became president.

The sweatshop women kept talking, for months, by their machines. Katy told Sally about Mrs. Kegan, who cared for children. Soon Mrs. Kegan was caring for Sean Marsh and Elliott Miller as well as her own six children and many others. Sally and Katy saw each other morning and night when they delivered and fetched their sons from Mrs. Kegan's basement.

Sally never forgot Katy's story, which seemed to grow in value in her mind now that Elliott Marsh's uncle had become the President. Long after Sally left the Asch building, traveling for new opportunities, she remembered thinking that her son Sean looked a lot like little Elliott.

Jimmy Sloan

Thursday, November 15, 1906

As President Roosevelt walked along the waterfront and Maurice Latta began to dress on the *Louisiana,* a different scene unfolded nearby at a gathering in a dingy saloon. In the city of Colón, just outside the ten-mile-wide American-controlled Canal Zone with its stuffy culture, there was plenty of room for drinking and other misdeeds. The Palms Saloon eased the way.

Secret Service agent Jimmy Sloan sat down at the head of a damp and dented table in the Palms, beside his host, a man he knew to be Police Chief George Shanton. Agents Larry Richey and Frank Tyree took the remaining seats. "Thanks for coming this far to help," said Shanton. Sloan raised his hand to signal, of course. Both men owed allegiance to Theodore Roosevelt. The President and Shanton had ridden together as Rough Riders in Cuba, forging a bond and leading to Shanton's appointment as Chief of Police for the Canal Zone. As for Sloan, the President pontificated that he could take care of himself while relying on the lead agent and his men for security.

Sloan knew that Chief Shanton had ordered the saloon to open at the ungodly hour of 6:00 a.m. An imposing man in his late thirties with a long face and sun-weathered skin, Shanton puffed on a Cuban cigar despite the early hour. He dressed like a military officer, with high boots and three gold medals, and five brass buttons on the chest of his khaki jacket. His was the only uniform in the empty saloon. Sloan and his agents dressed in undistinguished gray civilian suits selected to blend into any crowd. An observant onlooker circling the table might discern that the agents wore holstered guns under their unremarkable jackets.

"When I got your wire about the trip," the police chief said, "I'll be honest. Seemed like you didn't trust us. I have two hundred men in the force here under my command. They're used to drunkards and vagrants more than assassins, but they're good chaps. Most were in the army or on police forces in the States. The ones in the Zone are all white. I handpicked my men like Teddy handpicked me. I thought they could handle any threats. But now, after what I've seen this month, I reckon we have us a problem, just as you said, or maybe I should say problems.

The four men at the table knew they lived in the shadow of threats to leaders throughout the world. The previous twelve years had been bloody, with notorious murders in the news, one after the other. Sante Geronimo Caserio fatally stabbed French President Carnot in 1894. Three years later, Michele Angiolillio killed Spanish Prime Minister Cánovas del Castillo with a revolver. The next year Luigi Lucheni killed Empress Elisabeth of Austria with a sharp, four-inch file. Two years later, Gaetano Bresci, a resident of Paterson, New Jersey, shot King Umberto of Italy with a revolver. In 1901, Leon Czolgosz, born in Michigan, murdered President William McKinley. For the men sitting in the Palms Saloon, danger lurked in every nook and cranny. They were on edge, especially on edge about Italians or Americans with foreign-sounding names. Young agent Larry Richey spread his fears beyond Italians.

The bartender slowly walked to the table carrying a tray with two beers and two coffees. He showed no sign of being alert enough at the early hour to listen in on the conversation.

"George, we can move to first names, right? You and your men have done great work already," Jimmy Sloan said as he grabbed a coffee. "But we can't let our guard down. Too many bad signs.

"What you might not know," added agent Frank Tyree, sipping his beer," is that there have been lots of attempts on *this* President." Sloan nodded to Tyree to continue. At thirty-three, Tyree had added too many pounds for his position as second in charge on TR's protective detail. But Sloan knew Tyree to be a good agent, watchful, and eager to train Richey. "Captain Shanton, half the culprits are what we call cranks, deranged idiots we lock up in madhouses. Kehl, the Chilean you locked up, he's probably in that group. We'll get to him in a minute. But some of these troublemakers are anarchists. Larry, want to list just a few for Captain Shanton?"

Sloan appreciated that Tyree passed the conversation on to Larry Richey. "Yes, Richey, you may be the youngest, but you have the best memory around here." Sloan and Tyree chuckled.

Richey picked up the account. He had the list down cold and had no trouble talking as he drank the other beer. "Jerome Kehl, the man in custody, we know he sailed from Santiago, Chile. He came to America three years ago and threatened to kill TR unless he protected patents for his crazy invention, a floating propeller. Sounds crackbrained, right? A floating propeller. Jimmy Sloan here sent him back to Chile, we thought forever. Next was Henry Weilbrenner, who lived on Long Island. He drove his buggy to Teddy's house there, with a pistol, and planned to kill him. There was also a Swedish immigrant, Peter Elliot. Elliot had a pistol and bullets coated with poison, but Jimmy overpowered him before he could do any damage."

"Damn, I didn't know. Well, at least we got Kehl," Shanton said, smiling. He drank his coffee as he looked with envy at the beers. Agent Sloan had wired Shanton two weeks earlier to tell him to employ his Zone police to search all arriving ships for suspicious travelers. The telegram included a long list of known suspects.

Shanton put down his coffee, took up his cigar, and kept talking. "I sent my men to check with the captains and the manifests at the ports. You made it easy, Jimmy, by circling Kehl's name at the top of your list. What's next?"

"First, we'll question Kehl to make sure he acted alone. George, most of these fellows are part of well-financed plots, hatched down to the last detail, but we think Kehl really is just a lone crank. I wish I could tell you now that we have him, that our work's done, but with all the rumors we've picked up, I can't be sure. Also, our Pinkerton detectives, we have some on the payroll, they've fed us rumors about suspects we should hunt down. Those snoops are more accurate than ever these days."

While Shanton had checked ships arriving in Panama, as an extra precaution, Sloan had monitored the passengers of every ship departing New York for Panama. General Peter Haines and Admiral Mordecai Endicott oversaw that operation. Sloan had gone right to the top.

"The general and admiral, the men I wired you about, they had every person who boarded in New York scrutinized by our agents, and they arrested two men for questioning. Their names were, let me look at my notes, Alberto Agresti and Lorenzo Zampa, ha, A to Z—turned out to be businessmen trying to sell equipment directly to the Zone commissaries and enterprises." As he said "Agresti" and "Zampa," Sloan glanced over at Richey. As expected, the young man dropped his eyes, stared at his beer. "The Secret Service agents said those men were in the clear. Their bosses vouched for them. I had them released. You can see we're taking no chances."

Tyree and Richey looked at each other, grinned. Shanton squinted, not understanding. "Excuse us, Captain Shanton," Tyree said. "Just our joking. Jimmy's 'we're taking no chances' is his motto.

Used to this tease, Sloan kept talking. "Tell me, George, how many steamers land each day, and at which ports?"

"Three a day in Panama City, but the real activity is here in Colón, with ten a day. The steamers from Kingston and Bridgetown bring the colored laborers and some from Europe. South America too."

"I know you organized your men to search each ship," said Sloan. "Great job getting Kehl. Keep your men at it for another few days. We're especially worried about anyone who looks or sounds Italian." Sloan could think of no way around saying that, or his next sentence. "If you need a translator, summon Larry Richey." Sloan pointed to the young agent, who was just finishing his morning beer.

Shanton, puzzled, stared at Richey, but returned to the plan for the day. "You'll see twenty of my best coppers at the docks at 8:00 tomorrow. You'll recognize them because their uniforms, the ones I picked out, are like the Rough Riders. Slouch hats, khaki trousers and leggings, high boots, red kerchiefs around their necks."

"George, thanks, sounds good. We won't all stick around Colón. But thank your men for us. If you catch any suspects, hold them for questioning, better yet, hold them 'til Teddy leaves on Saturday."

"What about your protection detail?" asked Shanton. "Do you have enough agents?"

"Two of us will be with the President when he's in crowds," answered Sloan. "And one will either investigate a problem or go on ahead to search the next stop. We should be fine. Teddy doesn't like a protective detail and would duck us if he had his way. He thinks only royalty have bodyguards. But Mrs. R. tells him he has no choice. She's been scared stiff by the threats and won't listen to him. Oh, and you probably know from your days riding with TR that he carried a gun—that pearl-gripped Browning M1900—and knew how to use it. It's smaller and easier to carry than the Colt revolver most of the other Rough Riders used in the war. Well, he still carries that Browning now. He thinks he's his own best protection. He doesn't understand the determination of these bloody anarchists. Ha, George. You know Teddy. Doesn't want me using anything stronger than bloody. That's become my favorite word."

Shanton laughed. "Ya, bloody. Here in the Zone, bloody hardly dings the ears."

"Time to go catch up with Teddy now," continued Sloan as he motioned to the bartender for the tab. "We let him row along the coast and explore the waterfront with the *Louisiana*'s marines this morning, but I know he's chomping at the bit to set his feet on Panama." Shanton went to reach for his wallet to pay, but Sloan slapped his hand away. "Richey, you're in charge of checking out Kehl. Then meet back up with me and Tyree as soon as you can."

Sloan and Tyree lingered a minute in front of the saloon as Richey raced off to interrogate Kehl, seemingly proud of his assignment. Shanton pivoted to leave.

Sloan's hand lightly brushed Shanton's shoulder. "Got a minute? Shanton nodded.

"I want you to understand why I trust Larry Richey with Kehl. The lad's young, I know, just twenty-one, the youngest agent we've got. But he's special. He's from Pennsylvania, grew up in Philadelphia in an Italian family." Sloan ignored Shanton's frown. "When Richey was a kid, he played ball on the streets with boys from his neighborhood. One day his ball rolled half a block to an old building, well, anyway, that's the story. The ball stopped at a basement window. Richey bent down to get the ball, and through the window he saw three men, busy printing money."

Sloan saw Shanton's eyes widen. Shanton had seen a lot of action in Cuba, but here was something new.

"Yeah, a counterfeiting ring. Some boys would have ignored what they saw. But Richey, he knew something wasn't right. He finished his ballgame then went to tell the local copper. This copper was friendlier than most to the Italians. The copper did a little surveillance, determined Richey was on to something, and called in Treasury agents. The counterfeiters were arrested and convicted. After that, the coppers began to pay Jimmy, mind you, he was only fourteen at the time, to spy for them. He could blend in well among the Italians, and he knew the language. After two years, Richey did so well that the Treasury Department hired him as an agent, at age sixteen. Now he's been working with us, more than carrying his weight. I want you to understand why I trust him."

"Ya know, Jimmy, I was curious. Damn good story. Good man to have on your detail. He looks strong too. Let's hope we don't need to put his strength to the test."

The men said their goodbyes. Sloan and Tyree left for the train station and Shanton for the port. All three remained on alert.

Larry Richey

T he waters remained peaceful as the USS *Louisiana* sailed from Maryland to Panama the second week in November. While Edith Roosevelt read Sabatier's *The Vitality of Christian Dogmas* and studied maps of the isthmus, the President read Milton and then Gustav Frenssen's novel, *Jorn Uhl.* If TR fretted about his decision to dismiss without honor 167 soldiers from Brownsville or his choice to remain silent on the Atlanta riots, there is no record of that.

The President and first lady were not the only passengers with time on their hands. The sailors and officers on the USS *Louisiana* had light duty, considering they were on a battleship. They gravitated toward cards and storytelling. Teasing too. Agent Larry Richey, a lad who had never been out of the United States, served as a fine target.

Richey took the teasing in stride most days. He considered it a sign of acceptance, or envy of his proximity to TR. Only one taunt lingered in his mind. He made the mistake, over the ship's card table, of admitting his fear of snakes. It was just a quick aside in a conversation about Panama's fauna, but the marines, intent on fun, would not let him forget his phobia. Although none of the agents told the ship's crew that Jerome Kehl had been arrested, the marines knew of the search for possible assassins. They knew suspects would be imprisoned. They knew agents would need to question those suspects.

The sailors grabbed their opportunity. They described the snakes and reptiles slithering on the walls of the prison Richey would likely visit. With each card game, the monsters in the jail grew bigger and meaner. Alligators swim right up to the foundation, Midshipman Busby warned. Snakes crawl up the walls and through the barred windows, added Warrant Officer Oliver. By the time Richey entered the jail to question Jerome Kehl on the morning of November 15th, even this brave young man felt anxious, though he had hidden that from Jimmy Sloan in the saloon that morning. Richey prepared mentally for something that looked like the reptile house in the zoo in his hometown of Philadelphia. Instead, he found a typical backwater jail, where the monsters were the likes of rats and roaches—yellow isthmus rats and giant cave cockroaches, to be specific. Those specimens were more familiar to a Philadelphian than snakes.

The jailor at the prison's front gate led Richey to the cells in back, which held only one star prisoner. Agent Richey would have the honor of grilling this alleged mastermind. Richey saw a policeman, dressed in the uniform Chief Shanton had described that morning, standing guard at the cell door. The officer motioned toward the corner where two stools had been set up. He looked eager to talk but knew to let the visitor begin.

"Larry Richey, Secret Service Agent. Here to question the prisoner. What can you tell me?

"Pleased to meet ya. Never thought I'd be talking to a Secret Service agent. I'm Steven Bonner, on Chief Shanton's police force. I was with the team, just two of us, that found Kehl and arrested him. Chief Shanton asked me to do guard duty this week. Usually that would be a rotten assignment, but not in this case, when the prisoner might be fixin' to kill the President of the United States." Richey kept his eyes on Bonner, thinking all this breathless chatter could be useful. "And, ya know, I like guard duty more than my regular duty, keeping an eye on West Indian laborers, looking for the ones who are raising hell or loitering." Bonner lowered his eyes, shook his head, kept talking. "Back in El Paso, we call that spying. Anyway, Chief Shanton knows I'm smarter, more sharp-eyed too than some of the other fellers on the force. Sorry, I suppose that's braggin', but you can judge for yourself.

Oh, and I can speak Spanish. If you don't... " Richey shook his head. "I can translate when you question the prisoner." Richey smiled in appreciation, then listened as Bonner explained, with a twang and embellished detail, how his team had found Kehl.

None of the Canal Zone police had expected the search of arriving ships to lead to an arrest. Chief George Shanton proved them wrong. Beginning in early November, he stationed armed police, two at a time, at each ship arriving in Colón's Limon Bay, not just ships sailing from Europe or the U.S. On November 10th, Bonner and his partner waited in the hot sun for a ship that had sailed from Santiago, Chile, then stopped in Barbados to pick up laborers. The policemen watched the colored passengers disembark but watched the other passengers more carefully.

The next part of Bonner's account took Richey by surprise. Bonner was indeed observant. He recounted that as the first few laborers walked off the ship, unsteady after days at sea, their eyes fixed on the holstered Colt pistols that Bonner and his partner carried. Coming onto land, wobbling, the laborers looked terrified and huddled together. They had no reason to worry, Bonner explained. They were not the target of this show of force. The police were on the lookout for Italians, men who were lighter than the laborers but swarthy in color, men who may or may not have provided their real names upon sailing. As Bonner checked the passenger manifests against the list Agent Sloan had wired to Chief Shanton, the name Jerome Kehl was a match. The policemen stopped Kehl before he could leave the ship. They did not expect his fair coloring. His Spanish accent was close to Italian, Bonner thought. Maybe it was Italian. But Kehl said little at first, so Bonner could not be certain. By the time the prisoner started to gab, Bonner and others had figured out that Kehl's Italian was Chilean Spanish.

"Officer Bonner," Richey said, "thank you for this background. And for remembering so well."

"I filled in the blanks for you, sir. Wanted to give you the full picture. By the way, if you ask me, the prisoner's too crazy to plan mischief. You'll see."

The two men entered the cell. Richey's first impression was of welcome, cool air. Since the sun never entered, the cell felt less sweltering than many

55

places in Colón. His second impression was dismay at the pathetic prisoner. Kehl, in his forties, sparse hair awry on his pale scalp, paced and twitched.

"Get me out of this blasted hell hole. Teddy. Teddy. Bring me to Teddy now. You can't keep me away from him again. He must protect my patent. My floating propeller." These were the yelled words of the brutal assassin, Jerome Kehl, translated and cleaned up by Texan Steven Bonner.

Bonner's translating responsibilities proved easier than he expected. Kehl's arms alternately flailed in the air, and then circled his head as though to outline his invention. That pantomime alone may have gotten the idea across. But Bonner didn't need to translate floating propeller because Kehl used English to name his creation. As for the word patent, Bonner had no trouble recognizing the meaning of la patente. To both Bonner and Richey, Kehl looked more deranged than dangerous. And he reeked. He probably had on the same clothes he had worn when he left Santiago three weeks earlier.

"You know you were forbidden to enter the United States after your escapade there a few years ago, threatening the President and yapping about your propeller patents. Why travel to Panama?" Bonner translated Richey's question.

"Panama is not the United States. I reckoned that if I couldn't see Teddy in Washington, I could see him here in Panama. Colón is not part of the Zone. You can't lock me up. You have no authority."

With a rare bit of rational thinking, Kehl thought he had found a legal loophole. He knew that the Canal Zone, a strip of land about a mile on each side of the future canal, was under U.S. rule, and he knew that the ports of Colón and Panama City, just outside the Zone, remained under Panamanian rule. But Kehl had an imperfect grasp of the deal that TR's negotiators had made with the Panamanians. He did not know the fine points. In fact, the U.S. could act in the interest of public safely throughout the country, when necessary. In emergencies the U.S. police power went beyond the Zone.

Agent Richey understood that Americans, espousing law and order, would take advantage of that loophole. "Not only are we locking you up," he said, "but we will keep you here until the President leaves, and then we are putting you back on a ship to Santiago. Steerage. No rations. We could care less about your stupid patents."

Richey waited for a translated retort, but there was none. Kehl started to whimper, then to cry in earnest. Although Richey was too young to have experience with assassins, this prisoner didn't look or sound like he could hurt anyone, other than himself. Leaving the cell, Richey felt disgust that Kehl caused such unnecessary worry. As the agent reached the heavy exterior door to exit the prison, Steven Bonner tapped him on the shoulder.

"Agent Richey, is this dang Kehl the only threat? I'm just a poorly paid Canal Zone policeman, but I pay attention." Larry Richey took a good look at Steven Bonner.

"As far as we know, right now."

"I guess that's good."

"Bonner, is there something you want to say?

"I reckon it's nothing. But I can't help thinking. On Tuesday nights, I play poker, at an all-night house in Colón. It's out of the Zone. That means gambling, and, well, you know—it's all legal there. I play with a guy named Jeffrey Fowler. He's one of the engineers leading the excavations at the Culebra Cut. Fowler doesn't just gamble there. He also visits a lady of the line." Richey raised his brows. "A whore," Bonner said. Richey lowered his brows and offered a slight smile. "Besides Fowler, she had a customer the other night who acted strange.

Richey listened, carefully.

Maurice Latta

Thursday, November 15, 1906

My first morning in Panama, I tried to relax on the train, reviewing my duties, going over notes on TR's schedule. The straw seat felt comfortable enough, but the rain persisted, and I kept shooing bugs away, though I had been assured that the mosquitos no longer posed a health threat. The President's train headed southeast, entering a town or hamlet every twenty minutes or so. At each settlement where white workers lived, I observed that the ICC had built two-story gray and white housing with porches—some of the muckety-mucks on the train called them galleries—on each level, covered with screens. Every family had indoor plumbing, so I was told. The buildings looked freshly painted and clean, with manicured lawns. Upon second glance, I saw mud beginning to invade the grassy area, but I blamed that on the rain. To my eyes, these dwellings were better than the dreary farmhouse of my youth and better even than the small house Clara, and I and the boys lived in a mile from my desk at the White House.

Not everyone merited suitable housing. I stared out from the train, disheartened as we sped past villages of wretched shacks and more disheartened as we stopped at two of them. Remember, this was 1906, just forty-three years and eleven months after the Emancipation Proclamation ended slavery. At each settlement where Negro workers lived, the ICC had built shacks on low ground, with raised platforms to keep the chickens from drowning in the mud and the smelly latrines.

I kept my thoughts to myself. Mr. Loeb had asked me to accompany the President to perform a job, not to voice my opinions. But after touring alternating clean towns and squalid towns for an hour, I lost my self-control. "The housing in Cristobal and Empire is impressive," I commented to the friendliest of the minor officials sharing the second car with me. "But it is different than what I am seeing in Silver City." I thought I could make such a matter-of-fact statement without causing a stir.

The minor official smiled and leaned in toward me. "Yes, Mr. Latta, some are gold towns, and some are silver." For a second, I was reminded of what I had witnessed years earlier in Oklahoma Territory—comfortable homesteads on good land, shabby homesteads on bad land, and unspeakable hovels for the few remaining Cherokee. I served as a clerk in the land office of a little town, Perry, just after the last land rush. Some Negroes joined the rush, at the back end, or bought lots advertised by Negro businessmen. Most of the time Negroes and Whites registered their claims peacefully, but once, in 1896, I was pulled into a dispute. I remember the men's names because they were ridiculously commonplace. Wilbur White alleged Isaiah Washington had stolen his land. No need to tell you all the details, but you should know that the land they fussed about was rotten land, hard to farm, and that White's signature on the deed did not match the signature on his wedding paperwork.

The head clerk listened to White and Washington argue. As junior man in the office, I stayed in back. I heard little except for a tone of outrage. Then I was told to draft a ruling in favor of White. I did. By law Washington had thirty days to vacate his lot. The next day his shack went up in flames. He escaped with his family. His mules burned.

Most days since 1896, I managed to forget that episode, but it didn't take much for me to feel the twinge of guilt. The shacks I saw in Panama along the railroad tracks and the chatter of the minor official in the second car turned the twinge into a creeping itch. "The separation of towns keeps everyone in their place nicely," he said. "It's connected to the payment system, you know." I tilted my head. I didn't know. "Americans are paid in gold, which is actually worth something. The colored workers are paid in silver, worth less. They should be happy for what they get if you ask me." I narrowed my mouth into something like a smile. I did not debate the man.

Ignoring the heavy downpour, the President left the train at each village to accept greetings and to examine the housing. Mrs. R., mindful of the weather, remained on the train. Most of the White House staff thought her aloof, though devoted to the President. And he to her. But the staff made allowances for the woman, given the demands of her five children, well, six if you count the wild stepdaughter. (Seven if you count the wild husband.) As for me, I would never think of Edith Roosevelt as aloof again, not after last's night's tete-a-tete. I would have liked to remain on the train with her, well, in the car behind hers, and walked up to reassure her about the absence of new threats. Instead, knowing my place, I followed TR at each stop, tromping through the rain with the others.

At Red Tank—that was our seventh village, or you might say our second silver village—the President noticed that the floors of the workers' huts were little better than swamps. "Are these floors, no, I should say are these mud floors, these filthy mud floors, what all the workers from the West Indies have?" He addressed his question to Jackson Smith, the bespectacled, abrasive ICC official in charge of quarters for the men. Smith's reputation had traveled far and wide, with stories circulating about him among White House staff in advance of our trip. His claim to fame was that he had helped to build railroads in Mexico and Ecuador, but those skills did not prepare him for duty in Panama. "Square Foot Smith" was his nickname, fixed in my mind decades later. He allowed each unmarried American worker one square foot of living space for every dollar earned per month. He doubled that to two square feet for married Americans and allowed each child five percent of his father's space for each year of the child's age. As a rule-follower myself, I hung back from joining others in Washington in making fun of those formulas. I changed my attitude upon learning that Smith followed his rules only when they served his needs. He kicked out workers from their housing whenever he sought space for cronies.

"Yes, Mr. President," Smith replied firmly, not anticipating where the exchange was headed. "These floors are typical for the laborers. If you remember that last stop, houses for Americans have new oak floors." He stretched out the words "new" and "oak."

"Mr. Smith, improve these floors, in this town and the towns like it, by the first of the year. You may use pine or local wood, but you need real floors."

Smith turned red, slackened his lower lip. "Yes, sir."

The demand for wood floors was only the first of many orders TR delivered that day. I had to write them down on the spot for the President's records. He would use these later when he delivered an address to Congress about the canal. In my mind, TR's admirable concerns with the quality of flooring helped balance out his ill-considered Brownsville dismissals. I was one of only a few men keeping score that week.

As we returned to the train, I scrambled toward Larry Richey, matching my steps to his fast pace. I knew he had interrogated suspect Kehl that morning. "Larry, how did you manage with the Chilean?" I tried for an offhand tone.

"Such a waste of time. He's cuckoo. Not a threat."

"What a relief. Now you and Frank and Jimmy can relax."

"Maybe. While I was at the jail, I heard some talk that made me wonder if Kehl's the end of it." Now Larry lowered his voice. I knew better than to pry further.

After nearly three rushed hours, we arrived at La Boca, the port near Panama City. Mrs. R. and many of the dignitaries on the train rested there while I accompanied the President and Surgeon General Rixey aboard a tugboat to tour the bay. Mr. Palmer and Mr. de Lisser were to continue with us on the boat and anywhere else they wished. As we waited for the tug to pull to the pier, I saw Mr. de Lisser off to the side, speaking with Mr. Bishop. I gestured to Mr. Palmer, wanting a few minutes alone with him. "Mr. Palmer, I hope I am not out of order in asking if you can understand the seating arrangements on the train this morning."

"No problem, chap," he replied with a small smile I interpreted as a sign of understanding. "And call me Frederick. Or better yet, Fred. We will be together for a few days. We might as well drop the formalities."

I felt relief. Fred did not bristle at being paired with a Negro journalist. I decided to share what I had just learned on the train and to watch for reactions.

"Then Fred it shall be. And please call me Maurice. Fred, I wonder, did you know that the towns where the Americans live are called gold towns and the towns where the laborers live are called silver towns?"

"Really? I did not know. . . But now I understand the mystery," he said as he pulled a wrinkled map from his jacket pocket. Moving a few inches toward me, he pointed to the scribbled words next to the town names.

"Apparently, this nomenclature grows out of payment arrangements," I added, parroting what I had heard that morning from the minor official. "The Americans are paid in gold, and the West Indian workers are paid in silver, which I understand is worth less."

At first, Fred said nothing more, but then he half rolled his eyes, pulled on his broad mustache, and added, "Poor fellows might as well be paid in Confederate graybacks."

By sharing local knowledge, I may have set a friendly tone, for my comments seemed to give Fred an opening. "Now, let me ask you a question that might be out of order on my part. I heard rumors in New York before I sailed, rumors that there might be threats against the President. Anything to worry about?"

I had been sworn to secrecy by Larry Richey while we were still on the *Louisiana*, and I kept the confidence when I had tea with Mrs. R. Why did I weaken now? I wanted to make a rare friend among these dignitaries, snobs, and bigots.

"They caught someone and questioned him in Colón. This is not for the magazine," I said sternly, but with a smile. "And I hear there could be more," I whispered as we saw de Lisser walk toward us. I realized Fred needed to ensure his continued access to the President, and befriending me would help accomplish that goal. For my part, I needed company, then and later.

Arthur Sitwell

Sunday, May 10, 1903, and earlier

T he Chicago & Alton Railroad linked Chicago to East St. Louis, exposing the little town of Lincoln, smack in the middle of Illinois, to the flow of current events. None of the members of the anarchist cell on Chicago's near west side had heard of Lincoln until May of 1903. Along with six other men, mostly Italian-born, Anthony Santelli had devised a plan. To carry it out, he offered to recruit their comrade Sitwell, one of the two non-Italians in the cell. Santelli would talk to Sitwell alone, speaking for the others. The fewer men who knew the details, the better.

On a beautiful spring evening in Chicago, with the din of children at play coming through the open window, Arthur Sitwell met with Santelli at his Taylor Street apartment. The two men sat at the kitchen table, which was bare except for a large map of Illinois. An observer might have expected to see cards along with pitchers of beer and cigars, but this night's gathering was not for revelry or even comradery. Sitwell sat upright. He noticed his host also sat upright and had not offered him a drink.

The men chatted for a few minutes about the Chicago White Sox winning a sloppy game against the Detroit Tigers and thoroughbred Judge Himes winning the Kentucky Derby. Santelli had not placed a bet on either event. He was broke. Sitwell had bet on the Derby and lost. As the conversation slowed, Sitwell yelled encouragement to Santelli's boys, playing ball in the yard. Sitwell knew that this evening's small talk served as a warm-up. He braced for what was coming.

"Hey, blonde boy, you worked with explosives in Cuba and maybe back in, what was it, Sheffield, right?" Santelli had learned English, necessary for his work grooming horses in the stables on Maxwell Street. But any native-born American listening or watching would pick him out as foreign-born the few times he missed the "th" sound and the many times he gestured.

Sitwell ignored the blonde boy's taunt. He was used to the anarchists mocking his hair color and usually his long, lanky legs and British accent. He knew better than to give it back by mocking Santelli's olive skin and patchy beard. Sitwell concentrated on the question about explosives, which was not truly a question. Rather an invitation.

"Yes, but you and the other men—you're better with explosives than me."

"We may be better, but coppers are always looking for Italians. For piezahns." Santelli raised his palms, in a gesture of resignation. "You're not such a familiar face. You don't look or sound like you just got off de ship from Naples. Coppers will think you belong where we're going to send you. And if any hired Pinkertons come around, dey won't get suspicious either. Oh, and another reason. Sorry to bring it up. You ain't married. No family to support, at least none you're admitting to. Rest of us have big broods."

Five seconds of silence, then, "So what's your plan, and where's the money coming from?" Arthur Sitwell told himself to speak with assurance, to focus on the details.

"TR's heading back from his endless vacation in Yellowstone," Santelli said. "Think he knows what it means to work a day? Now listen. He'll be in Illinois on June 4th. What I hear is he'll take the Chicago & Alton line from Bloomington to Springfield, and visit the shitty town of Lincoln in between, at 9:00 dat morning." Santelli jabbed at Lincoln on the map. "The railroad bosses won't allow other trains on de track for three hours before.

"Ya know Colin Martin, my snitch from operations, guy who played cards with us once at de Wednesday game?" Sitwell didn't know. "The only other non-Italian in our cell?" With that hint Sitwell began to remember Martin. He worked as an operations engineer on the Illinois Central. Now Sitwell could picture Martin, nodded yes. "Martin's pa was shot by police during de Haymarket business." Santelli's hands kept moving, this time conjuring up a pointed gun. "Seventeen years ago. His pa was demonstrating for an eight-hour day, and some guys, anarchists like us, stood near him when the riot broke out. Afterwards, four anarchists were hung. Martin was only ten. He's been helping us for a while now. He's scared, but we can trust him. He's sure about de train schedule. Sitwell, your job's to leave a satchel of dynamite next to the tracks. Set it off when you see the train. I'll be in Lincoln too, for, what do dey call it? A diversion. Our guy who works on the Illinois Central will loan me his overalls. Don't worry about dough for expenses. Won't need much. I'll raise some. And for a lawyer too. He'll say I'm a hobo waitin' to catch a train. You'll run so you won't need a lawyer. The bluebloods will be generous with cash as long as we don't use names and we do all the dirty work. Capeesh?"

Arthur Sitwell, though at least as committed to the cause as Santelli, felt lightheaded. He understood the mission, understood why he had been selected for it. But he didn't like the burden, the fear. Maybe there was a way out. This strike was hardly targeted. "What about the other passengers?"

"Yeah, we'll get more than a president in our net. We have to up de ante."

Sitwell spent only three seconds dwelling on that problem. He trusted Santelli, who at least pretended to be the brains behind their operations. But the stakes were high, especially for Sitwell. He knew government was evil and means to end it were just, even killing innocents. At the same time, he didn't want to get the noose like the Haymarket martyrs. Or the chair like Czolgosz. Or shot like Booth. Since Czolgosz murdered McKinley, it had become harder and harder to plot in secret. Roosevelt was on the warpath. For TR, anarchists were murderers. He told Congress that "the anarchist, and especially the anarchist in the United States, is merely one type of criminal, more dangerous than any other because he represents the same depravity in a greater degree." Then Congress passed the Alien Immigration Law, barring anarchists from entering the country. Now, thought Sitwell, if Americans believe anarchists were murderers, he might as well murder the right enemy.

Five years before getting the Lincoln, Illinois assignment, Arthur Sitwell, bored with driving a hansom cab, enlisted to fight in the Spanish American War. For two years in Cuba, his commanding officers had him caring for horses. Occasionally they had him placing explosives. He saw little action, but he did save his wages. Returning to Chicago, he bought the hansom cab business and made modest improvements. He found a stable on Taylor Street where he could rent reliable horses for a cheap daily fee. The horse groomer there, Italian Anthony Santelli, greeted him warmly each day, sometimes chuckling if Sitwell used the word "bloke" when telling tales of his day. The two men had little in common, other than their appreciation for horse flesh. That would change on September 14, 1901. Sitwell brought his carriage horses back to the foul-smelling stable and waved a hello to Santelli. "I'm not saying he deserved it," mumbled Santelli, reflecting on McKinley's assassination. Santelli fiddled with his sparse beard, narrowed his eyes. "But it might send a message about us working men."

Sitwell, stunned to hear such a sentiment uttered aloud, pried carefully, hoping for an unexpectedly like-minded ear. "You're questioning whether our presidents are working for us?" he asked, with just a slight smirk.

Santelli hesitated for a minute before returning the smirk. He did not know until a few months later that Sitwell had grown up in Sheffield, England, where his cherished next-door neighbor was William Broadhead, the union leader at the center of what became known as the Sheffield Outrages. Broadhead wanted to help working men in the cutlery factories, where pay was low, and work with grinders used to create the empire's silverware was dangerous. Sitwell was not one for book learning, but he had read what Friedrich Engels wrote about grinders. "By far the most unwholesome work is the grinding of knife-blades and forks, which, especially when done with a dry stone, entails certain early death. The unwholesomeness of this work lies in part in the bent posture, in which chest and stomach are cramped; but especially in the quantity of sharp-edged metal dust particles freed in the cutting, which fill the atmosphere, and are necessarily inhaled. The dry grinders' average life is hardly thirty-five years, the wet grinders' rarely exceeds forty-five." As a child, Sitwell knew that when men who refused to join the grinders union came to Broadhead's attention, he taught them a lesson. He delegated well, hiring his followers to intimidate and sometimes to kill. Broadhead never espoused anarchism, but he did pass on to the neighboring Sitwell family an ability to ignore the morality of methods in the interest of a just cause. He passed along, as well, an elementary knowledge of explosives.

Sitwell spent his childhood in Sheffield with an insolent father who was rarely home and whose opinions paralleled whichever mate he last boozed with at the Red Lion. The locally famous Broadhead was steadier in all ways. He enchanted young Sitwell.

Decades later, when Sitwell heard the Italian horse groomer utter a comment sympathetic to the working man, a seemingly unlikely association began. After a few more exploratory, probing conversations, Sitwell was inducted into the Taylor Street Anarchist Cell.

Paul Pearson

Thursday, June 4, 1903

T he three thousand and fifty-three men who lived in Lincoln, Illinois, in 1903, mostly farmers and tradesmen, along with a couple of drifters, eagerly awaited June 4th, whether they had voted for Theodore Roosevelt or for William Jennings Bryan or not voted at all three years earlier. Even the three thousand one hundred and forty-nine women of the town, who, of course, never voted, eagerly awaited the day. The two thousand and seven children too. Most residents of Lincoln had never seen a president before. A few old timers had seen Andrew Johnson when he traveled through the aptly named Lincoln in 1865, but they barely remembered that event.

On the morning of the 4th, the Lincoln station master of the Chicago & Alton Railroad woke up even earlier than usual. He liked his job, monitoring the train schedules and managing the little station. At age thirty-eight, average height, with just a few extra pounds, he blended easily into the central Illinois landscape. On this particular day, Paul Pearson anticipated that he would be the most important resident of his town. The problem, at least the problem for him, was that no resident of Lincoln would know that.

What the residents did know was that President Roosevelt, finishing his eight-week swing through the West, was finally headed back East in early June. His special train—cars borrowed by the Chicago & Alton from the Pennsylvania Railroad—was scheduled to leave Bloomington, Illinois at

68

8:15 on the morning of the 4th, to arrive in Lincoln at 9:05. TR would stay for twenty minutes, then continue to Springfield. In early May, the district manager of the Chicago & Alton sent station master Pearson a letter, marked confidential, reporting on that timeline. For security reasons, the district manager directed Pearson to keep the schedule secret until June 3rd and to share it with just a select group of local officials. Pearson regretted that he had included the town clerk in that select group. At the Logan County Decoration Day celebration on May 30th, the holiday later known as Memorial Day, the over-eager clerk announced the schedule from the raised platform near the band shell. Now the entire town knew the precise timing of the President's upcoming visit.

At 5:00 in the morning, Pearson told his wife he was leaving to inspect the viewing area set up beside the station. He had lied to her before, once about his cigar habits, once about the money he had lost at poker, and once about a minor flirtation with a neighbor's daughter. He was not a practiced liar. Standing over his wife in the dark bedroom, he strained to modulate his voice. Fortunately, she was still sleepy. She did not take note of his uncharacteristically soft yet high-pitched tone. Their toddler son remained fast asleep.

Inspecting the viewing stands had been Pearson's original plan before he received a telegram on June 2nd, marked "highly confidential," a noteworthy step above the mere "confidential" on the district manager's letter a month earlier. "Anarchist plot discovered for Lincoln for June 4," read the telegram. "Meet Treasury Agent James Sloan and Pinkerton Detective Timothy Schneider at train station at 6:00 a.m. on June 4. Information not to be shared with anyone. Failure to comply is federal crime. Wire confirmation of receipt of this telegram. Leslie M. Shaw, Secretary of Treasury."

Pearson had received telegrams in the past. They were instructional in nature—orders to modify schedules, to close the station for holidays, to host work crews. None of those previous telegrams had an intimidating tone. None had been signed by the Secretary of the Treasury. None had mentioned a Pinkerton. For decades the local papers had reported on the Pinkertons' scare tactics to control labor unrest in steel mills and coal mines.

In central Illinois, most of the residents admired the detectives as law-and-order heroes, while others considered them thugs. The station master was an admirer. After rereading the telegram a hundred times, he hid it in his office safe.

Pearson needed only fifteen minutes to grab a cold breakfast, use the outhouse, shave, dress, and comb his sparse hair. He checked in the hall mirror to make sure his station master's uniform, pressed by his wife the evening before, looked as crisp as it could in Lincoln's humidity. According to the *Lincoln Courier*, the day promised to be unseasonably warm, with a gusting wind to counter the heat.

Pearson took six minutes to walk to the Chicago & Alton station. On other days he might have felt the welcome breeze, or heard the familiar robins, or noticed the buttercups lining his path. This day, in the dark, he concentrated on the uneven path and on the instructions in the telegram. The station he approached was more substantial than the traffic in the town deserved. The frame building, white with green trim, housed three spaces—Pearson's office, an office for the ticket agent who would arrive at 8:00, and a waiting room with the usual long wooden benches.

At 5:29, Pearson reached the station. He saw two men on the platform, huddled together, smoking. Both wore suits. The one talking was clean-shaven, average height, with full cheeks. The one listening was thinner, with hair blowing in the wind. As Pearson saw them, he hustled, worried that he had mixed up in his mind the time for the meeting. The men spotted him.

Pearson couldn't tell who was in charge. He decided to speak first, then realized that to recall names, he had to look down at the notes he had written. He pulled them from his pocket with a shaking hand. "Good morning." His voice squeaked, and he could hardly be heard. He tried again. "Good morning." A bit better. "I am station master Paul Pearson. I am looking for Agent James Sloan and Detective Timothy Schneider."

"I'm Schneider," said the thin detective. I work for the Pinkerton Agency out of Chicago. Never been out this way before. Real farm country."

"And I'm James Sloan," said the round-faced man authoritatively. "Call me

Jimmy. I'm a Secret Service agent from the Treasury Department and head of the President's protective detail." Pearson listened carefully, concentrating. Lincoln was not a town where new people were introduced regularly, let alone two strangers at once.

"Let me get right to it," Sloan said. "No time to waste. Last month one of the railroad's operations engineers heard a report of an anarchist plot. We suspect he may have been in on it, then he got cold feet, maybe because he remembered what happened to Czolgosz." Pearson heard Chowgawsh. As he was sorting out the name in his mind—he had seen the name of McKinley's assassin in writing but never heard it spoken—Pinkerton Timothy Schneider provided a confirming visual demonstration, jolting his thin torso as though he had been hit by an electric current.

Jimmy Sloan gave the detective a quick frown, then continued. "The operations engineer told the Washington police that a gang of anarchists plans to blow up the railroad near Lincoln when the President's car comes through. Then the police informed the Treasury Department. Shaw, Secretary Shaw, he put me on the case and offered additional help. The department doesn't have enough detectives, so they called the Chicago Pinkerton agency. That's how we got Tim Schneider here to help investigate.

"I'll share what we know, Mr. Pearson. This plot has been hatched by Italians again, probably from that bloody den in Paterson, in New Jersey. They're not going to place the explosives until this morning because they want to limit the time the charges can be found. We need to spread out and look for Italians who are sneaking around. We need to be quiet if we want to catch them in the act. We can't take any chances. Hmmm. Sorry, if my men were with me today, they'd poke fun at that chances line. It's my motto. Anyway, we need to grab the dynamite, get rid of it, and arrest the infiltrators."

Sloan took a breath, smiled at Pearson. "I was born in Danville, ya know, three counties to the east. My father was a detective for the Chicago & Eastern Railroad. Happy to be back in this neck of the woods."

"Two country boys," Schneider said. "We need to get you up to the big city."

Jimmy Sloan, resident of Washington and bodyguard to the President, gave Schneider a second quick frown, then turned back to Pearson. "Truth is, we need your help."

The station master had been trying to work out the mystery for the last two days. He didn't want the treasury agent and the Pinkerton detective to think of him as a dumb farmer. Yes, he was born and bred in central Illinois, but he was an upstanding citizen of America, with a head on his shoulders. Since receiving the telegram, he had guessed at the details of the plot. He was not surprised at the danger, just that it was centering on his isolated station. And he was scared that he would not come through for the President. After all, he had voted for him.

"I'm not trained as a detective. Wish I was. I'm just a station master—a pretty good station master, though. How do I help?"

"Here's what Jimmy and me are thinking," Timothy Schneider said, adapting a businesslike tone. "You know the route. You know where the track is hidden by crops and bushes and where it's visible to the farmers. We want you to pick out the places most likely for an attack. The gabby operations engineer tells us that the damn gang is looking at spots between the farmland and the town on the north side, the Bloomington side. Not so far out in the wilderness that they'll look conspicuous. Not so close that they'll be watched. He says to concentrate on the tracks a mile or two northeast of the station. TR's train will be traveling south. We need to focus on the route just before the train gets to the Lincoln station."

"Good details," Sloan said, smiling. Tim Schneider smiled back. Pearson guessed the Pinkerton thought he had regained the agent's confidence.

With the hints Schneider provided, Pearson could make a guess. He knew every inch of the tracks, from Lincoln to the next stations in each direction. He had played in the area as a child, and even now, he walked the tracks often, searching for obstacles and recommending repairs. The anarchists would be either near the abandoned Streeter barn, or hiding in the berm just beyond the barn, where the raised sides hid the tracks. But what if he got it wrong? His father had fought admirably in blue, at least so he recounted, at Chickamauga. Forty years later there were no widespread wars where the station master could show his own grit. This was his chance to shine or to fail. His young son would know either way.

"I can see two possibilities. Most likely is the Streeter barn. Sid Streeter walked away from his farm when his wife and daughter died last year."

Three Men on Edge

Wednesday, June 3, 1903, to Thursday, June 4, 1903

Anthony Santelli wore work clothes borrowed from his anarchist pal who repaired tracks for the Illinois Central Railroad. Gray overalls, white shirt, and cap. No one questioned Santelli on June 3rd as he rode the Chicago & Alton line, traveling farther south in Illinois than he had ever been, through the towns of Joliet, Normal, Bloomington, and finally Lincoln. None of the passengers realized his uniform did not match the train line.

The sympathetic, German-born brother-in-law of another member of the Taylor Street cell had scouted the area around Lincoln the week before, identifying the Streeter barn as abandoned and isolated, but close to the tracks. He also identified another area, further north, with a rise in terrain that could serve as cover. Santelli chose the barn for himself. After arriving at the station, he walked north. To anyone watching, he would look like another railroad man checking the tracks. With ease, he found the barn—substantial, with a cross-gabled roof that had separate portions jutting out in opposite directions. The wood was rotting, but the red paint remained intact. Clumps of white and purple plants grew between the tracks and the barn. He would not need to hide among the flowers.

Santelli found piles of straw and settled in for the night. He slept, knowing he had given himself an easy assignment, requiring more dramatic skills than courage. Rising early, he drank the cold coffee he had brought along.

74

Just after dawn, he left the barn, taking no precautions, and began to walk slowly along the tracks toward the Lincoln station. Once he got halfway to the station, he turned around and walked back to the barn, the wind now at his back. Then he turned around again. And again. He paced this half-mile path until 7:30. At last, he saw a thin man in a suit approach.

Walking toward Santelli, the thin man rounded the curve of the tracks. According to the accounts Santelli read later, the thin man would say he saw a laborer just ahead of him, wearing work clothes. He would also say that the laborer had swarthy coloring.

"Stop," the thin man shouted. "Pinkerton, working for the U.S. Treasury Department. Detective Timothy Schneider." He drew his pistol and pointed it. Santelli raised his hands high and shouted as loudly as he could, using Italian, to insist he was stopping and unarmed. He forgot to tremble.

* * *

On the evening of June 3rd, Arthur Sitwell rode the train from Chicago to Lincoln, wearing nondescript clothing over farmer's overalls, carrying a satchel. A quarter mile northeast of the Streeter barn, he found the spot. He hid between two types of plants, in undergrowth near the berm, mercury blasting cap at his side. Then he waited in a cramped position. Too old for this, at age 43. His shoulder ached. His long, lanky limbs resisted bending. His bladder kicked into gear, forcing him to crawl from his lair every few hours. Just before dawn, he placed the explosives on the track in the dark. Sitwell was already out of sorts by 7:30 when he heard a commotion down the tracks in the direction of the station. It had worked. The Pinkerton would be busy with Santelli, who was a stranger in town but had no weapons or explosives on him. Sitwell could breathe more easily now and concentrate on the blasting cap.

* * *

Taking no chances, agent Jimmy Sloan headed southwest as Pinkerton detective Timothy Schneider headed northeast. Sloan scurried almost two miles at a fast clip, looking at the few structures along the tracks, and then walked back again. He repeated the walk. Just as he returned to the station, worried and sweating, he saw the Pinkerton drag a dark-haired man onto the platform. Sloan ran ahead, waving and grinning.

"The guinea was walking along the tracks near that barn," Schneider explained without further details. Sloan, Schneider, and the detainee squeezed into the station master's office, barely glancing at Pearson, who had been waiting and pacing the platform. Sloan spotted no passengers in the station yet. All the regular morning passenger and freight trains had been canceled.

"What the hell," the men heard a gasp and looked up to see a balding man, mouth agape.

"This is our ticket agent, Harvey Bell," Pearson explained.

Sloan frowned and nudged Pearson into a corner for a private chat. "You do what you have to do to make sure Mr. Bell keeps his eyes closed and his mouth shut. You did great, telling agent Schneider where to look, but you bloody well know I'll arrest you and Mr. Bell if you share any information. Your job now is to mingle with the passengers, the fools who didn't realize their trains were canceled, and with folks who come early to see TR's train. Act as though everything is going smoothly. If anyone asks about us, say we're the president's advance team." Pearson nodded his understanding. He looked like he savored both the praise and the task.

Sloan put his hand on Pearson's elbow to keep him out of his own office. Schneider pushed the Italian into a chair and pulled up other chairs for himself and Sloan. The Pinkerton closed the office door and, without asking, took the lead in the interrogation. "Hey, dago, where did you plant the dynamite?" No answer. "What's your name? Who else are you working with?" The man scratched his sparse beard, said a sentence or two in Italian. Schneider scowled, then showed his clenched fists. The Italian didn't put up a defensive palm. Seemed ready for blows.

An uneasy feeling lingered at the back of Sloan's mind. A few threads, loose, not threaded in the needle. He had made a career out of keeping criminals away from the President, taking no chances, and had learned to trust his instincts. The Italian was not sweating—Sloan and Schneider were the ones sweating—and the Italian seemed to understand the questions, never looked puzzled. Why wasn't he terrified? Sloan squinted at the logo on the patch on the man's overalls. As the son of a railroad man, Sloan knew logos. The patch bore a horizontal diamond symbol, the logo connected to the Illinois Central, not the Chicago & Alton. The C&A had used various symbols—a triangle, a horseshoe, banner—but never a diamond. Possible for an IC worker to end up here, but not likely.

Sloan got up, left the room, and approached Pearson, who was sitting outside on a bench with the bald ticket agent. Talking in hushed tones. Pearson must be trying to persuade the quivering ticket agent to ignore what he had seen. "Let's talk," Sloan said.

A slow but steady stream of over-eager men began to enter nearby Elm Park, slated to be the site of festivities, just one hundred feet from the station via a temporary sidewalk. Two men in the park put finishing touches on the viewing stand, one hammering and one smoothing out the bunting. Band members arrived, toting their instruments. Keeping an eye on all of them, Sloan walked farther along, gesturing to Pearson to join him. Harvey Bell knew to stay behind, knew to relax his features, and to look elsewhere.

Once out of earshot of all but Pearson, Sloan asked, "The Pinkerton found this Italian in that barn, right? What was the second place you had in mind?"

"I can show you. Just follow."

Ten minutes later, Sloan and Pearson passed the Streeter barn. "We keep going," Pearson said. "A little way farther." By this time, his voice had grown steady, more confident. Strong breezes blew from the southwest to the northeast.

Those breezes, welcome on a warm day, carried a muted tone of voices to Arthur Sitwell's hiding place. He had a moment of horror when he could feel the wind knocked out of him, although he had barely moved all morning. He peeked around the underbrush. Two men were in the distance, walking with a purpose, one in a uniform, one in a suit. Not farmers. Shit. Shit. Shit. Sitwell staggered up. His long legs had fallen asleep. But somehow, he ran, leaving the detonator and explosives behind, useless without a helping hand.

Jimmy Sloan saw a tall, lanky, blond man wearing the clothes of a farmer leap out of the bushes. He thought about drawing his pistol and shooting but hesitated. Why would he shoot a farmer of the prairie?

Sally Miller

Tuesday, November 6, 1906

T uesday was usually a slow day in Panama City's La Boheme brothel. This Tuesday was particularly slow. Many of Sally Miller's regular customers were meeting with Theodore Shonts and Joseph Bishop from the Isthmian Canal Commission. Those officials were busy planning the details of the President's upcoming visit. Sally could relax and remain in her silk wrapper all day. But her son Sean still had work to do, sweeping and mucking out the stables in back. At fifteen, he knew what was going on inside La Boheme, but it was the only life he had known for the last three years, since Sally told him they were leaving New York's lower east side.

Life in Cocoa Grove, in Panama City, had been good to Sally and Sean. La Boheme was a world away from places like the Navaho in Bottle Alley in Colón, with its rows of filthy cribs surrounded by mud and its equally dirty customers. There, the girls were from the West Indies, a few from China. Those whorehouses bore little resemblance to Sally's house. La Boheme, with its brocades and punch bowls and women who looked like they could be walking down Main Street if they were dressed differently, served the engineers and the division heads and senior clerks, and everyone respected that difference. Last year business was brisk since most wives and girlfriends remained in the States. Americans were just beginning to bring their wives over now that Dr. Gorgas had eradicated Yellow Fever. The ICC may have banned prostitution in the Canal Zone, but brothels flourished in Colón and Panama City. Those port cities were not part of the Zone when it came to gambling and whores, thanks to the genius of some enlightened treaty writer.

Sally knew her son liked Panama, especially the weather. New York had been cold and dreary. During those years, as Sally sewed in the Asch building, Sean stayed with Mrs. Kegan downstairs in her tenement. Mrs. Kegan had six children of her own and a few more to care for, including Sean's playmate, Elliott Marsh. Mrs. Kegan always said the two boys looked like brothers. They even played and squabbled like brothers. Sean cried when he said goodbye to Elliott, not just for the night but for good. The boys were twelve by then—it was to be their last year with Mrs. Kegan. They had made plans to pal around once they were on their own, not foreseeing their separation. Sean never forgot his friend. But in Panama, Sean had more freedom and a higher class of company, well, both higher and lower. And Sally had more money, though not enough. Anyway, not enough for her.

Sally's Five Points connections had led not only to her fling with Sean's worthless father years earlier, but also to her new profession. In New York, she had chummed around with another Five Points hoodlum, this time a prosperous one. The hoodlum's brother went to Panama to set up a teamster business, first for the French and then for the Americans. The brother sent back news of endless opportunities, especially in the brothel business, and then died from Yellow Fever just as his recommendations, including a site and a name, were sinking in. The hoodlum honored his brother's memory by partnering with Sally to open La Boheme in Panama City's Cocoa Grove. On her end of the business, Sally was to send her backer, by money order to New York, fifty percent of what she took in. He was a money-grubbing scoundrel, always suspicious that she held back his fair share, but what he received, once a month and on time, filled his pockets enough for him to ignore his hunch. The dead brother had been right. Business was thriving. Sally knew how to pick the girls, how to keep order, and how to cook the books.

In September, Sally heard of President Roosevelt's plan to visit Panama. She had an early source of information in the form of John Connell,

Theodore Shonts's assistant chairman at the ICC. Connell was one of Sally's first regulars. She put up with his pretensions, a mild sin in contrast to the sins of her other regulars. "I'm ordering those buffoons at the Tivoli Hotel to ready a room for a presidential suite," Connell said, raising his voice so all the girls could hear. Sally knew Connell had little power at the ICC and daily kowtowed to his boss, Theodore Shonts. But then Sally read more details about the trip in the *Star and Herald*. Connell may have preened about his responsibilities, but he had his uses.

Her plan began to take shape. It was bold, but she thought foolproof. First, she wrote a short letter with a little help. Now she needed to bring Sean into the plan. He was a smart boy. Could he connive? She called him in from the stables and asked him to sit in the empty parlor. He scrunched up his face at the odd request. She allowed him into the parlor most nights, but only to serve whiskey to the guests. Now he sat on the richly upholstered settee, asking why she had called him inside. He looked down at the horse manure on his boots, careful not to rub the soles into the carpet. Sally shifted in her chair, then handed him a letter.

"Go ahead, Sean, read it. It's a copy of the original."

"Dear President Roosevelt," Sean read aloud. "I am Sally Miller, a resident of Panama. In 1891 you were informed that my son, Elliott Marsh Roosevelt, was the son of your brother, Elliott Bulloch Roosevelt."

Thanks to a few years of school in New York and the new school in Panama, Elliott read acceptably, struggling only over the unfamiliar Bulloch. "Shit, what are you saying? Elliott Marsh is still in New York with his ma. Why are you saying he's your son? And what's this with the name Roosevelt."

"Just keep reading." She shifted again in the chair, now sitting on the edge.

"This is stupid." Sean's face reddened. His voice faltered. He cleared his throat, then read on.

"I asked your family for $10,000 to maintain my son in good health and comfort, since his father, your dissolute brother, failed to honor his financial responsibilities. Your own lawyer allegedly gave my lawyer $4000 to give to me, but my lawyer then disappeared. I never received a cent. I am now asking you for $5000 to ensure the well-being of my son."

81

As Sean read aloud, Sally was impressed once again with her letter. She had made a good decision, asking one of her best clients to help her draft it and to handle related arrangements in return for a year of complimentary customized favors. John Connell earned a good salary as Shonts's chief assistant, but Mrs. Connell, back in Des Moines, had the mind of an accountant and would know if her husband's remittances, for her and his four children were slighted. Here was a way for him to cover the cost of his peccadillos.

"If I do not receive this amount," Sean read aloud, "I will need to take other action to guarantee my son's well-being. I know you will want assurances that Elliott Jr. is indeed your nephew. I am now living with him in Panama City, where you will be traveling in November. I will make plans for you to see him then. He looks like his father, as you realized years ago. I advise you to bring the $5000 with you to Panama to avoid trying to obtain funds while you are on your visit and in the public eye. You may write me in confidence in care of John Connell at the Isthmian Canal Commission office. He can be trusted. Yours sincerely, Katy Marsh."

"Katy Marsh?" How did she give you this letter? She's in New York."

"Sean, calm down and think about this. Think hard. For the next few weeks, you need to see me as Katy Marsh, and you need to be Elliott Marsh, the nephew of President Roosevelt. Do you understand what I'm saying? I'm going to say it just one more time. We're going to convince the President that you're his nephew. His bastard nephew. Katy left New York years ago with Elliott. I think for California. She won't cause any trouble."

Sally could see Sean's eyes narrow as he tried to puzzle out what he had just read. He whispered, "$5000?" but said nothing else.

Still on the edge of her chair, Sally handed Sean a second letter. This one was short, on different paper. Thick paper, with a gold leaf crest encircling three flowers. Years later, Sally would realize that the flower chosen for the crest was related to the family surname.

Sean began to read again, slowly now. "Dear Miss Marsh, my secretary, Maurice C. Latta, or his emissary will be in touch with Mr. John Connell upon arrival. Sincerely yours, Theodore Roosevelt."

William Karner

Thursday, December 15, 1904

"Those Jamaicans don't trust us, whatever we do." John Findley Wallace, Chief Engineer of the canal, whined to his dependable Assistant Engineer, William Karner. The two men, dressed in nearly identical white, wrinkled suits, sat in large leather armchairs in the administrative offices of the Isthmian Canal Commission in the Panamanian town of Balboa. They wore similar thick-soled shoes. Mud clung to their cuffs. Both sported neat gray mustaches and wore rimless glasses on their noses.

William Karner recognized that his friendship with Wallace and their similar appearances masked different statuses. John Findley Wallace was a Canal Zone luminary. At a salary of $25,000 per year, he was the highest-paid federal official other than President Roosevelt. Karner, earning a sixth of Wallace's pay, did not resent his boss's good fortune. Instead, Karner had chosen long ago to hitch his wagon to a star.

Karner admired his boss, who deserved every dollar he earned. Wallace had worked his way through college doing menial jobs for the Chicago, Burlington, and Quincy Railroad. Rising in station and salary, he moved from railroad to railroad. When he became General Manager of the Illinois Central, he hired Karner and then brought him along to the next job—Panama. The two men had worked side-by-side for over a decade.

Karner appreciated being called to the Chief Engineer's office for a chat.

Wallace, at fifty-two, was a fine boss by the standards of the rough-and-tumble railway business and remained a fine boss in the more sedate Canal Zone. This afternoon, though, Karner thought Wallace looked grumpy. He had brought his wife to Panama, so at home, he lived in constant fear for her health, and at work, he faced the stupendous challenge of digging a canal to connect oceans. When Wallace complained about the Jamaicans, he was not talking about the thousands of Jamaican laborers who helped the French in their failed efforts to build the canal. He was referring to Jamaica's unfriendly governor, Sir Alexander Swettenham. Word had reached Wallace that Secretary of War William Howard Taft, who had just visited Jamaica to seek laborers for the canal, failed in his talks with Swettenham.

"I counted on Taft to bring us workers. Big mistake. Maybe he did the best he could," Wallace said. "But he left Jamaica without a single digger for us. Bill, we need thousands and thousands more laborers, fast. Maybe 15,000." Wallace drew out the number, pronouncing each syllable separately. "You and I can't dig the canal ourselves, though if you look at our cuffs, it seems we were doing just that. Let's remember to avoid inspection tours in the rain."

Karner chuckled, then sat back in the armchair, happy to have in his hand a whiskey with some rare ice in the glass. For a minute, he could join in the banter, ignore where the conversation might be headed.

"I heard Taft all but kissed the governor's ass," Karner said.

"Well, he should have done that and more."

Both Karner and Wallace knew the details of Taft's offer. He had sworn to Governor Swettenham that the ICC would pay passage home for Jamaican laborers who worked on the canal for at least 500 days and then asked to return. The Jamaican authorities didn't trust Taft's offer. They still smarted from paying to repatriate stranded Jamaican workers the French left behind six years earlier. Swettenham offered Taft counter proposals, but they were too pricey and cumbersome for Taft to swallow.

Karner and Wallace repeated the unworkable terms to each other, using what they imagined to be Swettenham's aristocratic British accent. When they tired of laughing, Karner changed targets. "I hear Swettenham made

Taft sweat. Though given Taft's heft, I suppose anything would make him sweat."

Noticing a smile on Wallace's face—the man enjoyed gossip too, despite his serious demeanor—Karner continued. "I'm sure Taft isn't used to failing. Karner took his fourth sip of whiskey, keeping pace with Wallace. Or more than keeping pace.

A moment passed. Karner saw Wallace turn his glass in his hand, listen to the ice clink, scoot forward in his chair. The signal was clear. The time for jocularity had ended.

"Bill, we need to find another solution to our labor problem."

No canal official admired Jamaican laborers, but the canal wouldn't dig itself. Knowing Wallace well, watching his jaw set, Karner braced for what was coming. Wallace would hunt for labor wherever he could get it. The two men paused their talk as a West Indian waiter entered the office, pouring whiskey refills without being asked or thanked. The man looked down at the glasses, hurried out.

"Bill, I've been checking around. We could try to bring in more workers from Spain, and maybe Italy or Greece. Those workers have a solid reputation. Some of them, or their fathers, or maybe grandfathers, helped build railroads. And a few here tell me to hire Chinese. Won't work. Most of the men don't want coolies. Problem with all these groups is they don't speak English and it's expensive to bring them across the ocean." Wallace put down his drink and fixed his eyes on Karner. "So now I'm thinking about Barbados. Make the switch. Put all our attention there. I hear those men don't work a full day, just like the Jamaicans, but it's worth a try because at least they know our language—after all, they're British citizens—and I hear that, unlike the Jamaicans, they respect authority. Right now, the price of sugar is low in Barbados. Hard for the Negroes there to keep it together. The planters don't have the money to put them to work anymore. Thoughts?"

Karner put a hand on his knee to restrain his left leg from bobbing up and down. He was right to anticipate being pulled into the vortex.

"I know you've been working on the reservoir here," Wallace continued

85

without waiting for Karner's reply. "That construction's almost done. Soon we'll have clean water. What do you say, can I redirect you? To recruit for us? You're a great engineer. You'll make an even greater Chief Recruiter. And the pay's better."

Karner thought little of backwater Bridgetown, which would be his destination in Barbados. He weighed that against his loyalty to Wallace, who always seemed to have a new job for him. Coming to a quick decision—probably the only available decision—Karner tried to see this proposed exile as an opportunity. Perhaps he could make his mark, could succeed where even Secretary of War Taft had failed.

"I'm willing to give it a try. What's your timetable?"

"How soon can you pack?"

Understanding an order, Karner immediately booked passage to Bridgetown on the Royal Mail Line Steamer *Atrato*. Upon arrival, he checked into the prestigious Marine Hotel, believing that he should appear as a man of means if he was to convince others that he could pay for workers. His immediate concern was to figure out how he was going to afford the bill at the Marine, since due to the ICC's red tape, he couldn't get travel expenses up front, and he had no idea when he would see evidence of his increased salary. While fretting about that personal problem, he developed a plan for the personnel problem. He would save the canal. He would save his boss's reputation.

William Karner

Wednesday, January 4, 1905, and the next four months

William Karner took a few weeks to adjust to Barbados's capital of Bridgetown and devise a plan of action. Early in January, he handed his credentials to the Colonial Secretary, an Englishman who listened attentively to the Isthmian Canal Commission's new proposal for laborers. "Sensible plan, old chap, sensible plan," he said, to Karner's relief. The Colonial Secretary himself took responsibility for the next step, arranging for Karner to meet with Barbados's Governor Gilbert Carter. Karner could address his host as either Governor Carter or Sir Gilbert, whichever he chose. Neither came easily to Karner, but he settled on the more familiar Governor Carter.

Karner worried he would receive a cold shoulder, like Taft's treatment by Governor Swettenham in Jamaica. Instead, Governor Carter welcomed his American visitor with warmth, showing him around the palatial Government House. Carter seemed desperate to get rid of his starving and unemployed subjects, whereas Swettenham couldn't think beyond his distrust of Americans. Also, Governor Carter's second wife was a wealthy Bostonian, and perhaps incidentally, an artist and an architect. Was she a true patriot, putting in a good word for Karner? Or did the Christmas season help? Whatever the case, Karner soon received the coveted permit to contract for labor in Barbados. He had taken a key first step. He could not have known that his accomplishment would soon change, some might say for the better, the lives of tens of thousands of people and the future of an island country.

At the meeting in Government House, supportive Governor Carter suggested Karner hire an assistant, Barbadian S.E. Brewster. Brewster, the sixty-year-old scion of a family of planters who had failed even in good times, proved more capable than his forbearers, according to Carter. Brewster had been the sanitary inspector of St. Michael's Parish, a road inspector, and an agent for a steam packet company. He knew the ways of the island and if given an opportunity, could be of help. Karner, trained as an engineer, recognized the potential value of a local assistant.

Karner wasted no time hiring Brewster. Within a day, Brewster recommended where to set up shop—an abandoned loft between Bridgetown's Trafalgar Square and the warehouse district. Karner happily signed a two-year lease for the space. Brewster knew to advertise for workers in the local papers, the *Jamaican Gleaner* and the *Advocate*. Those who could read would read aloud to those who could not. Brewster knew to send runners to the parishes to spread the news. Brewster knew to offer scouts a bonus for every man they sent to the recruiting office. Brewster knew that Dr. Ward in Bridgetown could follow the ICC's medical requirements. By early February, Karner & Brewster were in business.

Nothing went as planned.

"Why did only fourteen men show up today?" Karner snapped at Brewster a week later. At this rate, how were they going to deliver for Wallace? "You told me this would be like shooting fish in a barrel. Dr. Ward stands around with little to do."

"You are usually so cordial, Mr. Karner. I hear your frustration today. Let's talk this through. The men here still remember stories about the workers who went last year and who went in the '80s for the French. They died of all those disgusting plagues. Bad way to go. Why should they sail to their deaths, even for your good wages? Tell me the truth, are you sure conditions are better now? How do you know? I hope you didn't hide anything from me." Brewster had never been to Panama. He had to rely on Karner for the latest news, just as Karner had to rely on him to understand

Barbados.

"Brewster, I told you, I talked to Dr. Gorgas myself. You can trust the man. He tells me Yellow Fever is over. My pals on the isthmus say they might even send for their wives. These men are telling the truth unless they've had enough of their wives and want them to suffer a miserable death."

Brewster, though happily married, managed a chuckle. "Then it's a matter of time," he assured Karner. "Be patient. Word will get back to these men that the isthmus isn't a death trap, not anymore. As soon as a steamer comes back from Panama with healthy workers taking a break to see their families, the tide will turn."

To help that tide a bit Karner wrote a letter for the local *Advocate*, explaining how conditions had improved and stressing good wages. He would stretch the truth if he had to, but there was no need. Within six weeks, the tide did turn. Just as Brewster predicted, a few Barbadian laborers who worked on the canal came back for a brief visit, loaded down with pockets of money they flashed around to their countrymen. "Money like apples on a tree," was the chorus heard around the island. A week later, the line of applicants at the recruiting office, snaking around the block, nearly overwhelmed the fledgling operation. Karner hired Barbadian police to keep order in the line while he and Brewster divided up their increasing responsibilities. Brewster manned the door to the office and let in one hundred men at a time, twice a week. Karner told the young ones and the old ones to go home. A few scrawny boys claimed they were twenty. Karner saw through that ruse.

Once the eligible men entered the office, Dr. Ward took charge. He rolled back their eyelids to screen them for trachoma, ignoring the wailing protestations heard up and down the line. He told the recruits to strip and listened to their chests, again ignoring protestations. Any poor fellows with TB were kicked out. He checked for hernias. More whimpering from frightened applicants who had never been touched by a doctor.

The tests winnowed each group of a hundred down to forty. Next came the smallpox vaccinations. Karner & Brewster wouldn't take anyone who already had three little vaccination scars. Those men wouldn't have been vaccinated in Barbados, so the marks meant they had already been to the canal and had given up for some reason that wouldn't be good news. The isthmus needed fresh recruits. Dr. Ward vaccinated the men remaining in line, of course, under more noisy protests.

The recruits cheered as Karner handed them contracts he had printed up. In return for working 500 days on the Isthmus, each laborer was guaranteed free passage there and back, free lodging, free medical care (though Karner said it wouldn't be needed), and ten cents an hour, in silver, for a ten-hour day. This daily wage was three to four times more than they were accustomed to on the sugar plantations.

Karner signed a contract with the Royal Mail Steam Packet for steamers to take the recruits from Bridgetown to Colón. To begin with, two steamers a week. They weren't enough. He chartered a third steamer. He was doing his job for the canal, for his country, and for Chief Engineer John Findley Wallace, who had mentored him. Karner didn't know then that one-third of the young men from Barbados would spend time on the isthmus, changing lives for themselves and lives back home.

Karner also didn't know, until a few months later, that John Findley Wallace had resigned as Chief Engineer. Though Yellow Fever no longer threatened him and his family, he felt drained from the fear. He was also annoyed that Roosevelt opted for a lock canal rather than a sea-level canal and was even more annoyed with red tape in Washington. While bureaucrats there slowed down Karner's travel money, they also slowed down requisitions for essential supplies and equipment.

Unsociable John Stevens would replace Wallace. Stevens was not a fan of either Barbadian or Jamaican laborers. In a letter to ICC chairman Theodore Shonts, Stevens wrote, "I do not believe that the average West Indian…is more than equivalent to one-third of an ordinary white northern laborer." Nonetheless, Karner knew that his recruiting efforts were essential. Stevens depended on Karner & Brewster to bring him the West Indian laborers he needed. In the eyes of many, the Assistant Engineer turned Chief Recruiter, who recruited thousands, would make a greater contribution to the canal than the Chief Engineer who had hired him.

Meanwhile, William Karner continued to worry about his bill at the Marine Hotel in Bridgetown. He would not receive travel funds or an increased salary for six months. Outperforming William Howard Taft in the recruiting department, Karner would reap praise in Panama. But unable to pay his hotel bill, Karner would be a deadbeat in Bridgeton.

Selina Thompson

Thursday, September 27, 1906, and the next six days

Selina Thompson carried over her shoulder a light canvas sack stuffed with the two muslin dresses she owned, one church dress, undergarments, and a tin plate. Her Aunt Aletha, at twenty-one, just six years older than Selina, didn't have much more in her own sack. "You keep near when we get on board," Aletha said. Carlyle Bay in Bridgetown teemed with people, some sweating through laborer's clothes, others sweating through linen suits, all miserable from the heat. Carriage drivers rumbled up to the wharf to unload baggage. Teamsters handed off satchels of mail to dockworkers. Market women hawked bananas and mangoes. Mothers and children shouted goodbyes, good wishes. Selina and Aletha had heard such a level of noise only in the sugar mills of Barbados, with their grinding and crushing machines. Most of those mills had closed the year before.

First to see their boat, Selina pointed to a large steamer with *La Plata* stenciled on the side in large letters and Royal Mail Steam Packet Company in smaller letters. It rested at anchor in the water, just beyond the dock. Selina saw a smaller boat bobbing to the side of *La Plata* and guessed it would take passengers to the steamer. Six or seven police boats floated by too. A show of force. The police sitting on the decks looked bored. Folks in the crowd may have made a racket, but no one acted rowdy.

Selina counted three rows of passengers standing on the dock, in the area closest to *La Plata*. White men queued in the front line, each holding papers and leather suitcases. They stood still, keeping their distance from each other. Colored men queued in the middle line. A few good lookers. One or two noticed her. Besides holding papers, they carried their baggage, usually a sack like Selina's, a deck chair to sit and sleep in, and sometimes an accordion or guitar. They looked jumpy, chatty. Island women waited in the third line, dressed the usual way—threadbare, bright dresses with flounced skirts and white head scarfs. Selina felt relieved they wore no special clothing for the voyage, or maybe they were saving their finery for later. Only one of the women had pale skin. None of them seemed to talk, other than sharing the sailors' directions that some heard, and some didn't.

Selina and her Aunt Aletha lingered, unsure where to go. The third line seemed likely, but they were wary, had never been to Bridgetown before, wanted to be certain. Sometimes Selina looked to Aletha for an explanation of what they were watching. More times Aletha, gnawing on her bottom lip, looked to Selina with her left eye, the one that didn't wander. Aletha took an extra bandana from her satchel, wiped the sweat off Selina's brow, then her own. After ten minutes, they sorted out the pattern. Little activity in lines one and three. Lots of movement in line two. A white man in a suit keeping watch on the second line would shout a number, hard to hear, then a black man would move forward and hand over a small sheet of paper, which the white man matched up with his own papers.

"We don't get in line with de colored men," Aletha said. "Just like we thought. We don't have recruitment numbers. We get in with de women, third class tickets."

Selina and Aletha walked to the back of the third line, taking their place behind the last woman, really a girl, who offered a sullen glance. The sun continued to blaze, Aletha continued to swipe sweat. The women watched the front line of white men move toward the steamer. Then the middle line of colored men. After an hour, a British sailor walked toward the women's line, stopped fifteen feet away. "Time to move. Hand me your ticket before you jump down." He shooed the women onto the small boat, which he called a lighter, then on to the steamer. "This way, on the deck to the right," he shouted above the rumble of the engine. "Find a spot. That's where you'll bed down for the trip. Men went to the stern, women to the bow. No need to go below deck. We'll bring you food here. Remember, no need to leave the bow."

Selina and her aunt grabbed a spot and watched the others settle in. Within a few minutes, the women started to talk, to share stories. Maybe they talked because they were comfortable now, sitting, or maybe because they knew they'd be shipmates for nearly a week. Sue, the sullen girl who had stood ahead of Selina in line, planned to meet her boyfriend. He had sent her the fourteen shillings she needed for the passage from Barbados. She saw no need to get married, though she promised to say she was married if any white person asked. Charlotte, who clung to a satchel protecting her wedding dress, also planned to meet a boyfriend. This boyfriend was already arranging a church wedding. Emily, the pale woman, stayed mostly quiet, with a way of talking that none of the others recognized. She would look for work, she said, fiddling with the head scarf that covered most of her straight brown hair. Later she became chattier, talking about her Irish family in St. Johns Parish. Selina and Aletha had heard of poor Irish in Barbados. They had never met any of them.

On the first day, Selina sat back while Aletha shared their own story. "My mate Michael want me and his niece, Selina here, to be with him in Panama. Her parents dead. We her family now. He save up and send tickets for both of us. It hard, he wrote, for a worker there with no woman to keep house. We both scared, but no reason to stay in Barbados." Just then Selina felt the ship sway. She had been in little boats before, fishing. Never a big steamer. Six days of this would be fun. For some.

By day six, Aunt Aletha had stopped vomiting over the railing and had started to eat again. Selina was luckier, using the voyage to make friends. Charlotte, still holding tight to her satchel, kept the women amused with stories from her boyfriend's letters. He wrote about the glories of the canal, but Charlotte said he couldn't write. Someone else must have helped. In the letters he complained about noise from monkeys and about tasteless food. Mostly he bragged about good wages. Selina thought these letters seemed a lot like the ones Uncle Michael had sent to Aunt Aletha. Except her uncle would have written those himself. Other young women on the steamer added to the chatter, one teasing Selina that at age fifteen, with her looks, she should already have a young man, one warning her against men. Especially those she might find in Panama, full of themselves. As for the young colored men who ogled Selina on the Carlyle Bay dock, she never got to the *La Plata's* stern to see them, and they never got to the bow.

The scene changed as day six dawned. The colored men from the stern scrambled in a pack toward the women at the bow. Selina wondered if one of the good lookers would spot her until she realized their eyes were not on the women, but on the horizon. "Land soon," one of them said. Selina pushed her way to the railing, looking for the shore. Within an hour, the steamer pulled into the dock at Limon Bay in Colón, even noisier and more crowded than Bridgetown's Carlyle Bay. The women reached into their sacks and put on their Sunday clothes and bonnets. Little did they know how much mud awaited them. Selina and her aunt dressed as best they could. Aunt Aletha, happy to see land, took extra care. She donned the headscarf and beads she knew Michael had liked. As the steamer reached land, neatly dressed men and women in stylish clothing came into view. Selina saw her aunt chewing her bottom lip again, willing her right eye to behave. "These island clothes," she said, "they look shabby."

First to debark, the businessmen in their wrinkled linen suits hobbled off the ship. Then the workers, also unsteady, were herded down the ramp and over to waiting officials who looked them over carefully. Finally, the women were steered off to find their way on their own. Selina and Aletha were lucky. Michael Thompson—one of the Barbadians Karner & Brewster had hired after clearing him for trachoma, a hernia, and tuberculosis and vaccinating him for smallpox—stood waiting for them.

Godfrey Moody, Steven Bronner

Monday, November 5, 1906

T he recruits rounded up by Karner & Brewster and laborers coming to Panama on their own faced back-breaking work. Much would be familiar—long hours, sweat, abuse. Abuse had been part of their lives as far back as they could recall, and before then, according to stories passed down. Gradually, sometimes cautiously, laborers began to wonder if abuse on the canal was different, less predetermined than abuse where they had come from.

Thousands of these men, divided into work crews, began to prepare the earth at the Gatun Dam site for what would become the largest dam in the world. Godfrey Moody, a young laborer from Barbados, adjusted the dusty bandage over his ear, the result of standing too close to a swinging crane. He listened to his crew leader, Alejandro Calvo, the Spaniard with the gold tooth and the odd accent. The only Spaniard on their crew. If you listened to Alejandro, you might keep your limbs. Alejandro knew dynamite, knew how to keep Godfrey and the other six men on the crew out of trouble. How to remind them to hold their shovels carefully so they didn't strike the explosive charges. How to dig to just the right depth. His instructions on dynamite rang clearly through the air as the work gang crouched in the mud.

Now Alejandro lowered his voice. "Tonight, at 8:00. We need you." He whispered the invitation only to Godfrey. Alejandro knew Godfrey came from Barbados, but he must have guessed that of them all, Godfrey would be the only one to listen, the only one who would have followed stories about unrest among the workers.

"Vienna Hotel. Near the Culebra Cut," Alejandro added, again just for Godfrey. "Virden will be there." Godfrey and Alejandro both looked up to check that the foreman was too far away to hear. John Cunningham, a white man from Ohio, was not among the worst of the foremen, but his crew knew he had orders to make sure the men worked a full day, and emphatic orders to put a stop to any unrest. Cunningham turned around, walked back their way. Godfrey raised his palm in a clear warning to wait for a work break.

An hour later, the crew emerged from the ditch for their break, all dressed in the standard laborer's uniform—khaki pants and a blue shirt—now coated with mud. Only Alejandro wore a different cap, one he had brought with him from Spain. Cunningham gave the crew leader latitude on headwear.

Alejandro and Godfrey sat together, leaning against the same piece of machinery. "Not sure if I come," Godfrey said. "Virden don't want us." Godfrey emphasized "us." Alejandro pursed his lips, frowned.

"*Cobarde*," Alejandro said, spitting out the word, turning his head away.

Godfrey did not know Spanish, but he knew the Spanish word for coward. He had heard it before. But why would he, or any other worker from Barbados, help Virden, a white miner who had been running around the isthmus clamoring for an eight-hour day, for his kind. He hadn't made much progress.

"Virden, white man, he gold, and you boys from Spain, you gold too," Godfrey said. "Well, you sometimes gold. Me and my mates, we silver. That never going to change." Godfrey understood the order of things on the canal. White men at the top, paid in gold. Colored men like himself at the bottom, paid in silver. Men from Spain or Italy or Greece like Alejandro, somewhere in the middle, but paid in gold.

"Sí. Virden is gold," Alejandro said. "And he wants more for white workers. That's good. But we need to tell him that if he is going to be *activista— cómo se dice*—an activist for better wages, he should stand up for the rest of us. If he wants a strike, he needs us to strike too."

Godfrey knew Alejandro Calvo's story. He was one of two hundred Spaniards, most from impoverished Galicia in northwest Spain, who had sailed to Cuba to build a railroad at the turn of the century and then been recruited to come to Panama. He had learned explosives and enough English to get by. Isthmus officials were hardly in love with the Spaniards. They called them Gallegos, rolling their eyes as they said the word. But the officials believed the Spaniards, along with other European workers, were more skilled than the West Indians. The Spaniards were paid twice as much as the darker laborers and had separate mess halls and quarters—better than the West Indians' but not as fine as the Americans'. Godfrey knew this and more because he read all the broadsides plastered in the bars in silver towns, read them before the police tore them up. He knew that by recruiting Spaniards, the officials had another goal. They thought if the labor force was made up of groups from different countries, speaking different languages, the men were unlikely to collaborate to ask for better wages or shorter hours. The officials had not anticipated a worker like Alejandro, a worker who managed to get his hands on treatises from across the ocean and had grown up in a town where he learned the language of internationalism.

Godfrey leaned in closer to Alejandro. "Why you bother?" Godfrey asked. "You gold."

"Maybe no more. Stevens, he wants to move all the Spaniards and Greeks to silver." Alejandro spit on the ground in disgust. "The ICC is arguing about all that now. Men who came from my town in Spain, the ones in the crew at the spoil cars, they want me to speak up."

Godfrey pictured John Stevens, the Chief Engineer. This man knew how to build a canal. He understood the need to improve the railroads first, to take away dirt the workers dug. But he hated the diggers. "Stevens want you to use the silver bathrooms with us?" Godfrey asked. "And go to the silver pay window with us? And the silver entrance to the commissary?"

"Sí. System is bad for you. And would be bad for us, too," Alejandro said. Another crew, not on their break, started drilling, helping to cover sounds of talk. "Stevens has us all working against each other—competidoras. You gotta see that. Virden thinks he knows about labor, but all he knows is American. The miners' Cripple Creek strike in Colorado. The meat cutters in Chicago. In Spain, sí, wages and hours, they're important, but we also want *colectivismo*." Godfrey squinted his eyes. "Collectivism. Sounds strange to you, right? In my town in Spain, we have councils that work together. They organize rent strikes, food riots."

Godfrey tilted his head, trying to understand. John Cunningham blew a whistle and Alejandro led his crew back to work.

Four hours later, as the men drank from the water van on the site and broke up for the evening, Alejandro grabbed Godfrey by the sleeve. "We need you. Bring your friends. You West Indians just accept everything. Time to change."

Godfrey had heard that before. Everyone thought the men from Barbados and Jamaica were placid, looking for just enough money to live on, never trying to get up in the world. He knew some of his buddies fit that tag, but most of them worked hard, especially once they got to Panama. But that word—*cobarde*—most of the men who had thrown that word at Godfrey had been louts, not worth bothering about. Alejandro, though, he was a good man. Looked after his crew.

"You wrong," Godfrey said. He paused, his face contorted. "Maybe I see you at the Vienna."

Godfrey took the worker's train back to Silver City, where he shared a shack with Tom Gordon, the meat peddler who came to Panama from the same village in Barbados. Tom would not join him that evening. Said he had heard too much about police thugs. On his rounds from house to house, talking with ladies and their maids, Tom picked up a lot of news, but he picked up airs too—thought he was better than some of the boys he'd come over with.

Godfrey walked the muddy paths of Silver City and found two mates with no plans for that evening.

* * *

Texan Steven Bonner took off his Canal Zone policeman's uniform and donned khaki trousers and a blue work shirt. Looking at the small mirror in his boarding house, he parted his hair differently and replaced his cap with a slouch hat favored by skilled laborers. Bonner smiled at his reflection. Not his best look, but suitably unremarkable. He took a train to a tavern near the Culebra Cut and chose a stool away from others, at the end of the bar. After two beers, he was as ready as he would ever be. He trudged to the Hotel Vienna, timing himself to enter the barroom just after the meeting began.

Bonner loitered in a corner of the back room, smoking a cigar and fussing a great deal with cutting, lighting, and puffing, using his hands to mask his face. The smoke mingled with the sour smell of dozens of sweaty men. Usually at ease with his nonstop mouth, Bonner knew that today he needed to keep quiet, focus on his eyes. He saw about twenty workers, ranging in color from light to dark, and enough light-skinned patrons—boiler makers, brakemen, dredge operators—so that he didn't stick out in the crowd.

"We don't get overtime. Skilled workers don't get overtime. Why should we stand for that?" grumbled Joe Virden, the white miner the men had come to hear. Virden perched himself on the bar, his legs dangling. Looked like he was enjoying his audience. "The colored workers get overtime."

At a table to his right, Bonner saw four colored men with beers. They had been quiet, listening to Virden rile up the crowd, but now the man with a bandage over his left ear stood up to talk. "Yeah, but you get paid twice as much as we do."

"What about de work week?" one of the other colored men at the table said. Some say five days. Some say six days."

Now a man with lighter skin stood up—a worker, wearing a different cap than the others. "I'm a Spaniard. We've been on the gold rolls." He grinned, pointed to his gold tooth. "Now Stevens says we don't belong on gold, that we're not white. He's trying to move us to silver. How do we stop him?"

The banter went on. The colored man with the bandage had a lot more to say. His buddies echoed his words. The Spaniard kept talking too. And others, some with accents, some without. Bonner couldn't help but admire

100

Joe Virden. The man was listening. Doing his best. "We've heard a lot," Virden said. "If we're going to, you know, do what we've been talking about, we're going to need to agree on demands."

Bonner tuned out from the rest, concentrating instead on trying to get the names of the rabble-rousers while fading into the crowd. But the men were on guard, giving away little. Finally, the colored men to his left, who'd been doing more drinking than agitating, started to banter among themselves. "That Godfrey, he usually quiet. Now he talk. Looks like he can still hear, even with that bandage. But he need a bandage on his mouth."

Godfrey. Bonner suspected a lot of Godfreys worked at the canal, but not too many to check into. He unclenched his jaw, rounded his shoulders.

Bonner understood the rules. Workers could gather, could talk. Just not agitate. He knew that his boss, Chief Shanton, already had Virden's name from past surveillance. Tomorrow Bonner could provide another name. One should be enough to satisfy Shanton. No need to stay longer. Bonner left the meeting, sliding his right hand down his left sleeve, his left hand down his right sleeve, trying to push away his unease. Five days later, Bonner would be reassigned to ship duty, checking the passengers who disembarked in Colón. Three days after ship duty, he would be particularly observant during a poker game. Two days after the poker game, he would have prison duty, guarding Jerome Kehl, with a chance to share his observations with agent Larry Richey.

Jeffrey Fowler

Monday, April 3 and Tuesday, April 4, 1905

On April 3, 1905, at 3:00 in Bridgetown, eighteen months before Selina and Aletha boarded *La Plata*, assistant recruiter S. E. Brewster offered Michael Thompson a one-page contract for 500 days of pick and shovel labor, at ten cents per hour, in the Panama Canal Zone. One hour earlier and 1,821 nautical miles away in New York City, a recruiter handed Jeffrey Fowler a three-page contract, stipulating forty-two days paid vacation, thirty days sick leave, nine paid holidays, and a salary that was twice what he had been earning on the Erie Canal.

Late that night, Jeffrey Fowler returned to his red-brick Greek Revival row house on Liberty Street in Troy, New York. The house looked grand from the outside, but both Jeffrey and his wife, Liza, knew it needed a new roof and plumbing repairs. As Jeffrey limped downstairs the next morning, he smelled his usual breakfast of toast, eggs, and coffee. He saw that his wife Liza had placed the *Albany Evening Journal* next to his plate, while she fed baby Gregory. The morning routine would last two more minutes.

Jeffrey sat forward on his chair, fiddling with his eggs, forgetting to butter his toast. He neglected to rail about yesterday's shenanigans in the Albany legislature. He stared at the same spot on the front page of the *Journal*. Liza showed no sign of registering these peculiarities.

"You must have come back late," she said, her voice rising. "Never heard you come in."

"Yah, it was late, near midnight." Jeffrey paused, doing his best to modify his shallow breathing. He put his cup down, hoping Liza would not notice his trembling hand. "The truth is that my meeting was not down the road in Albany. I went to New York. The city." Another pause. "We need to talk, Elizabeth."

She stared. She looked alarmed at his strained tone, at his use of her full name. She would insist he tell her why he lied. She would suspect the usual. Drink. Whores. Not this time.

"I'm unhappy at the canal." He had rehearsed these words on the train the night before. "The work is tedious, and I don't know when I'll ever get to be senior engineer. You want that for me, too, right? We both want that title and the salary. My experience with the Erie Canal is valuable, even more than I realized. Last week I saw an article in the *New York Tribune*. The people Roosevelt appointed to run the other canal, the Panama Canal, they're looking for people like me. So I went to New York yesterday and talked to one of their representatives, a recruiting agent. Didn't want to tell you because I had no idea if this made sense for us. But the arrangements are perfect." Yet another pause. "I signed a contract."

He forced himself to meet Liza's eyes. Everyone in Troy, at least everyone who paid attention, believed his wife had married up. While Jeffrey Fowler's father owned a lumber mill in Troy, Liza's father was an irregularly employed handyman. Now she had married an engineer, a professional man, lived in a row house in town. True, Jeffrey knew he was not the best-looking of her suitors. A childhood accident left him with a limp and Liza chided him on his expanding waist. With her looks, she could have found a more attractive husband, but Jeffrey had the most promise. And she cared dearly about that promise, that climb up Troy's ladder.

Before Liza could spit out an angry response, Jeffrey continued, racing through the selling points he had rehearsed. "The pay's twice what I make here. The canal Commission will give us free housing and free transportation. They're building clubs with dining halls and planning social events. You'll have servants to help with the house and with Gregory. The medical authorities are cleaning up diseases there. The engineers and administrators talk about bringing their wives over. You'll meet swell new friends and be in good company, good society. And I'll get to work on what looks like the biggest engineering project of the century. My title will be Senior Engineer in the Department of Excavation and Dredging. That's in the Department of Construction and Engineering. Everything has a long name in Panama."

As he talked, Jeffrey Fowler could almost forget what had pushed him to yesterday's New York City appointment.

He had graduated five years earlier from Rensselaer Polytechnic Institute with a degree in civil engineering., with his family cheering him on. Uncle Daniel Fowler was one of the loudest cheerers. Uncle Daniel owned a factory on the outskirts of Troy that produced building supplies and concrete. He played a role in local affairs and spoke to some of his pals about nephew Jeffrey's new skills. Before long Jeffrey accepted a position at the Erie Canal to help design a new lock system and a deepening of the canal. In these years experts and politicians debated changes to the route and depth of the Erie and how much those changes would cost, debates that in some ways paralleled the squabbles over the Panama Canal. The State of New York asked for estimate after estimate, for this plan and that plan. Jeffrey served as a member of the group that arranged for bids. In late 1904, Troy Building Supply was awarded a multi-million-dollar contract for concrete. It didn't take long before the New York State Committee on canals realized that Troy Building Supply was owned by Uncle Daniel Fowler. The agitated State Engineer summoned Jeffrey Fowler for questioning. Did Jeffrey leak word of the other bids? Did he tell Uncle Daniel what the New York canal Commission would give greatest weight to? Did he alter the bid after it arrived? Jeffrey admitted to nothing, stating repeatedly that Uncle Daniel always came cheap. The State Engineer had already weathered numerous scandals. Said he couldn't afford another. He encouraged Jeffrey to resign. After hours of wrangling, they came to an agreement. Jeffrey would resign, and in return, no charges would be pressed. The story would be hushed up.

For the rest of his life, Jeffrey Fowler would worry that Liza might learn the true story behind their move to the isthmus. But at least for now, the

State Engineer honored his part of the bargain. Jeffrey saw Liza's face change with every detail he added to his rundown of arrangements. Her taut mouth and sharp blue eyes softened. Maybe this would all work out for the better. Neither Jeffrey nor Liza had ever been south of New York City. Now Liza would have a chance to see the world as a refined lady. And Jeffrey had a second chance to build.

Liza Fowler, Jeffrey Fowler

Wednesday, October 31, 1906

The ants, both red and black, attacked the bread. Disgusting. They carried crumbs, crumbs bigger than the ants themselves, across the kitchen floor.

"Not again. Not again." Liza Fowler screamed at the marching line, then at that girl, Selina. "Last month, roaches and mice. Then lizards and bats. Sometimes a scorpion. Now godawful ants. Can't you keep this house cleaner?"

The girl looked down, muffling a laugh.

"Miz Liza, do you want to know how we get rid of ants in muh—my—house?"

"Is this going to be some bit of West Indies hocus pocus? Give me a solution, not magic."

Liza couldn't believe how stupid her new girl was. Karen, the ignorant Jamaican girl she had before, was almost as bad, though she had been in Panama for longer and knew at least something about American ways. As Karen started to show more and more of a belly last month, Liza had to dismiss her. Maybe Tom Gordon, that Barbadian who peddled meat each afternoon in the Fowlers' neighborhood, had stuck around too long. Handsome man, even with that dark skin. Liza wasn't worried about how Karen would fare. She knew Karen's family would care for her, unlike families with such scandals in Troy. Now Jeffrey had brought Selina into their house in the lovely gold town of Empire. A girl fresh from Barbados.

A girl who might be the prettiest damn maid on the isthmus. What a gift. Selina had never seen a doorbell before. She called it a squealing button. She had never seen a watch before. She called it a pocket engine. She had no idea how to set the table for supper. She had boiled a Porterhouse steak. She could barely pronounce basic English sounds. How would this West Indies girl know how to eradicate pests?

"We put kerosene on plates and put table legs into four of dose—those—plates," Selina said. She raised her eyes, lowered them.

Liza looked again at the marching line of ants. Shrugged her shoulders. "Shit. What do I have to lose? You fetch the kerosene from the storeroom. I'll get the plates."

Both women bent down to place the dishes under the table. Liza, wearing her flower-print daytime dress of fine cotton and still cursing, by accident rubbed up against Selina's simple muslin shift. Twisted away. Just then, they heard a door open and looked down the hallway to see Jeffrey Fowler. He was never at home at this hour in the morning. She should remind him to take off his boots—they'd be filthy. Selina wouldn't get around to cleaning the hall floor for a while, and Liza certainly wasn't going to mop. But today, she was so startled by Jeffrey's early arrival and by the look on his face that she ignored the mud. She didn't even bother to see if Selina looked away from him, as usual.

"My God," swore Liza. "What's happened?"

"We were getting ready to dig out the next level. Everything was in order. I followed all the rules. I asked the foreman to set out the tubes. Michael was going to help the foreman." Jeff looked over at Selina as he said this, then looked away. "I'm so sorry about your uncle, Selina. You better go find your aunt and tell her what happened. Michael's shovel hit a tube. It exploded. His foot got real bloody. The men put him in the ambulance car. You'll need to get to Ancon to find him in the hospital. Just take the day off."

Selina said nothing. She ran off.

"Liza, I've got to get back to the site," Jeffrey said. "I'll need to do an accident report for Stevens and find another man to take Michael's place." She heard his uneven gait as he left.

Gregory had been crawling along the floor, too close to where the ants marched. Liza scooped him up and went out on to the house's veranda. She was annoyed that Selina would be away for a few hours. Jeffrey had told the girl to take the day off as though that were nothing, nothing at all.

From the veranda, Liza looked out over the yard, her yard, even if she shared the house with other families. The ICC had built the impressive two-story building the previous year, thinking about both practicalities and appearances. The builders screened the porch, top and bottom, with fine copper wire to keep out mosquitos. They used corrugated iron on the roof to protect against drenching rains. They planted gardens of hibiscus and bougainvillea, with lawns of green grass surrounding all the houses in the neighborhood. Liza never took those details for granted. She lived now in a grand manner, by the standards of Panama and certainly by the standards of Troy. Yes, four families shared the house, two on the first floor and two on the second. But the spaces were large and private, and the families were all led by professional men, division engineers like Jeffrey, or ICC officials.

Liza knew, too, that her town of Empire had a perfect location. The town was adjacent to Culebra Cut, where most of the excavation in the Zone was underway. Laborers lived on the other side of the railroad, on lower land, in either Red Tank or Paraiso. Selina lived with her aunt and uncle in Paraiso. Liza would never go there. She would stay on the exclusive side. Could she overlook the vermin? Yes.

Liza had met Michael Thompson, Selina's uncle, once when he picked up his niece. She remembered that Jeffrey considered the laborer reliable. Today's accident was the second this month. The first was worse, but it was under another supervisor's watch. An empty train car, too light to make noise that rose above the other noises, rolled down a hill after its brakes failed. A worker loading a different train car was crushed to death.

Liza's thoughts did not linger on the newest accident. She would have to manage today without the girl. Listening to her neighbors, Liza had learned that ladies had no choice but to work around the tragedies of their help. Now, without Selina to do the chores, Liza would need to walk to the train station to pick up her day's supply of ice. She would need to haul water

108

from the tank. She would need to hunt for meat that looked palatable and bread that looked fresh. All this while carrying Gregory. She could handle the extra work for a day, but Selina better get herself back soon.

* * *

Jeffrey Fowler hustled, as fast as he could with his limp, just over a mile back to the muck of the Culebra Cut. The mud, which reached halfway up his high boots, was oddly welcome—it allowed Jeffrey to focus on keeping his balance, not on the accident. As he approached the site, through the haze he could see crews on every level of the terraced earth. Even though he had left the site to report on Michael Thompson to his niece Selina, Jeffrey saw that the laborers had not taken advantage of his absence. They had filled two spoil cars, almost full, with dirt and would soon send them downhill to the latest dump site.

The men worked silently. No singing, no banter. They had seen the accident. This time they had no body parts to pick up. The explosion had decimated Michael's toes. After a minute of searching, Jeffrey found the foreman he was looking for among the workers from Michael's crew on the third tier.

"His niece knows now. She'll tell his wife. And I'll get a report from the hospital tomorrow." Jeffrey spoke quietly to the foreman.

"Michael, okay. Just toes. Not as bad as de other guy last week. Thanks." The foreman was thanking Jeffrey for not yelling. Both men understood none of the workers were at fault. The foreman guided his men well and Michael knew the dangers, paid attention. Sometimes the explosives were so buried that not even the most careful diggers could see them.

Most days Jeffrey Fowler appreciated his job. Good, honest engineering work, work he had trained to do. He could look at the land, assess the slope, estimate the pounds of rock and mud, schedule the week's work, and then manage his many crews. The men trusted him and knew him to be fair. And yet he had failed Michael Thompson. Yes, he had assigned Michael to an experienced foreman who had been on the isthmus for six months.

But that wasn't enough. Jeffrey knew that as a division engineer, he was ultimately responsible for every death, every missing limb, and even every toe, whether Chief Engineer Stevens cared or not. Jeffrey would fill out a report, which Stevens, busy with so many details, might glance at. Jeffrey was certain the accident would not lead to any reprimand, especially since his weekly reports of excavation progress continued to be outstanding. He had learned quickly—it was the dig that mattered.

Today, as he did many days, Jeffrey brooded over his worries. He knew some men pushed their problems aside. He preferred to think them to death. His work on the canal, with its responsibilities to his men and his bosses, was in the forefront now. But then there was Liza, his beautiful, shrewish wife, and Emily, his resourceful, agreeable new Irish whore. He needed Liza because he had never expected to attract such a comely wife. He liked looking at how men looked at her. He needed Emily, well, that was all about lust, but he also needed her because she admired him without reservations. Jeffrey had been raised to know all this was wrong, but not so very wrong. He had a third worry, too—the secret of his past record on another canal. Third, for now.

Jeffrey Fowler

L a Boheme was not the only establishment of its kind. Laborers frequented the filthy stalls of Bottle Alley in Colón. Boilermakers and yardmasters frequented the bars and brothels of both port cities. Professionals and managers frequented the lavishly decorated La Boheme at the top of the heap. In Panama City, The Luna occupied a place somewhere along the spectrum. Upstairs were five small, seedy rooms usually occupied by whores and their patrons. Downstairs were games of chance, including poker games. Division engineer Jeffrey Fowler liked The Luna. Every Tuesday, he visited Emily Byrne in room four before he moved on to the poker table. He had married, it was said, the most beautiful woman in Troy, New York, and she accommodated his bedtime preferences. But Jeffrey wanted more, with variety not easily available in Troy.

Policeman Steven Bonner liked to join the Tuesday game, which he said provided relief from the boredom of his prison guard duty and the anxiety of his surveillance duty. Fowler and the other fellows liked to hear Bonner's chatter about police escapades. Bonner seemed to like their chatter, boasting about tons of earth moved.

On the night of November 13th, Jeffrey Fowler reminded his wife he needed to complete his weekly status reports for Chief Engineer Stevens and would return home after midnight. He took the train to Panama City, assuming he would see Emily at the same time he had for the last three

111

weeks, 8:00.

"Mister Fowler, you'll have to wait. A new customer came first." The Luna's madam lowered her eyes as she gave Fowler the news. She didn't like to disappoint her regulars.

"Really, who is it?" Fowler regretted his angry tone. Not the madam's fault.

"Didn't say. A tall, blond stranger."

Jeffrey frowned. Decided to use his unexpected free time wisely, at the poker table. As he approached, Bonner and the other players nodded, a subtle welcome. After an hour of small losses and smaller wins, and of keeping his eyes on the staircase, Fowler saw a tall, lanky, pale man descend from the second floor and head outside. Fowler had never seen him before. He was good-looking, a fact that registered in Fowler's mind. No excess weight around the middle. No limp. A few minutes later, the madam tapped Fowler on the shoulder. He climbed as fast as he could up the staircase to his delayed pleasures.

"Not easy waiting for you," said Fowler in a bit of a huff. His mind fixated on the stranger's looks.

"Sorry. That man was here first. I had to be with him." Jeffrey loved hearing Emily's Irish lilt, but he remained sullen. "Don't worry," she added quickly. "Judging from his wee wanger, he had something else besides me on his mind."

Jeffrey smiled. "I haven't seen him before." Then he looked at Emily for a name.

"Said he was here to photograph TR's visit. Most men don't talk much. He never shut up. Wore me out with questions about where the President would be going. How would I know? He was good-lookin' but off his nut—crazy. And he had a British accent. Odd because said he was from Chicago and had a name like he was from Sweden. Ahhh, don't worry, he was clean."

Enough talk. Jeffrey got down to business. After an enjoyable hour, when he forgot all thoughts of jealousy, he returned to the poker table.

"So you had to follow a good-looking new customer," Bonner said, with a teasing stress on good-looking. "I saw that gent go up there."

"Yah. But Emily says he was an odd duck. Asking a lot about the President. Said he was a photographer. With an accent that didn't make sense." Fowler looked at his watch. "Just enough time to catch the last train home."

"Me too," Bonner said. "Good timing since I've run out of money. Tell me again, what did your girl up there say about the stranger?"

Emily Byrne

F ar away in time and space, Oliver Cromwell invaded and conquered Ireland. The Wars of the Three Kingdoms were brutal. In September of 1649, an Irish soldier named James Walsh was taken prisoner at the siege of Drogheda, north of Dublin. When the siege began, he was one of 3100 Irish Royalist soldiers. Most perished. The 200 who survived were transported on ships, ships they considered slavers, from Cork to Bridgetown, Barbados. By law, the prisoners of war were indentured servants, with contracts stipulating that the period of their indenture would be three to seven years. This detail proved meaningless. Their alleged freedom was freedom into continuing poverty and degradation. In Barbados, English overseers removed James's chains so he could work in the sugar fields of a small plantation, Rose Gate, in St. John's Parish. His imprisoned shipmates did not fare any better. Planters and slaves came to think of these Irish as Redlegs because their skin burned under the intense sun.

A year after James arrived in Barbados, Sarah Murphy, the young widow of one of the unfortunate Irish Royalist soldiers, descended into poverty, taxing the limited resources of her Irish village. Against her will, she, too, was transported to Bridgetown, where she was hired on as a cook for the overseer of Rose Gate plantation. She met indentured servant James Walsh the day she arrived. They married six weeks later.

Emily Byrne, born in St. John's Parish over two centuries later, in 1890, would never know that Sarah Murphy and James Walsh were her ancestors: ten greats before the word grandparents. What she would know is ostracism by her non-Redleg neighbors, both wealthy whites and poor blacks, as well as hookworm and other diseases, poverty, and loneliness. When she was fifteen, her older cousin, who worked as a maid for a plantation owner near Rose Gate, secured Emily a job there as a laundress. A year later, Emily met Jason, a carpenter working on repairs to the main house. His status as a skilled black man was higher than hers as a pale Redleg, although that would not be hard. Jason spent less time with bottles of rum than did most of the Redleg youth of St. John's, although, again that would not be hard. The first time Jason visited Emily on the porch of the washhouse, both were shy. The second time, both smiled. The third time, they looked around to make sure they were the only occupants of the porch. No Redleg Emily knew, and certainly, no virginal girl, had taken up with a colored worker. To do so, she had been told, would be to go against the dictates of nature. At some point, Emily stopped thinking about dictates. By the sixth time the two were together, half-dressed and with hands all over each other, Emily's cousin eyed them. She had come from the big house to the washhouse to gossip on a slow day when the plantation owners were away. From that moment on, Emily's life in Barbados became untenable. She would not lose her job because the cousin was too ashamed to tell the owners about Jason. But the cousin didn't hesitate to tell Emily's parents and neighbors. Now Emily was spoiled for the Redleg boys, as though they weren't already spoiled by rum. Her parents gave her a week to move out of their shack. A single route was left for her—the same route many of the young men around her were taking. On September 27, 1906, she walked half a day, arrived in Bridgetown, and boarded *La Plata*, lining up in the same queue as Selina and Aletha Thompson.

The sea voyage had gone better than expected, with its comradery among the women on board. After a few days, they warmed up to her, the only white woman. She soon realized that most of the others were going to meet boyfriends and husbands or had pre-arranged jobs working for families on the isthmus. She would need to scramble.

Though Emily managed to avoid Bottle Alley, she couldn't get on at La Boheme. The proprietor, Sally Miller, considered Emily the wrong material. Her customers preferred less familiar-looking girls. Within three weeks, Emily was one of the most popular whores at The Luna.

Maureen McGowan

Ancon Hospital straddled the top of rocky Ancon Hill, one of the highest spots near the Canal Zone. The main building stood at the center of two dozen detached, smaller buildings. A staff of four hundred—doctors, nurses, and laborers, hardly any born in Panama—worked in the complex. Looking down from the hill, employees with a minute to spare could see Panama City and the Pacific Ocean. In the distance, they could see the new Tivoli Hotel, and if they squinted, they could see workers readying it for the president's arrival. Like the hotel and other grand buildings on the isthmus, the main hospital was a white, wooden structure surrounded by wrap-around porches and screens.

The hospital staff had worked frantically in the years leading up to November 11, 1905, when officials reported the last case of Yellow Fever. Before that landmark announcement, panic had spread, rumors had abounded. The staff heard that Chief Engineer Wallace imported expensive metal caskets for himself and his wife. If the couple succumbed to Yellow Fever, they were prepared for burial. Who could blame them? Wallace's valet and cook were stricken with Yellow Fever. His architect, his auditor, an executive secretary, and the wife of another secretary died from it. And Wallace was only too aware that his predecessor under the French, Jules Dingler, had suffered even more. Dingler's daughter died, then his son, then his daughter's fiancé. Nurses and doctors could do little for any of the patients other than make them as comfortable as possible.

That was to change. The Chief Sanitary Officer, Dr. William Gorgas, knew from his experience in Cuba that mosquitoes caused Yellow Fever, but he couldn't convince Wallace to request funds for cleanup. Wallace feared the disease, but doubted the little mosquito was to blame. After he resigned and Stevens became Chief Engineer, Stevens approved funds for a virtual army of workers and for enormous amounts of supplies—wire screens, netting, fumigation materials, tools to pump out standing water. Gorgas sent sanitation workers throughout the isthmus, concentrating a force at Ancon Hospital. The workers' mission was clear: kill mosquitoes. They checked screens weekly for holes, burned pyrethrum powder on porches, sprayed with a mixture of crude oil and kerosene, drained puddles and ponds, filled thousands of pottery dishes with oil, and set those dishes around the once beautiful hospital garden. In the sick wards, the workers placed the legs of beds in basins filled with more oil. The fight against mosquitoes was intense on hospital grounds and throughout the Zone, and the fight succeeded.

Now doctors and nurses faced medical problems that were no longer deadly, but still serious. Nurse Maureen McGowan, with her long gray dress, starched white apron, and demure cap, walked the first-floor halls of the West Indian ward, moving quickly from bed to bed. She shrunk from this assignment. At least the rotation on the first floor lasted only a month. Then she could go back to caring for the white men on the second-floor ward. Not that many white men filled the beds any longer. With Gorgas's cure, the second floor had emptied out. The few men lying in the white ward mostly suffered from the ravages of malaria, still a torment to everyone in Panama. Those men were too ill to be of romantic interest to Nurse McGowan.

When she first arrived on the isthmus, Maureen had grown skilled at tending to the patients on the second floor, the last of the poor souls who had contracted Yellow Fever just before the cure. She knew she could make those men, professional men, white men with yellowish skin, more comfortable as they vomited and bled through the nose and mouth. It had been terrifying for both patients and staff. The first-floor ward terrified her in a different way. Nothing in the Cleveland Training School for Nurses had prepared her for what she still saw on the first floor—colored men without limbs, without faces, with rips in their middle. Explosives, falling cranes, and runaway trains took their toll. When Maureen signed up for three years in Panama, an honest recruiter said she would be nursing people of all colors. At the time, her need for adventure overshadowed her concerns. Then she had neither a sense of how many colored laborers worked on the isthmus, nor of how their bodies would get torn up in the effort to dig the canal. Nor how uncomfortable she would feel treating them, touching them.

Looking down the hall of the first-floor ward, Maureen saw Dr. Robert Peterson approach. With his sloping shoulders and receding hair, he was less of a catch than many of the other young doctors at Ancon. Somehow, though, he stood out. His interests seemed broader, at least broader than pure medicine and rapid advancement. As she hovered between beds seven and eight, he looked at her, then away. She had already cared for the patients in beds one through seven. It would not do to backtrack. She busied herself with straightening chores at bed seven, while noting the doctor's gait and voice. He took his time with these patients, asking them about their pains and staying for their answers. She waited to treat the patient in bed eight until Dr. Peterson continued his rounds and neared her. As he reached bed eight, Maureen began to change the temporary dressing on eight's foot, gently, more slowly than she might have on another day. "How are you feeling, Mr. Thompson? Michael?" the doctor asked. Maureen now made a mental note of the patient's name.

"What happen?" Michael asked, with a West Indian dialect.

"You were knocked unconscious when you fell from an explosion. I'm afraid you lost three toes on your right foot. We're giving you morphine that will help with the pain. And make you sleepy."

"Trouble don't set up like rain."

Peterson leaned to Maureen to explain, "That doesn't mean it's raining. It means you can't always see trouble coming." He smiled—it really had started to rain. Bending toward his patient, Peterson said, "I am going to need to clean up and sew the wound." Michael nodded assent.

Peterson and Maureen worked together on Michael's foot for ten minutes. Then Maureen slowly reorganized supplies as Peterson finished his rounds.

She followed him into the hall. He lingered, smiled.

Panama had very few respectable places where a single gentleman could entertain an unmarried lady. The only rules of engagement for either Nurse McGowan or Dr. Peterson were the ones they brought from Cleveland and from Philadelphia. No one watched to see how those rules worked in the tropics, but Maureen knew that the doctor strove for the gloss of decorum—a public setting, unchaperoned. "Would you like to meet again for dinner at the International?" he asked. "Seven o'clock?"

An hour later, Maureen returned to Michael Thompson's bed. She wanted to make sure no infection had set in. She also wanted to test herself a bit with this colored man. He looked like many of the others on that ward—dark, young, suffering. Nice-looking for a colored man, except for a gap in his front teeth. He had seemed surprisingly comfortable with the doctor, not frightened as some of the other men on the first-floor ward. She had learned that most of the colored workers had seen a doctor only at a recruiting station. They were frightened of the white men who touched them, hurt them. Did Michael understand more than others? Did he see that she and Dr. Peterson could help, at least with the pain? Maureen noticed that Michael's skin was a middle shade of brown, lighter than the patient in bed seven and darker than the patient in bed nine. She examined his foot. They talked.

After her ten-hour shift, Maureen went to the nearby nurses' quarters in a cottage that had never lost its damp smell. She changed out of her soiled uniform, putting on one of the flowered cotton dresses she brought with her from Ohio, the blue one, and her best shoes though she noticed they were wearing thin. She had heard enough comments to know that the staff considered her pretty, especially since the competition was modest. Except for the nurses, few white women lived on the isthmus, and many of the nurses were older veterans from the wars in Cuba and the Philippines. They looked as war-weary as they felt.

Maureen walked from her cottage to the front of the hospital, where Robert would wait for her, as he had the week before. They would take a carriage to the International. Their last dinner had gone well. They talked about Dr. Gorgas's successes, Chief Engineer John Stevens's tactics, and the coming visit of the president. The conversation went much the same as the talks she had with other doctors, both on the wards and during social occasions. Except that Robert seemed to probe. At their last dinner, he told a story about a patient and a story about Canal Zone policy and then waited for her responses, unlike the other doctors who just talked. Tonight, she would be ready.

The International was elegant by the standards of the isthmus. White tablecloths, chandeliers, crystal glassware, colored waiters in livery. A few of the doctors claimed the food was the best in Panama. Perhaps Cleveland had an equivalent. Maureen wouldn't know because she had frequented only modest establishments in her hometown. As she entered the International on Robert's arm, she set her mouth to a casual smile, as though accustomed to such elegance.

Maureen did not wait long into the fine meal to see if she was right about Robert's interests. "Do you remember Michael Thompson, in bed eight on the first floor?" she asked.

"The patient who lost three toes? I hope there's no sign of sepsis."

"No, I checked the wound. He'll be alright. You know, though, these colored workers don't get sick leave. With no money coming in, they usually return home, back to Barbados. In his case, he won't be sick enough to go back, and I'm not sure he'll be well enough to stand and dig all day long. He told me about his worries. He said there was a rumor that the ICC paid $500 to any man who lost a leg. Can that be possible? He said he doubted that was true, and even if it was, he couldn't imagine what he would get for three toes."

Robert sneered. "We could ask Square Foot Smith—you remember, the snot who assigns housing space—to apply his methods of allocating housing to wound measurements. What portion of a leg's surface is made up by three toes?"

Maureen matched Peterson's sneer, then continued. "He also heard that if an injured man can work, just less than before, wages are cut from ten cents to five cents an hour. Michael has a young wife, well, she may be his wife, he brought her to Panama. And he's the guardian, well, maybe an informal guardian, for his dead brother's daughter. Selina, that's her name—the niece's name. He needs to earn money. And every week, he sends money back to Barbados, for a grandma who needs help. Also, he asked me for a bible. I saw him reading it. He's smarter than the others."

As Maureen spoke, she watched Robert put down his soup spoon and look at her intently. Encouraged, she continued.

"I know we can't help every colored laborer on the ward, but can you think of any possibilities for Michael?" She felt his leg brush against her dress, linen against soft cotton, felt his ankle touch her shoe.

That night, Robert and Maureen spent an hour in his office on the third floor of the hospital, before he walked her slowly to her cottage. They could see the Southern Cross as they glanced at the sky, smiling.

Robert Peterson

Most of the doctors at Ancon Hospital worked there for all the right reasons. They enjoyed travel, they sought knowledge of tropical diseases, they wanted experience with trauma patients. A small number traveled to Panama for the wrong reasons. They had earned the displeasure of their supervising physicians, or they feared retribution from a badly treated patient.

Dr. Robert Peterson did not belong exclusively to either camp. In 1892 he worked briefly with Dr. Walter Reed at Johns Hopkins School of Medicine, where he gained expertise in bacteriology. Later, he followed from afar the experiments in Cuba to find the cause of Yellow Fever. He knew he would have an opportunity to learn even more in Panama.

As his profession taught him ways to ease suffering, so did the Abolition Movement and its aftermath. Peterson was born in 1865 to a family in Pennsylvania. His beloved parents and grandparents had been active in the Movement and the Underground Railroad. Peterson followed in the family tradition. He served on the board of the College Settlement of Philadelphia, both when it was in a Negro neighborhood and when it moved to a neighborhood of new immigrants, and he contributed to its programs for the poor of the city. Peterson had read about Panama and realized he could honor his family even more by practicing medicine there. But his leanings played only a small role in motivating him to give up his creature comforts and his medical practice in Philadelphia.

The doctor did not let his sparse hair and sloping shoulders limit his love life. He kept company with a string of lovely young women living in the suburbs along the Main Line of Philadelphia. They seemed to appreciate his charm, or his status, or his concern for the unfortunate. Sometimes all three. Most were chaste, waiting until attention turned to courtship, and courtship to engagement. Their waiting proved fruitless. Peterson enjoyed his life just as it was. The fourth of these women, Adelle Hart from Marion, decided to gamble. She traveled to Baltimore, supposedly to meet an old school friend, as Peterson traveled there to the secluded hotel he had frequented as a medical student. A man of his era, Peterson was more experienced than Adelle. He started with a position she expected, then moved on over the course of the weekend to positions requiring some agility. Adelle kept up with him.

Seven weeks later, Adelle confronted the good doctor. Her plan took courage, so he realized she must have felt certain that engagement would follow her news. Unknown to her, Robert Peterson had an ace in hand. When he was ten, he was diagnosed with mumps, the most severe case the family physician had seen. His parents expected him to die. He developed orchitis, an inflammation of the testicles. As a young man, he had visited specialists who confirmed his sterility and were unable to reverse the damage. He told Adelle, then chose to forget her spirited reaction. Was she inventive or promiscuous? No matter, he was off the hook. But if he remained in Philadelphia, Adelle might be a thorn in his side and could sully his name. He sailed for Panama the next week.

After a year in Ancon Hospital, Dr. Peterson felt good about his move. He helped Dr. Gorgas with sanitary activities leading up to the win against Yellow Fever. He tended to poor laborers in need of medical attention. He learned about a wide range of illnesses from his fellow doctors and taught them as well. Those accomplishments left him contented, almost. When he met Maureen McGowan, he hoped for an attachment, his usual sort of attachment. She was a looker.

Their talks had been easy. They exchanged views on the patients, the other doctors, the isthmus. First, that was all. No conversation extended beyond pleasantries. Maureen mentioned her discomfort with the Negro patients, probably expecting that he would concur. He said nothing. After one or two dinner engagements, Peterson began to reconsider. Although Maureen may have felt uncomfortable on the Negro ward, she had taken an interest in the patients, or at least in one of them. She had learned more about Michael Thompson, the patient missing toes, than he had. Could her discomfort be more habit than belief?

In early November, he received a letter from his parents, the usual missive filled with news from Philadelphia and the Main Line—the Parker family, the Smithvilles, the Harts. The Harts. Adelle Hart. Now she was engaged to Lucas Crary, also from Marion. In the letter his mother begged for more information on how he was faring. He knew what that meant. More information on his romantic life.

The news about Adelle struck him as freeing, around the same time that he started to see Maureen in a different light. He felt attracted to her, and, he thought, she fancied him. He began to obsess about his fateful bout with mumps. Did she have a right to know? Or not? How long could he wait? There would be a festive reception at the pier at the end of the President's visit. The staff of the hospital were all invited. He would declare his intentions, as the saying went, and maybe let her know his one limitation. Maybe.

Emilio Santelli

Most anarchists sat at home, dreaming of a better world. The few who planned mayhem scrambled to find funding for their operations, except for one fortunate anarchist who found money falling into his lap. The series of events that led to this stroke of luck began in an impoverished neighborhood in Naples, as nineteen-year-old Emilio Santelli longed to follow his brother, Anthony, to America. Anthony wrote to his family in Italy that he had become a Chicago horse groomer, making good money. Emilio wrote back, asking if the horse stable owner could take him on too.

Brother Antonio didn't want Emilio to join him in Chicago. In Anthony's next letter, he used code words the brothers had invented in childhood. Too much danger. Anthony encouraged Emilio to avoid Chicago and to find his way to an uncle's home in Ohio. Emilio thought, why not? Ohio is closer. Unfazed by traveling alone to a new land, he landed in New York harbor and quickly ripped off the card pinned to his jacket by an immigration officer, the card with the initials w.o.p. for without papers. Emilio took the train to Cleveland and walked to his uncle's tenement in the Big Italy neighborhood along Woodland Avenue.

Emilio didn't take long to find work. He started in the Standard Oil Refinery as a night watchman. He barely qualified for that job. His bear-like looks and determined attitude helped him pass muster. Most nights, he struggled to stay awake at his post. One night, as he began to drift off, a gang of marauders sneaked to the refinery, planning to wreak havoc. Sitting on his watchman's stool, hiding behind a half-open window, Emilio heard the gang before he saw them. Though his own Neapolitan dialect differed slightly from the dialect he heard, which he guessed was Sicilian, it was close enough. Emilio listened as the thugs bragged to each other about how they would destroy the equipment Emilio was guarding.

The refinery was among the first of the businesses in Cleveland to have a phone. Emilio had never used it before. Took three tries. The English lessons he had begun two months ago at the Hiram House Settlement gave him just enough phrases to communicate the threat. Perhaps Emilio was a good worker, or perhaps he anticipated the benefit of doing the right thing. While waiting for the coppers to arrive, he strode out of the office, holding his stool to his chest as a shield, and arching his broad shoulders. That bought him one minute, enough time for the gang to hear the bell of the arriving police van. Although the gang ran away before they could be caught, the police reported to refinery owner John D. Rockefeller that the night watchman had averted catastrophe. Not for two decades would Emilio realize that the gang leader was Joe Lonardo, later known as Big Joe, who would become a boss of the Cleveland crime family.

Soon after the incident, Rockefeller made his quarterly visit to the refinery. When Emilio arrived at work the night before, he saw on his watchman's stool a note from the security chief. The chief ordered him to show up at work the next day, an hour before his shift started, and to wear a suit. Claimed it would be worth his while. Emilio had two sets of clothes, no suit. He borrowed his uncle's, used only for funerals, and admired himself in the looking glass. This country—not so bad.

At the appointed time, Emilio found the security chief who led him to elegant offices hidden away on the side of the refinery. John D. Rockefeller, with his pinched face, sat in a wing chair waiting for the two men. Emilio did not know enough about American tycoons to feel intimidated. He shook less than the security chief. All three walked to a platform in a central area that had been readied for a formal address to the workers at their shift change. Emilio listened while Pinched Face spouted statistics—so many barrels of oil last month, so many this month, quotas for next month. The man paused, motioned to Emilio. Come here to the platform.

"Men, I want to introduce you to Emilio Santelli, our night watchman. This fine boy has been with us for only a short time. Even though he is new to America, he works hard for our company. Two nights ago, he single-handedly thwarted a gang of hoodlums, intent on destructing property. I commend his dedication to his job and hope the rest of you feel inspired by his heroism. I believe in the value of hard work and industriousness, characteristics that have served me well and that Emilio seems to share. Emilio, accept this check in appreciation for your vigilance." The man handed Emilio an envelope. Despite his English lessons, Emilio was unsure of the meaning of vigilance. *Vergine?* Virgin? He took the envelope, happily.

With that $50 payout, John D. Rockefeller had more in mind than a thank you. The rest of the story came to Emilio slowly, over the years, as he pieced together what he read in the papers, what he heard from his uncle in Cleveland, and what he learned from his brother in Chicago. Rockefeller was discretely hunting for a back channel, a way to end the career of the President. Theodore Roosevelt, known as a trust buster, wanted to break up the Standard Oil monopoly. 1906, the year of Joe Lonardo's attempt at destruction and Emilio Santelli's attempt at safeguarding, was the year TR's administration filed an antitrust case against Standard Oil.

The tycoon knew that Emilio had been on the right side of the law this time. Nonetheless, he bet Italian immigrants could be persuaded to be on the wrong side. His questionable assumption paid off. The day after his visit to the refinery, Rockefeller talked to a man on his payroll, Milton Anderson. This former Pinkerton detective, freelancing for Standard Oil, took it from there.

Anderson requested Emilio's address from the security chief. A well-compensated emissary, chosen because of his fixed scowl and broad chest, was sent to the uncle's tenement in Cleveland. The emissary spoke the language of persuasion. The uncle didn't want his nephew to lose his job, right? Wanted the nephew to continue to pay for his keep, right? Surely the uncle knew fellow wops looking to change the world. Better if they were local, but anywhere would do.

Within a week, detective Milton Anderson found Emilio's brother, anarchist Anthony Santelli, near Taylor Street in Chicago. Anderson, trying to ignore the smell of horses wafting from Santelli's jacket, finalized the deal and handed over the money, Standard Oil money, in cash. He handed over as well news of TR's impending international travel to a place where bodyguards would likely be few and far between, and escape routes would be plentiful.

Now Santelli, the mastermind of the Taylor Street cell, had the stash he needed to put his plan in motion, a plan that would cost more than sending a man one-hundred-and-seventy miles south, a man wearing nondescript clothing over farmer's overalls. "I have the right man for the job," Santelli assured Anderson. "A man who don't look like me. Won't be spotted." Santelli didn't need to mention that Arthur Sitwell, having failed once three years ago in Lincoln, Illinois, would be determined to succeed. At all costs.

Emilio would learn of his uncle's role, his brother role, and Milton Anderson's role, but he'd still be short one conspirator—a young shop owner from Panama City.

Shing Wong

S hing Wong's father had provided an example of hard work, leaving to his son a thriving shop carrying silks and spices, along with the occasional map, situated in the heart of Panama City. The father had not intended also to bequeath to his son a mission of revenge.

While growing up, Shing Wong listened to his father's stories. Wong Kong Yee was one of thousands of Chinese laborers recruited by the French to come to Panama to build the railroad and the canal. He left a region of little food and less opportunity, arriving in Panama City in 1882, a month before President Arthur signed the first Chinese Exclusion Act. Wong Kong Yee knew nothing about the Act, which then had little relevance to Panama. He stayed on in his adopted country, even after the French engineers gave up in despair, to be followed by savvier American engineers.

The suffering Wong Kong Yee first experienced in Panama killed most of his countrymen. The French steered their Chinese workers to the backbreaking job of clearing land using picks and shovels. With no immunities, hundreds fell sick with Yellow Fever and malaria. They were buried unceremoniously along the railroad tracks. But hundreds somehow survived. Wong Kong Yee was one of the lucky ones at this point. He survived, saved his wages, and started a store. At first, the store was little more than a shack along the tracks, selling food—oranges, eggs, and beans—he picked up each morning at the port. Then Wong Kong Yee took the profits from that trade and made two decisions. First, he sent for his wife, as he had promised he would. She arrived in 1886. Next, he gradually added to his inventory. Around 1896 he gave up the shack and moved his business to Panama City. His store, still small, was frequented by the wives and servants of the neighborhood as well as visitors to the port. Then he expanded again into a shop near the central plaza. Shing Wong heard that part of the story from his father.

The next part of the story, Shing Wong experienced for himself. He often visited the shop, where he completed his schoolwork in the back room and helped as needed. When Wong Kong Yee closed his shop for the day on November 3, 1903, "cigars arrive tomorrow" were his last words to a customer. Wong Kong Yee went to the family's home on Salsipuedes Street while Shing Wong and his mother went to spend the night with friends in a town farther from the wharf, which seemed safer in view of a growing rumor that Colombian soldiers might be closing in on the city.

The next part of the story, Shing Wong had to learn from newspapers and chatter in town. Around the time the shop owner said his last words, bickering had intensified among three factions—Americans who wanted a canal, Colombians who had taken over Panama and wanted to hold on to it, and Panamanian revolutionaries set on reclaiming their country. The Colombians, represented by two Generals, needed to move hundreds of their troops from Colón to Panama City, to meet up with approaching Colombian battleships. If the generals could mass their warriors, then they could dissuade Panamanians from fighting to retake the isthmus. The Colombian plan was stymied by American James Shaler, serving as Superintendent of the Panamanian Railroad. Shaler delayed transporting Colombian troops, while appearing neutral. Perhaps he knew TR thought it would be easier to negotiate a canal with Panamanians than with Colombians. The third faction, the Panamanian independence movement, was led by Manuel Amador, soon to become President of Panama. The Panamanian revolutionaries had money, American money, and put it to use. They understood one of the Colombian generals was dispirited, as were the soldiers he led. They had not been paid for months. Fifty dollars to each Colombian soldier, $10,000 to each junior officer, and $30,000 to the dispirited general worked magic, buying treason. The Colombians soldiers offered no resistance to the Panamanian revolutionaries.

What of the Colombian battleships that had been sent to back up the Colombian army? Without knowledge of the turnabout on shore, those sailors chose action. On the evening of November 3, 1903, the gunboat *Bogata* bombarded the Panama City shoreline, just as the Panamanians declared independence. The shelling amounted to little, Shing Wong read in the papers. According to the official diplomatic report of the incident, from Vice-Consul General Felix Ehrman to Francis B. Loomis, Assistant Secretary of State, "the city of Panama was bombed with about six shells, one of which killed a Chinese in his bed and another one a donkey that was in the slaughterhouse." A cable sent from Panama City carried the same information, reporting that the shells "killed a Chinaman in Salsipuedes Street and mortally wounded an ass." Ten months later, Ignacio Molina, owner of the boardinghouse where the Chinaman lived, sued Panama for five hundred pesos, the cost of the damage by the shells to the roof of his house. No one, according to the recorded history, mourned the Chinaman, Wong Kong Yee.

Except for Shing Wong. The young shopkeeper was sixteen when his father died.

Shing Wong's anger could be distributed widely. Were the Colombians to blame? They lobbed the shells. Were the Panamanians to blame? They secretly collaborated with the Americans to bring on the U.S.-supported revolution. Were the Americans to blame? Their zeal to build a canal lay behind all the shenanigans, and they never properly reported on the one casualty, giving Shing Wong's beloved father the same attention as a donkey. The young shopkeeper could choose his enemy.

A bit of history made his choice easy. The United States Congress, which passed the Chinese Exclusion Act in 1882, renewed it for the first time in 1892, and for the second time in 1902. The country of freedom for all prohibited the immigration of Chinese laborers. Whether this applied to the Canal Zone was debatable. In the end, the Act triumphed. The Exclusion

Act would be the law of the land for decades.

By April 16, 1902, when the Act was extended, few Chinese laborers remained in Panama. Those who remained weren't likely to read a newspaper. But Shing Wong was among the best students at his school in Panama City. For a few years, until the authorities got organized enough to segregate, the school taught everyone—not just the Americans—to read, in English. And Shing Wong had access to a wide range of newspapers as he helped in the shop. He took pride in reading to his father and translating for him. On May 5, 1902, eighteen months before a Colombian shell killed Wong Kong Yee, a customer left on the shop's counter the April 17th edition of the *San Francisco Call*. "Senate Passes Bill Continuing Chinese Exclusion Laws" rang out the headline. Shing Wong, as he often did, translated the story for his father, grimacing over each phrase. Senator George Turner of Washington State "spoke of the Chinese, declaring that two-facedness is a characteristic of that people." Shing Wong considered not translating that sentence for Wong Kong Yee. He would never know the difference. The youth made a fateful decision, rendering the English into Chinese as closely as possible. The look on his father's face would haunt him. Theodore Roosevelt was the President of the country that allowed this hate.

Arthur Sitwell

Monday, October 15, 1906, and Wednesday, November 14, 1906

Arthur Sitwell, who had immigrated from Sheffield to Chicago, became Magnus Gustafsson, who had immigrated from Stockholm to Chicago. With that change, he cast aside his former self—a coward who failed to set off an explosion along the tracks of the Chicago & Alton Railroad three years earlier. His new name, alongside his slight British accent, would confuse people. They would be too busy trying to discern his country of origin to wonder if he hailed from a land of assassins. He chose Magnus Gustafsson for more reasons too. The new first name signaled magnificence. The new surname signaled gumption. With these words in mind, he would make headway. He would choose his weapon and order new clothes. Easy tasks.

Moving on to a harder task, he needed to find an escape path. He was not suicidal like some of his fellow anarchists, the long list of those who had murdered heads of state and swiftly been brought to justice. He thought more strategically than those martyrs. The $10,000 Anthony Santelli had given him—thanks to detective Milton Anderson's work on behalf of robber baron John D. Rockefeller—exceeded the actual costs for murder. If Gustafsson could hold in reserve $3000 of the Rockefeller money, that might buy additional detective services. Gustafsson would offer to give Anderson back some of the cash if he could identify a helper or a means of escape. Santelli told Gustafsson how to contact Anderson.

The Oyster Bar saloon on the south side of Fort Wayne, Indiana, halfway between Chicago and Cleveland, served as a fine meeting place. Five weeks before the president's trip to Panama, Magnus Gustafsson, feeling well disguised in his new identity, rode the Twentieth Century Limited east to Fort Wayne. Milton Anderson, leaving a bit later, rode the New York, Chicago & St. Louis Railroad west to Fort Wayne. Gustafsson arrived first. He slipped the saloon barkeep a sawbuck, for use of the back room. Dark, paneled, private. As Gustafsson nursed a whiskey, he reminded himself of why he had chosen his name. His confidence just began to rise when the saloon's front door squeaked open. He envisioned the barkeep pointing the customer toward the back room. Slow footsteps. A man entered. Clean-shaven, thin lips, no expression. The two men fixed their eyes on each other, after a second each offering a nod. Gustafsson introduced himself—the first time he said his new name aloud to anyone other than Santelli—and ordered two more whiskeys from the barkeep who appeared, staring at his new patrons. Gustafsson felt ready. He stretched out his long legs under the table. Began with a bit of small talk about Fort Wayne. Such a backwater.

"Your friend hinted that you wouldn't look Italian," Anderson said. "But what are you? I hear more of England than of Sweden."

"I'm just what you want," Gustafsson said. "You can see, I don't look like a man out to kill a tyrant, right? Especially at my height. No way I can fade into the background."

Anderson kept staring at the tall, blond stranger. Finally, bobbed his head up and down and smiled. "Right."

"I need an accomplice, a man who won't be suspicious, who can hide me away until it's safe to leave. I'm asking you to travel to Panama next week and make a connection for me. Can't do it myself. Can't be seen traveling there twice, and I can't stay for a month, unemployed, without arousing suspicion. You understand, right?"

"Lemme think," Anderson said, rubbing his chin slowly.

Gustafsson understood the gesture. "Three thousand. I'll give you back $3000."

More chin rubbing, faster now.

"I've snitched on laborers, started a fight at labor rallies, snuck guns to the right people." Hearing Anderson boast, Gustafsson tensed his jaw. How did he end up in a saloon with this man who must see his drinking partner as a kindred spirit? "Now," Anderson continued, "I've hired an assassin. Shouldn't be hard to find a getaway man."

And it wasn't. Once in Panama City, Anderson contacted an old buddy, another former Pinkerton detective who had hired on to provide security for the Isthmus Canal Commission commissaries. Although John O'Malley no longer did detective work, he remained both inquisitive and suspicious. By habit, O'Malley had in his head a list of those Panamanian residents who were unhappy with the United States. The list included a couple of liberal politicians, three disgruntled office workers, and, at the top, a young Chinaman shopkeeper with superb English and a sharp bone to pick against Americans. Anderson explained that he needed a man to hide a European-born detective traveling to Panama to smoke out American labor organizers. O'Malley loved his fellow Americans, but not labor organizers. He passed along a name.

Milton Anderson returned home from his errand to Panama. He sent Gustafsson a letter, using the Caesar cypher they had agreed on in Fort Wayne, a simple system where each letter was replaced by a letter three ahead of it in the alphabet. Gustafsson now had the name of a Panamanian who would assist him. With $7000 remaining from Anderson's payment, Gustafsson purchased a first-class train ticket from Chicago to New York, first-class ship passage to Panama City, and three new suits. On the ship, he looked like just another businessman, this one tall, thin, and blond. He kept to himself when walking the deck or dining. If asked any questions, he had a standard reply. "Hope to expand my Chicago photography business with a shop in Panama. Full of opportunities with men coming from all over." He decided to stick with Chicago rather than inventing a new home. If any of the ship's passengers wanted to chat about hometowns, at least he would know what he was talking about. "Yes, I love the Midway," he would say. "The Ferris Wheel was the highlight of that Colombian Exposition, the world's fair. I rode it three times." As for his slight British accent alongside a Swedish name, that was easy to explain. Born in Stockholm, he spent his youth in London learning photography, then moved to Chicago. Passengers' memories of him would center on his migration story, nothing else.

Of all the purchases Gustafsson had made in the last month, he was proudest of the newly designed Winchester semi-automatic rifle, which had a greater range than a revolver. He would need the distance. He didn't want to be grabbed a foot from his prey, like McKinley's assassin. He also purchased photography equipment, including a tripod, camera, and a plain, black case, the longest and widest he could find.

Once in Panama City, Gustafsson selected a boarding house, the Gomez. In these comfortable surroundings, he would continue to marshal his courage while exploring the geography of the plaza and surrounding streets. On the morning of November 14th, he sat at Señora Gomez's breakfast table, eating a surprisingly British breakfast of toast and tea. He asked the comely maid for a second helping, while noticing that the talkative, bald lodger at the table kept his eyes on her. Gustafsson had no such interest because he was remembering with satisfaction the previous night. It had been too long since he'd been with a woman. The whore he found at The Luna, the brothel recommended by a loquacious fellow shipmate, excited him. With luck, he would survive his assignment, and Emily would not be his last fuck.

Dressed in one of his unremarkable suits, Gustafsson fit in with the other lodgers eating breakfast. Only one man had dressed informally, as though he was heading to a jungle or a wasteland. No one seemed curious about anyone else. Just the usual chit-chat among businessmen in a strange country. One little snippet gave Gustafsson pause. "How far is the cathedral, the one in the central plaza," he heard the man dressed in casual clothing ask Señora Gomez. She answered in English, "Just a few blocks, to the right." The other men at the table commented or murmured agreement while Gustafsson studied his toast. He planned to visit the same spot, but now he needed to wait until the sightseeing lodger had a head start. He fidgeted in his chair, then caught himself and willed his lanky limbs to stay still.

When the sightseer finally left the boarding house, Gustafsson walked past the front desk in the crowded room that served as the Gomez's entrance. No one was behind the desk, and Señora Gomez stayed with her lodgers around the breakfast table. He checked the register, fiddled with the mail in the sorting boxes behind the desk. The man dressed for the jungle must be Frederick Palmer from *Collier's*. Right to keep a distance.

Gustafsson left for the cathedral, keeping an eye on Palmer ahead of him. Once Palmer had his fill of the public square, Gustafsson entered the same space. It was quiet this time in the morning, aside from the sounds of workers hanging bunting. Gustafsson looked at the cathedral, on the western side of the plaza. With luck, the towers would block the setting sun, so if he faced the cathedral late the next day, he would not be blinded. He focused on the buildings across from the cathedral, with their arched entrances and wrought iron balconies. He needed to find a room with a balcony that he could rent for a time. His accomplice, a young Chinaman he had met the day before, had urged him to move quickly. On one of the buildings that overlooked the plaza, Gustafsson noticed a sign, in English, "The Broadmoor. Caldwell Isthmus Properties. Mr. Roland Caldwell, Manager." A temporary "For let" sign had been tacked up next to the permanent sign. These balconies would undoubtedly be popular the next day. Again, Anderson's money would come in handy.

Gustafsson remembered seeing a plaque for Caldwell Isthmus Properties on a building he had passed on his way to the plaza. He easily retraced his steps until he saw the plaque again. He knocked. A young man, stylish, opened the door, stared.

"Good morning. I am Magnus Gustafsson. I am exploring property around the central plaza."

"Please come in. I'm Roland Caldwell, property manager. My assistant usually greets our customers. He's out today." Gustafsson followed Caldwell into a paneled office, with green damask draperies bracketing two tall windows. Gustafsson settled into the leather wing chair Caldwell pointed to while Caldwell sat behind his desk. The décor belonged to another era. Or was selected to look that way. Strong cigar smoke. Maybe the smell of stale coffee. Neatly stacked documents were piled an inch high on the middle of the desk. A ray of light coming in from the crack in the draperies highlighted a layer of undisturbed dust on each side of the pile. Gustafsson did not think he had interrupted any activity besides smoking. He saw no separate room or desk that could have been an assistant's.

"Mr. Caldwell, thank you for seeing me without an appointment. Do you manage the Broadmoor on the central plaza?"

"Yes, one of our best located properties. Facing the beautiful cathedral."

"Let me explain my interest. I'm a photographer." Gustafsson paused, contemplating how much to add. "I work for a newspaper." He decided to name the city. "A New York paper. They assigned me to photograph the President's visit. Can I rent a room or an office on the third floor for a week? I need to bring in photography equipment and have use of a balcony." Gustafsson usually subdued the British accent of his childhood. This morning, he purposely slipped back to something close to those sounds, careful to lend a genteel gloss to his Yorkshire accent.

"I'm sorry. The Arenas family—have you heard of them—they're one of the leading families of the city, they asked for the use of that room that's for let because the ladies want a good view of events tomorrow afternoon. Oh, I suppose the exact timing is a secret, but Señor Arenas has friends at the ICC, that's the canal Commission, who say 4:00 is set for the speeches." Caldwell grinned, tapped the cigar on a plate already brimming with ashes.

Gustafsson relaxed his jaw, trying to mask his satisfaction at having the schedule confirmed. But the room had been spoken for. Did he have other options? The plaza was smaller than he had expected. Maybe this property manager could use some extra business.

"Would you mind telling me what the family offered you for the week? I can triple the amount and pay in U.S. dollars."

Roland Caldwell

Roland Caldwell moved to Panama to get as far away as possible from the Caldwell family of Burlington, Vermont, and from the cackling and clucking of Burlington society. The Northern Vermont Lumber Mill had been passed down through four generations of Caldwell men with much predictability and no disputes. For the first two generations, each Caldwell proprietor groomed his oldest son to run the mill. The third-generation proprietor sired only one male. No contention during that era. The fourth-generation proprietor sired two males. The oldest was considered simple-minded, needed to be fed. No contention then, either. But the fifth generation presented Papa Caldwell with a problem, for he had sired twin sons, Roland and George. Roland asserted he was five minutes older, but no one in Burlington, not even the attending doctor or Mama Caldwell, could recall which son came first. Growing up, the brothers assumed their father would divide up the mill, more or less equally, in some yet-to-be-determined manner. Then, unexpectedly, business declined. Papa Caldwell put aside the expansion.

Roland knew his father favored George, the solemn and crafty twin. George negotiated with loggers and mill workers, giving them pittances while making them feel good to be working for Northern Vermont Lumber. Papa Caldwell labeled Roland the bumbling and handsome twin. Roland did his best. He enrolled at Bowdoin, made lots of friends, never graduated. He kept the books at the mill, entering in numbers when he remembered, aiming for the correct column. Papa Caldwell frowned at the jumble. Meanwhile, Roland courted the wealthy mayor's daughter. Marjorie Hunter, hardly the beauty of Burlington, was at first taken with Roland's dark curls, good form, and prospects. After a three-month courtship, she changed her mind, marrying one of the city's young doctors.

When Roland and George turned twenty-one, Papa Caldwell called them into his office. He spoke bluntly, without regret, stating that son George was best suited to manage the mill, with its hundred workers, changing technology, and complex finances. In ten years, when Papa Caldwell turned sixty, the mill would be George's.

Roland's anger went beyond what anyone could have imagined until Mama Caldwell found a solution. She went for a walk with Roland, explained that her social standing and George's depended on the success of the mill, and that when she could push aside her husband's unapologetic demeanor, she knew he made the right choice. She loved Roland, though, and offered him the inheritance she had from her own family, to begin afresh somewhere else where he could escape the embarrassment of being the dismissed twin, dismissed by his father and dismissed by his sweetheart. That embarrassment was the talk of the town in February 1900, when the cold and the ice kept people indoors, prattling near their firesides.

Roland let Mama Caldwell do the research for him. Argentina held promise, but he worried about learning Spanish. Australia held promise, but he wasn't sure he could survive the long sea voyage. Then his mother read about Panama. The country, she said, seemed to be a mix of Spanish, English, and French. Roland thought he could manage that shorter voyage, especially when she promised $15,000 to set him up.

By 1901 Roland Caldwell had established himself as a landlord in Panama City. Upon arrival in the port, he began to socialize with some of the families, especially those eager to marry their daughters to men of standing. He himself lacked standing, but he had capital, almost as good. In a few years, when he turned twenty-five, he married one of the elite's daughters, Caterina, a member of the celebrated Alcalde family of Panama. Thanks to his nest egg and his newfound family contacts, he bought up valuable property and started to make a living. He somehow managed to buy property when it was cheap and sell when it was dear. That good fortune, which even Roland knew was not the result of wise judgment or shrewdness, lasted a year or two. When he did trouble to look at his messy account books, he saw that he wasn't earning enough to fulfill his promise to the Alcalde family, or even to hold on to his business.

On November 14, 1906, when Roland Caldwell sat at his dusty desk smoking a cigar, trying not to doze off, he heard a visitor knock. The man calling himself Magnus Gustafsson asked to rent a room with a balcony on the plaza. Awkward—Roland had made other arrangements. Because of his wife's connections with the leading families of Panama, he often mingled with the Arenas family. He had been happy to offer Tomas Arenas the room on the plaza, at just slightly over the going rate, in between permanent tenants. Now, though, Roland had a chance to make a windfall that would buy him time before he had to shutter his office.

"I have no choice," Roland Caldwell explained an hour later to Tomas Arenas, "but to rent to the gentleman who approached me this morning. He's the official photographer for the President's visit. He needs to be on the balcony to record the gathering tomorrow."

In perfect English, Tomas Arenas grumbled, then settled down. "I promised my daughters, and my fussy wife too, a view of the platform in front of the cathedral. That room of yours looks right out on the plaza. I should wring your neck, even if you married my daughter's best friend." A pause, as he lowered his shoulders. "But a photographer, for the President? The President who will build the canal, the canal that will bring riches to families like ours? I will tell everyone I gave up a viewing space so the visit could be recorded for posterity."

John Connell

J ohn Connell looked forward to a fine day as he relaxed at his desk in the Isthmian Canal Commission offices in Ancon. His boss, Theodore Shonts, known by ICC workers as The Other Teddy, was out of the office, traipsing around the isthmus, trying to keep up with the true Teddy. Connell was not technically in charge of the office in Shonts's absence. Shonts, the most arrogant man Connell knew, never delegated. But Connell would comport himself well if any emergencies arose. Slouching in his chair, imagining what he might accomplish as senior man in the office that week, Connell heard the Jamaican houseboy formally greet a caller at the door. "Letter for Mr. John Connell," the caller said. Connell peeked out the window. A marine. Most mail arriving by messenger was for Shonts. A delivery for Connell would impress the houseboy.

Connell resisted the urge to rush up to collect his letter. After three long minutes, the servant knocked. "Letter for you sir."

"It's about time," fussed Connell, ripping open the envelope embellished with a gold crest.

> *Dear Mr. Connell,*
>
> *I will get right to the point. I understand you know Mrs. Katy Marsh and her son, Elliott Marsh. I must see the son, briefly, when I am in Panama. I will not meet with his mother. Bring him to my rooms at*

143

the Tivoli Hotel at 7:00 in the morning on Saturday, November 17th. Tell the guard who you are and that you are introducing me, as I have requested, to the son of an engineer who died in Panama. Do not ask or answer any questions from Elliott Marsh, Katy Marsh, or the guard at the door. I insist that you keep my correspondence and the meeting unknown to anyone beside the Marshes and yourself. Send a letter acknowledging these arrangements to my assistant secretary, Maurice Latta, at the Tivoli Hotel.

Sincerely yours, Theodore Roosevelt

Maurice Latta

fter my hushed exchange with Frederick Palmer at La Boca over seating arrangements, silver and gold towns, and matters I should have kept confidential, our group boarded a tug. We chugged around the bay, despite non-stop rain. When our tug passed other boats, the sailors and passengers saluted, cheered, blew their whistles. Every boat in the bay unfurled flags, sodden like everything else in the country. Felt like a parade, except that a parade in the States would have been canceled in such weather.

William Gerig, the ICC officer who steered our tug, babbled to the President about the canal's technology, explaining how workers build dams. I couldn't follow Gerig's details. Didn't try to. I passed the time berating myself, silently replaying what I had said to Fred ten minutes earlier. "They caught someone." Then I remembered worse. "I hear that there could be more," I had added for Fred, as though I held special knowledge, as though I carried weight. And why? To ingratiate myself with Fred? To make a friend?

Unlike me, the President stayed attentive, fascinated by Gerig's onslaught of facts about engineering feats that could expand the empire. When Gerig exhausted his supply of details, he moved to anecdotes, one of which I remember. He had almost been late that morning, for his moment in the sun. In the rain, really. He depended on the rails to go from place to place,

145

and the President's train had forced all other trains to slow down. Later I saw this comment as an omen, since in the coming days, few would manage to keep up with the speeding President.

When the tug brought us back to land, I was still furious with myself. Soon my attention pivoted from my failings as a confidential public servant to my failings as a scheduler. Out of the corner of my eye, I saw the President meet up with Mrs. R., who had stayed on shore. They began to walk, unannounced, into the nearby ICC mess hall. I nervously and repeatedly scanned my official schedule. I had no choice but to remind the President, respectfully, of course, that the Tivoli Hotel was hosting a formal lunch for him at 1:00. He ignored me, none too politely. The title of Assistant Secretary didn't carry much weight. (I quickly wrote an apology to the Tivoli hotel manager, alerting him that we would miss lunch in his dining room, and sent a messenger to deliver it.)

Ahead of us, I spotted the manager of the mess hall pat down his hair and dash to the front to greet the President. "We are delighted to see you, Mr. President, though we were not expecting you."

"No problem, chap. I simply wish to see how the workers eat." I knew from previous discussions that disfavored journalist Poultney Bigelow had written articles berating the food served at the mess. I suppose the President wanted to assess that for himself.

Walking past the cashier, TR saw that lunch cost thirty cents. He carried no money. He asked me to pay for him, Mrs. R., and myself. I did, despite the mess hall manager's insistence that we eat on the house. I grumped to myself about this development because I suspected the President would forget to pay me back, but in view of Teddy's reputation for honesty, which I was and still am reluctant to contradict, there was nothing to be done. Needless to say, he did forget to pay me back the sixty cents, and after his death, none of the Roosevelt children honored that debt. I never mentioned the obligation to Mrs. Eleanor, though that would have made for a good laugh with her.

The President led us to an empty table near the workers, who stared in astonishment. I saw that the mess for white workers split into two spaces.

On the left, the men were in shirt sleeves, and on the right, they wore suits. The President selected the shirtsleeve side. (I learned later that the ICC ran three messes—the one we were at, for White workers, a second for workers from Spain and Greece, and a third for Negro workers who stood while eating.) Secret Service agents Larry Richey and Jimmy Sloan followed us into the mess hall, and Fred ambled over to sit with them on the same side of the table as the President, probably craving an opportunity to gather news for *Collier's*. Dr. Rixey, who quietly accompanied the President everywhere, sat across from TR and Mrs. R. I sat beside the doctor, with a good view of everyone.

Mr. de Lisser seemed to have disappeared. Then I realized de Lisser was not the only missing member of our entourage. A door opened and agent Frank Tyree, carrying a few extra pounds, rushed in. He squeezed between Jimmy and Larry and put his head so close to Jimmy's that anyone else would have concluded they were long-lost friends. Next to them, Fred Palmer tensed his shoulders, edged his head almost an imperceptible inch toward the couple.

As I watched this scene, a waiter came to the President's table to offer us a drink, called a Panama cocktail—quinine, for malaria, mixed with a little brandy. The President declined the drink but seemed aware of the ritual because he pulled out of his pocket quinine pills for himself and for Mrs. R. He forgot about me and the others in his entourage, so I accepted the cocktail, the worst drink I have ever had. The toxic taste lingered, canceling out the rest of the meal of soup, beef, mashed potatoes, peas, plum pudding, and ice cream. The President, who did not have the taste of liquid quinine in his mouth, appeared to enjoy the food. I suspect that he had been subjected to the quinine drink on his previous travels to Cuba and knew its perils.

While gulping water, I stared across the table. Frank continued to whisper to frowning Jimmy. Larry seemed to hear his fellow agents. Fred stretched to try to hear. The four looked locked in an odd tableau. Only when TR stood, ready to move on, did Frank lift his head from Jimmy's.

Now another break from the schedule. With three gloomy agents, one journalist, and me trailing behind, TR strode to the mess's kitchen, surprising the Negro workers as he had surprised the mess hall manager. The President bombarded the kitchen staff with questions and listened to complaints about pay, overtime, and the low quality of yams. I must explain the business with yams, which I heard about for the first time that afternoon. Standing in the kitchen, I was astounded that the President was attentive to the discussion of this food. Later I would read that yams were crucial for the diet of West Indian workers. They were accustomed to inexpensive, nutritious, fresh yams, which were hard to obtain in Panama. With hindsight, I think the situation might be the equivalent of American workers complaining about sour milk or stale bread. TR seemed to understand this before I did. My new friend Fred, busy writing in his notebook, would report the following week for *Colliers's* on the President's peculiar interest in yams. Herbert de Lisser was not present to take notes.

As I type these remembrances, in 1947, my readers will be familiar with Harry Truman, son of a farmer and a haberdasher by trade. Until Harry, most of our presidents had grown up in privileged surroundings. They would not have stood in a kitchen talking about yams. Not Harrison, not Cleveland, not McKinley. Though good men, they were used to talking with the powerful. So was Teddy, but his love for talking knew no class bounds.

After the mess hall and the kitchen session, now ahead of schedule, we set off for an inspection of Ancon Hospital. By messenger, we sent word ahead to Dr. Gorgas, who rushed to meet the President so they could ride together in the coach the ICC provided. The two reporters (Mr. de Lisser had been waiting outside the mess), the three agents, and I followed in a large but simpler coach. By now, the rain had stopped, and the sun blazed down, but I felt a chill. The agents said nothing and sat stiffly. Frederick Palmer fidgeted with his shirt collar. Herbert de Lisser looked from man to man.

Until this point, while in Panama, TR had kept to the strip down the middle of the country, the Canal Zone, which since 1903 was technically American soil. The only exception was the hour he spent on the Colón wharf, but no reporter seemed to count that. Ancon Hospital, everyone knew, sat on a hill in a part of Panama outside the Zone. When the President's coach crossed the Caledonia Bridge at the foot of Ancon Hill, he made history. Never before had a president been on foreign lands while in office.

After arriving at Ancon, TR, Dr. Gorgas, and the hospital's flustered director, also surprised by the President's early appearance, inspected the White and Negro wards. At the door to the wards, the group divided, with the President, the doctors, and the Secret Service agents walking forward while the reporters and I stayed in the hall. I was not eager to breathe in more of hospital smells, which had seeped into the hall, or to see broken bodies.

I ignored the reporters standing next to me. Fred kept up his fidgeting. After a few minutes, I said I needed to find the toilet. Fred perked up, said he'd keep me company. Fred and I entered the Whites Only toilet.

"Maurice, they think there's an assassin on the isthmus. Have you heard anything?"

I felt my blood sink to my feet. "No, Fred. I'll see what I can learn." My resolve to lie low wilted.

Magnus Gustafsson

Thursday, November 15, 1906

Standing in front of the boarding house mirror, Magnus Gustafsson adjusted his clothing with care. If he kept his wits about him, this new suit would never see the inside of a coffin. He settled his bill with Señora Gomez, using Rockefeller cash. As agreed, the day before, Shing Wong carried the valises and the cases carefully selected to accommodate photography equipment and more. The young man seemed an eager accomplice, especially after learning that his new boss was not hunting labor organizers, as O'Malley had said. Anyone in the plaza would see a tall, blond man, accompanied by a Chinaman fittingly burdened with baggage, zigzagging around the puddles left from Panama City's heavy morning rain. They arrived at the Broadmoor Building on the central plaza at 2:00. Shing Wong hauled the gear up to the rented room, then returned to his shop. In three hours, he would hide Gustafsson behind bolts of silk in the backroom until the trail of the assassin turned cold.

Upstairs in the Broadmoor, Gustafsson paced. He had overpaid that twit property manager, knowing Caldwell's balcony was not the only balcony around the plaza, but not fully realizing the problem. People on adjacent balconies could see his balcony, as could people on the balconies on each of the plaza's sides at right angles to his side. Already, men decked out in formal suits and women wearing wide-brimmed hats stood against the railings to view the plaza, hours before the President's scheduled address.

150

He noticed a man pouring what appeared to be whiskey and passing it around to smiling takers. Gustafsson could not simply stand with his semi-automatic Winchester stabilized by the iron railing and aim across the square.

He had planned for contingencies, throwing a black cloth in his camera case while still in New York awaiting passage. Newer camera equipment did not always require protection against light, but he doubted most Panama City residents would know that. They would think instead that it was routine for a photographer, using a tripod, to drape his head and shoulders and the back of a bulky camera with a black cloth. Using this method, the photographer would exclude extraneous light to ensure a good view of the projected image on the glass plate. Today, inside the rented room, Gustafsson experimented to determine if the cloth would hide both his head and his rifle. No matter what position he took, the forty-inch rifle stuck out in front of the drape.

Bollocks.

For a horrid few seconds, he knew he should abandon his post, run. Then he looked out at the festooned speakers' platform, with the Roosevelt family crest attached to a drape. Set up for the powerful, the men who grabbed.

He took a breath, two breaths, rethought his plan. On the balcony, he would slowly and deliberately set up the tripod, camera, and cloth. Spectators on the surrounding balconies would see a professional hard at work with complex arrangements. Then, with a few minutes to spare, he would move the equipment inside the room, with the French doors leading onto the balcony open two feet. He would be less visible. The rifle would be visible behind the open French doors, but only if spectators studied the inside of a dark room rather than looking at the speakers' platform or the parading horseback riders and marching bands scheduled to start the festivities.

Shing Wong would return to the plaza at 3:00, as planned, to observe preparations. The shopkeeper would anticipate a ten-minute point before the speech. He would remove his hat, wipe the sweat from his forehead, and replace the hat—the prearranged signal that all looked as expected from the ground. Then he would return to his shop to await the assassin.

Weeks before, Shing Wong had measured the plaza, laboring with his calculations at 2:00 in the morning, scrambling to avoid the light from lamp posts. 503 feet from east to west, the dimension that mattered. He had telegraphed Gustafsson the number, along with a detail about roses facing east, buried in a message that appeared to be a misdirected order for goods. Armed with those details, Gustafsson had selected his Winchester. Now, from 503 feet, Gustafsson subtracted eight feet because the speakers' platform stuck out a bit. He added four feet to allow for his position inside the room. He needed to shoot 499 feet, well within the Winchester's effective range of 200 yards, or 600 feet. Gustafsson could put the rifle under the drape and add to it the telescopic sight, a new invention that he had imported to Chicago from Austria, and then added to his luggage. As Arthur Sitwell he had practiced with the gadget for days in the countryside west of Chicago.

Gustafsson used a corner of the black cloth to wipe the sweat from his neck. His hansom carriage company required long days, but not much physical endurance. The sedentary life onboard ship during his passage took a toll too. He didn't anticipate how he would tire from hauling and rearranging his equipment. He tried to ignore the sweat still dripping onto his white collar, vowed to succeed, and waited.

Maurice Latta

Thursday, November 15, 1906

A t Ancon Hospital, I saw no sign that Jimmy Sloan had provided updates to the President. TR remained at ease, walking the wards and talking with the hospital staff and patients. As best as I could see from my perch in the hall, never once did TR flinch as he passed by men missing limbs or eyes.

After an hour, I gently reminded the President that it was time to leave for the hotel to change out of his wrinkled, muddy white suit into his formal white vest and black frockcoat. His valet had insisted that the schedule allow time for the President to freshen up in advance of the coming hoopla. Attentive to my duties, I prided myself that our carriages pulled up to the new Tivoli Hotel on schedule. We now had our first glimpse of the magnificent four-story building, wrapped by porches and encircled by palms. Even more attractive than the Willard, Washington's best hotel.

As part of my duties, I registered all of us—Dr. Rixey, TR and his valet Amos, Mrs. R. and her maid Bonnie, the three agents, one reporter, and me. Amos had stood behind the grounds waiting for our entourage to arrive because he knew he needed the credentials I carried if the manager was to allow him a basement room. Paperwork done, I followed the President to his lovely suite on the second floor for quick dictation. Then I rushed to my room to change into a fresh suit. In the hall, I spotted agent Frank Tyree hunting for ice. How to start? I found an opening.

"Frank, I saw you were late for lunch today. Hope you are feeling fine."

"Ah, yes. Jimmy sent me on a mission, not exactly aboveboard. No way I'll tell the missus about this one."

I pursed my lips, waiting. Frank scanned the hall. Empty.

"Suppose it can't hurt to tell you, given your duties here. Jimmy asked me to talk to a whore. I see you're surprised too." Frank rubbed his chin three times. "See, a copper told Larry, and then Larry told Jimmy about a poker game in a brothel, where the players see the men come and go. One fellow, a stranger, he went with the whore, Emily Byrne's her name. Nice girl, Irish lass, works in a decent house, not a crib. I went to see her while you were cruising on that tug. She told me the guy was tall, lanky, blond. He gave the madam and Emily a Swedish-sounding name—neither one could remember it—but said he was from Chicago. Funny thing was he had a British accent. And he talked a lot about TR, about the visit, the schedule. Nervous. Claimed he was a photographer. Eventually, after jabbering a lot, he got down to business. Smells of fish to me." Frank bit his bottom lip.

"Oh, my," I said, stumbling for words. "Hope he's simply a talkative customer." I glanced at my pocket watch. "Nine minutes before we leave again."

We separated, to ready ourselves for what we thought would be the highlight of the day, probably the highlight of the entire visit—the ceremony in the central plaza, where TR would give an address. One I had helped to write, or anyway, one I had proofed and typed. According to plan, the President's carriage, with TR and Mrs. R., stopped at the palace to pick up President Amador and his wife, Maria. She dressed like a twin of Mrs. R., all in white, large hat, veil. Another carriage for the three agents and Dr. Rixey followed. A buggy for the journalists—de Lisser, unwelcome at the Tivoli, had been waiting off to the side—and for me, trailed behind the agents. Looking toward the front of our cortege, I could tell that President Amador, the only bi-lingual passenger in the presidential carriage, seemed busy translating for his chatty wife.

Nearing the central plaza, we heard the noises of spectators chatting, horses snorting, and band instruments warming up. By the time we arrived

154

on the edge of the square at 3:30, the noise made it impossible to hear each other. The three agents separated from us, undoubtedly for business connected to their protection detail. I suspected they were searching for a tall, blond man. Fred Palmer and Mr. de Lisser and I pushed our way through the throngs. We recognized the short ICC Secretary, Joseph Bishop, with his neatly cropped gray beard, and walked with him to a good vantage point. I looked around, partly to take in the beautiful square, with its balconies and ornate wrought-iron railings, and partly to keeping an eye out for danger. We could see the speakers' platform in front of the cathedral, decorated with wilting flowers and droopy flags and bunting. I stared at what appeared to be the Roosevelt family coat of arms, pinned to one of the soggy drapes at the platform. TR would immediately see it as an imagined and simplified version of his true coat of arms, but he would take care not to laugh.

Waiting for the festivities to begin, I wondered if Fred would ask Secretary Bishop about the threats. Apparently, the long friendship between Bishop and Fred didn't allow for gossip. Instead, Fred turned to me and asked about the Brownsville affair, maybe realizing that was safer to discuss in public. "Maurice," Fred shouted above the noise, "do you mind me asking you about that affair down in Texas? The killing spree? Where the President dismissed without honor all those Negro soldiers? Have you heard anything more about Negro disenchantment with the President?"

Fred seemed to have no hesitation asking these questions in front of Mr. de Lisser, who listened carefully. "I wonder too," said de Lisser. "My friends in America tell me the proof against the soldiers was trumped up." When I think back, I realize there may have been tension between the two reporters, each eager to get the best story. But at this moment, they were united in their curiosity, both hoping to benefit from information I might share. Bishop, for his part, seemed disinterested, focused more on surveying the crowd to find friends than on what an assistant secretary might say.

Indeed, I knew a lot about the Brownsville affair, simply by reading telegrams and letters that came through our White House office and the *Louisiana*'s telegraph operator. Booker T. Washington had urged TR to

155

rethink his strategy of punishing 167 Negro soldiers. That entreaty fell on deaf ears. I continued to think of the President as fair-minded, so I simply added a vague statement of my trust in his judgment. I suppose I may have added just a detail or two about the investigation, nothing Bishop would have considered a breach of confidence. Fred would want a story, needed a story. I took pride in the fact that he sought it from me. Maybe I wanted to pay him back for the information he had shared in the hospital bathroom, even though Frank Tyree had just confirmed that information, in the Tivoli hall an hour earlier.

As we talked, more spectators squeezed into the plaza. They cheered, waved, elbowed for space. Ladies fluttered ivory fans—I made a note to myself to buy one for Clara—and men mopped their foreheads with linen handkerchiefs. I smelled the sweat of the crowd and the growing aroma of horses whose riders sought their designated place for the processional. Soon the sights overtook the smells. A dozen Panamanian officials jockeyed for space on the speakers' platform, reminding me of the scramble on the train that morning to be near the President. I felt the swelling crowd push in on us from every direction. Bishop looked pleased with the size of the gathering. I suspected he was in the dark about danger.

At 3:46, TR and Mrs. R. and Manual and Maria Amador left the carriage where they had been waiting and took their places on the platform, amid another swell of cheering, the loudest yet. TR began to watch the processional in his honor.

Ernest Hallen

E rnest "Red" Hallen, setting up his camera on the central plaza, would have preferred to be with his wife and daughters in Jersey City, New Jersey. But he couldn't turn down a job. Back in New York, brothers Elmer and Bert Underwood had looked out for him, even when he was too young to be considered a professional photographer. For the firm of Underwood & Underwood, Hallen produced stereographs, double image photographs that captured what the left eye and the right eye saw, as well as more conventional photographs. The Underwoods had sent him to cover the Greco-Turkish War in 1897, then sold his remarkable images to newspapers and magazines. Although he wasn't allowed to add his name—purchasers knew only the brand Underwood & Underwood—Hallen had become respected among members of the minuscule circle of American and European photographers who traveled to war zones. Now the Underwood brothers asked him to go to Panama to record the construction of the canal. The brothers said they felt confident in his ability to talk himself into the right circles, to get permission to take photographs.

Hallen had heard over the grapevine that three American photographers had already gone to Panama, at the invitation of the Isthmian Canal Commission, and had failed. He knew all three and predicted their failure. Chief Engineer John Findlay Wallace had hired and fired the first, who

157

was just no good, and the second and third were too persnickety about conditions. When John Stevens replaced Wallace as Chief Engineer, Stevens had decided he didn't need pictures of mud. But once actual construction became visible, Stevens changed his mind and started to look around for the right talent.

The Underwoods had employed Hallen when they could, but the jobs were unpredictable. He knew that if he were on the isthmus, working freelance for the company but recognized in a semi-official capacity by Stevens, he might then latch on to the permanent ICC job in the Zone. Such positions were rare, especially for a thirty-one-year-old, self-taught photographer, with no useful connections.

But Hallen did have one connection.

He had been in the coastal port city of Volos during the Greco-Turkish War. That war, like all wars, was a nasty business. The reporters sent to cover it shared information and hung out together in the cafes and bars of Athens and Volos, waiting impatiently for military action. The group had included Frederick Palmer, reporting at the time for the *New York Press,* and the more famous Stephen Crane. Lonely, fledgling photographer Red Hallen had latched onto these men.

When Hallen arrived in Panama nine years later, he called on ICC Secretary Joseph Bishop, who handled contact with journalists and photographers. Hallen, guessing that Palmer and Bishop knew each other from New York, mentioned Palmer's name as a reference. A quick telegram confirmed Hallen's worth and got him the access he needed to set up equipment along the canal. Bishop understood that newspaper editors had started to clamor for photographs. He also believed that illustrated stories could help build Congressional support for the canal. Bishop hinted that Teddy needed that support and that Hallen had a good chance of becoming the Zone's official photographer if he excelled at capturing the President's visit.

On November 15, 1906, in the central plaza, at 2:00 in the afternoon, Red Hallen began to set up his equipment. A Kodak Film Plate Premo, a cumbersome stereograph camera, a tripod. (No black drape.) He chose a corner, just to the side of Avenida Central, a street that fed into the plaza. Not under the balconies on the second and third floors near the cathedral, where the overhang would block the sun.

Maurice Latta

Thursday, November 15, 1906

At 3:41 in the plaza—I checked my watch often—I stood beside Frederick Palmer, Joseph Bishop, and Herbert de Lisser. We crowded together, next to a group of three women adorned in multiple layers of finery despite the blazing heat. Mr. Bishop tilted his head, stared at the oldest of the women. "You know," he whispered in my ear, "I mingle with wealthy families here. Part of my job. Give me a minute to offer regards."

"Señora Arenas, good to see you on this glorious occasion. Let me introduce my colleagues if I may," Mr. Bishop shouted above the din. He named me and the journalists, in turn. Señora Arenas introduced her daughters, though I could not hear their names. I noted that de Lisser was in no way sidelined, and I guessed that Señora Arenas had a good command of English.

Rising noise curbed more talk as the processional began. Marchers streamed into the crowded plaza from the side streets. Schoolchildren sang the national anthem. Uniformed soldiers paraded in formation. Musicians played patriotic tunes. Mounted police, led by Chief Shanton, rode into the plaza. Dressed as rough riders, they waved their slouch hats, while their horses' hooves sounded a regular beat. At the end of the processional, on foot and on horseback, marched two hundred members of the leading families of Panama.

160

When the band paused between songs, Mr. Bishop addressed Señora Arenas again. "I suppose you ladies are here unaccompanied. I know Señor Arenas is marching into the plaza with the other men of the leading families. I just saw him come down the side street a minute ago. The President is watching all this pomp and circumstance. He'll talk soon." Mr. Bishop could speak with authority, for he had helped plan the day. "I do hope you can see TR on the platform."

"I can if I crane my neck," shouted Señora Arenas, with a frown. She held a perfumed handkerchief over her nose, hoping to mask the smells of sweat and manure. "I like to think I am a forgiving Christian woman. But I may never forgive that photographer."

Mr. Bishop winced. "Oh, yes, I know him. Fred—Mr. Palmer—knows him too. We spotted him in the corner a minute ago and thought we'd say hello once we can nudge our way through. Red Hallen's a good man, been on the isthmus for just a week. What in the world has he done to annoy you?"

Señora Arenas looked puzzled. "No, I mean the photographer with a Scandinavian name who stole the balcony from us. Magnus somebody. He convinced my husband that the room he had reserved for us so we could stand above the crowd—she turned slightly, looked over her shoulder, and pointed up—should be forfeited to this Magnus somebody. So he could photograph the event. Did you have a hand in this act of thievery?"

Now Mr. Bishop looked puzzled. "Señora Arenas, I select the photographers allowed to follow the President. Only Red Hallen should be recording today's festivities."

My brain twisted away from the heat and the noise and spun. Mr. Bishop didn't know what Frank Tyree had told me about the prostitute's customer, a talkative photographer. From Sweden. Or England. Or Chicago.

"Excuse me, Señora. I must check. No one should photograph the President without my approval," He pivoted. I followed at his heels. De Lisser and Fred joined in behind, sensing something amiss, probably curious to see Mr. Bishop berate a devious photographer. We pushed our way through the crowd for thirty feet, until we saw a red-headed man surrounded by photography equipment.

"Red," shouted Mr. Bishop. "Good to see you."

"Remember me?" added Fred, shouting too. "The last time we saw each together, oh, eight or nine years ago, we were boys dodging bullets in Greece, gossiping about Stephen Crane, who managed to report about the war while never leaving the bar for the battle. Oh, and this chap with us, meet Maurice Latta. He's Assistant Secretary to Teddy."

Hallen shook my hand, paying more attention to the others. "Of course, I remember you, Fred. You were always the most inventive of that group in getting your story to New York, no matter how far we were from a telegraph office. Looks like you're wearing the same explorer clothes you wore in Greece. Ha. And thanks for vouching for me last month." He turned his smile to Mr. Bishop and then back to Fred. "Great to see you again after so long. What a day this is going to be. I hope these crowds don't destroy my equipment. I have everything ready to go. I can't talk long—this is my big opportunity." He glanced again at Mr. Bishop.

"Right, not much time to talk, if they keep to the schedule I gave them." The procession was ending, and the minor dignitaries were arranging themselves on the platform "Tell me, Red, you are alone, right? You don't have an assistant, do you?"

"An assistant? What a joke Mr. Bishop. You know my other bosses, the Underwoods, would never pay for a second passage to Panama. Not even on steerage.

"No chap with a Scandinavian name? Magnus someone? Stationed up in a balcony?" Hallen shook his head firmly as he maneuvered his camera to photograph the end of the processional, focusing on his job. Mr. Bishop tensed, but only because some would-be photographer up on a balcony somewhere had gotten the better of him.

My spinning brain stopped dead, spun again. I alone made the connection. I ran toward the speakers' platform, weaving around the crowds.

Magnus Gustafsson

Thursday, November 15, 1906

4:15. He stayed focused. He would succeed this time. He had practiced in his head, again and again. He had worked through the few changes. Contraption inside. Tripod one foot from French doors. Black drape. Rifle. Bullets. Scope. Look around room for identifying possessions. No cigarettes. No initialed handkerchief. Just straw hat on hook to grab while running, to throw off spectators. Now wait. Ha, just another day with smell of horse manure. Wait. Surging noise from plaza. Practice sight with Amador, remember he is taller. Amador steps back. TR steps forward. Starts. After every sentence, clapping, yelling. Lower rifle slightly. Watch. Get it right. This time get it right.

Maurice Latta

Routine desk work fills most of my time in the White House office. While I forget most of my tasks after completing them, like most Americans, I do remember historic events—McKinley's assassination, Wilson's declaration of war against Germany, Pearl Harbor, Hiroshima. But even more, I remember ten minutes of the late afternoon on November 15th, 1906. The second most vivid ten minutes of my life. I believe I remember what I truly remembered, not what I want to remember. Others may decide I exaggerate my own role, which amounted, quite literally, to a gesture. I ask, what would have happened in the absence of that gesture?

In Panama, I felt responsible for knowing where to find everyone in the entourage at any time, though that was not easy. No one thought it necessary to report to an assistant secretary. In view of what I had learned from agents Larry Richey and Frank Tyree, and from my friend Fred Palmer too, I kept an eye on the agents during the central plaza festivities. Jerome Kehl might not be the sole threat. Lead agent Jimmy Sloan stood at one side of the speakers' platform. Frank and Larry were out of sight, probably stationed on the platform behind the President, their backs almost touching the front door of the cathedral.

Pushing through the crowd, I spotted Jimmy. He stood at the front corner of the platform, six feet from President Amador, who was speaking to

164

formally welcome the President. Jimmy's head moved left, then right, left again, looking out at the crowd. On my mind, and I suppose on Jimmy's, were the events in Buffalo five years before. Leon Czolgosz had wrapped a bandage around his hand to hide his gun and then walked up to McKinley to shoot him at close range. Jimmy, on the slightly raised platform, could look down and out.

Almost at the platform, waving frantically, I caught Jimmy's attention. I raised my right hand, pointed to the third-floor balcony Señora Arenas had pointed to a minute earlier, and then made a gesture I had never made before. I brought my raised arm toward my head and pointed my finger. Jimmy could not misinterpret my gesture, and I was not known for clowning around. No one besides Jimmy paid me any attention. All eyes were on President Amador.

Except Jimmy's. He followed the direction of my pointing finger. He darted to the back of the platform, where he must have found Larry and Frank. Then our President, oblivious to danger, succeeded President Amador at the front of the platform. TR began the speech I had typed on my Oliver typewriter aboard the *Louisiana* and had handed to the President during lunch. "For the first time in the history of the United States it has become advisable for a President of the United States to step on territory, not beneath the flag of the United States, and it is on the territory of Panama that this occurred, a symbol and proof of the closeness of the ties that unite the two countries, because of their peculiar relations to the gigantic enterprise of digging the Panama Canal." As he spoke these words (and as I was too preoccupied to lament the regrettable repetition of "United States"), the agents moved from the back of the platform to the side. Jimmy pointed to the balcony. Larry and Frank separated and barged forward, each swinging around the plaza by a different side.

TR spoke for four minutes, holding his top hat in his hand. The two presidents' wives looked on, admiringly. Actually, I assume admiringly. Each was veiled. While the President blathered on about the promise of the canal, I looked not at him, not at the dignitaries, not at the wives, but at the agile members of the President's protective detail, darting through the crowd, and at the third-floor wrought-iron balcony of the building across the plaza.

For the first few minutes of the President's speech, I saw nothing more to worry me. Did I raise an alarm needlessly? Would Jimmy forgive me?

I lost sight of Frank and Larry, but I kept looking. And listening. Although the President wrote his remarks himself, I had taken them down in dictation, typed them, edited them lightly, too lightly, and knew what was coming. "Nowhere else in the world at this moment," he bellowed to the crowd, "is a work of such importance taking place as here on the isthmus of Panama, for here is being performed the giant engineering feat of the ages and it is a matter for deep gratitude that I am able to say that it is being well and worthily performed."

As TR got to the "feat of the ages" phrase, I saw what I thought was a scuffle through the French doors that opened onto the balcony across the way. The movements were hard to make out from where I stood. I might have dismissed from my mind what I thought I saw, except that after fifteen seconds, Larry Richey came out on the balcony. He looked over at Jimmy Sloan, who had stayed near the platform to guard TR. Larry gave a faint wave with uplifted arm, an arm I knew to be powerful. I looked around to see if anyone else in the crowd witnessed the same wave. But the spectators were still looking at the platform, not away from it as I had done. Even Fred, Mr. Bishop, and Mr. de Lisser, who I could just make out still standing near Red Hallen, stared ahead at the speakers. When I glanced back at the platform, I saw that Jimmy had abandoned his post and hustled across the plaza toward the building where Larry stood. Then I lost sight of Jimmy as he disappeared into the throng. Recalling these events, I wish I could add that I rushed to the balcony along with the agents. It never occurred to me to do so. I commend the agents for their speed and muscle. For myself, I take pride in my moving right arm.

Edith Roosevelt

Thursday, November 15, 1906

E dith Roosevelt wondered if Maria Amador also suffered from the heat on the speakers' platform. Maria may have built up tolerance. The two women wore the full uniform of first ladies in the tropics. Layers of white linen covered every inch. Like Edith, Maria would be wearing a corset, would feel sweat under her hat and veil. They sat three feet apart on the speakers' platform in front of the cathedral, looking out at TR's broad back, too broad, and at President Amador's narrow back and perfect posture. The heat and her husband's familiar patrician voice made Edith groggy. She had heard her husband's words many, many times, and with five children, well, six with Alice, to worry about, she could focus on only so much. Perhaps Maria could concentrate more squarely on the occasion. Edith knew she ought to follow what she imagined was Maria's attentiveness. Easier to drift off for a minute or two.

She caught her eyes closing, pinched her arm as a signal to stay awake, to look out at the crowd. Tilting her chin up half an inch, she saw balconies filled with bystanders, men holding drinks in their hands. Undoubtedly spirits. Her mind wandered to Elliott, her alcoholic brother-in-law, now dead for twelve years but still bringing shame. Just before he died, Edith had learned, to her horror, that he had fathered a child with his maid as his wife lay dying of diphtheria. Stories had leaked to the papers. Edith, devout, upright, reserved, had counseled Theodore to pay off the maid, Miss Katy

Marsh. That payment would end the matter, would keep the stories from recurring. Theodore assured her the story had been hushed up.

A few weeks before departing for Panama, Edith had caught Theodore in the White House family quarters, oddly stooped, staring at a sheet of paper, looking distracted. When she pried, he silently handed her the letter. No crest, thin paper. "I know you will want assurances that Elliott Jr. is indeed your nephew. I now live with him in Panama, where you will be traveling in November. I will make plans for you to see him then. He looks like his father, as you were told years ago. I advise you to bring the $5000 with you to Panama to avoid trying to obtain funds while you are on your visit and in the public eye.... Yours sincerely, Katy Marsh." Edith sank down on the bed, light-headed. Theodore stood at the window, looking out at the White House grounds. She rose, put her hand firmly on her husband's shoulder. With that touch, they silently shared their anger toward Elliott, the brother Theodore had loved. Aside from commiserating with her husband, Edith would not speak of the shame. She could not foresee that she would remain silent even twenty-seven years later, when she turned seventy-one and the bastard nephew's half-sister, Eleanor, became First Lady.

A sudden movement jolted Edith out of her brooding. She saw what others failed to see. A man barging up to Jimmy? Mr. Latta, that secretary who stuck by the rules, wouldn't share? Pushing? Pointing across the plaza? Oh, my god, that gesture. Jimmy Sloan raised his head, pivoted, scurried to the other agents. Another false alarm? Don't stir. Trust Jimmy. Sit still. More movement. Agents shoving. No gunshot. False, false again. A minute. Two minutes. Her eyes stayed across the plaza. Now she saw it. Larry signaling to Jimmy. Dizzy. Light. The taste of lunch rising to her mouth. The veil, with its white dots, provided privacy, allowing her to grimace and work through her breathing without others noticing. She thought about grabbing for Maria, looking for comfort, sharing. Her reserve triumphed, for now. She remained aloof, upright. No one in the crowd would see her terror. No one would read about it.

George Shanton

S till mounted, Police Chief George Shanton motioned to his men. They had comported themselves well in the processional, adding to the festivities with their Rough Rider uniforms and fine horsemanship. Time to lead them out of the plaza.

He saw a tall man with a round face run toward him. Jimmy Sloan. He had just seen him that morning in the Palms Saloon. Sloan raised his arm, swung it, a clear instruction to dismount. Shanton walked his horse to the corner of the plaza, leading Sloan to a spot where they could talk.

"A damn shooter perched up there." Sloan pointed. "Today, I'm saying damn, not bloody. We got him just in time."

"What? I didn't see a thing." Shanton grimaced with anger and shame. He had ridden with Teddy in Cuba, and now the president, his president, had been threatened on Shanton's own watch.

Sloan, panting, ran through the events that led to the room at the Broadmoor. He paused to catch his breath, then added that agent Frank Tyree had noticed a sign for the real estate agent who managed that building.

"George, I need to learn who the shooter is. To learn if he's alone. He won't give us his name."

"I've got it. I'll report back." Shanton galloped to his office to change from his rough rider costume into his police uniform. Ten minutes later, he knocked at Ronald Caldwell's office. No answer. With little effort, Shanton

169

broke down the door. He saw a beautifully appointed real estate office, a bit stuffy, with a small stack of files on the desk. He looked quickly through the files and immediately found, on top of a surprisingly small number of signed leases, two documents of interest—a lease for the plaza space signed by Tomas Arenas, with a big x through it, and another lease for the same space signed by a Magnus Gustafsson. Shanton pocketed those documents. Now he had to locate Caldwell, to learn more about Gustafsson. Rummaging through Caldwell's desk drawer, Shanton found the address he needed. A lovely house six blocks from the plaza. A maid answered the knock.

"Ronald Caldwell," Shanton said, using his command tone. "Tell him it's the Chief of Police."

The maid looked stunned. *"Un minuto."* Then catching herself, "One minute, please."

The Caldwells seemed to be finishing dinner at their dining room table, just in view of the front entrance. Ronald sat beside his wife, Caterina. Shanton already knew she was part of the elite Alcalde family. None of this made sense. Caldwell's office was substantial, his house was grand, he was ensconced in the Panamanian elite. The Caldwell and Alcalde families were not the sort to shelter an anarchist, whether he was Italian or Swedish.

The maid leaned over the table between Caldwell and his wife. Shanton could not make out the maid's whispered words, but guessed she was warning her employers that the caller had not used a genteel tone. Caldwell stood, a confused look on his face, and told his visitor to step into the parlor. The maid closed the squeaky double doors separating the parlor from the dining room, leaving a half-inch opening.

Shanton raced through a cleaned-up rendition of what happened in the third-floor room off the plaza. He spoke of a dangerous intruder, not of an assassin.

Caldwell looked stunned, chewed on his bottom lip. "The man seemed fine. Blond. Tall. Nothing suspicious. Said he needed to photograph the proceedings. I'd never met him before."

"When did he sign a lease for the room?"

"Yesterday."

"Wasn't that space rented to Tomas Arenas."

Caldwell winced. He must wonder how that information got out.

"Well, yes, but then Mr. Gustafsson came along and said he really needed that room and that balcony. For his newspaper."

"That meant you had to cancel arrangements with Tomas Arenas. I know Arenas. He is wealthy and powerful. Why would you cancel for a stranger?"

Caldwell said nothing for a minute, squirming and lowering his eyes. Shanton continued to stare.

"I have had some reversal of my fortunes," Caldwell said quietly. "Mr. Gustafsson offered me a large amount of money. If you have seen the two leases—I wonder if you broke into my office—you know he paid three times what Tomas Arenas was going to pay. I have loans that come due on December first, and I needed to come up with resources."

"You fucking idiot." Caldwell opened his mouth to utter an expletive of his own, then thought better of it. Without a goodbye, Shanton rode to the Tivoli to report to Jimmy Sloan that Roland Caldwell was a bumbling upstart, not a conspirator.

Shanton didn't know and wouldn't have cared that within three months Roland Caldwell's wife would ship her penniless husband back to Mother Caldwell in Burlington, Vermont. Twin brother George would employ Ronald at the Northern Vermont Lumber Mill, where his main duty was to order food for the loggers. Neither brother, nor their parents, would ever know that a Caldwell had harbored a would-be assassin.

171

Chapter 40

Thursday, November 15, 1906

When festivities on the plaza ended, a remnant of our entourage slowly gathered around the carriages that were to take us back to the Tivoli. We were missing Mr. de Lisser, who roomed elsewhere, and agents Larry Richey and Frank Tyree. Jimmy Sloan, looking glum, told me not to wait for them, then he moved on to talk to TR and Mrs. R. and Dr. Rixey. TR had his arm entwined through Mrs. R's. Though they were about the same height, he appeared to support her. President Amador and wife Maria were off to the side, awaiting their ride to the palace. Mrs. Amador chatted to her husband and waved to friends in the crowd, seemingly unaware of events. For my part, I stood with Fred. We were both speechless, me because I was dazed and Fred because he knew not to ask, with the others nearby, why I had run off when Joseph Bishop asked Red Hallen if he had an assistant photographer.

Back at the Tivoli, I entered the lobby just behind Jimmy. I saw Mr. Bishop sitting in an armchair, which surprised me because he lived in Panama City and was not a guest at the Tivoli. I also saw a policeman, dressed in a uniform adorned with brass, run into the lobby, breathless. Jimmy put his palm out to Mr. Bishop in a wait-a-minute motion and huddled with the policeman as I walked to my room. I loosened my tie and poured tepid water over my face, then flopped down on the bed. Ten minutes later, a messenger knocked, telling me to meet Mr. James Sloan in the hotel bar.

Was I about to be reprimanded for putting my nose where it didn't belong? As I entered the bar, I saw Jimmy, Mr. Bishop, and Fred, all waiting for me. We ordered drinks. I was not much of a drinker—still the case—but that evening would be an exception as I waited for a public dressing down.

"I'm going to tell you what happened. Then it goes no further," Jimmy said quietly after we took seats at a booth. "Teddy wants all stories to focus on the canal, on progress with digging and sanitation, Yellow Fever, and such. No distracting news. Poultney Bigelow's stories about dirt and disease did enough damage. Any more bad publicity about the Zone won't go down well with Congress. Think 'uplifting.' Also, I don't want imitators. Those anarchists learn from each other." Fred looked puzzled.

"No bloody stories in the news," Jimmy said again, looking pointedly at Fred, who nodded slowly in assent. "And no stories to the missus," he said, looking at me. I followed Fred's lead, nodding in assent. I suppose Jimmy and Mr. Bishop already had an understanding about silence because Jimmy never glanced at him. They must have talked in the plaza and Jimmy must have asked him to come to the bar. "One more thing. No talking to Mrs. R. She knows something happened, and she's spooked enough. Don't make it worse.

"But for the three of you, I owe you the story. Maurice here, God bless Mr. Maurice Latta, pointed at the balcony and made a trigger motion. I could see an open door and a lot of something black inside the room. Didn't look good. And no spectators on that balcony. I signaled Larry and Frank to run in separate directions over there and enter any way they could. They found a back street behind that row of apartments and pushed their way through the locked door at the street level. They ran up. Found a few doors off the hall. Most of them were open, and the agents could see people inside, people who looked harmless. They kicked in the one hall door that was closed. No one heard because of the noise from the plaza. The agents saw the arse of a tall man. That is if you could tell by his legs.

"He could have been a photographer, since he bent under a black cloth. But his head was higher than his camera. He tried to stand. Larry and Frank grabbed him and wrestled him to the ground. He dropped," Jimmy looked at me, "a rifle. A brand-new semi-automatic Winchester." I felt my blood drain down and my whiskey come up.

"The shooter was blond," Jimmy continued, "definitely not Italian. He whimpered. Didn't resist much. Said nothing. But Larry had been alerted by a Zone policeman—Frank confirmed this—that a tall, blond stranger in town was acting oddly.

"After Larry signaled from the balcony that he had everything under control, I left Teddy and went to the building myself. I thought the shooter looked slightly familiar, can't be sure. We're keeping him in the apartment 'til dark, under guard. Larry and Frank are on him." Jimmy snickered for an instant. "Together, that's three hundred and fifty pounds of muscle and bulk." Later we'll take the man to one of the tugs following the *Louisiana* and grill him again. His loaded Winchester is all the proof we need to hold him.

"I doubt this thug is part of a larger conspiracy. George Shanton—he's the chief of police you might have seen in the lobby—learned that the shooter's name is Magnus Gustafsson. If he's using his real name. The real estate manager who rented out the space did it for the money. The manager claims he'd never seen Gustafsson until he offered a bundle for the room. But we'll stay watchful—we're not taking any chances. That's my motto.

"Now remember, this is all to stay hidden away, forever. I don't think Magnus Gustafsson is going to find himself a lawyer. As a matter of fact, I don't think he'll ever make it to a courtroom."

Not only didn't I need to worry, but Jimmy paid for my whiskey.

Herbert de Lisser

Thursday, November 15, 1906

As darkness came on, Herbert de Lisser found his way to Mrs. Hunter's boarding house, a slightly tilted two-story structure needing paint—the best he could do in this part of the city. His room was little better than a cardboard box, without a window for a breeze. De Lisser could have afforded better.

On the way to Mrs. Hunter's, he saw a watering hole and considered a drink. Peeked in a few feet. His shoes stuck to the sticky floor. He registered the stares from the bedraggled Negros at the bar. Wearing his well-tailored suit, he might be as unwelcome in that establishment as he would be in the saloons frequented by the President's entourage. He reconsidered, turned around.

When he reached the boarding house, Mrs. Hunter handed him a message. "Man with round cheeks sitting at hotel bar with young, bearded man in explorer clothes and another young man with high forehead and one short older man with gray beard. Older one, not hotel guest. Round cheeks talking to them." De Lisser could not view this foursome himself—he could not enter the bar—but the day before, strolling in front of the hotel, he had listened to the bellhops chat with each other. He enlisted the help of the one who seemed the smartest to watch the men around the President and send observations by messenger, for a fair price, to the boarding house. The messenger had just made his first delivery.

175

De Lisser knew that the men in the President's retinue thought he had no eyes or ears. Didn't understand that he had learned to make sure every sense was on high alert, always. An hour or two earlier in the plaza, he suspected something was amiss. Though his view was partially blocked by heads and hats, he saw Maurice Latta rush across the plaza to signal to Jimmy Sloan. Then he thought he saw Sloan giving directions to Frank Tyree and Larry Richey. He watched Maurice Latta, trying to follow his movements. Again, too many large hats. In frustration, de Lisser turned to look at the platform, where he had a clear sight line. Edith Roosevelt sat still on the dais, wrapped in white and veiled. Suddenly she jerked. Next, her shoulders rose as she tensed her body. She saw something.

Frederick Palmer would hear from Jimmy Sloan what happened in the plaza. Had to be a threat against the President. Nothing else would have caused the sequence of movements de Lisser witnessed. Palmer seemed a decent chap. But he had the nice hotel and ready access to the President in mess halls and bars. He would be the first to gather news. For *Collier's*. Galling.

Maurice Latta

A fter the terrifying scene in the plaza and after the revealing conversation in the Tivoli bar, two more events remained on my official schedule for that night. President Amador, who still seemed unaware of the threat against TR, hosted a dinner at the palace for twenty canal officials and Panama's leaders, followed by a reception for three hundred people at the Commercial Club. I had not made the cut for the dinner, but I was among the masses invited to the reception. I donned my new evening tailcoat, too distracted to pay much attention to my new look, swiped the worst of the mud off my shoes, and rode to the Club with Fred (who did not seem to own evening apparel). He stayed at my side, probably feeling uncomfortable too. We spotted Mr. Bishop—not easy given his short stature—hobnobbing with the crowd and TR and Mrs. R. making the rounds. Fred and I stuck to the sidelines. We grabbed flutes of champagne, which was another rarity for me and then found our way to the terrace, out of earshot of other guests. I sensed Fred was eager to talk too.

"Maurice, do you know how hard it is to keep my promise of secrecy? I could earn a fortune reporting on the actual events. My reputation would be sealed among the fourth estate. But I'd never get past Jimmy Sloan to meet with Teddy again. I'd have a minute of fame, and then my career would go south fast."

"For me, I just wish I could share with my wife, Clara. She thinks I have what we call a desk job behind the scenes. She would be dumbfounded to learn what happened. (By now, I had had too much alcohol. I cannot be certain I used the word dumbfounded.) And I'd like to tell my sons, too, when they get a little older. But I would never go against our oath. I guess you could call it an oath. And I will admit there's more on my mind than ethics. If the story got out and TR or Jimmy traced it back to me, I'd be out of a job. I don't have connections to find another one."

After these confessions, Fred asked how I had known the would-be photographer was really an assassin. Earlier that day, in the hospital toilet, Fred told me about bits of a conversation among agents he overheard at lunch, and we both heard Jimmy at the bar, but Fred did not know about the information Frank Tyree passed along in the hotel hall mid-afternoon. I erred yet again, admitting to Fred that Frank told me about a lady of the night at The Luna who had entertained a talkative Swedish photographer. Fred smiled at the story, perhaps because he could imagine the scene at The Luna, perhaps because of my skill at making connections.

At 11:00, we returned to the Tivoli. The President called me to his suite for dictation and correspondence. I thought he might thank me for my role, but he never mentioned events on the plaza. He seemed full of energy, while I could barely keep my eyes open by the time he dismissed me a half hour later. I collapsed in bed. I thought the drama was over, and I felt satisfied with my role, my historic role, in pointing to the balcony. I thought of the crank, Kehl. I thought of hapless Gustafsson. I was certain TR was safe.

Edith Roosevelt

Thursday, November 15, 1906

E dith Roosevelt had known two first ladies—Frances Cleveland, twenty-one when she entered the White House, and Ida McKinley, long an invalid. Edith rarely thought of either, except when she assessed the official china passed from administration to administration. Maria Amador, though, seemed a first lady cut from a different cloth. Edith had spoken to Maria on the *Louisiana* the night before, with the help of a translator. Maria followed politics, knew the importance of the canal, the importance of this visit. Wives of high-ranking officials in the ICC had told Edith that Maria's father served as chief justice of the supreme court of Panama, partly explaining the role she played in politics, helping with strategy, behind the scenes.

Maria did not know English. Decades ago, Edith had learned both Latin and French, felt unsure with each, and knew no Spanish. Returning from the terror of the central plaza, she struggled with what to do and how to do it. Discretion should prevail, as always. Edith appreciated better than anyone what Teddy hoped to accomplish. But she was a woman of faith, loyal to her God as well as her husband.

Teddy sat in the parlor, reading dispatches. Amos had been efficient—Teddy was already in his formal wear. Bonnie was efficient, too, helping Edith change into another white gown, this one more formal. While changing, she strove for a nonchalant voice, asking Bonnie to keep an eye out for anything odd—no harm in that. She told Bonnie to keep to a simple updo. Finally, Bonnie left.

Pen in hand, uncertain about her decision and her words, Edith sat at the bedroom desk and labored over a card with the help of a Spanish dictionary. She hid the card in the pocket of her gown, praying she could trust Maria.

* * *

Maria de la Ossa de Amador would never forget the embarrassing deal her husband had helped negotiate. A few years earlier, under his watch, the United States paid the New Panama Canal Company—a French company—$40,000,000 for the outdated, rusted equipment the French had abandoned. Not a cent came to Panama. Then, in an additional deal, the U.S. leased the land for the canal from Panama for a trifling $10,000,000, plus $250,000 annually, also trifling. Her husband was at the mercy of selfish officials and businessmen, but he needed to take some of the blame.

The Panamanian elite had wanted the canal to go to the Americans, believing that arrangement would bring in money and end fighting between the Conservatives like her husband and the Liberals. Panama had had fifty-three riots in fifty-seven years, or so the American president liked to say. Others called the fighting the War of One Thousand Days. The price of coffee had sunk, killing Panama's economy. Roosevelt's canal could turn things around, usher in prosperity. Maria felt heartened, pleased about the presidential visit.

At fifty-one, Maria was six years older than the other first lady, the woman she would entertain at the palace and the Club tonight. Maria did not obsess about comparisons. Neither did she ignore them. Mrs. Roosevelt was taller, and maybe prettier, though not by much. Maria's American friends had shared gossip. Edith Carow Roosevelt came from a family with culture but without means. Her drunkard father started out in the shipping business, then lost a great deal of money. The family struggled to pay for lodging and schooling. Theodore Roosevelt may have admired Edith, a childhood friend, but as his first wife he chose a beautiful woman from higher ranks of society. And the friends mentioned scandal. They heard TR's brother had fathered a child with his maid. Not so unusual, Maria thought, but apparently shameful for Americans.

No matter. Maria felt close to Mrs. Roosevelt, despite the brevity of their acquaintance. On the *Louisiana*, helped by a translator, they had chatted about the canal—the technology, the prospects. In the carriage ride to the ceremony on the plaza, with only Manuel to translate, Mrs. Roosevelt had said little and seemed aloof. But from her smile, Maria sensed they shared pride in their husbands. On the ride back from the plaza, Mrs. Roosevelt had said even less, probably tired from the heat.

At the reception that evening, Maria saw her counterpart approach. "Mrs. Amador, may I have a word with you?" An aide translated the request. Edith Roosevelt led Maria toward a corner, with a light hand on her elbow. After shooing away the aide and checking that he was out of hearing range, Edith spoke.

Maria heard words she did not understand. An apology about language limitations? Then Edith reached into her pocket and handed Maria a small note, motioning to open it, to read. The grammar and choice of words were all wrong, but the meaning was straightforward: There was an assassination attempt on my husband today. Take care. Do not tell your husband, I implore you. Return this note to me now.

Maria read the note twice. She looked up, as she sensed tears forming in her eyes and winked to keep them there. She nodded and handed back the note. *"Muchas gracias. Eres muy amable."*

Edith's face was half grimace, half smile, as she returned to the gathering. Maria would keep the confidence. And she would ensure that her husband was out of harm's way.

Larry Richey

L arry Richey felt as though he'd had ten cups of coffee. He'd been guarding TR, then ran to the lair, then tussled with the blond man, then guarded him. Finally, George Shanton had come to provide relief. Larry and Frank Tyree could go back to the Tivoli, rest. Jimmy was at the reception guarding the President, along with some of Shanton's men. But Larry couldn't imagine sleeping. He had a better idea. Mrs. R would be at the reception too. Without her maid.

Bonnie Clifford heard the knock. Three fast raps, one long rap. She must have realized they wouldn't have much time—they never did—because she had already undressed and had on her wrapper. Larry looked around. At this late hour, no one was in the hall. He entered, closed the door, locked it, then put his shoulder on her smooth neck, seeking for a moment more comfort than lust, careful to slacken the muscles in his upper arms. He knew he smelled of sweat. She smelled of Mrs. R.'s scent, Guerlain's Apres l'Ondee Bonnie had said.

"What happened? Missus was odd tonight when I dressed her. Quiet like. Didn't fuss about her hair. Kept fiddling with that veil. Wanted to wear it, even to dinner. I said there won't be mosquitoes in the palace or the Club. She wouldn't take it off. And then she said, 'Bonnie, I suppose you hear gossip in the White House and maybe here too. You know I worry about Quentin and Alice, my troublesome children. I also worry about the President. He has enemies. And I worry about other things as well. You'll tell me if you hear anything I should know, right?' She looked embarrassed, having to ask her lowly maid for information. I didn't know what to say. I wouldn't admit that I knew about that bastard nephew, Elliott's son. And I wouldn't admit that you hint at what the agents face. And then you disappeared. Couldn't find you."

Larry had been afraid Bonnie would feel him shake. But her shaking hid his. Would she understand if he said nothing about tonight? He took the comforting embrace up a notch, let one arm crawl down her back, farther. Let his muscles tighten. Here they were, an Italian from the tenements of Philadelphia, a maid one generation from County Mayo. In the middle of a ghastly commotion.

Bonnie, do you have cool water here? Can you wash me before we shag?

Alberto Agresti

Sunday, September 16, 1906 to Wednesday, September 19, 1906

Pinkerton Detective Schneider stubbornly insisted the terrorist plot against President Roosevelt in Lincoln, Illinois, in 1903 originated in an anarchist den in Paterson, New Jersey. He was wrong. A home on Taylor Street in Chicago served as the lair. But Paterson would remain one of the movement's centers, and in 1906 Alberto Agresti would become one of that center's heroes.

Since 1900, a sensational rumor had circulated: eight anarchists, including Gaetano Bresci, once stood in a circle, drawing lots to see who would assassinate King Umberto I of Italy. Bresci, an Italian silk weaver who moved to Paterson then traveled to Milan, did indeed pull the trigger. The smarter of the anarchists doubted he became a killer because he drew a short straw. They understood he hated the King, who had given an order to kill hundreds of blameless Italians. Nonetheless, the story of the lots lived on. Silk weaver Alberto Agresti remembered it vividly.

Six years later, one of the New Jersey groups that Bresci had belonged to, perhaps Gruppo L'Era Nuova, perhaps Gruppo Diritto all'Esistenza, did decide to draw lots. Many members worked as silk weavers or were friendly with weavers. All were committed anarchists who believed there was no place on earth for rulers.

The back room of the Straight Street Tavern in Paterson usually filled up Sundays. Most silk weavers had abandoned religion, making Sunday a

184

favorite day to carouse. The previous week, during work breaks—factory foremen allowed seven minutes, twice a day—the men had begun to plan. They agreed to work out details Sunday at the tavern. The bartender, an anarchist himself, would tell unfamiliar patrons the bar was closed for a private party.

Of the eleven men expected that night, the bartender unsurprisingly arrived first. Then Alberto Agresti entered, always on time, his full head of dark hair parted in the middle as usual. The bartender offered greetings, and Agresti greeted back, pleased he could control his voice. He watched as fellow weaver Stefano Grandi strode in and began to tell jokes. Within a few minutes, five others arrived. Three avoided each other's eyes. Two entered with large strides and shoulders thrown back. All remembered that the assassin Bresci had been sentenced to penal servitude for life on Santo Stefano Island in the Mediterranean and had either died or been murdered in prison, far from his family. The three weavers who never showed up at the tavern claimed illness or emergencies, or forgetfulness. Their absences would never be forgotten.

On this evening, Stefano Grandi, speaking loudly and in his native tongue, ordered a round of beer to start the proceedings, then ushered the men into the back room. He took charge, as was his custom. "No point waiting for those three cowards. Time to start. How do we draw lots?" he asked.

Alberto Agresti, focusing on details, responded first, also in Italian. "Let's put eight small, folded slips of paper in a bag. I'll write the tyrant's initials on one. The others will be blank." Checking in with the bartender, Agresti located two blank pieces of paper and a scissors, then methodically cut each sheet into four perfect rectangles, which he called lots. He wrote on one and folded each twice until he had eight small lots that looked identical. The men watched carefully, without comment. Then it came time to settle on a bag.

"Let's use an empty flour sack from the kitchen," added one of the men, pointing with his index finger to his forehead, gesturing to pay attention to his idea. The weavers, along with the bartender, were a noisy group, usually interrupting each other with stories and boasting. Today was different.

185

After more dallying and restrained discussion of the relative benefits of different containers, Grandi had enough. He gathered the slips and threw them into a flour sack. He passed it around. Urged each man to shake.

"Who picks first?" asked one of the weavers.

"Go in alphabetical order," said another. None of the men would argue with that proposal.

"I guess I'm first," Alberto Agresti said. He reached into the sack, confident that he would breathe deeply in a minute. His quivering fingers selected a folded scrap. Pulled it out. A cloud of flour filled the air. He opened the lot. Bits of remaining flour stuck to the slip.

Agresti saw the initials TR, in his own handwriting. Mouth open, he held up the unfolded slip for all to see. He lowered his hands to the stool, hiding his tremors.

To make sure there had been no skullduggery, the others selected their slips, in turn. The remaining seven, also covered with a dusting of flour, were blank.

For the next few days, Alberto Agresti kept to himself. Not a religious man, he never considered talking to a priest. He would talk about his mission to only seven men—those who knew which lot he had drawn. They were sworn, the Naples way, to secrecy. He hoped that code prevailed in America. But it was accepted that he would talk to his wife, Ernesta. About business. She had to know she would be provided for. He waited a few days, until Stefano Grandi, the boisterous silk weaver who happened to have connections, pinned down the money.

Ernesta put the children in bed. She stood washing up at their sink, stained with years of food, her face away from him. He looked at her slim back, the back he had put his arms around, caressed, knowing that this moment at the sink was the end of the first part of her life.

"We've never forgotten how Roberto fought for the workers, right?" Alberto knew his wife adored her brother. Took pride in his political activities, despite the outcome.

"Of course. We remember him every day, every hour. Why are you bringing him up now?" She turned from the sink, to look at him.

"I was his friend. I believe in what he believed."

"I know." Her lips stretched.

"Ernesta, I drew the marked lot on Sunday. You know the story about the lots?"

"Gaetano Bresci?

Alberto nodded his head slowly while staring at his wife. Beyond that stare, he didn't need many words.

As she stood still, he began with the abstract—doctrine, honor, legacy. She remained still as he moved to details she needed to know. He would be well paid. The backer would provide $10,000 now and a final $20,000 after the deed—to Alberto if he was alive and free, or to Ernesta if Alberto was dead or imprisoned. The final payment was guaranteed, even if Alberto failed at his task. Just not if he turned coward.

"Ernesta, Stefano worked out a good deal. He's a loud-mouthed bastard, but he feels responsible. Cares about you and the boys. He's working on a scheme, a safe scheme."

The source of the cash was unexpected. Alberto did not name names. He gave Ernesta only a simple summary. An unnamed Colombian businessman, about forty years of age, unknown to most, would bankroll an Italian American from Paterson.

That morning before work, Agresti had listened carefully as Stefano Grandi explained arrangements. Five years earlier, this businessman's beloved father, a Colombian diplomat, felt Roosevelt's diplomats had bested him in complicated negotiations over the canal, leading to his humiliation among his countrymen. His son, a clever businessman who married into a wealthy family, overdramatized his father's shame. The son determined to seek revenge. Whenever he traveled to New York for business, he read the American papers, hunting for articles about anarchist activity. Grandi guessed that the businessman knew that a principled anarchist might come cheap, needing expenses but not much more. On a 1906 trip, the businessman made discrete inquiries in Paterson, New Jersey, a town with a growing international reputation for unrest. It took only two days for him to find Stefano Grandi, known as a loud-mouthed rabble-rouser.

And only two hours for Grandi to negotiate a future for the Agresti family, or whatever would be left of the family.

Ernesta Agresti

Thursday, September 20, 1906

A ll forms of government oppress people, Ernesta Agresti believed. She had heard those words, sometimes in English, sometimes in one Italian dialect or another, for as long as she could remember. Growing up in Naples, where the rising price of wheat made bread scarce, labor unrest was woven into the stories she overheard. And more than stories. Eight years earlier, her older brother Roberto linked up with a group in Naples that incited strikes. Wanting to broaden his circles, Roberto traveled to Milan with his friend Alberto Agresti. Her suitor. The two joined a bread riot. A policeman armed with a baton hit Alberto, knocking him out. He never saw the policeman who shot Roberto. The young men had been friends, listened to the same speeches on anarchism, shared the same beliefs. Roberto's death led Alberto to seek a fresh start in America, while sharpening his hatred of merciless governments and their rulers.

When Alberto wrote home that he'd been hired as a silk weaver in Paterson, New Jersey, Ernesta joined him there. Alberto rented the basement flat of a tenement, with a coal stove that barely kept up with Paterson winters. At first, Ernesta focused on the attractions—a toilet off the common hallway, running water, gas lighting. After a few years of looking at the poverty near her and listening to anarchists on the lecture circuit, she knew the abuses overshadowed the attractions.

"Alberto makes twice at the mill here what he made in Italy, but it goes half as far," Ernesta said to her friend Maria Roda, known as Roda, as they shopped on Market near Main, Paterson's unimaginatively named streets, pushing baby carriages. The women spoke in a mixture of languages, like most of the shoppers darting in and out of the bakeries and apothecaries on the crowded sidewalk, all too busy to attend to the chatter of others.

Ernesta usually invited Roda to shop together, but this time Roda invited Ernesta. A good sign, Ernesta thought. At age thirty, Roda was an institution in Paterson's anarchist circles. Always out front, writing, organizing, lecturing, despite a houseful of children. Roda had once been imprisoned in Milan, adding to her reputation as a firebrand. Ernesta knew that her own beliefs were hemmed in one layer beneath her domestic responsibilities as she fussed around her two young children. Somehow Roda kept all her priorities high in her head, hemming in nothing.

Could it be that Roda knew, that she wanted to calm Ernesta, to reassure her? True, Ernesta needed calming about violence, and how it could backfire. She also needed something more than calming. Time to poke about.

"Whatever Alberto brings home, it's never enough, especially during the months the mill closes." Rambling on, Ernesta added details about the cost of food, now twenty cents for a loaf of bread and twenty-eight for a dozen eggs. She linked her remarks on food prices to stories in *La Questione Sociale*, the anarchist paper where Roda published her essays. Ernesta needed to keep the conversation going.

"That Roosevelt, he hasn't done much for us yet, Roda. Yeah, when he was police commissioner in New York, he promoted an Italian from patrolman to police lieutenant. Maybe, ha, just so the man could root out crime by Italians. One promotion won't get him our support, right? Should we give up on TR?" Ernesta had ably moved the conversation where she wanted it.

"That President," Roda said, shrugging her shoulders. "He's rich. His family owns lots of big, beautiful houses. He doesn't care about working people. Or the price of bread. What kind of president stands by while we starve? Like you've heard me say, and your husband too, we need a stateless society, not a centralized authority. Remember, Emma Goldman talked to the crowd about this when you went with me to New York last year."

"But she didn't mention violence." *Violenza.* Now Ernesta was getting close. Maybe too close.

"Not in so many words. You know that's what she meant."

"How can you be sure?"

"You have to listen to what she doesn't say." *Tacito.*

Emma Goldman was a legend for Roda and her friends. McKinley's assassin, Czolgosz, visited Goldman and heard her speak. Officials believed her anarchist associates helped Czolgosz. Goldman was on the run for a while, but detectives never found proof of her complicity. That was hardly the end of it. She had a lover, Alexander Berkman, who was imprisoned for trying to kill Henry Clay Frick, manager of Carnegie Steel. When Roda mentioned Goldman, anyone in the Paterson circle would understand the connection. Goldman denied she advocated violence, but violence surrounded her.

Ernesta settled her mind. Roda must know. Roda's mention of Goldman was the clue. They couldn't talk about the lots because the women needed to claim ignorance if questioned, but, yes, Roda knew. Secrecy, the Naples way, had its limits.

"Roda?" Ernesta stopped mid-block, ignoring the restless toddler who expected to be pushed. Ernesta stared at her friend, who stopped too.

"Yes, sometimes we must act. Are you bearing up? Can you get through this?"

Ernesta stiffened. Roda wanted to offer only solace.

"Roda, I am alright. Scared shitless, but alright. I need to say something." Ernesta saw that Roda faced her, listened. "You are a force, you work for what you believe. You see me as a wife, a mother, while you write, and you agitate. I can't write about ideas. I won't ever be famous. But I am not just muddling by. Now, in my own way, I can stand up. I can aid the cause. I can make love to my husband, then kiss him goodbye and say, as the classic saying goes in my family, desperate times call for desperate measures." *Ai mali estremi, estremi rimedi.*

"Yes, Ernesta. You'll do your part."

Ernesta Agresti, at peace, hearing the promise of recognition, pushed the

191

carriage forward. Her sacrifice would not go unnoticed.

Salvatore Scarpetta, Alberto Agresti

1818 to Tuesday, November 6, 1906

Seventy miles separates Paterson, New Jersey, from Georgetown, Connecticut, where the once great Gilbert & Bennett Manufacturing Company made its home. Benjamin Gilbert founded the smelly tannery in 1818. Gilbert soon realized that tanning gave him a by-product of abundant horsehair, less smelly than hides. What to do with horsehair? He started a business weaving it into sieves to separate bran from meal in cooking and cheese making. Benjamin Gilbert and Sturges Bennett, who joined as a partner, did not themselves take up the tedious process of weaving. They enlisted industrious women for that task.

When the Civil War began, Gilbert & Bennett could no longer sell to the South, forcing the company to seek new markets. One of their entrepreneurial employees, never named in company histories, experimented with metal wire, using it for sieves and chicken wire fences. When the company accumulated a surplus of wire mesh, employees experimented further with a new product—wire screens for windows. The commercial weaving of wire by hand was impractical, and machinery for such a purpose unknown. The company improvised again, borrowing and adapting a neighbor's carpet loom.

By 1887, sheets of galvanized wire mesh reigned at Gilbert & Bennett. With this innovation, Americans could open their windows without worrying about insects. Expanding to meet demand, Gilbert & Bennett provided work for 600 content employees, many newly arrived from countries throughout Europe. Salvatore Scarpetta was one of them. Scarpetta's brother-in-law was cocky silk weaver Stefano Grandi, of Paterson, New Jersey.

While Gilbert & Bennett workers rolled out wire mesh in Connecticut, 1400 miles away as the crow flies, doctors in Cuba tried to prevent Yellow Fever. Dr. Carlos Finlay believed the humble mosquito caused the disease, but never proved it. Building on Finlay's ideas, Dr. Walter Reed designed conclusive experiments. He placed volunteers in a screened-in hut, where they slept on beds used by Yellow Fever patients and wore infected clothing covered in the vomit, blood, and excrement of those unfortunate people. He placed other volunteers in a hut where the bedding had been disinfected, but the inhabitants included fifteen infected mosquitoes. The mosquito-bitten volunteers—no one can be certain they understood the risk—contracted Yellow Fever. The volunteers protected from mosquitoes by screens remained healthy. Filth was excused. Mosquitos were blamed. The case for screening became incontrovertible.

In Cuba, Army doctor William Gorgas, working under Reed, heeded the experiments. Soon after, Roosevelt wisely selected Gorgas to be Sanitary Officer for Panama. Once Chief Engineer John Stevens approved money for insecticides and for screens, Gorgas worked magic, eradicating Yellow Fever.

The life-saving role of screens in Panama made news in the States. Salvatore Scarpetta, by now a trusted foreman at the entrepreneurial firm of Gilbert & Bennett, read stories about the medical miracle. Unfortunately, E. T. Barnum Wire and Iron Work in Detroit, not to be confused with P. T. Barnum, had a monopoly on screens for Panama. That irritated Scarpetta and the other proud employees of Gilbert & Bennett. Around the same time, Scarpetta learned that his brash brother-in-law, Stefano Grandi, was rustling up something unsavory down in Paterson. The brothers-in-law met in New York to hatch a plan. Following up quickly, Scarpetta talked to his ambitious boss, a Mr. John Marston.

"If you want to open new markets," Scarpetta said, "hire my friend. He can sail to Panama and work as a sales representative for the firm. He's a skilled salesman. Knows how to close a deal. I can vouch for him. Name is Alberto Agresti."

John Marston listened, scratching his cheek, then his chin. "Panama? I thought Yellow Fever was gone already."

"Yes, Mr. Marston. It is. Because of screens. Barnum screens. But they will rust soon in that climate. Time to replace them with a better product, right? And you know we Italians work hard—just look around your factory."

Scarpetta realized he could be fingered if all went as planned. He would return to his hometown near Naples to aid his ailing mother. He, too, had been raised in a community of anarchists. The townspeople would hide and shelter him if it came to that. Scarpetta was grateful for a chance to contribute to the cause by bringing Alberto Agresti to John Marston's attention. Scarpetta would create an alibi for Agresti, to give him a reason to be in Panama. Scarpetti's task was easier than Agresti's.

* * *

Two days later, Alberto Agresti traveled to Georgetown, Connecticut, for his interview. "Tell me about your experience as a sales representative," asked Marston. Agresti saw the company manager's stare, sizing him up. Marston would see a nice-looking man, early thirties, solid of build, curly black hair parted sharply down the middle. Marston would hear that the applicant was clearly Italian, but with better English than expected. Agresti sat on his right hand, to hinder his usual gestures.

"I've sold silk for the William Strange Mill in Paterson for three years. My territory is all of New York City north of Houston Street. I exceed my manager's goals each year." From weaver to salesman was only a slight stretch of the fabric.

"That's silk. What do you know about wire mesh?"

"Both are woven. For each, the quality and durability of the weave is of upmost importance to the customer. Also, I studied the mesh offered by E.T. Barnum. I have a sample at home. It is weak, and it rusts easily. I don't

195

think it will be hard to take business away from them."

"I understand from your friend that you don't mind leaving your family and going to Panama. You might be there for a few weeks or months. And you might need to make return visits to check on customers. Can you do that?"

"I sailed from Italy to New York. No sickness on the open seas. And my family in Paterson is supported by other members of our family. Everyone helps everyone else, just like in the old country. I don't know Spanish, but most of your potential customers will be English speakers, right? You can hear, my English, yes, it's accented, but it's good, better than most of my chums. I studied in Italy while they played. And I can leave soon."

Agresti sailed to Colón on the steamer *Allianca*, on Gilbert & Bennett's dime, with rolls of mesh wire hiding his Smith and Wesson .32 long revolver, purchased with funds from a Colombian businessman. The voyage was uneventful except for one memorable day. During a stop in Ponce, Puerto Rico, two U.S. marines boarded the *Allianca*. They identified the American passengers, then questioned them about the purpose of their travel. Agresti calmly pointed to a letter he carried from John Marston, spelling out the conditions of employment and the terms of commission. The marines, ordered to watch out for suspicious Italians, scurried to their Ponce headquarters to cable Gilbert & Bennett. Two hours later a telegram arrived, confirming employment. The *Allianca* sailed on to Colón, bearing a silk weaver turned sales rep turning assassin.

Michael Thompson, Alberto Agresti

Tuesday, November 13, 1906

"Remember, like I told you yesterday, don't pull rusting screens off the windows until you nail on new screens," Aaron Blake explained to his helper, Michael Thompson. "If Dr. Gorgas sees no screen here for even two minutes, he'll blame me for a new epidemic. I'll lose my job."

Thompson paid little attention to his missing three toes, blown off two weeks before, and a great deal of attention to his new boss, the carpenter at Ancon Hospital. Aaron Blake had come to Panama from Jamaica long ago, to work under the French, and knew the ways of the isthmus. Hardly sounded Jamaican anymore. His good talk reminded Thompson to work on his talking. And Blake liked to teach, maybe because he could see Thompson learned quickly. Last week they repaired the wood on the porches. Today they tackled the windows. "How often we change screens?" Thompson asked.

Blake kept up his training talk. "E. T. Barnum's guy says these screens should last years. I fit them into the windows six months ago, and you can see the rust." Thompson looked up from his work to see a hospital orderly arrive, escorting a sales representative who wanted a word. Thompson was not surprised. He had seen reps call on the colored carpenter before. Noticing Thompson's surprise at these calls, Blake had explained. Drs. Gorgas and Peterson trusted their carpenter. Had given him a great deal of latitude with suppliers and budgets. Even now, after Yellow Fever had ended, the medical staff had their hands full with malaria, pneumonia, and trauma.

The approaching salesman was a well-dressed man in his thirties, wearing a bowler hat and carrying a large sample case. He removed the hat, showing dark hair parted in the middle. "I'm Alberto Agresti," he said, presenting his card. Blake glanced at it for a second, looked at the ground, and handed it to his helper. Thompson looked at the card more carefully, noting that this visitor was from Gilbert & Bennett, in Georgetown, Connecticut. For a second, he thought fondly of St. George Parish, just north of his own parish of Christ Church. Blake introduced himself as the hospital carpenter and introduced Thompson as his helper.

"Gentlemen, I know you are busy, so I won't take much of your time." Gentlemen? For Thompson, that was a first. "Are you satisfied with the window screening? Looks like you're making repairs." The salesman had a very slight accent. Maybe Italian?

"We were happy with Barnum's screens until now," Blake said. "But look here. You can see holes and rust starting to take over." Thompson remained quiet, happy to have the carpenter take the lead.

Opening his case, Agresti showed his samples and made his practiced and convincing pitch about the comparative merits of Gilbert & Bennett's wire mesh window screens. Thirty minutes later, Blake and Agresti shook hands on a deal for 500 linear feet of screening, with the promise of a larger order down the line. Blake assured Agresti that he could easily get formal approval from Dr. Gorgas, who loved nothing better than quality screens. Blake acknowledged that payment might take a while. Now the salesman moved on from the business at hand. In my country, he said, we seal deals with a drink. "Can we find a welcoming bar?

Blake pursed his lips. Thompson rubbed his tongue over the gap in his teeth. They knew what had gone unsaid. Can they find a bar where two colored men and an Italian could drink together?

"Give me a minute to think. Beer sure would help with this heat," Blake said. I like Balboa Lager. You should try it. From a small distillery down the road, just starting operations."

"But you can't top Hinchliffe Lager from Paterson," Agresti said proudly.

"Where's Paterson?" asked Blake.

Thompson listened, expecting the answer to be near Georgetown, Connecticut, the place on the salesman's business card.

"Oh, New Jersey." The salesman's voice turned to a quiet mumble.

Thompson, remembering Georgetown, Connecticut, on the business card, thought it was odd that this salesman would go to a different state for his beer. He had heard of Paterson before but couldn't place it.

The men never did find a welcoming bar.

* * *

Alberto Agresti felt flush following his sale at Ancon Hospital. He wanted to carry out his role as a salesman in a convincing manner, to establish a foolproof identity and a foolproof alibi. Maybe, just maybe, he could survive the next few days and return to the States alive. His next stop, as salesman, was the new Tivoli Hotel, designed by ICC officials to accommodate the managerial class of canal workers streaming to the isthmus.

Walking toward the circular driveway, he saw at the crest of a hill a grand hotel—a white wooden structure shaped like the letter E, with a central brick section, distinctive wrap-around porches on each level, royal palms lining the entrance, and a view of the bay. Carpenters and painters had rushed to complete construction, ensuring the hotel would be ready for the President and his party. As Agresti approached the main entrance, he walked past uniformed bellhops and observed, with satisfaction, that the wrap-around porches had no screening. He could further cement his new identity and more.

He sought out the harried hotel manager.

"Sir, have you thought about screening the porches on the exterior of the hotel?"

"We barely have the ballroom completed. I haven't had time to arrange for screens yet. But don't report me to Dr. Gorgas." He chuckled. "I already told him I'll get to it next week. All new guests will use the interior halls until screens are in place."

"Well, you're in luck. I certainly am not here to check on you. I am the authorized sales representative from Gilbert & Bennett, the largest screen manufacturer in the East. Here's my card. If you like, I can give you a recommendation and an estimate. First, I'll need to walk around the porches and take measurements. I can show you samples of wire mesh of different qualities, and we can discuss costs."

"Good. But I have very little time. We're still readying the President's suite. He'll be here in two days." No sign that the hotel manager was troubled by the accent he heard. Maybe he was accustomed to a variety of accents, like that carpenter and his helper. The manager pocketed Agresti's business card with barely a glance.

"I won't get in your way," Agresti said. "I'll deliver an estimate tomorrow." The manager pointed to the entrance to the porch with a quick nod. Agresti found his way and walked around the ground floor perimeter. He tipped his bowler at the construction workers and decorators—all working industriously—so that they would feel comfortable with his presence on the porch. Taking out his tape measure, he measured and re-measured within their view, stretching the tape out with wide and purposeful arm movements. He did the same on the second and third-floor porches. On the second-floor porch, in the front of the building where the view was the best, he saw even more activity than elsewhere. He needed to be sure.

"Sorry to be in your way. I'm measuring for screens. I'll be out of here long before the President moves into this suite. Lovely furnishings, from what I can see."

Agresti spoke these words to the men busily arranging opulent carpets and pots of orchids and buckets of cut flowers in a large suite. They wore suits, not the work clothes of the hotel cleaning staff. He guessed they were native Panamanians. All he cared about was that they understood his English. The men didn't look up, just absentmindedly nodded assent. This was the room. Or it would be more accurate to say the sitting room. Through a door to the right of the sitting room, Agresti could just make out a bedroom. He could smell the strong odor of fresh paint and the subtler odor of wood shavings. After poking his head in, he withdrew and turned around to get his bearings. He counted doors, railings, palm trees. Then he counted a second time. He could return to this precise spot.

Agresti was about to leave the Tivoli when he spotted two young men on the lawn, rounding the corner of the hotel. Going to the end of the gallery and looking down, he saw that they entered a side door. He stretched his tape measure across the railing, in such a way that he could continue to observe the door. Over the next ten minutes, three more men and two young women entered the same door. He had accidentally found the service entrance. Taking a side staircase, he found his way to that door, then downstairs to a basement hall. The hotel was so new that the management had not yet thought about security for the service entrance. Agresti held his tape measure at his chest in case anyone noticed him, but the service hall was empty. He stopped at the sound of voices. Pretending to measure the hall, as though for wallpaper, he listened. Chattering bellhops put on their uniforms in what must be a changing room to the left, and in the room to the right maids did the same. He waited until they left, presumably when the 4:00 to midnight shift began. No one paid any attention to him. Then he quickly entered the room on the left, scanned the garment rack for a large bellhop uniform, and stuffed it, and a hat, into his briefcase. Suspecting that the service hall led to a staircase to the first-floor porch, which led to a staircase to the second-floor porch, he walked far enough to check. Smiling for the first time in weeks, he exited the hotel.

Alberto Agresti

Wednesday, November 14, 1906

On the very morning that would-be photographer Magnus Gustafsson and property manager Roland Caldwell negotiated a blind for hunting on the plaza, Alberto Agresti put aside his goal of establishing himself as a salesman, focusing instead on another detail of his mission. When would the President give his speech? Roosevelt would talk in the central plaza, in front of the cathedral, on the 15th. But when? The newspapers never provided a precise schedule.

Just in time, Agresti discovered the information he needed.

Agresti knew from fellow weaver Stefano Grandi that the Colombian businessman bankrolling the plan wanted to meet in person to size up his new hireling. Grandi explained that the businessman traveled frequently to Panama as well as to New York to check on his banking concerns, and additional interests. He would plan another trip to Panama City, to coincide with the American president's visit, and with Agresti's visit.

Their meeting was arranged through half a dozen coded international telegrams using Stefano Grandi in Paterson as go-between. The business-man chose a genteel bar close to the Metropolitan Hotel, where he was staying, and not too far from the Paramount where Agresti was staying. At the appointed time of 6:00, Agresti arrived, predictably first. He sat at the bar, nursing a beer. He saw this was not a working man's bar, like his usual haunt, but a bar where men conducted respectable business. The thick smoke in the bar felt familiar. The cool tones of the surrounding conversations did not.

Agresti, thick hair parted neatly down the middle, wore a green necktie, as agreed. He spotted the businessman enter at two minutes past six. The man wore an orange necktie, also as agreed. He was tall, light-skinned, attractive, impeccably dressed, about the same height as Agresti only slenderer. Agresti had taken particular care with his appearance that day. Nonetheless the silk weaver turned screen salesman realized that his suit, though new, lacked the style and bespoke tailoring of his benefactor's. The Colombian recognized Agresti immediately. The two moved to empty stools at the quiet end of the bar. Taking a stool to the man's right, Agresti could sit on his own right hand without that odd motion being noticeable. He could avoid his usual gestures that way, raising his hand just to drink. "An old fashioned, *por favor,*" the newcomer said. Agresti saw the bartender pour a bourbon whiskey and hoped his own choice was not ill-advised.

Even with their codes and costumes, each man took care that the other was not an interloper or an informer. They began their talk with banalities, or at any rate, news they perceived as banalities. A deadly train wreck in Indiana, government efforts to dissolve Standard Oil under the Sherman Antitrust Act, even the dreadful isthmus weather. Checking each other out. It wouldn't do to discuss details with an undercover Pinkerton. Somewhat reassured, after ten minutes, the Colombian broached the central topic.

"I am happy I found you. I've been waiting years to settle a score, a grievance, you might say. A private family matter." Agresti didn't change his expression. No need for the businessman to know that Grandi had explained the man was using his wife's money to exact revenge. "Hope you're up to the task. Let me get to the point. Can I expect results soon?"

"I am checking. I am working on the timing," Agresti said, squaring his shoulders, raising his chin. He needed to focus on his best English. "The papers are vague about where our prey goes each day. He wasn't supposed to arrive until tomorrow, but I heard a rumor at my hotel that he is already here. The papers report on a gathering at the central plaza tomorrow afternoon. The stories never mention precisely when he will appear. Maybe on purpose.

I cannot hang around for hours. De location. . . ." He caught himself. "The location of the square works best for me, but if I cannot predict when he arrives, I have a backup plan. I've already started advance work for that other plan." The Colombian puckered his lips. He wanted more. "The Tivoli Hotel. Just in case."

Neither man spoke for a moment, as Agresti drank his beer, and the Colombian fingered his old fashioned. "You know, Mr. Agresti, I am paying you for this job. To do it on your own. I shouldn't offer any help, but I am impressed that you are thinking ahead about problems and about options. Here's what I can do. After our drink, I head for La Boheme." Agresti looked blank. "You know, the classy brothel on Calle Boquete. Last time I visited La Boheme, in the parlor I met a man, a *cliente*...." Ah, Agresti thought, the businessman must work at his English too. "A regular customer I think, who is close to Theodore Shonts. Shonts, the man at the head of the ICC. The Chairman. Maybe I can buy this man, I think his name is Connell, a drink and gather information on the schedule." Agresti saw the Colombian twist his nose, as though averting a bad smell, when he named Connell.

"Would that help?" the Colombian asked.

Agresti sat up straighter. "Please, sir. That would be excellent."

The Colombian Businessman

Wednesday, November 14, 1906

A t La Boheme, the Colombian businessman had come to expect, and to experience, flesh in every hue. Including Mei. He could get the same treats in Bogota, but little privacy. Too many of his fellow Colombians, of his status, knew him. Also, although Panama City was not part of the Zone, and so not controlled by the Americans, he was certain these girls would be healthier. His chums in Bogota often complained of the clap. After frequent excursions to La Boheme, he saw no signs of disease.

At 9:00 in the evening on November 14th, the Colombian checked in with the shapely proprietress, Sally Miller. When she warned of a long wait for Mei, he requested Madeleine, a tall, young Jamaican. He had enjoyed her on his business trip last summer. Sally extolled his choice and said he was third in line for Madeleine. He settled himself on the lush cushions of a sofa in the parlor. About ten other men sat waiting, drinking, or just appreciating the mood of the evening. As the Colombian had hoped, one of these customers was John Connell, the Assistant Chairman of the ICC. Connell looked in his forties, paunchy for his age, with a full head of graying hair. He slumped in an armchair, whiskey in hand, reading a much-used *Harper's Weekly*.

"Good evening. We met a few months ago when I was here on business."

"Oh, yes, yes," Connell said. The Colombian watched Connell's eyes, knew the official would gradually recall the social position and wealth of the man

205

talking to him.

Earlier that evening in the bar, the Colombian had not told Alberto Agresti much about John Connell. The year before, the Colombian had hired a private investigator to gather information on Connell, and also on Connell's boss, ICC Chairman Theodore Shonts. If the two officials had sources of capital, they might be lured into investing in the businessman's ventures in Bogota.

Connell, the Colombian learned, was born in Manhattan, a few blocks from the Roosevelts' home. Just a year younger than the President, Connell had walked the same neighborhoods, though never moved in the same circles. Connell's father, a banker, provided for his family well, for a while. When Connell turned fourteen, his father suffered in the Panic of 1873. The family moved to Iowa, where the senior Mr. Connell found a new position, earning enough to send his son to college and law school in Iowa City. Eventually, John Connell caught on with the Baker, Drake, & Shonts law firm in Iowa. The Shonts on the masthead was Theodore Shonts, later to become Chairman of Panama's ICC. The Drake on the masthead was Francis Marion Drake, later to become governor of Iowa.

In 1881, Theodore Shonts, positioning himself well, married the daughter of senior partner Drake. Soon Drake enlisted his son-in-law to manage one of the firm's railroad clients. Proving his value by hounding workers to meet a deadline, Shonts became General Superintendent of the Illinois & Iowa Railroad, eventually becoming President, and still later becoming President of the Toledo, St. Louis & Western Railroad. He took Iowan John Connell, who was eager to move almost anywhere easterly, to Toledo with him as assistant president. When Shonts got the call from TR to head the ICC, he again kept Connell by his side.

Due to the diligence of his private investigator, the Colombian may have been one of the few people to know that Shonts had secretly taken up with a New York socialite. The investigator could not know that fourteen years later, Shonts's widow would sue the mistress, alleging alienation of affections, in a sensational case that would make national headlines. Even John Connell, sitting in a brothel in Panama while his own wife languished in Toledo, may not have registered his boss's impropriety—he was too busy with his own impropriety.

"Good to see you here again," said Connell. "I'm waiting for Sally—she is in debt to me, so to speak, a nice condition." Slight wink. "It's busy tonight. I have to wait until things slow down and she can get away. Who are *you* waiting for?"

"Ah, Madeleine, and it will be a while for me too. I see your glass is empty. Can I buy you a drink while we wait?" Good, Connell was as talkative as ever. The Colombian motioned to the proprietor's young son, Sean, who was helping with drinks.

At first, the two men discussed the business of the Canal. Next, they discussed the girls. "I like this establishment," offered the Colombian. "The girls seem healthy, and they will do what my wife won't, you know what I mean." He stretched out the last part of the sentence, inviting comments.

Connell, in tight with the proprietress, knew which girls would go beyond expectations, which girls were freshest, which girls were too tired for fun. He enjoyed sharing this information, in detail. The Colombian listened and asked follow-up questions, particularly about activities beyond expectations. No point in getting to the larger topic on his mind prematurely. Once it was understood that the men shared certain peccadilloes—St. George and two activities where French, not English, was an international language, *soixante-neuf,* and *menage a trois*—the Colombian could move to a less intriguing conversation without attracting undue attention. Stag talk had worked its magic.

"So, you must be busy with the President's visit. Has he landed already?

"Yes, ahead of schedule, which doesn't make my Mr. Shonts happy. He's trying to catch up with Teddy now. Ha, the two Teddies.

"Does TR have a hectic schedule?

"Crazy. Crazy. The secretary sent us his itinerary. Activities every hour."

"Do you think I'll get a chance to see him?

"Well, there's the gathering and speech in the plaza tomorrow at 4:00. You might squeeze your way in. I would try to get you invited to one of the more private events, but you know that Teddy dislikes Colombians, right?

Hope you understand, chap."

"I understand. I had heard of a program for tomorrow afternoon. I wasn't certain when Teddy would be there. He's going to the plaza? At 4:00? And that's not what you Americans call a decoy, to fool us? Won't that be dangerous?"

"He has protection—two or three agents on his protection detail. He should be safe."

"I hope he's going to get some rest. The bellhop at my hotel tells me he heard from his friend, the bellhop at the Tivoli, that the staff there are scrambling to ready a wing for him.

"Right, a second-floor suite. Don't know why they bothered. He'll hardly be there."

The Colombian gathered more information than he expected. Now if Madeleine were ready for him soon, it would be a grand night. He could dream about Mei next time. Or maybe Mei with Madeleine. He preferred the Spanish, *un trio*.

Edgar Winston, Liza Fowler

Edgar Winston looked nothing like his boss, Sir Claude Coventry Mallet, the British Consul to Panama. Sir Claude was fair-haired, short, stout, with thin lips and the usual wide mustache, while Edgar Winston was dark-haired, tall, slim, with full sensuous lips and a hairless face. Despite these outward differences, they both understood their official roles as they sat side-by-side to receive endless complaints. Every Barbadian or Jamaican laborer with a bone to pick, whether over the food supply or mistreatment by a foreman, lined up at Sir Claude's office door, seeking protection as an Englishman. Winston and Sir Claude met with each complainant. Sir Claude expressed concern and offered to investigate, then Winston made inquiries. The diplomats rarely managed to bring peace, but they did just enough so that the dark citizens of the Empire felt they had at least a tidbit of standing as British citizens.

Sir Claude had served as the only British diplomat in Panama until he complained to the Foreign Office about the increasing number of aggrieved British laborers, more than he could handle. The obliging Deputy Foreign Secretary posted junior diplomat Edgar Winston to assist. Winston fit the bill. At age twenty-eight, he wore the bespoke suits of Savile Row, the choice of textiles modified for the isthmus's climate, and he shared his boss's upper-crust English. Although Winston considered Panama an undesirable posting, he preferred it to the other available options, British Guiana and

Uganda, and he knew Sir Claude welcomed his help and congenial company.

The Foreign Office provided Winston a dreary room in a boarding house. After months of grumping about the accommodations, he found an apartment to rent, and under the terms of his employment, he now qualified for a furnishings allowance. Shopping list in hand, Winston hastened to the new ICC commissary at Balboa, near Panama City. Using the portal for gold workers, he entered the warehouse-like building, hardly a Central American Harrods. Winston deemed the selection of goods unsatisfactory but knew he would find nothing better in the smaller shops nearby. Most of those were owned by Chinamen, who would have no idea how to outfit a British gentleman's quarters. Making the best of things, Winston gathered up linens and pots and wrote down the item numbers of the bed and chairs he selected. He presented himself and his wallet to the young commissary clerk. Winston began the transaction with polite chit-chat about the weather and the inventory of goods. That chit-chat was a mistake.

"Excuse me, sir, but hearing you speak, I believe you are an Englishman. This commissary is under the jurisdiction of the ICC, the Isthmian Canal Commission. It is for Americans only."

Winston heard a tremble in the clerk's voice. He'd put the young man in his place. "Haven't you ever had a British customer before? You need more of us. Might help the ambiance of this place."

"Yes, we have had British customers before. They are the colored, and they come in through the silver door."

Winston pushed his chin toward the clerk's chin. "I am losing my patience. Take my money. Wrap my items. Deliver my furniture."

"Sir, we have rules here. You see, the shopkeepers in town import goods that are taxed, while the commissary imports untaxed goods. Shopkeepers couldn't compete with our low prices. To keep them happy, Secretary Taft agreed that the commissary would be for ICC workers. To keep out native Panamanians and foreigners. If I serve you, I will lose my job."

This quivering dolt was standing his ground. Winston put his elbows on the counter, leaned forward. "I have never, never, been unwelcome in a shop. Surely, I am entitled to do my shopping here. Why wouldn't I be? I work with Sir Claude. Sir Claude Coventry Mallet, British Consul. He is in the same set as Mr. Theodore Shonts, your ICC Chairman. Mallet dines with President Amador. He had audiences with King Edward VII, Bertie." Winston sensed that the more he tried to achieve diplomacy, the angrier, and less American, he sounded.

The clerk's slack mouth firmed up. He pointed to a set of six regulations next to his cash box and read them aloud, more stiffly than Winston expected.

The twit needed a dressing down. "Arsehole. I am not leaving. I will remain here until you complete the transaction."

"Sir, I will seek a manager." The clerk walked to the back of the commissary.

Twenty feet away, a man of unremarkable appearance listened to the hubbub. Winston did not see the stranger, and even if he had, he would not know that the man was John O'Malley, a former Pinkerton turned security officer for the commissary, who would soon tell his old friend, detective Milton Anderson, that Shing Wong would make a fine getaway man. Seeing that the outraged customer was a well-dressed white man, O'Malley chose to overlook the fracas. He saw the clerk approach the commissary's assistant manager and knew the matter would soon be settled.

* * *

A second person in the commissary overheard the hubbub—Liza Fowler, wife of Division Engineer Jeffrey Fowler. Liza was shopping for dining items, preparing for visitors, while Selina watched the baby. In Liza's native Troy, she was used to the shrieking arguments of her uncouth Father and his buddies, but not to rude banter with an English accent. As the clerk stepped away to seek out authority, Liza offered the trim, handsome stranger some solace.

"Don't mind the clerk," she said, aiming for a refined tone. "He is just trying to interpret Secretary Taft's latest set of rules. There are rules everywhere you go here."

The gentleman turned to see who spoke, looking annoyed that anyone overheard his tirade. She knew once he saw her, his expression would change.

"Oh, my. I apologize for my behavior. I did not realize I had an audience." He pulled back his chin, to the benefit of his full lips. "Have you been on the isthmus for long?" he asked, recovering from embarrassment.

"Oh, no, only a short time. But long enough to know the foolish rules." Liza stretched out "foolish."

They continued to talk until the clerk returned, accompanied by an assistant manager who sized up the situation quickly. After Winston answered a few questions, the manager apologized profusely and gave the clerk a look that could kill. Winston asked for his purchases to be delivered, provided an address, and then stepped aside to let Liza pay for her purchases. She planned to carry them.

"How far are you walking with those?" he asked.

"To the train, just a few blocks."

"Let me help."

The dalliance that followed suited Liza. Her husband's interest in their maid Selina had grown intolerable, provoking revenge. And Edgar, in his posh suit and leather shoes, attracted her more than her flabby, crippled husband, in his dusty pants and muddy boots. Edgar finished too fast in bed, no better than Jeffrey, but she held modest expectations. She herself acted quite the vixen in bed, eager to please in ways old and new. Falling quickly into a routine, Liza went to the commissary every Wednesday while Edward told Sir Claude, he had signed on for a Wednesday afternoon Spanish lesson. Sir Claude admired his assistant consul's dedication.

Only the maid, observant Selina Thompson, knew better.

Alberto Agresti

Thursday, November 15, 1906

Alberto Agresti walked past the Paramount Hotel's front desk toward the dining room readied for breakfast. The reception clerk wagged an envelope at him, a sealed envelope bearing only a room number. The clerk's eyes searched fruitlessly for a hint of the content. Guessing the envelope was from the Colombian, Agresti clutched it, reversed his steps, and returned to his room. He had with him Henry James's *The Ambassadors*, the novel the Colombian had mailed to him in Paterson to function as the key for decoding messages. After a tedious ten minutes, working from page numbers, line numbers, word order, and letter order, Agresti learned when his prey would pontificate in the central plaza and to keep alert for agents. He had a good eye for that danger, given his experience with unrest in Paterson. Escape from the plaza, however—that could prove difficult. Luckily, he had begun to work through a second option.

Agresti checked his watch - 8:00. He used a cigar to burn the Colombian's message, then returned downstairs and thanked the clerk for the envelope, adding over his shoulder that the sender had confirmed his next sales call. Walking into the dining room, the smell of coffee almost turned Agresti's stomach. He sat at the table, forcing himself nibble, to calm his fidgeting leg, to push his shoulders back, to talk casually about the rain, to ignore the thick butter the guests slathered on their toast.

213

After twenty minutes, Agresti left the Paramount, raising his umbrella. He heard a growing racket as he entered the central plaza. Men in linen suits shouted directions. Laborers in work clothes nailed sodden drapes on the speakers' platform and trimmed with greenery. Others tied bunting and flags to balconies, ignoring the rain dripping off the fabrics. Two boys, maybe street urchins, swept mud from the paths. Agresti could not know that a day before journalist Frederick Palmer had toured the same plaza as part of his research, and Magnus Gustafsson had done the same, less innocently.

Agresti walked diagonally across the square. If he intended to cross a second time, he would need a simple change. He found a shop a few blocks away with an array of goods. He entered, selected a Panama hat with a wide brim and a high crown, and picked up a newspaper. He purchased these from the talkative Chinaman at the counter, exited, reluctantly threw his reliable bowler into an alley, and doffed his new hat. Returning to the plaza for a second view, Agresti would look different, even to agents who might be on duty.

He sat on a bench, still holding his umbrella. He raised the newspaper over his face while scanning the plaza. Those balconies could give him height and a great sight line. But they would be crowded with spectators and out of his revolver's range. Better to stay on the ground, slightly below the level of the speakers. He watched workers move potted plants and vases of flowers onto the platform, leaving space for the President, who would stand in front of the cathedral, facing east. If the sun set behind the cathedral, then spectators in the plaza would have to look into the sun. When would the sun set? Maybe he should stand to the side. But it would be harder to hit his target from that position. Then he saw a bench that would work as a compromise, just slightly off to the left as he faced the cathedral. The bench would serve as his signpost, marking the best spot.

A group of women entered the plaza, lowering their umbrellas as the rain eased. They seemed to monitor foot traffic, probably wondering how soon they needed to station themselves there to ensure a viewing spot. Agresti stared. As a silk worker, he paid attention to women's dress. Fashion kept the mills going. While the women in Paterson wore sensible blouses with high collars and gored skirts, the women in the plaza leaned toward excess fabric. Their sleeves either widened out a few inches below the shoulder, or ballooned out even fuller, leg-o'-mutton style. They wore extravagant hats, too, broader and more feathered than what he had seen in New York. Just what he needed.

After what he deemed sufficient time to have read the newspaper, he walked toward the Paramount. He stopped at a café, ordering tea and *pan micha*, the lightest lunch he could find. He barely tasted his meal, maybe his last meal in freedom.

At 12:30, Agresti returned to the hotel, waiting outside until he could see through the window that the nosy clerk still loafed at his station. Agresti climbed upstairs to room 323, waving hello to the clerk, catching his eye. Now, crucial preparations. Agresti took apart and reassembled his Smith and Wesson .32 long revolver with its five bullets. The damn dampness. He needed to make sure the gun would fire. It seemed too bulky for the pocket of his pants or his jacket. Although sewing was not part of his skills as a weaver, he found supplies in the wardrobe and managed to sew a pouch, using two handkerchiefs, into the inside crown of his new Panama hat. He had selected one with room to spare. He experimented, holding the hat in front of him at waist level. He tried to withdraw the revolver quickly. Tried three more times. He had sewn too tight a pouch, and, moreover, onlookers on a day that had turned sunny might wonder why another onlooker held a hat instead of wearing it. His pants pocket would have to do.

Just before 2:00, Agresti collected his remaining papers and identification and burned them in a tobacco tin, saving only his return steamer ticket, his money, and *The Ambassadors*. He might need the book again, so he placed a scrap of paper in the middle, as though to mark his place, and scribbled "From Mary with love" on the title page in a flowery script. He started to leave money on the bed to settle his bill so that if he was shot or captured, the common people might think him an assassin but not a deadbeat. Then he changed his mind. If the maid collected the money in the afternoon and he managed by some miracle to return to the hotel afterwards, then he would have to explain his premature payment.

The bellhop uniform presented another problem. If he carried out his mission in the plaza, he wouldn't need the uniform. But leaving it in his room could arouse suspicion. No time to devise a creative solution. Agresti waited at the top of the staircase, an agonizing eleven minutes, until the desk clerk left his station. If the clerk went to the toilet, Agresti had a minute. Walking briskly downstairs with a package under his arm, he ducked into the dining room, then found a nearby pantry. Sacks and cartons lined the shelves. He hid the package behind the stored items, hoping the cook would not discover it for a long time, and by then, have no clue as to its origin. He dodged out to the street.

By 2:30, Agresti reached the plaza. The area around the bench he had identified was filling up fast. He walked around, mingling with the crowd at different places in the plaza. He shifted his head and eyes, as though looking for companions, while he checked for agents. No, they must be with the President.

When the parade of musicians and marchers began, Agresti returned to the area of the bench. As he had hoped, groups of men and women stood shoulder to shoulder. He studied the women. One looked taller and wider than the others, with a full skirt, gathered sleeves, and an elaborate hat. He staked out a crowded position a foot behind her, hoping his proximity simply echoed the other close encounters in the plaza. He tried to ignore her pungent perfume, the mole near her hairline, the perspiration shining on the back of her neck.

In the space between the feathered hat and the full sleeve, Agresti had an acceptable view. Adjusting his head, he spotted, near the platform, a tall man, round cheeked. Another one, brawny. Another, beefy. Each glancing into the crowd, each unaccompanied by a woman. With luck, agents on or near the speakers' platform could not see a rising hand behind a wide-brimmed hat. He would shoot, drop the revolver, run. Seeming to check the balconies for familiar faces, he turned around frequently, craning his neck to study possible escape paths. All appeared encumbered, but some led to streets while others led to dead ends. He tried to remember the best of them. In the chaos, he could run back to the Paramount.

A surge of noise and movement on the dais as the ceremonies began. Agresti rotated his shoulders. Shook out his arms. Tried to ignore the sweat dripping down under his straw hat. First, Amador, looking old, standing straight. Now Roosevelt, younger, heavier. The crowd clapping, yelling support in two languages. Agresti felt himself breathing too rapidly on the wide lady's neck. He tried to slow his breathing, reminding himself that he would need to do so when he aimed. He hoped the woman couldn't smell him. He could smell her.

As he heard "giant engineering feat of the ages," he feared TR was winding down. Only a few seconds to act. The crowd looked forward. He gripped the revolver in his pocket, fingered the trigger. For a split second, he envisioned Roberto, his friend, his brother-in-law, martyred in Milan. He tried to hold the image. Couldn't. He turned around to take a final look at his escape path, all his senses on alert. Fuck. On that high balcony. Maybe scuffling, inside the French doors. The men he had eyed earlier? Or was he a nervous coward, imagining a snag, allowing a distraction? Seconds passed. The President nodded goodbyes. Then the brawny man came out on the balcony, making a slight gesture of success.

Alberto Agresti would never know that Larry Richey's gesture was observed by only three other people—Jimmy Sloan, Maurice Latta, and Edith Roosevelt.

The crowd drifted out of the plaza. Agresti let himself be carried along. At 4:30, he was alive. Alive, as a coward. *Codardo*. Why didn't he aim sooner? He missed his best chance. Now he had just one more.

He walked back to the Paramount, kicking the trash that had accumulated in the streets. His shirt, damp with sweat, stuck to his back. His *pan micha* rumbled down his insides. Relieved to see the desk clerk attending to an impolite guest, Agresti hurried upstairs. Then he realized it wouldn't matter if the clerk thought the guest in 323 had returned to his room or remained out, since nothing had happened.

He allowed himself a few minutes of painful remorse. Enough. He had to pick up the pieces. He knew the Colombian might begin to lose faith in his investment and wonder why he heard no news from the plaza. Agresti composed a short, coded letter. "No opportunity today. Moving to second option." He did not need to sign it.

Caretaker of Catedral Basílica Santa Maria la Antigua

Thursday, November 15, 1906

At 3:30 the old man thought he deserved a break after sweeping the floor of the cathedral until it was spotless, especially since he would need to sweep again the next day, to wipe out all remnants of the celebration. He had never seen such hustle and bustle before, not even on Saints days, not even on Christmas morning. He felt tired, and his knees hurt, but he had just enough energy left to trudge up the stairs of the white bell tower on the south side of the cathedral. From 118 feet above the plaza, he took in a scene he would never forget—thousands of people standing shoulder-to-shoulder, hip-to-hip, men in top hats and women in feathered hats. A sea of hats hiding bodies and feet.

On the side streets extending out from the plaza, the caretaker saw hundreds of marchers and a brass band. He thought he spotted his nephew playing a horn. Then the school children. Was that his grandson? Then mounted police, men from wealthy families. Smells of sweat and horse manure wafted up. Sounds pounded his ears. Hoofs, clapping, songs, trumpets. Next silence, or something close to it, as the President of Panama, what was his name, Amador, spoke. More clapping and shouting. Then the man they called TR.

The caretaker could not see the speakers' stand, hidden from his high perch. He looked out at the crowd, craning to pick out his wife. She would not be dressed well like the people in the plaza, so the police might have kept her at arm's length. Ahhh, he saw her at the far edge, smiling like the others, clapping too. The caretaker waved, though he doubted his wife could see him. But she knew to look up toward the tower. Her smile widened.

He had worried that the Americans, with their canal, would be no better than the Colombians or the French. The spirit in the plaza gave him hope.

John Connell

Friday, November 16, 1906

ICC Assistant Chairman John Connell had never visited La Boheme in daylight. He took a seat on the settee between the madam, Sally Miller, and her son Sean. Connell ran his fingers through his abundant gray hair, hoping to take Sally's attention upward, away from his paunch. She looked different, dressed for business this morning, but not her usual business. No delicious decolletage. Connell had never seen her parlor so empty, bereft of eager men waiting in armchairs for their turn.

"Say as little as possible, Elliott," Connell said, with emphasis on the name Elliott. "Remember, you are young Elliott Roosevelt, nephew to the President, not Sean Miller, son of a, a businesswoman. Fine to look fifteen. You also need to look like you are to the manor born. Ya know? Look like once you had a rich father, and you need to be rich again."

"I know how this works," Sally said. "I know men. Teddy will think my Sean is Elliott Jr., the son of his brother Elliott. He'll want that, even if he's still pissed after twelve years that Elliott whored around with his maid and drank himself to death. Teddy wants to know that some part of Elliott lives on. They say Teddy loves Elliott's daughter Eleanor. He'll love Elliott's son too."

"But what do I say if he asks me about my pop? I don't know anything. Even the real Elliott, the little guy in New York, didn't know anything." As Sean fussed, his cheeks flushed pink.

"That's the point, "Sally said. Little Elliott didn't know anything. Katy told me she got nothing from Elliott's pop. She said the same thing every day we sat at those damn sewing machines. No money. No help. And TR never met his nephew. You don't need to lie about what you remember. You remember nothing. Just say that we lived in New York, then we moved here to run a boarding house. Remember, a boarding house. No details. And one more thing Sean. I mean Elliott Jr. Can't you stop that blushing?"

"Yah, no rosy cheeks, ha, even if you'll be pretending to be a Roosevelt. And I'm just a friend of the family," Connell said with a slow wink at Sally. "Elliott, Elliott Jr., I'll have a carriage pick you up at 6:30 tomorrow morning. Dress sharp. We're going to see the President." He gave Katy a look, a smirk of anticipation.

Menora Bradford, Sean Miller

Friday, November 16, 1906

At first, the ICC officials were too busy with arrangements for recruiting and digging to think about education. After a while, they realized that to attract good men, family men, they needed schools. The first American school opened in January of 1906 in Corozal, a short train ride from Panama City.

The school superintendent hired two groups of teachers—young, educated men from Jamaica, like Henry Coleman, to teach the Negro students, and young, educated women like Menora Bradford, wife of an ICC accountant, to teach the White students. This arrangement proved satisfactory, for the most part. In early November, Mr. Coleman took ill with malaria. The superintendent asked Mrs. Bradford to take over Mr. Coleman's classrooms.

On November 16th, Mrs. Bradford began her day with reading lessons for younger White children while the morning assistant handled the classroom for younger Negro students, asking them to draw turkeys in preparation for Thanksgiving. After an hour, Mrs. Bradford dashed to the classroom for the younger Negro children for a modified reading lesson while the assistant gave the turkey assignment to the White students. Then Mrs. Bradford swapped places with the assistant for a math lesson with the White children while the Negro children moved on to drawing Pilgrims. At noon the assistant and the younger students went home. Mrs. Bradford, already exhausted, grabbed a quick lunch. She opened the windows, which the ICC had screened, but felt no breeze to help with the heat.

Now time to move on to the older students, who were just arriving. She had decided to quietly gather the Negroes and the Whites together since only two Negroes had enrolled in the upper level.

The previous month, before she knew she needed to fill in for sick Mr. Coleman, Mrs. Bradford had assigned *Huckleberry Finn* for the month of November. *Huck* had met a mixed reaction back home—some called it coarse—but she thought the book would hold the interest of a group of students who were also on the move, like Huck.

Mr. Coleman, when he was up and about, taught the Negroes, and she had no idea what he would have assigned them. She discovered that the two in the upper level read so well that it made sense to assign them *Huck* along with the White students. Now, though, with the Negro students sitting with the White students, she worried that she made the wrong decision. In the homework assignment, she left out the question about the various meanings of slavery and freedom. That still left her with four questions: How does Huck change, and why? What does it mean to be civilized? How does Huck show social responsibility? What does friendship mean to Huck? All safe questions for a mixed class.

* * *

After leaving New York, Sean Miller had attended a passible municipal school in Panama City. One of his mother's customers learned of the better ICC school about to open in Corozal, intended for residents of the Canal Zone. Although La Boheme was not in the Zone, this customer, hoping to curry favor with La Boheme's madam, fiddled with admissions paperwork, providing a Zone address for the Miller family.

Sean liked the new school and always completed his reading, even the difficult *Huckleberry Finn*. On November 16th, he joined in the class discussion along with the nine other White students, all sweltering in the hot room. The two colored students in back never raised their hands, and

Mrs. Bradford never called on them. Sean was not uncomfortable about the occasional comments on slavery that crept into the discussion. He never looked behind him at the two silent students. He did become uncomfortable about other parts of the discussion that day, especially when the know-it-all girl sitting at the desk beside him spoke about Huck's conscience, Huck's confusion over right and wrong. Mrs. Bradford liked what the girl said, asked her for examples. Liked her examples too. Sean used his shirtsleeve to wipe the sweat from his neck, then stared at his damp cuff.

Maurice Latta

Friday, November 16, 1906

I slept poorly Thursday night, thinking how close Americans had
come to having Charles Warren Fairbanks, the Wall Street puppet,
as president. No one remembers that vice president's name now, for
good reason. I took comfort in my role in avoiding calamity. Decades
later, I remain amazed at the sequence of events the previous day and at
the international cast of characters. Emily Byrne, an Irish woman of the
night born in Barbados, told Jeffrey Fowler, an engineer from Troy, New
York, about a Swede. Fowler told Steven Bonner, a policeman from Texas.
Bonner told Larry Richey, an agent from Philadelphia. Larry told agents
Jimmy Sloan, from Danville, Illinois, and Frank Tyree, from Charleston,
West Virginia. Frank told me. Señora Arenas mentioned the Swede. ICC
Secretary Bishop knew the Swede could not be legitimate. I pointed and
gestured. Jimmy acted. Larry and Frank wrestled.

I had made the connection. In my heart, I knew I saved the President. In
my head, I knew saving him depended on each improbable link in the chain.
I did not realize that the chain would grow.

Friday morning, I expected my suit to have dried overnight. It remained
damp, and then the rain started again. None of us in the President's
entourage wanted to leave the Tivoli, but we knew TR would forge ahead
to inspect the Culebra Cut, the site of all the action. After breakfast, we
boarded the train. Along with Mrs. R, who wouldn't look at me, the group

226

in the front car included Dr. Rixey, Mr. Bishop, and Chief Engineer Stevens. I rode in the second car, again with Frederick Palmer and Herbert de Lisser. We saw no sign of President Amador or his wife.

On the way to the Cut, we saw marvels of engineering—steam shovels reaching up, men drilling and blasting, a maze of spoil cars. Dirt, and more dirt. Even though the French had removed sixty million cubic yards of it, Americans still needed to remove fifty million more. Looking out from the train, we saw two remarkable machines. First, the track-shifter, invented by the general manager of the Panama Railroad, who would host our dinner the next day. The huge, crane-like machine could lift a section of track, including rails and ties, and shift it in another direction. Second, the ninety-five-ton monster Bucyrus steam shovel, which could haul up 4800 cubic yards of earth every eight hours and could load a spoil car in eight minutes. Mr. Bishop gave us a lesson in pronunciation. "Say byoo and then Cyrus, like the first name." These statistics and pronunciation guides went into my notes, the ones I still read today.

When TR saw the magnificent Bucyrus, he could not contain himself, not that he ever tried. He gestured to us to leave the train and gather around the shovel. The President jumped up, giving the startled operator no choice. As we know from Red Hallen's photographs, Teddy, looking like a contented beached whale in his white suit and mud-splattered canvas leggings, surrounded by gears and beams, climbed high up into the driver's seat and operated the behemoth. Red Hallen caught this on camera with images that went around the world. As a side note, those pictures proved lucrative for the Bucyrus Foundry and Manufacturing Company, as it competed in the market for powerful steam shovels to build roads and rails. For me, those pictures signify the power of the trip, for better or worse.

TR's love affair with the shovel made an impression on Fred too. "The President," Fred would write the next week in Collier's, "went up the steps in the manner of a man who had just bought a half interest in the implement and was about to ascertain what it could do." Of the two journalists, only Fred made notes every time we heard a detail about technology.

I never managed to read Mr. de Lisser's articles in the *Gleaner*, but I remembered that his comments aboard the *Louisiana* centered on workers, not machinery.

When Red Hallen took a break from his camera, I overheard a chat between him and Fred. They never saw me because so many of us from the train and the dig crowded around the Bucyrus.

"Red, those photographs will make your reputation. I want one for *Collier's*."

"Hope the photographs get me a permanent job here. Hey, yesterday, when you came to see me in the plaza, the man with you—you said his name was Ladder or something like that—he ran away, sudden like. A problem?"

I prayed the machinery around me would stay quiet, so I could hear Fred's reply.

"Nothing much. Latta's the name. He had to work out arrangements for the schedule. You know, he's filling in for Teddy's Secretary. Needed to get the attention of one of the President's men."

Red Hallen seemed satisfied. Or too busy to ask more. He returned to his camera. I saw that Mr. de Lisser stood nearby and may have listened to the same conversation.

Suddenly everyone in the crowd looked up at the cab of the Bucyrus. Taking advantage of the President's hip-to-hip proximity, the shovel operator started to complain. All the Bucyrus operators had a reputation for being smug—they considered themselves the royalty of the skilled workers. Mr. Bishop and I conferred, wondering if we should protect the President from grousing, but we lacked the means to muscle our way through the crowd and didn't want to ruin Red Hallen's photographs. Everyone quieted down, wanting to listen in. The Bucyrus operator fussed that he did not receive overtime pay. The President called for Chief Engineer John Stevens to join the gripe session. After listening to both sides, TR determined that the operator should get overtime but that this ruling did not necessarily apply to other ICC men. Then TR took the opportunity to ask about working conditions more generally. Now we get to what I call chapter two in the great yam story. The shovel operator said the West Indian laborers often quit because they did not like yams from Panama, preferring instead yams from Jamaica. He thought better food would make them work harder.

Overhearing these conversations, many in our entourage—I could tell from their expressions—could not believe the focus on yams, or on one man's salary, amidst the most massive construction project in history. I felt no surprise. Our President loved detail and longed for stories. Mr. de Lisser took out his notebook and began jotting something down. I wasn't sure if the yams or the wages had caught his interest.

The rest of the day passed as a whirlwind, TR style. I frantically scribbled notes to myself, either reminders for follow-up letters (there would be hundreds) or observations for the President's future talks. We visited field hospitals, more housing, canteens, machine shops. At the houses for white employees, the President asked why promised furniture had not been delivered and demanded results. He chatted with everyone—machinists, clerks, health officers, Negro laborers, wives. I reminded him of the names of the managers he had appointments to meet, but I could not know the names of the others. I felt unfit for the job. Thankfully, TR seemed satisfied, or too preoccupied to care.

None of the agents sat on the train. I spotted them separately, at our stops. They must have carried out advance scouting, on high alert. At one stop, I glimpsed Larry Richey trying to fade into the background in a machine shop. I met his eye. He stared at me for a couple seconds longer than I would have expected, then looked away. I think he just tried to make a connection, between two who knew.

The schedule had us lunching at Chief Engineer John Stevens's house, close to a railroad station. Mr. de Lisser lingered at the side of the station. I saw Mr. Bishop confer with Mr. Stevens, who wore his grumpy face, then walk over to Mr. de Lisser. The two men talked for a minute, then walked together toward the house. De Lisser sidled up to Fred as we entered and found our places at the table. I surmised that while a Negro reporter may not have been welcome in our hotels or messes, he was sometimes accepted, or maybe reluctantly accepted, in a private home. Only now, on my third day with Mr. de Lisser, did I realize the full awkwardness of the situation, which went beyond the seating arrangements in a train car.

After lunch, we continued the inspection tour. The unease I had felt at the Cut, speared on by Red Hallen's question, reached a high pitch. At one of our stops, I got Fred's attention, leading him away from the crowd. He looked at me curiously, wondering if I had more information, I suppose.

"Fred, are you feeling as anxious as I am? Yesterday was a near calamity."

"Maurice, I suppose you could say I am experienced at terror. You know, reporting has taken me to awful places. I'm familiar with canons blasting, men dying. To tell you the truth, it's hard to get as close as I want to the action. You witnessed chaos yesterday, maybe your first time, and I understand, that's always nerve-wracking."

I had just a moment of, shall we say, reflection, when Fred minimized my participation to that of a witness.

"But I'm upset for another reason. *Collier's* sent me here. They paid for my passage and they're paying my expenses. They expect me to get the story, the best story I can. You know we had to promise Jimmy silence."

"Yes, and though my job is not the same, I feel this too. I need to report back to Mr. Loeb. He expects a full accounting. And I made the same promise you did. I'm not sure if Jimmy thinks Mr. Loeb would be an exception. And I usually share everything with Clara. My wife."

We exchanged sulks, then both saw Larry approach, looking like he, too, needed a moment of sharing. Although I had caught his eye an hour earlier, we hadn't talked since the events on the plaza. "Larry, how are you doing," Fred asked. Larry ignored Fred, looked over his shoulder to ensure others were not standing near and turned to me.

"Maurice, you saved our hides yesterday."

I will remember those six words forever. Fred looked down, then at me, then smiled.

"Is he safe now?" Fred asked. Before Larry answered, Jimmy Sloan walked over and motioned him away. The agents had to move on to clear the next stop. Although the conversation with Fred and Larry took only a minute, and I should have been annoyed at Fred's airs, instead I felt a swell of belonging, belonging to a group of good men who understood each other and who stood at the center of events.

Soon the train engineer herded Fred and me back to the train. We arrived at the commissary's grocery, where we heard the third chapter in the yam saga. TR asked a clerk about the supply of yams. The clerk shrugged. "Mr. President, the yams we import rot fast here. It's too humid." Then his shrug changed to a smirk. "If the laborers purchasing them are unhappy, they can return them."

TR frowned but seemed at a loss for words for the first time on the trip. Or so I thought until he turned to leave and whispered under his breath, for only me to hear, "or let them eat cake."

In the evening, the President and Mrs. R. dined alone at the Tivoli. Then he met with the British consul, Sir Claude Mallet, while I took notes. Although our President had dark hair and Sir Claude had light hair, their waists, visible through their unbuttoned post-meal dinner jackets, seemed a perfect match. The counsel struggled with a difficult job because most Negro laborers came from the British West Indies and looked to him for assistance. He helped in egregious cases but seemed realistic about his ability to improve the workers' lot. He related typical examples. I recall just one of many. A foreman publicly insulted a Barbadian laborer, but the poor man, illiterate, could not read the instructions on the machinery. TR smiled in sympathy at the stories but had no intention of intervening in the British empire as he tried to establish his own empire. Sir Claude moved on to gossip about parliamentary affairs in London, of surprising interest to TR. Realizing he did not need me to take notes about British gossip, the President released me.

On the way out, I motioned to the President's valet, Amos, that I wanted a word.

I had been fretting through the meeting with Sir Claude, uneasy that Mrs. R. would no longer look at me. She must have thought I knew of the threat on the plaza and had ignored my promise to keep her informed. I felt certain that neither the President, who dismissed all threats as minor, nor lead agent Jimmy Sloan, who took discretion too far, would have discussed events with her.

231

If the President's wife thought ill of me, that did not bode well for my career. And separate from my ambitions, I regretted her disapproval. As I left the President and the British counsel, I asked Amos to get word to Mrs. R. early the next morning that I wished to see her about a matter of Central American protocol and would arrive in the sitting room at ten to seven. I would take her aside and explain my ignorance. And maybe add in a word about my fortunate instincts in the plaza.

Only later did I realize that this hectic day, Friday, constituted an interlude, a short breathing space.

Alberto Agresti

Friday, November 16, 1906

While President Theodore Roosevelt met with Sir Claude Mallet at the Tivoli, Agresti cleaned his revolver for the second time, again to make sure the gun, with its five bullets, would be at its best. Then he trudged through the dark to the central plaza. As an anarchist he believed in neither government nor any spiritual higher beings, but he felt drawn to the cathedral he had stared at that afternoon. He sought a place for contemplation, not for salvation.

"*Buenos noches,*" he said to the elderly caretaker sweeping the entrance. At the floor end of the broom Agresti saw the debris from the day before—bits of hay, half-smoked cigars, drying petals. The caretaker dipped his head, pointing to the mess and mumbling something in Spanish. Probably fussing that it was taking him more than a day to return the cathedral to a pristine state. Agresti entered, shuffled down the left aisle with his head bowed, and sat on a wooden bench. No one else in sight, aside from the caretaker. Not even a priest. Cool air for the first time that day. He fixed his thoughts on his wife. Ernesta believed in him, wanted him home but wanted him to carry out his mission too. She understood that mission. She believed success would honor her brother Roberto. Without praying, Agresti tried to take strength from these memories. He looked at the marble alter, at the black and white tile floor, at the stained-glass windows, dull in the darkness. At the flat images of Christ. Nothing there to draw strength from. He needed to rely on his brain, his wits, his luck.

Returning to the Paramount Hotel, he sat on his bed for two hours, peering out the window at the street life. He saw less activity than usual, thanks to patrolling police and marines. At midnight he heard the Paramount's night clerk making his rounds. Agresti ran to the pantry to retrieve the bellhop uniform, moving only when he guessed the clerk would be in another area, with an impeded view of the hall. Agresti put on the uniform, now feeling foolish as well as fearful. In the mirror, he saw himself in gray pants with a stripe down each side, a short red jacket with a high white collar and two rows of brass buttons down the front, and a hat that looked like a cake pan. He laughed, surprising himself. He took off the uniform, refolded it into the package, then put on a dark suit.

Agresti left the Paramount and walked toward the Tivoli, striving for a routine pace, carrying the package and his Panama hat. He selected a cluster of three palm trees facing the hotel. Was he selecting a gravesite? He folded himself into the damp foliage under the tree, peeking out to look for night watchmen or a guard detail. He saw no one other than bellhops and a few inebriated guests, staggering in late. Agresti tried to find a comfortable position, tried to avoid the sharp, notched leaves of the ground cover, tried to ignore the black beetles crawling under him. He looked at the sky, thinking the same sky hovered over Paterson, straining to imagine he lay there, not coiled in the foliage on an isthmus, waiting to kill. Unable to picture himself elsewhere, he watched the gas lights of the hotel and counted the rooms on the second floor. Then counted again.

Just before dawn, Agresti rolled into a position so he could pee without wetting himself, then put on the uniform over his suit. A difficult task, especially sitting on the damp ground, avoiding the puddle he had just made. He had to tuck his suit jacket beneath his shorter uniform jacket. He would need that suit to escape. Fortunately, the uniform had deep pockets that could accommodate the revolver. He started to use his finger to part his hair down the middle, then he realized his part didn't matter as he doffed the odd bellhop hat. At ten minutes to seven, he shook out his arms and legs to free his muscles and to quiet his mind. He quickly entered the service entrance, carrying his straw hat. He had placed his steamer ticket back to the States in the unused pouch he had sewn into the hat. Where to leave it? Out of desperation, he placed the hat in a corner next to the door, behind a trash bin. If he succeeded in an escape, he could grab it then, while discarding the bellhop uniform at the same time.

Agresti thought back to the beginning, the drawing of the lots two months ago. He knew he had used the time since wisely. Was his planning enough? Nothing left but to push through to the end. He would not have a third chance.

The Colombian Businessman

Friday, November 16, 1906

When leaving La Boheme Wednesday night, the Colombian asked Sally Miller to put in his request for both girls, for Friday night, two days hence. He assumed this trio would make for a good celebration following events in the plaza. On Friday, as he entered the parlor, he knew he had erred. No news of success. No matter, the wait would go quicker if he had some fun. Despite his advance reservation, both Mei and Madeleine were finishing with their current patrons. Scowling at the proprietor, the Colombian found a seat in the parlor. Again, John Connell sat there too. He must be a regular. He puffed on a cigar, of inferior quality, and slugged his whiskey, this time forgoing *Harper's Weekly* and glancing instead through the *Railroad Man's Magazine*. These Americans—always thinking of work.

"Great to see you again," Connell said, glancing up. "You like the services here as much as I do?"

"Even better than my Bogota haunts, and with a classier library," the Colombian said, winking, pointing to the *Railroad Man*. He took a nearby seat. "And here we have many possibilities, as you and I discussed earlier. I have reserved two of La Boheme's beauties."

"Ah, a man of good taste. I will have a more standard evening tonight. Need to be up at the crack of dawn tomorrow."

"At dawn?" I thought you officials kept banking hours."

"Most of the time, yes. Not tomorrow. Can I tell you in confidence?" Without waiting for a reply, Connell continued. "Few people know this—Teddy has a bastard nephew. Believe it or not, that nephew is Sean over there, the lad emptying ashtrays. Amazing, right? Tomorrow I am acting as intermediary. I am taking Sean to the Tivoli to see Teddy. Early."

"Early?" asked the Colombian, casually.

"Have to be there at 7:00. Before the day gets going. That's the schedule Teddy wants." As he got ready to get to the details, Sally appeared through the French doors. She motioned to the Colombian that all was ready.

"Have fun," Connell called out. The Colombian strode in the direction Sally pointed. He tried to make and retain a mental note to send Alberto Agresti a coded message about Connell's early morning visit to the Tivoli. Agresti didn't need complications. The mental note fell into the background, behind the Colombian's beating heart and swelling enthusiasm. Even if the Colombian had remembered to send a message, Agresti, who had already left his hotel, would never have received it.

John Connell

Connell rose early. He dressed in his best cream-colored suit and selected his new leather shoes, the ones free of muck. He directed his carriage driver to collect Sean Marsh at La Boheme. The youth skulked in front of the brothel door. Without meeting Connell's eyes, Sean climbed into the carriage. He wore a gray suit of moderate quality. Connell shook some stray hairs off Sean's jacket, straightened his tie.

"Good morning. Big day for you. We're going to meet the President." Connell spoke quietly, in a singsong manner, turning away from the driver. "Or maybe I should say you're going to meet your uncle." Still using a hushed tone, Connell strung out each word, smirked. Sean showed no reaction. "Come on, son. No slumping. You're doing your mother a favor. Don't you think she can use some help?"

"What am I supposed to say?"

"Remember, you say nothing. Let me do the talking. If he asks, you say you like Panama but wish you could afford to go to school instead of working in a stable next to the boarding house. Nothing else. And don't mumble."

"I do go to school, already. The good ICC school. Do you want him to think I'm dumb?"

Connell sighed. "Damn, boy. Think of your mother. That woman deserves a break."

They traveled in silence for five minutes. As the driver pulled up to the circular path in front of the Tivoli, Connell straightened his own tie and strode into the lobby. Sean trailed, eyes to the ground, cheeks flushing. Connell approached the reception desk, knowing this would be the first and last time in his life he could announce himself this way: "John Connell here, with Elliott Marsh, for an appointment with President Theodore Roosevelt." The desk clerk nodded in the direction of a man standing to the side. Burly, ordinary suit. A bodyguard, Connell guessed.

"You are here for your 7:00 appointment?" asked the bodyguard, checking a list. "Sorry, I need to search both of you. Follow me." The guard led them behind a screen, then patted them down with excessive care. Connell adopted a posture of disdain. He saw Elliott look alert for the first time that morning, intrigued by the protocol.

"Over there to the second floor, please." Another "follow me."

Entering the hall, Connell admired the décor. Elliott straightened up and looked around too. They saw wide halls, flocked wallpaper, sparkling chandeliers. La Boheme was the nicest brothel in Panama City, but a modest establishment when measured by Tivoli standards. The threesome ascended the stairs then walked past five or six doors. Connell spotted a young man, muscular, in a chair at the side of a paneled door. Must be another bodyguard. The man raised a brow, looked for a sign. The older guard signaled something with his left hand. The younger guard stood, then knocked, three quick knocks, a pause, one more. A light-skinned colored man answered, distinguished looking. He wore a short jacket over a vest, which Connell registered as the clothing of a butler or valet.

"Good morning, Amos. John Connell and Elliott Marsh, here for the President," announced the older guard, again consulting his notes.

"He is getting ready, Mr. Tyree. Please sit here for a minute, gentlemen," added the valet, pointing to a dark blue settee along the wall of an impressive sitting room. May I offer you coffee or tea?"

Elliott, shuffling, pink rising to his brows, knew not to answer. Connell answered for both. "Coffee for me, nothing for the lad."

The valet went to a gleaming silver set and started to pour.

239

"Bye, Amos. I'm going to relieve Larry." The guard turned to leave.

Connell looked around the sitting room. He saw a slender man with a high forehead, holding a portfolio and a notebook, drinking coffee. The man looked expectantly at the door to the President's bedroom. The door opened. The President, ready to meet? No. Connell smelled the perfume, fresh, not cloying, of a woman who must be Mrs. Roosevelt. She began to walk through the door into the parlor. Connell strained his neck to see. Saw the first two inches of her white dress cross the threshold.

A gunshot.

Connell sensed the wall behind him vibrate. The slender man dropped his coffee and dashed into the bedroom. He embraced the woman. Pulled her into the parlor. The guard leaving the sitting room reversed direction. Knocked over the coffee pot. Tripped over the embracing couple. Ran into the bedroom. A second shot. A thump. The hall guard, running, dashed over the couple. Ran into the bedroom. A third shot. A man's yelp. Damn—Sean jumped up, ran into the bedroom with the valet. Moaning. Groans. A fourth shot.

Connell still sat on the settee as silence came.

Maurice Latta

Saturday, November 17, 1906

Our two and a half days in Panama seemed like months. I felt exhausted. My suit, laid over a chair, had barely dried again. We had one final day to get through. I awakened earlier than usual, to see Mrs. R. at ten to seven and to pack because we would not be returning to the Tivoli. As I dressed, a hotel clerk knocked on my door. He handed me telegrams that arrived the night before or early that morning, so I could prioritize them for the President. Two of the telegrams related to the day's routine arrangements. I went quickly to the third, from Secretary of War William Howard Taft. I explained earlier in this account that TR had dismissed 167 Negro soldiers following the Brownsville affair. He was irritated that none would squeal on the alleged perpetrators who were thought to have killed a bartender. Several Negro leaders had asked Taft, charged with all military matters, to intervene. Taft's telegram, now in my hand, urged TR to reconsider the dismissal order, pending a trial and investigation. Taft implied that as Secretary of War, he might rescind the order himself in the President's absence. I bore responsibility for triaging telegrams, not judging them. Although I usually avoided judging policy matters, in this case, I had strong opinions. I agreed with Taft. The President, usually a friend of the Negro, had erred. I placed the telegram in my portfolio.

Walking to the President's suite to see Mrs. R., I rehearsed in my mind what I planned to say to her. Larry Richey sat guard at the door. We exchanged warm smiles. He knocked. Three quick knocks, a pause, one more. Amos let me in.

The next five minutes did not proceed as expected. Amos offered me coffee, which I eagerly accepted. I held the cup with one hand and my portfolio and notebook with the other. He knocked on the bedroom door to tell Mrs. R. I had arrived. As I drank my coffee, Frank Tyree entered, escorting two visitors unknown to me, the first paunchy and middle-aged, the second young and nervous. They sat on the blue settee against the wall shared with the President's bedroom. I puzzled over the identity of the visitors. They were not on my schedule. Then I heard Frank announce their names—John Connell and Sean Marsh. I recalled that the sealed envelope the President handed me two days ago had been addressed to Mrs. Katy Marsh, in care of John Connell. Amos offered them coffee. The plump man accepted. I started to introduce myself as Frank turned to leave.

The bedroom door opened. Mrs. R. adjusted her collar, then took a step toward the sitting room. Gunshot. A crackling sound. Sudden, unmistakable, unforgettable. TR's upper left arm, I learned later. Mrs. R. screamed. "Teddy." I dropped my portfolio, my notebook, my China cup. Took four steps ahead, wrapped my body around hers. Dragged her away from the bedroom. Scent of orange blossoms or roses. Why do I remember that? Bodies rushed past into the bedroom. Frank, then Larry. A second shot. Frank's thigh, I learned later. A rush of men into TR's bedroom. Amos and the lad. A third shot, a different sound. The assassin's arm, I learned. Grunts of a tussle. A fourth shot. The assassin's hip. Silence.

I tried to force Mrs. R. onto the settee, next to the plump man, but she would have none of it. She raced into the bedroom, with me behind.

Carnage. Larry had slung himself across the President, pressing him down on the unmade bed. The President, in shirtsleeves, mouth agape, with shaving cream on his face, held a smoking pearl-gripped Browning M1900. He rolled every which way, trying to push Larry off. I saw a fist-sized stain of blood on TR's left shirt sleeve. Bonnie Clifford, who must have been arranging Mrs. R's wardrobe, curled on the floor, grabbing up at Larry.

She stayed silent, maybe in shock. Frank Tyree, blood gushing from his leg, groaned on the floor, a foot from Bonnie. Amos and the lad held down a bellhop slumped over the windowsill, blood streaming down his gray sleeve and pant leg. He screamed in pain and babbled in a foreign language. Larry shouted back at him, also in a foreign language. Only those two in the room could understand. Days later, Larry filled me in. The bellhop had denounced TR, so Larry had responded, *"Puoi pensare di far finire il governo da una cella di prigione."* You can think about ending government from a prison cell.

I no longer smelled Mrs. R's perfume. Just gunpowder.

The tableau I described has appeared in my mind every night for forty-one years. Sometimes I see myself helping to restore order, sometimes I see myself leaning against the wall, shaking.

You might think all this noise would have awakened the dead, but the wing that had been readied for the President's stay had no other guests who heard the commotion. The President's entourage, which included me, Jimmy Sloan, and Dr. Rixey, were all housed on the third floor in another wing. Larry, despite his young age, took charge. He rose from the bed, verified that the President and first lady were all right, and yelled at me to fetch Jimmy Sloan and Dr. Rixey. I returned with them at a run three minutes later. Jimmy, wearing his pants and undergarments, assessed the dreadful state of affairs. Dr. Rixey, still in his dressing gown but alert enough to have grabbed his medical bag, tended to TR, who insisted that the bullet had just nicked his flesh. The doctor then treated Frank, applying a tourniquet and administering morphine. Last, Dr. Rixey looked at the bellhop, who had collapsed on the floor. The doctor felt for his pulse and eyed his wounds. Blood ran onto the carpet. Jimmy riffled through the bellhop's pockets, which offered no clues, and reported that the man wore a suit under his uniform. Jimmy collected three weapons—the President's, Amos's, and the stranger's, which had fallen on the floor, and checked them in various ways beyond my expertise.

Bonnie Clifford? Well, I think we ignored her. Even Larry. I'm ashamed to say we may have ignored Amos too.

All of us wanted to talk to Jimmy Sloan at once, to explain the sequence of events. He told us to slow down, asked a few follow-up questions, and checked out sobbing Mrs. R., **a** woman we knew to be calm and formal. He asked Dr. Rixey to give her a sedative. Then he asked me and the two agents, the lad, and Mr. Connell, who had been sitting in the suite all this time, to wait in the hall for a few minutes. Jimmy took the President, still in his shirtsleeves, still with shaving lotion congealing on his face, aside for a conference in a corner of the sitting room. We stepped around broken China cups and puddles of coffee and cream. On the way to the hall, I picked up my portfolio and notebook, covered with a thin film of coffee.

Out in the hall, we didn't talk, but instead strained to hear the muffled voices in the suite. When Jimmy called us back, I learned a plan had been hatched, on the President's orders. No one was to know that the first of the assassin's bullets nicked President Roosevelt. No one was to know that the assassin's second bullet hit Frank Tyree. No one was to know that the President, using his pearl-gripped Browning, shot the assassin in the left arm. No one was to know that a lad, a stranger to us all, had held down the struggling, bleeding assassin and pommeled him. No one was to know that Amos, who kept a pistol in his valet's jacket, had ended the attempt on the President's life with a well-timed, decisive shot, narrowly missing the lad. No one was to know that a lone bellhop, or a killer dressed as a bellhop, had come close to murdering the President of the United States. No one was to know how many times Jimmy used the word "bloody" in his directives to us. Jimmy looked directly at me and the two agents, ignoring Dr. Rixey, Connell, and the lad. "You three know the drill." I understood what he was saying—the same instruction that followed the struggle in the plaza.

As Jimmy spoke, Amos fetched a basin and towel. He cleaned off the presidential cheeks. Then TR added a seal to Jimmy's orders. "Absolute silence," he said, staring at each of us in turn. "This expedition is about the canal, and progress, and absolutely nothing else." TR's eyes, narrowing, reached Mr. Connell. "Sir, you are John Connell?" The man nodded once. TR's eyes moved on to the lad who had pommeled the assassin. Those eyes lingered, appraised.

"One more thing," Jimmy said, looking at Mr. Connell. "We're arresting you, sir, and the boy with you. It's too strange that you came here at precisely the moment the assassin broke in. You'll be detained for questioning."

Both the President and Mr. Connell looked confounded. After seconds of silence, the President spoke. "It is all right, Jimmy. I know why this gentleman and the lad arrived here. They had an appointment with me. Since we are sworn to secrecy about this morning, I will add a new secret for you. This youth—I will tell you—is the son, born out of wedlock, of my dear brother Elliott. Looking at the boy, I cannot deny it. Edith and I must keep this story quiet, for the sake of Elliott's memory." He paused. "Give me a moment, Mr. Connell."

The President entered the bloody bedroom while the rest of us shuffled our feet and avoided locking eyes. TR returned two minutes later with an envelope, which he handed to Mr. Connell. "This assumes full discretion."

TR walked up to Elliott, shook his hand, looked him in the eye. "We will never meet again. Know that your father was a good man at heart. I have placed more in that envelope than requested." The President's mouth curled up. "And thank you for stopping my assassin." He gave the lad the gentlest of shoves out the door.

Mr. Connell, who had lost all color, placed the envelope in his pocket without a word and followed Elliott out the door. The rest of us looked at each other, with frozen expressions. Amos said he would take care of the remaining details, which I guessed meant disposing of the bellhop's body and tending to Frank. As Amos left the room, Jimmy cocked his head, remembering a detail. "Larry, talk to Bonnie Clifford. Swear her to secrecy if she wants to continue to tend to Mrs. R." Larry slowly moved his chin slightly down, slightly up. He understood. Jimmy waved me out, a signal to get on with the day. The day an insignificant assistant secretary may have saved the life of the president's wife.

In later years, I occasionally met two or three of the men who had been in the suite at drinking holes in various cities to share our memories. We could speak only to each other about what we had witnessed. Some details grew clearer in the telling and retelling, some less clear. We recognized changes in each other's versions, not in our own.

Sean Miller, Sally Miller

Saturday, November 17, 1906

S ean Miller exited the Tivoli, gazing out at the palm trees around the circular drive. John Connell shuffled alongside, clutching his jacket to his stomach. The waiting driver stood at the carriage, smoking, with several cigarette butts on the once-pristine gravel. The driver drew his bottom lip over his top. "Was to be only a half-hour, right?"

"Mmmm, sorry," Connell said. "We were delayed. Unexpectedly."

On the trip back to La Boheme, Sean said nothing. Connell said nothing. When the driver pulled up in front of the brothel, Connell put his hand on Sean's shoulder. Gave a pat. Connell reached into his pocket for the envelope and handed it to Sean with one word. "Goodbye." Sean heard an air of finality. He leaped out of the carriage while Connell, who remained seated, told the driver to take him to the ICC offices. As Sean dashed to the door of La Boheme, he did not bother to look over his shoulder as Connell disappeared down the road.

* * *

Sally Miller spent an hour pacing. Now she waited at the window. How could the transaction take this long? Had Sean slipped, said more than he was supposed to? Were they both in jail now? She had locked the front door. At last, the carriage appeared. Only Sean stepped down, though she had expected Connell to return with the boy to give an accounting.

"Sean, I've been a wreck. What took so long?"

Sean ignored her question. He reached into his pocket and handed his mother a fat envelope.

"Whoopee. Glory be." She enveloped Sean in her arms, jumped up and down with him. "You did it. You did it."

After her third jump, Sally realized Sean had come alone.

"Where is John? We should celebrate with some liquor. Even you."

"I'm not sure you'll see him again," Sean said quietly.

"That's not possible. I owe him…money. I'm sure he'll come 'round.

"Look in the envelope."

Sally ripped it open. She saw cash, which she would count later. Must be the $5000 she had requested. She saw, too, a promissory note for $5000 to be honored by J.P. Morgan and Company.

"Sean, is this $10,000? Did Teddy make a mistake, giving us twice?"

"No, Ma." He paused. The pause barely registered for Sally, as she ogled the stash. "He really thought I looked like his brother."

After a few minutes, Sally probed further, but Sean's story of the day remained guarded, month after month and year after year. He talked only about the pat-down, the opulence of the hotel, the valet's livery, TR's stare. When Sally asked what John Connell had said to the President, Sean claimed he could not remember.

Sally Miller could not understand why John Connell never again visited La Boheme, never collected his debt. He wouldn't explain that not even her promised charms could wash away his shame.

Maurice Latta

Saturday, November 17, 1906

None of us had a choice. We needed to resume our roles, mine as Assistant Secretary.

In heavy rain, we boarded the train that morning, sixty-five minutes later than scheduled. Most of the waiting officials, used to delays, seemed unaware of the discrepancy. But the observant reporters pushed for an explanation. Following our routine, they sat down near me in the second car.

"Chap, we have started on time each of the other mornings, even if we fell behind during the rest of the day," Frederick Palmer said. "Why the delay?"

"The President had a lot of paperwork to tend to this morning." Positioning my head so Fred could see, and Mr. de Lisser couldn't, I rolled my eyes in a telling manner, suggesting I wished to say no more in a crowded train car. I knew this brief sentence would buy me time until lunch. I would use the next few hours to decide how to respond to Fred's curiosity.

Just before noon, the rain slowed to a trickle then ended, answering our prayers. We transferred to a spur line to reach the Mt. Hope Reservoir and nearby mess, slightly smaller than the mess we ate at previously. Chief Engineer Stevens, with a proud smile replacing his typical scowl, explained that the new reservoir supplied residents of Colón with clean water. Looking at mud oozing everywhere, I hesitate to imagine conditions before.

We walked on to the mess, dodging muck. Mrs. R. raised her veil, looked my way for a long second. As our eyes met, she conveyed gratitude and I conveyed what I might call solidarity. Later Dr. Rixey told me that she had refused a sedative, determined to continue with the tour. As we neared the mess, she grabbed her husband's right arm, hooking it through her left arm. I had never known this sturdy woman to trip. I suspected she did not seek his support on the slimy path, but through his jacket, felt for the flesh she had almost lost.

For lunch, our entourage expanded to include six engineers and Walter Tubby, superintendent of construction. He was the same surprisingly slim man who Theodore Shonts, ICC Chairman, enlisted to greet TR two days earlier at the crack of dawn. And Shonts, I now realized, was John Connell's boss. (I could not know then, but upon Shonts's death in 1919, his widow sued his mistress for a fortune. The pompous man's improprieties did not surprise me.) I had, at last, become familiar with the dozens of officials claiming some corner of power on the isthmus. Until that morning, my greatest source of pride in my job had been mastery of such details. Now I felt another source of pride.

No one bothered with the lunch ritual of quinine this time, though I suspect TR may have gobbled pills on the sly. If he suffered pain from his flesh wound, he didn't show it. I did not see Mr. de Lisser at the mess. He may have been waiting on one of the trains.

To almost everyone at lunch, nothing appeared out of the ordinary. Fred suspected otherwise. I should have avoided him, but that was not my inclination. Put simply, I had information he wanted, and that gave me a welcome sense of authority, rare for an assistant secretary from rural Pennsylvania.

Fred gestured to me to take a seat beside him at a table far from the others. "What can you share? I see Mrs. R. looks shaky. Is she ill? Does that explain the delay?"

"She is unwell, but not with an illness. Fred, you always look for a story. I can talk to you as a friend, not as a reporter. Can you promise to exclude what I am about to say from your writing? I realize Jimmy Sloan already swore you to silence, but for a different debacle."

He said yes to me, while shaking his head and spreading his arms, palms up. "You and Jimmy give me no choice. I will report only what I see with my own eyes."

Trying to keep drama out of my voice, but probably failing, I reported on the extraordinary events of the morning in TR's bedroom. As modestly as possible, I included a summary of my rescue of Edith Roosevelt. I explained the actions leading to the shooting of the bellhop. I added a bit about young Elliott Marsh. I ended with Jimmy's demand for silence, reinforced by TR. Fred's face, usually impassive, moved and stretched. His mouth opened. He scratched his ear. After a moment's silence, a moment when I cursed myself for my lack of discretion, Fred swore again to honor his vow of confidentiality.

And he did just that, for forty-one years so far, and I trust he will continue to do so. Why, you may ask, am I writing these secrets down now, for my family and others to read? Mrs. Edith Roosevelt is eighty-six years old. I will place this manuscript in my safe, to be read upon my death, and she is likely to die before me. I understand from others in the office that the other Mrs. Roosevelt, Eleanor, realizes that Elliott Marsh, the real Elliott Marsh, is her half-brother. Weighing what at this point would be a modest embarrassment to the Roosevelt family against the call of history, aren't forty-one years of secrecy enough?

Herbert de Lisser

Saturday, November 17, 1906

This time Herbert de Lisser could not resist a drink on his way to Mrs. Hunter's boarding house. He felt agitated and needed to calm himself. Maurice Latta had ignored him on the train that morning, favoring Frederick Palmer. Those two had spoken, heads together. And this was after that strange delay in starting the day's trip. What were they hiding? De Lisser chugged two beers while standing at the bar, avoiding stares from men of the same color. Once the warmth began to coat his nerves, he walked to Mrs. Hunter's.

A rap on the door. Mrs. Hunter delivered a long message from the bellhop at the Tivoli. First, the bellhop reported on a meeting between the President and the British counsel. Ah, de Lisser would love to have heard that. The counsel probably complained about Jamaicans—British citizens—his countrymen. Though the bellhop wrote that he couldn't hear most of the conversation, he did make out the council's whiny tone. Then the bellhop reported on some sort of fracas in or near the president's quarters early that morning. A maid heard sounds of scuffling and smelled ammonia. No workers he talked to could provide details.

But Mr. Latta had learned the details. And Mr. Palmer had learned the details. Those two posed as righteous, but they would never share.

Daniel Fowler

W hen observers think about the Panama Canal, most think about waterways and vessels. Some think about screens, Bucyrus steam shovels, and track shifters. They should add in concrete. For most of the nineteenth century, wood, brick, steel, and iron served as the construction supplies of choice. The list expanded after architect Ernest Ransome designed the Pacific Coast Borax Company Refinery, using reinforced concrete. The building survived a spectacular fire in 1902, providing an unforeseen advertisement for concrete. Influenced in part by Ransome, engineers who had used masonry for dams began to realize the strength of concrete.

Chief Engineer John Wallace, the man who sent William Karner to Barbados to recruit workers, resigned from the ICC due in part to delays he faced requisitioning building supplies from Washington. His successor, taciturn John Stevens, had a slightly easier time, though he still faced delays. Stevens needed not just the expensive Bucyrus steam shovels in the historic pictures—seventy-seven of those—but also 100 smaller steam shovels, thousands of feet of iron pipe for the water supply, thousands of feet of terracotta pipe for sewer lines, 100 pneumatic rock drills, 1500 electric motors, 500,000 linear feet of steel rails, 3.2 million board feet of lumber, 30,000 tons of coal, 1,000 spoil cars, 500 flat cars, 120 tons of pyrethrum powder. Even 3,000 garbage cans, 4,000 buckets, 240 rat traps.

And increasingly concrete, huge amounts of concrete. The ICC solicited bids for most of these supplies, slowing down improvements but containing costs. And for the most part, guarding against favoritism.

* * *

Back in Troy, New York, Daniel Fowler, owner of Troy Building Supply and uncle of Canal Engineer Jeffrey Fowler, enjoyed the profits from his sale of concrete to the Erie Canal. Though exhausted from the effort of winning that bid and delivering on it, his greed outbalanced his exhaustion. Fowler and other concrete manufacturers read a government notice announcing the January 1906 ICC call for bids for concrete. He paid attention to the name of the official who signed off on that notice—Panama Canal Purchasing Agent David Ross. The ICC needed concrete to line drainage ditches to redirect stagnant water, to construct a refrigeration and ice-making plant, to build small dams needed for drinking water, and to erect trestle bridges.

Not a man to leave any stone, or barrel of concrete, unturned, Fowler imagined himself with a piece of the action. Word had gone around in the small community of concrete manufacturers that the ICC engineers had begun to design the Gatun Dam, including, at its center, an arched concrete spillway of massive proportions. In 1906 Fowler knew that eventually, David Ross would solicit bids for that enormous project. Fowler could not know then that the Gatun Dam bid would be for five million barrels of concrete, or that the Gatun Dam would become, for almost thirty years, the largest concrete structure in the world, or that the contract would be worth $5,500,000 in 1908 dollars. But he did know that his best chance of competing for the contract for the Dam in a year or two would be to first win the contract for the more modest projects.

When he had bid on the Erie Canal years back, Fowler connived with his nephew Jeffrey to peek at early bids. Now he needed to figure out what might work in Panama. Jeffrey, a sociable man, must know all the people of influence employed by the ICC, including Purchasing Agent David Ross. Daniel Fowler booked passage to Panama.

Jeffrey Fowler

J effrey Fowler stood on the Colón dock, watching Uncle Dan wobble off the *Allianca*. Though disembarking passengers often looked peaked, Jeffrey could barely recognize his uncle. The man looked twenty years older than his age of fifty-one, and his wrinkled suit hung loosely on him. His partly gray hair had turned pure white. The sea must have been rough. Today would be the family reunion Jeffrey had dreaded since getting a letter that included babble about Fowler kin and toward the end, a disturbing sentence. "When I arrive, we can talk about new business opportunities."

Uncle Dan had been a central figure in Jeffrey's life, inspiring him to succeed, contributing to his tuition at Rensselaer Polytechnic. When Jeffrey announced his engagement to Liza, his father scowled, and his Uncle Dan commented on her feckless family, her beauty, and her bosom. Jeffrey's memory of tension over Liza faded into the background as he struggled with his deceit regarding the widening of the Erie Canal. He had made an ill-advised decision to help his uncle. Jeffrey lived with the fear that Liza, or maybe some of the engineers in the Zone who had friends who worked on the Erie, would discover his transgressions. He would not tempt fate again. Life seemed good now, with Liza at home and Emily at The Luna. And maybe Selina.

Uncle and nephew said little at first. Jeffrey wanted to delay the inevitable conversation and he could tell that his uncle felt unwell. After a while, they chatted on the train—the progress on the canal, the cursed weather. Jeffrey asked about the voyage, another safe topic.

"You know, I'd never been on a steamer before," Daniel said, speaking slowly. "Barges, rowboats, but always on lakes or the Erie, never on the ocean. We had mostly calm waters, but I vomited, couldn't eat."

Jeffrey forced his face into a semblance of sympathy. "Did you spend the whole trip in your cabin?"

"A few times, I tried to walk on deck. You know me, I like to talk to people. Wanted to meet the other passengers on board. The non-laborers. I tried to start up a conversation with the captain. And with one of the businessmen—a young man who was also into building supplies. Maybe screens. But I didn't have much energy."

Jeffrey and Uncle Dan walked from the train station to Empire, near the Cut. Despite his limp, Jeffrey had to slow down for his trailing uncle. Entering the front door, Jeffrey saw that Liza looked lovely, ready to impress. She had planned a wonderful spread. All week she had given Selina orders. Find the best beef, the freshest vegetables, cook them the right way. During dinner, Jeffrey watched Liza call for Selina repeatedly. She must want Daniel to see that the Fowlers had a servant. He paid little attention. Jeffrey wondered if his uncle was aging faster than expected—he barely glanced at Selina, who had a reputation as the prettiest maid in the town of Empire.

"How does Troy fare these days?" Jeffrey asked.

"Not good. All those insurance claims because of the San Francisco quake. They're hurting everyone, in all the states. Then there's the Hepburn Act, regulating, I should say overregulating, rail freight rates. The stock market is down too."

Jeffrey wished his uncle would elaborate—he usually droned on and on, until his listeners' eyes glazed over. At the dinner table, in front of Liza, Uncle Dan would not make any improper requests.

"Finances," Liza said. "I'm interested in ours, but not anyone else's. Let's talk about something more interesting now that we have Uncle Daniel here. How are the Stonemans? Did Matthew ever dry out? What about the Mortensens? Is the house they built as grand as they boasted?"

Daniel mumbled answers, but Liza looked like she wanted more.

"And Julia Grant?" Jeffrey knew his wife had been obsessed with Troy's Julia Grant, not the wife of Ulysses, but the daughter of a former Troy mayor. Julia, eight years older than Liza, had been the belle of Troy. She married a man who became mayor of New York City. Liza still sulked about the wedding notice in the *New York Times*. "The veil of tulle was held in place by a tiara of diamonds, the gift of the groom."

"Well, I hear that Hugh Grant is now caught up in all sorts of corruption messes in the city," Uncle Dan said.

Liza smiled. "No details for me, Uncle? Jeffrey, can you get your hands on any of the New York papers? I'd like to read about the Grants."

"Let's forget about Troy and all those snobs. Here," Jeffrey turned to Daniel, "we're making friends with the families of ICC officials, right Liza? Everyone has come from somewhere else, and they're eager to meet new people." Liza's eyes wandered to the side and then settled. She had not told Jeffrey about snubs from two of the engineers' wives, but he had pieced that together from overheard talk at a one of John Stevens's conferences.

Selina started to clear the table. Jeffrey heard her whisper to Liza. "Mam, your guest not like his dinner?" He sensed Selina worried that Liza would be angry.

Jeffrey and Liza looked at Daniel's plate, still piled with Selina's cooking.

"Uncle, do you still feel ill from the steamer? Or don't you like the foods we can get here on the isthmus? Maybe you don't like Selina's cooking." Liza glared at her maid.

"Sorry, Liza. Just not hungry," Daniel said. "I'd better go to sleep now."

Jeffrey showed him to his bed. Liza had moved the baby to the larger bedroom, freeing up the nursery. As Daniel mumbled goodnight, Jeffrey felt relief that his uncle turned in early. No evening session of smoking and plotting.

Listening attentively, he heard Selina close the door as she left for the night.

Jeffrey Fowler, Selina Thompson

Wednesday, November 7, 1906

T he day after Uncle Dan arrived in Panama, Jeffrey Fowler walked as usual to the work site he supervised, as Division Engineer. He observed with pride three spoil cars rolling downhill to a marsh. His workers would unload the dirt, then transport it for use as fill. The men had worked hard to finish excavations on this part of the Cut. Now he could direct the foreman to move the track to the next tier, where work would begin that afternoon. He trusted Bruce Lighter, the young foreman in charge of the operation.

It was Wednesday, so Jeffrey's mood lifted despite his uncle's arrival. Jeffrey knew that Liza would make her weekly trip to the commissary today, leaving baby Gregory with Selina. He knew, too, that Gregory napped at 2:00.

"Lighter, I need to check in with the manager at the machine shop this afternoon. Need to make sure the Bucyrus will be ready for us tomorrow and that we can get that operator we had last time. It will take me an hour or two. By the time I'm back, the track should be repositioned."

"No problem, boss. We got it." Lighter smiled.

The men had played this charade before. Jeffrey knew that Lighter knew the visit to the machine shop was unnecessary. Arrangements had been worked out before. Jeffrey also knew that Lighter didn't care about the dishonesty and considered his boss a decent chap. Lighter might even welcome two hours unsupervised.

At 2:00, Jeffrey hurried to his house. With his damn limp, the walk took fifteen minutes. He expected to surprise Selina. Approaching the yard, he contracted his stomach, squared his shoulders. A few feet later, he stopped short. She sat on the porch, next to a tall West Indian, a handsome man, dressed a bit better than a laborer in a clean white shirt and blue pants. He had left his cart on the side path and lounged beside her, with one hand on the bench, near her shoulder, and another arm on his lap. They were not discussing the age of the cabbage in his cart. As Jeffrey registered the scene, he saw Selina look out in the yard, spot him, then turn back to the man. He could continue into the house, explaining that he needed another pair of boots. No point. He pivoted on his good foot, turning back.

* * *

The first week of November Selina worried about her uncle Michael, recovering at Ancon Hospital. Even so, she looked forward to the next Wednesday, November 7th. Every Wednesday, Selina organized her time to do the family wash in the back yard at 2:00, around the time Gregory took a nap. She smiled to herself as she scrubbed Miz Liza's dresses, the ones with too many flounces. From the yard Selina could see the road leading to the kitchen. On Wednesdays, Miss Liza would stay away for the afternoon for her long shop at the Commissary. Except that Selina had a friend who cleaned at a small hotel a block from the Commissary, who knew otherwise.

Selina had had boyfriends in St. George Parish—boys she walked with through the fields and towns, boys who grabbed her hand, her waist, sometimes her breast. Those boys stayed in Barbados, probably beginning to work at the sugar plantations or mills, as their fathers did, if they were lucky. Tom Gordon, the neighborhood meat peddler, had left Barbados for Panama, even before the Thompsons did. He wanted to earn good money, Selina knew that, but he also wanted a new adventure. He became the best supplier, the vendor all the wives and maids waited for, the one who never, almost never, sold them bad meat. He was talky too—knew everything about everyone. And handsome. Broad shoulders, smooth skin. He always sought out Selina last, after doing business with the maids of the three other apartments in the building. That way, he could take his time, especially on Wednesdays. Selina had explained that was the best day for her to linger. The previous Wednesday, he brought his horse to a blacksmith, so had missed her. She had more than one reason to want Tom around on those days.

They sat on the porch bench. She sensed his hand moving to her shoulder. She would raise her hand, place it on his.

Dammit. The other one stood thirty feet away, staring. After last Wednesday, he thought Wednesdays were safe. He'd push her into a corner again, slobber on her. But he saw Tom.

Emily Byrne should have been enough for Jeffrey Fowler.

Selina had run into that Irish girl, her shipmate from *La Plata*, on an errand to fetch sewing supplies in Panama City. Emily Byrne had tried to pretend she didn't recognize Selina, but Selina had yelled a hello. After a few minutes of talk, Selina said she worked for the Fowlers. Emily's face twitched. After that, Selina yanked out of Emily the details she tried to hide. Jeffrey Fowler was her regular Tuesday night customer at The Luna. Selina promised not to tell Miz Liza about the arrangement, though she guessed Miz Liza had figured it out already.

Robert Peterson, Jeffrey Fowler

Saturday, November 10, 1906, to Thursday, November 15, 1906

D
r. Robert Peterson had completed his medical school education
at Johns Hopkins University, where he trained under William
Stewart Halsted, the celebrated doctor who performed the first-
ever surgery for pancreatic cancer. Thanks to this superb training, Peterson
took only a few minutes to diagnose his new patient, Daniel Fowler, fresh
from Troy, New York. The usual diagnosis when a white man arrived in
Ancon Hospital was malaria—the illness that not even Dr. Gorgas had
conquered. But Fowler showed no sign of sweat or chills, and he had been
on the isthmus for just a short time, not long enough to have contracted
malaria and shown symptoms. Instead, he had jaundice and pain in his
stomach and back. These symptoms pointed Peterson to Fowler's pancreas.
Hopeless.

* * *

Daniel Fowler had been in bed for two days, ever since the dinner he barely
ate when he arrived. Jeffrey realized his uncle's problem might not be
seasickness. With the help of an ICC ambulance cart, Jeffrey brought Daniel
to Ancon Hospital and stayed with him just until he was settled on a ward.
Happy to delay talk of business matters, Jeffrey did not visit for a few days.
When he felt he could stall no longer, he took the train to the hospital. In

no hurry, he walked around the hospital grounds, looking for his former worker, Michael Thompson. He found him in the supply shed, cleaning tools, standing straight and looking fit. Michael smiled, revealing the gap in his teeth.

"Michael, how is that foot? So sorry about your toes. You know we miss you at the Cut."

"Beginning to heal, Mr. Fowler. They good to me here. Why you at Ancon?"

"My Uncle Dan came from Troy to visit. Your niece—Selina—has met him. He must have gotten sick on the steamer coming down because he's in pain. Dr. Peterson is looking after him. Since I'm here, I thought I'd find you to see how you're feeling. I heard you're doing carpentry work for the hospital."

"Thanks. Dr. Peterson a good man. He put me with Aaron Blake. He the hospital carpenter. Lost my toes but this work safer. Dr. Peterson, he help your uncle too. And if you want, I keep an eye on your uncle when I do my hammering on the wards."

"Good. I'm glad you're doing well. Guess I better move on, find my uncle."

As Jeffrey Fowler entered the long, narrow ward, he saw a row of three patients. Uncle Dan, at the end, looked the sickest. His color seemed off and his eyes drooped. Jeffrey nearly choked on the sickening smell of vomit, mixed with disinfectant. He said hello to his uncle, patted down his unruly white hair, and waited a few minutes until his open mouth and loud breathing suggested sleep.

After searching the wards, Jeffrey found Dr. Peterson, an unexceptional looking man with narrow shoulders, and more bare scalp than hair. The doctor reported that he would try some mixtures to provide relief for Mr. Fowler's pain but couldn't offer much hope. Jeffrey shuffled on his uneven legs, arranged his features into a distraught look, and said he would return in a couple of days.

He let five days pass before returning. On his way to the ward, he saw a nurse leave Daniel's bedside. Beautiful woman, he hadn't seen her before. He raised a finger, asking her to wait. She looked down at his uneven gait, not with distaste but with a nurse's assessment. He pointed to Daniel's bed.

"I'm Jeffrey Fowler, his uncle."

"Oh, pleased to meet you. I'm Nurse McGowan. I work closely with your uncle's doctor, Dr. Peterson. You want to know how Mr. Fowler is doing, right? I'm afraid he's gotten worse each day. So very sorry to tell you. He was nauseated and vomited yesterday, though he barely ate. He has pain in his stomach and back. And you should know that he goes in and out of lucidity. As for a diagnosis, well, you'd best talk to Dr. Peterson."

Jeffrey found a wooden, straight-backed chair in a corner and dragged it to Daniel's bed. The scraping of the chair echoed through the quiet ward. Daniel opened one eye and winced.

"Uncle, "I'm sorry I didn't get here earlier. The work on the Cut is at a crucial point. Couldn't get away."

"Want to talk. Want your help. David. David Ross. Know Ross?" Daniel whispered these phrases, hoarsely. This could not be good. Jeffrey struggled to place the name David Ross.

"Uncle, don't talk now. Rest. Let me talk. I'll tell you about the excavators we're using and how close I'm coming, it's the halfway point, to meeting the goal for the month. My men are good workers."

As Daniel panted, Jeffrey droned on, to fill the space and the time. He did not want Daniel to interrupt with more rasping talk. Jeffrey could read the clock on the wall from the chair. After ten minutes, long minutes, Daniel seemed quiet again. Jeffrey waited another five to make sure, then touched his uncle on the back and said goodbye to the sleeping man.

On the way out, Jeffrey found Dr. Peterson again. "I am afraid your uncle's symptoms point to a problem with his pancreas, which is serious. We're still trying to relieve his pain." Dr. Peterson stretched his mouth, indicating a hopeless case. "You can try to talk to him, but he goes in and out of lucidity." The doctor and nurse obviously conferred about Daniel's state.

Leaving the hospital, Jeffrey struggled to put his finger on the name David Ross. Ross? Before returning to the Cut, Jeffrey detoured to the nearby ICC offices. Clerks had shelved the annual reports in an open hallway, accessible to anyone who appeared to belong in the building. He had used those reports before to check details about excavation regulations. He checked a different section this time.

Yes, as he feared. Ross served as the ICC purchasing agent. Uncle Dan didn't realize that Ross worked in the ICC office in Washington. With half the ICC staff in Washington, even Stevens, struggling to cut through red tape for supplies, couldn't break the logjam over a beer. And as for bids, no whispered offer of an exchange—a job for a cousin or building supplies for a house back home—would have any impact. Jeffrey had never met Ross and never would. If Uncle Dan recovered, a long shot, he might ask for help again. This time Jeffrey wouldn't be tempted.

Robert Peterson

Thursday, November 15, 1906

N urse Maureen McGowan and Dr. Robert Peterson conferred. Sometimes they did so in Dr. Peterson's small office, as she sat on his lap in the plaid wing chair, behind a locked door. Then their conferring centered on how far Dr. Peterson's hand might wander. Sometimes they conferred in the hall, about the state of their patients. About Daniel Fowler. He would die shortly, Peterson said, with conviction. They agreed it might be time for morphine, or the new wonder drug, heroin.

"Mr. Fowler," Dr. Peterson said as he and Nurse McGowan approached. "You have a serious illness involving your pancreas. I believe it is best to be honest with our patients. I cannot cure you. We want to concentrate on relieving your pain. Nurse McGowan is going to inject you with an opiate."

Dr. Peterson saw his patient open his eyes, listen. "No cure?"

The doctor shook his head. Twice to make sure Daniel saw.

Almost immediately, Peterson sensed that Daniel's abdominal pain took second place to his fever. He began to sweat, and his flesh turned pale yellow. His eyes watered, looked up. Peterson had seen this before—patients who couldn't move their bodies, upon hearing their fate, swung their minds, swung to a new state, sought grace. Maureen walked to a cabinet and pulled cool compresses from a box lined with ice.

"Need to make amends. Amends," groaned Daniel Fowler. Peterson pushed himself to remain silent and to listen, no matter how uncomfortable he grew. Maureen mirrored his stance. After three weeks of courtship, they communicated through eyes. They listened together.

"Tell him. Jeffrey. Sorry. Bad to ask. Bad to rig. Bad bids. Bids. Got him in trouble. Shoulda been me."

As Nurse McGowan wiped the patient's forehead and white hair with the cool cloth, he continued to ramble in a whisper, mostly words of regret. After a few minutes of tormented babble, he stammered, "Erie." Dr. Peterson heard "eery." Daniel Fowler worried about ghosts? Then Daniel managed the four key words. "Sorry about Erie Canal." Peterson guessed that the thoughts of bid rigging lingering on the man's mind did not involve the Panama Canal.

While the nurse and doctor stood watch over Daniel Fowler's bed, they did not see Michael Thompson, who kept a watch of his own. Carrying lumber through the ward, quietly, with just a slightly awkward walk, Michael lingered twenty feet from the patient.

Michael Thompson

Monday, November 12, 1906, to Tuesday, November 13, 1906

T he shack in Paraiso, surrounded by dozens of similar shacks and machine shops built by the French years ago, resembled Michael Thompson's shack back in Barbados. Two rooms, a dirt floor, mud all around, stench. Fruit rotted between the shacks, and worse, people threw dead cats and dogs into the ditches. He could manage the cheap rent. The ICC provided free housing for colored laborers, single men, but if Michael wanted married housing, he needed to show a marriage certificate. He and Aletha had never bothered with a ceremony. No point. ICC housing sat on mud too.

Aletha and Michael's niece Selina kept the shack in good order, even though they dragged through their own chores after days working as maids for the families of engineers. Selina especially. She usually came home by train with Aletha around 7:00. The women had to stand in the open boxcar designated for colored workers. Sometimes Selina came home alone, even later in the evening, if the Fowlers asked her to stay.

About two weeks after the explosion that cost Michael three toes, he sat eating dinner, fretting that Selina was late again. Aletha had prepared fishcakes and corn. She always managed to buy food and a little bit of ice.

"Bitchy Miz Liza," Michael said. "She ask Selina to clean up dinner? To put that baby to bed? Since I come home from the hospital, Selina late a lot. You think she acting odd? Quiet?"

Michael welcomed this chance to talk to Aletha alone. He finished his fishcakes, spooned out more corn from the pan. He eyed Aletha's fishcake. She saw, smiled. "For me, after that accident, everything better. Good work with Aaron Blake teaching me carpentry. But Selina, she got no family besides us. We need to keep an eye out." Michael saw Aletha grimace. "I'm not talking about your wandering eye. I love that eye just like your good one." He took a breath. You think those people Selina work for bad? The missus, Miz Liza, she no good, right? But her man, Fowler, he got me to the hospital fast. He OK."

"Yah," Aletha said. She pushed half her fishcake aside. Michael grabbed it. "When we come to Panama, Selina all jolly. Laughing. Now, I don't know. On days when she see that good-looking meat peddler—Tom Gordon—she happy. She sweet on him. I hear from other maids I see in town. He a fine man. Other days, especially if she stay late at Fowlers', she sad."

Michael told Aletha that his dead brother would never forgive him if harm came to Selina. Aletha tilted her head, nodded. "Yes, you remind me every day." They shared a laugh, then heard Selina come up the path.

"How it going?" they said in unison.

"Miz Liza a terror. I scrub the floor ten times a day, even when it clean. She yells and slaps. She tells me to stay late the night when Mr. Jeffrey's uncle come. No extra pay."

The next night, Selina returned to the topic.

"Now Miz Liza dock me. She take away some of my regular pay. The train this morning stop for an hour when it run over a worker. She say I get there late. Not right."

"She slap you again?" asked Michael.

"Yes, sir. Shake me too."

Michael helped Aletha clean up, washing and drying as Selina put her head down on the table in exhaustion. He gave Aletha a knowing look and gesture. Aletha understood—later. The shack offered little privacy. After Selina went to sleep on her cot in the kitchen, Michael slipped out to the alley behind their row of shacks. Aletha followed. The air had cooled, easing the smell of the outhouse and the rotting fruit.

"Not right. Not right." He saw Aletha chew on her bottom lip. That meant trouble.

"Miz Liza, she the one that make Selina stay late. That just hard work. Don't bother me. But I don't like what I hear about Miz Liza's man, that Jeffrey Fowler. You know, looking too much. The maids talk to me about the meat peddler. And they talk about Fowler too. I should'a told you before, but I don't want you worrying. And I know Fowler good to you. I think Selina talk so much about Miz Liza to cover up what she not say about him." Aletha spoke quietly until she got to the "him."

Florence Dauchy, Aletha Thompson

1905 to Wednesday, November 14, 1906

H and labor and steam shovels may have dug the canal, but railroads paved the way. Hundreds of men who had built America's tracks and trains moved to Panama, seeking money and adventure. They learned about job opportunities from each other, they recommended each other, they followed each other. The Illinois Central Railroad in particular served as a training ground for canal officials. John Wallace, William Karner, David Ross, and many others polished their skills there.

The Chicago, Rock Island & Pacific Railroad served as another training ground. William Bierd, inventor of the celebrated track shifter, had worked there, along with an engineer named Walter Dauchy who moved to Panama to become a division engineer. Dauchy hailed from Troy, New York, and attended Rensselaer Polytechnic. In between stints with various railroads, he and his wife Florence went back to their hometown. Though Walter Dauchy was fifteen years older than Jeffrey Fowler, the men had mingled in the same professional engineering circles.

Shortly after Selina Thompson went to work for the Fowlers, Selina's aunt Aletha went to keep house for Walter and Florence Dauchy, in the same town of Empire. Florence met Liza from time to time at the ICC Commissary or saw her at an afternoon tea hosted by division engineers' wives, but they rarely talked. Tom Gordon, the local peddler, did the talking for two households. Tom sold his wares every day on the Fowlers' street, then moved on to the Dauchys' street. He provided meat and produce, as well as the best scuttlebutt in the neighborhood. The day he met Selina he learned that her aunt Aletha needed work. He passed that news on to Florence's maid, who planned to leave to set up a dressmaking business. The next day, Florence Dauchy hired Aletha Thompson, unfazed by the young woman's wandering eye.

Florence Dauchy had servants when she lived in Troy—a housemaid, a laundry girl, and a cook. She prided herself on managing them well and carried those skills to Panama. Knowing that her new maid had never worked outside of Barbados before, Florence offered guidance. Aletha was to cook and clean. She was to buy meat from Tom Gordon and milk from a local dairy farmer. She was to scrub and hang out laundry every Tuesday and iron every Wednesday. She was to serve dinner from her employers' left. The young woman learned quickly. Florence could soon turn back to her luncheons and charitable events.

With Aletha trained in the ways of the Dauchy household, Florence paid scant attention to her maid in the evenings. Always talkative, Florence kept up her dinner table banter.

"Aletha tells me Daniel Fowler has been visiting his nephew but took sick. Came from Troy just to see him. She heard it from her niece, the one who works for Jeffrey and Liza Fowler down the road." Florence helped herself to a second portion of pork roast, in no hurry to finish dinner.

Walter, silent and sated, slumped in his chair, tired after a day of supervising laborers.

"Walter, can you listen? What do you think? Do those rumormongers back home have it right? That big contract Daniel got? Did Jeffrey have anything to do with it?"

"Ah, the Erie Canal, the Erie, again," sighed Walter. "So many opportunities for corruption. Jeffrey should have put his civil engineering to better use at a railroad. Instead, he wanted to stay near home and got into trouble. We're not supposed to know about the shenanigans."

"Shenanigans? Is that another way of saying bid rigging? I wonder if that floozy wife of his knows. She's dumb enough not to know, but in a way she's clever too. She does put on airs, to get ahead with what passes for society here. She tries to socialize with the Stevens and the Bierds. They're having none of it. In Troy she would be lucky to be taking in our laundry. But I see men looking at her. She's a beauty, I can't deny that."

"Nor can I," Walter said, chuckling.

Aletha brought the plates back to the kitchen, clearing from the right, walking quietly.

* * *

An hour later, Aletha Thompson returned to Paraiso, eating a late dinner of her own with Michael and Selina. "Miz Florence on a rant tonight," Aletha said. "Learn two things. Miz Liza from a poor family. She putting on airs. And her man, he in trouble at something called Erie." Aletha continued, providing all the details she knew.

Godfrey Moody, John Cunningham

Thursday, November 15, 1906

Journalists recorded the dramatic dangers that canal workers faced—mudslides, explosions, train wrecks. They did not record the smaller dangers that plagued every worker, every day—sodden clothes. Laborers spent their evenings washing mud off their one or two sets of clothing, hoping their shirts and pants would dry, then putting on damp clothes in the morning. Godfrey Moody, the skin near his ear still bandaged from a minor crane accident, struggled to get into his clammy garments—the khaki pants and blue shirt laborers wore regardless of the weather.

As Godfrey pulled on his damp pants, his roommate, the peddler Tom Gordon, grinned. "Hey, you play cards in Colón every Wednesday, right?"

"Mostly," Godfrey said. "Why?"

"Going tonight?"

"What in it for me?"

"I'll lend you clothes when you go to the saloon. My good trousers and shirt. Even damp, they're nicer than yours. And the girls like 'em."

"You mean the clothes you swagger around in?

"Need to look good for the ladies who buy my meat." Tom grinned. "They'll fit you."

"Deal, if you throw in your straw hat too. To take the girls' eyes off my bandage."

"Deal. Just don't come back 'til eleven."

The roommates joshed each other and helped each other. They both had grown up in Black Rock in St. Michael Parish, Barbados, and they came in on the same steamer. Tom paid for his passage, to join a cousin in Panama who had set up a little meat and produce business. Most of the fruit in Panama was sold by West Indian women, peddling what they could carry in baskets. Tom and his cousin had a bigger operation, using carts and horses. They picked up meat and produce from the new warehouse that had refrigeration and then made the rounds to sell to families. Unlike Tom, Godfrey had his passage paid because he had an ICC contract to work at the Gatun dam site, boring holes. He could have had free ICC housing—a canvas cot that folded against a shed wall. Instead, he rented a shack with Tom in Silver City.

Godfrey had no need to ask Tom why he wanted the shack that evening. Godfrey knew about Selina, the comely maid on Tom's route. The one who would say she had to stay late at her job to watch a baby. Ha.

Later that morning, Godfrey stood over a drill, trying to bore a hole big enough for six sticks of dynamite. His daily routine had returned to normal, a week after he surprised himself by speaking up at a labor meeting. Made him feel good. His crew leader, Spaniard Alejandro Calvo, had patted him on the back the day after the meeting. Calvo had smiled, his lips parting over his gold tooth. Godfrey wondered if Calvo planned to spout off more about internationalism.

The foreman, John Cunningham, blew a whistle for the ten o'clock break. His whistle sounded different, slower than usual. Cunningham's three crew leaders and twenty-one laborers trudged to the water van.

Godfrey didn't get far. "Hey," Cunningham said. He cleared his throat, looked down. "Let's talk." The foreman motioned to the far end of the site.

"Your timecard. It's wrong. You wrote down 8:00. But you didn't show up here until 8:15. Same problem, three days in a row." Cunningham spoke nervously, barely above the roar of machinery. Godfrey looked over at Alejandro Calvo, sitting still off to the side at the water van. Calvo's eyes were set ahead, not on his tin cup.

274

"Mr. Cunningham, you know, those trains don't run on time. I try. Can't help it if the train late."

"Three days in a row, Godfrey. Three days. That's it. You can't work here any longer. Get your gear and go home."

Foremen dismissed men every day, for one reason or another. Godfrey knew that the timecard was not the problem. Other men had bigger timecard lapses. Should he argue? When this happened in Barbados, and it did many times, he would slink off. But here? He needed his wages, for himself, and even more, he needed to keep sending money home to Black Rock. Every week he mailed a money order to his mother, as did most of his friends, especially the single men. Sometimes he chuckled to himself, imagining half of the residents of Barbados waiting for money orders to arrive.

As Godfrey worried over what to say, Cunningham tapped his shoulder and walked him farther from the work site, beyond the drilling. Lowering his voice to barely a whisper, Cunningham added, "You know that guy with the blond hair and the big birthmark on his cheek? At the small bakery in Colón. He's looking for workers. Pay's lousy, but you can give that a try. I have some advice for you. No more late-night meetings, ya know. Stay away from that crowd."

Godfrey saw Alejandro Calvo, still off to the side, sipping water and watching. He would figure out what was going on. When Calvo lowered his head, Godfrey couldn't tell if it was in sympathy, guilt, or anger.

* * *

That morning John Cunningham had focused his attention on his damp shirt. He had more changes of clothing than the men in his work detail, but still not enough. Today it was easier to fuss about the humidity than about the orders that had arrived the night before. They had not come from Chief Engineer John Stevens. They came from Police Chief Shanton, a man Cunningham knew only by reputation, in an envelope marked confidential. Ripping open the envelope, Cunningham had feared the contents would cite his own transgressions. Did Shanton know that he gambled in the Zone as well as out of the Zone? No, nothing about his gambling habit. "Upon receipt of this order, dismiss laborer Godfrey Moody, guilty of inciting labor activism at a secret meeting on November 5th. Do not refer to this offense. Find a separate justification. Confirm when done. Sincerely, George Shanton, Chief of Police, Canal Zone."

John Cunningham hated the timecard business. West Indians filled the cards in for each other, scribbled indecipherable times, forgot to make any notation at all. Cunningham didn't care what Godfrey's explanation might be. The man would lose his job over a minor timecard infraction. The crew would be down a fine worker.

Robert Peterson

Saturday, November 17, 1906

"Doctor, sir, have a minute?" Robert Peterson, writing reports in his hospital office, saw Michael Thompson approach.

"Certainly, Michael. I see you're adjusting. Hardly any limp. Have the stumps healed?"

"Yes, fine."

"And what about the new job?"

"Aaron Blake, he fine too. Teaches me carpentry. He give me a break so I can see you." Michael paused. Stretched his lips over the gap in his teeth. "I need to talk about Mr. Jeffrey Fowler, the man who limps worse 'n me. The nephew of the sick man in the ward."

"I've told Mr. Fowler that his uncle will probably die any time now. Do you know him?"

"No, but my niece Selina, she a maid for Mr. Fowler and his wife, Miz Liza. Mr. Fowler—he my boss when I lose my toes. The two of them," Michael looked down, paused, "they bad people. Miz Liza slap my niece. Dock her pay. Mr. Fowler, he do worse. I need to watch over my niece. Don't know who else to go to." Michael gnawed on his bottom lip. "You and the nurse, you be kind to me."

Robert Peterson had heard stories like this before. Some, he thought, seemed exaggerated. But he and Maureen had spent a lot of time with Michael, helping him. Maureen had been right in her assessment of

277

his abilities. Aaron Blake had reported that Michael took his new job seriously, learning quickly. Above all, Michael's lamentations summoned forth in Peterson his family heritage of extending help, whether it was in Philadelphia or Panama.

Michael continued to talk, recounting Liza Fowler's misdeeds. Peterson remarked, "oh my," several times. Michael took those interjections as an invitation to go further, picking up speed with each of the tales—Jeffrey Fowler's alarming interest in Selina, his weekly trips to The Luna, Miz Liza's weekly trips to a hotel. And rumors from his wife's employer of something Michael admitted he didn't understand called bid rigging. Peterson sighed. None of these transgressions surprised him, not even bid rigging. He had heard Daniel Fowler mumble the same words two days earlier.

"Michael, you are right to tell me about the Fowlers, and to do what you can to protect your niece. I can help. For now, leave this to me."

"I pay you back," Michael said. "Carpentry work? Shelves?"

"No need for payment. I will do my best for your niece."

Shortly after Michael left, Daniel Fowler took his last breath. Dr. Peterson sent a messenger to the Cut, with a note for Jeffrey Fowler. Then Peterson pulled on his boots and ducked out for a quick visit to Walter Dauchy at his job site. When Peterson returned, he entered the first-floor ward to check on his patients. He saw Jeffrey Fowler speaking with an orderly, heard something about an undertaker's services.

"Let's talk here," Peterson said, ushering Jeffrey into an office. Jeffrey stood a few feet away, in a hurry to leave. Peterson pointed to a chair and waited until his guest sat. "Mr. Fowler, I am sorry about your uncle. Like many dying men, he seemed to have a troubled soul. He did not die in peace. When I offered to fetch a clergyman, he shook his head. Nurse McGowan and I did what little we could to relieve his suffering. Do you have any idea what he said to us when the fever wracked his body, and he knew the end was near?"

Jeffrey Fowler tensed. His shoulders moved forward and met his ears. "No."

"I struggled to understand him. He talked about making a mistake, dragging you into it, and feeling bad about that. Something about a canal too. Hard to make sense of his mutterings at first. Then I talked to Michael Thompson. You remember Michael. He's the laborer who worked for you and lost some toes. He's doing fine now, helping our carpenter. Well, you may know his wife—I think she's his wife—Aletha Thompson. Works for the Dauchys. When she's there, she hears a lot. Then she passes it along to Michael. When Michael and I started talking, I could fill in the missing links. And more missing links after I visited Walter Dauchy earlier today. I know what happened. I know that you connived with your uncle to rig the bids for improvements in the Erie. And I know that you don't want anyone to know that, maybe including your wife."

Jeffrey Fowler's face contorted.

"I am not here to ruin your life, Mr. Fowler. I have a different goal. Michael tells me that his niece, Selina, works for your family. I suppose your wife might have limited experiences in managing servants." Peterson fiddled with the thin hair on his scalp. He was ashamed he had said this, with all it implied, but he continued. "Selina should have a good life here, working a normal day and being treated with dignity." Peterson repeated, "dignity," drawing it out.

Jeffrey Fowler put one hand over half his mouth.

"Liza tries. She does. She just doesn't always know the right way. And I, I'll be more aware of, of all this."

"Do you think you can persuade your wife to change? To treat Selina like a good worker who has a life of her own? And if Selina wants to leave, to offer a good reference? If so, then the story about the Erie—and everything else—will stay between us, and of course, Michael. And I suppose Walter and Florence Dauchy too. So far, they have kept the story about the Erie to themselves. According to Aletha and to what the Dauchys said, they believe it to be a rumor, and probably true, but not a fact. They are people of integrity." As Peterson said that last word slowly, he stared at Jeffrey Peterson, who looked away.

The men came to a prompt agreement, unspoken, with merely a nod. Peterson had one more card up his sleeve. Michael had told him that

Selina knew about Jeffrey Fowler's visits to Emily Byrne. And Michael had reported that Selina knew about Edgar Winston—the junior diplomat who spent Wednesday afternoons in a hotel room with Liza Fowler. Probably half the Canal Zone knew, though not cuckolded Jeffrey Fowler. But Peterson thought he had said enough. He could move on, to gather the courage he needed to talk to Maureen at the reception in a few hours, to tell her he could never father children. This would be a day of secrets revealed.

Maureen McGowan

Saturday, November 17, 1906

L a Boca, close to both Ancon and Panama City, was the site of the well-stocked main commissary. Before long, it would compare favorably to department stores in American cities. But ICC officials had just shifted the commissary from the auspices of the Panamanian Railroad to the auspices of the ICC. New managers needed to assess how much merchandise they could squeeze into the squat two-story, white building in La Boca, and how much they should spread across the Zone. A particularly imaginative manager decided to segment off shoes into another two-story white building, this one in Cristobal, with a lovely gallery on the second floor.

Ordinarily, the satellite location across the isthmus would annoy nurse Maureen McGowan, but not this day. She planned to accompany Dr. Robert Peterson to an evening reception honoring the President, and had decided her best shoes, the ones she wore to dine at the International, looked too worn for dancing on the pier. She had saved for a new pair. The reception would take place in Cristobal, the same town as the location of the commissary now dedicated to shoes.

Maureen donned her best frock, the dress with rose-colored flowers. She would take the train to Cristobal, make her purchase, and then wait for Robert who would meet her at a tea shop so they could walk together to the pier. Was Robert a good dancer? Would musicians play a Quadrille, waltz,

281

or maybe the newer two-step? Maureen smiled to herself as she thought about the coming evening, the first time the couple would be together at a festive event. She wondered if her suitor would use the occasion to declare his intentions. Her family and her set in Cleveland loved that phrase. "Has he declared his intentions?" they would ask if she decided to mention him in her letters.

By the standards of the railroad, the crash that afternoon was not terrible. During the year so far, thirty-two men had been killed in train accidents, including a laborer, cut in half, and two others, crushed. When Maureen's train raced through the part of the route near the Cut, where the excavations continued, a heavy crane fell on the tracks. The train engineer had been going fast, then slow, trying to stay well behind of President's train. The engineer saw the crane fall. He applied the brakes. The derailment may have resulted when the brakes, asked to do what they couldn't, failed, or maybe from the force of contact with the crane. Metal hurled across cars. One piece went through Maureen's rose-colored dress, then through her chest. Her old shoes remained on her feet.

Maurice Latta

After lunch near the reservoir, I reproached myself. Why had I confided in Fred? Looking back, with self-awareness brought by time, I realize I had few friends in the White House and welcomed my budding friendship with Fred. Even more, I enjoyed a heady sense of being in on something, of belonging, of moving from the edge to the center. I had been part of the group in the Tivoli that eventful morning.

Grabbing my portfolio as I boarded the train, I remembered the telegram from Secretary Taft that I had intended to give the President. I walked to the first car and handed it to him. He read it, maybe twice, and pushed it back to me for safekeeping.

An hour later, we visited the site where the Gatun Dam would be built to control the Chagres River. We heard more lectures on technology. TR seemed fascinated with details about borings and excavations. Unsatisfied with observing the site from below, he charged up the hill. Our President had sustained a flesh wound and fended off an assassin six hours earlier, but the effort didn't appear to affect him. With a grin, he took in the future shape of the dam that would stretch a mile across the valley of the Chagres.

Resuming our train ride, we stopped repeatedly so the President could inspect the towns and houses of employees, White and Negro, married and unmarried. He critiqued what he saw, this time grousing about the furniture. Next, we went to Cristobal, where we gawked at a bakery turning out 24,000 loaves a day and toured a cold-storage plant. I wondered if that plant would ease the yam fuss.

One of our last stops was a humdinger, according to Larry, who reported back in detail—I waited behind with the reporters. Teddy mounted a bay outfitted with a hand-made Mexican saddle and galloped with Shanton and Stevens and others through the streets of Colón. Crowds shouted approval. The riders raced down muddy Front Street, then across muddy Fifth Street, down the muddy saloon district known as Bottle Alley, along muddy Beach Road, and finally past beautiful Garfield House with its two floors of porches and ocean view. For Shanton and TR, the outing evoked their months as Rough Riders. As we stood waiting, Fred snickered that the men played soldier. But even during the frivolous ride, the President kept his eyes on details, commenting on the sewers, curbing, and lights, improved just for him.

In the evening, William Bierd, the railroad manager who invented the track-shifter, hosted our entourage for dinner at his home on the beach in Cristobel. Stevens and Shonts and their wives attended, along with me and Dr. Rixey, who whispered that Frank Tyree would make a full recovery. Jimmy and Larry dined nearby, keeping an eye on their charge. President Amador and Mrs. Amador, a couple I had not seen in two days, joined us for dinner. They kept to themselves, surrounded by aides and two of Shanton's police officers. Maria Amador sat quietly on the dais. Her eyes scanned the crowd, but she never turned her head for conversation.

Following dinner, we moved on to a reception hosted in a huge ICC structure at the largest wharf in Cristobel. Eight hundred people attended, mostly exuberant canal workers who had come to see their leader on his last night on the isthmus. We heard a band tune up for dancing, and marveled at beautiful decorations, rows of flags, and palms artistically arranged on the dock. Lanterns, glowing yellow and orange, illuminated the ships in the harbor, and magnificent fireworks added more color.

Mr. de Lisser had not been included in the dinner at Bierd's house, but he was invited to the reception at Mr. Bishop's request. I saw the journalist standing alone near the wharf, moping, looking at me. I interpreted his expression as discomfort in that setting. I approached, starting a conversation about what an amazing few days we had shared.

"M, Mr. Latta," he stuttered. I had never heard this elegant man stutter before. "You know I am here to report for the *Gleaner*. That is the major English-language newspaper in Jamaica. I am the Editor in Chief, and the only staff member qualified for this sort of reporting position. I feel a responsibility to write about events here. They are of worldwide importance and of particular importance to Jamaicans. To be honest, I doubt I have the complete story of this week." He paused, his face taut. "Anything you can add to what I have seen?"

Oh, how I must have looked. I made a feeble effort to hide my distress. Maybe I could trust Mr. de Lisser as much as Fred, but I had been uneasy with what I had shared already, and I did not want to compound my mistake. Is that all that stopped me? I don't know.

"Mr. de Lisser, the week has been full of events. Most are public, and I am pleased that Mr. Bishop has included you and Frederick Palmer in all of them. As you realize, I have access to certain communications and circumstances that are confidential. I am careful not to share those confidences with anyone, not my friends, not my family. I hope you can understand." I paused as I tried to interpret his expression. I realized, then and now, that I sounded smug. I continued, ill-advisedly. "I am, you know, a man of honor."

After a few seconds of silence, de Lisser responded. "Of course." He walked away. I have not seen or heard from him since.

I was not a man of honor. I was a man who craved an inch of spotlight. And a man who related to one reporter differently than another.

During the dancing, I saw Mrs. R. hover near the Amadors and, for a minute, hold hands with Maria Amador. I stood against a nearby wall, not dancing. Mrs. R's eye caught mine. She walked in my direction and handed me an envelope, with a simple note. "Thank you, Edith Roosevelt." Whenever I wonder if I imagined pulling her out of the presidential bedroom to avoid an assassin's bullet, I go back to that note, which is now in my safe deposit box in Washington.

Fred arrived late to the reception, looking more out of place than ever in his informal clothing. He had been working on his article for *Collier's*. He sought me out and handed me a flute of champagne—the servers had an endless supply. "Well, old chap, we had quite a time together," he said, winking, patting me on the back. I suspect our paths will cross again, as long as I stay in Teddy's favor. And I promise to stay in your favor, too," he added with a smile.

Just then, the President spoke, complimenting the workers. "As I have looked at you and seen you work, seen what you have done and are doing, I have felt just exactly as I would feel to see the big men of our country carrying on a great war." He spoke extemporaneously. I knew he had no written speech. Standing amidst the lights and the flags and knowing that in my pocket I had a note from Mrs. R., I could understand the importance of the trip for him.

I recall one sad note from the reception. Dr. Gorgas reported that an Ancon Hospital nurse had been killed in a railroad accident that afternoon, near the Cut. Her train had been following our train.

At last, the festivities ended. I joined the President's entourage on the tender returning to the USS *Louisiana*. The ship departed Panama at 11:00, headed to Ponce, Puerto Rico. I relaxed on the trip back. When Larry Richey had no guard duty, he and I walked the deck and talked, and visited Frank Tyree in the ship's infirmary. Larry brimmed with energy. As a young man of twenty-one, who grew up speaking Italian, he had saved the President's life during one assassination attempt and maybe during a second. I, too, brimmed with energy, believing my raised arm on November 15th had saved TR and my dragging embrace on November 17th had saved Mrs. R. Surely Larry realized the first lady had been in little danger, but he never made me feel anything other than brave. We talked and praised each other, knowing we could not share our experiences beyond our little circle.

But Larry did not share everything with me. Rumors circulated aboard that Jimmy Sloan had hidden two prisoners in the brig below decks. The marines who usually guarded the brig were told to leave guard duty to Larry and Jimmy. A talkative marine who saw the prisoners surprised me when he described one as very tall with light hair, and the other as a bandaged foreigner. The marines had no idea of the identity of the prisoners, nor would they.

Clara and the boys met me at the Navy Yard. I arrived with no gifts. I had noticed the women of Panama cooling themselves with ivory fans and had intended to buy one for Clara. Alas, no time. I promised her I would send for one, and I promised the boys I would buy them models of the Bucyrus steam shovel.

The next day I met with Mr. Loeb to go over my impressions of the trip. He filled me in on Brownsville. On the return voyage, Mr. Loeb thought TR must have brooded over Taft's implied plan to take matters into his own hands by rescinding the order to dismiss without honor the Negro soldiers. Then I remembered. Taft indeed made a threat in the telegram I had handed the President on our last day in the Zone. Focused only on danger to the President, I failed to realize, until Mr. Loeb's rendition, that Taft's message could be seen by TR as a threat to his presidency, as treachery. When TR didn't respond to Taft, using silence as a tool, Taft evidently thought better of his threatened assumption of power and never did rescind the nasty dismissal order. It went into effect during our return trip.

For four days on the isthmus, I stood at the center of events, not at the edge as usual, though I returned to that edge the minute we made landfall. I had tried to highlight my time in the center by sharing, ill-advisedly. If Fred had not been Fred, I would have been undone. I now understand that the center carries problems of its own, including the need for discretion and the inability, or lack of will, to cure injustice. And even those of us at the center didn't know the whereabouts of Arturo Agresto and a man with the born name of Arthur Sitwell.

Back in Washington with Clara, I managed to keep working for TR, then Taft, Wilson, Harding, Coolidge, Hoover, FDR, and now Harry. I would remain in the background, comfortably in the background. But I knew I could rise to the occasion, if needed.

Ernesta Agresti

E rnesta Agresti heard slow footsteps. She had a visitor on Sunday, on Monday, and now here was a new visitor, climbing the stairs to the third floor at 85 Cianci Street in Paterson. This time it was Stefano Grandi, carrying the usual four newspapers—the *Sun*, the *New York Herald*, the *New York Tribune*, and the *New York Times*.

Shaking his head, Grandi said, "still nothing Ernesta. *Ancora niente.*" He placed the papers on the table, knowing that after he left Ernesta would try her best to read them, just to be sure.

"No stories, no telegram? How could he do this to me? You think he's dead? Did he run away? He is no coward. I am certain."

"But you are OK, right? I mean with money. Rent? Food?"

Yes, she might be a widow, but she was not *stupido*.

"Stefano, I visited Paterson Savings and Paterson National," she answered with half-hidden pride. "Both. National was better. My money is safe there. $10,000 should last us ten years. And if dat man honors his promise, $20,000 more is coming, whatever happened in Panama." Stefano bobbed his head up and down, signaling appreciation. He might be a loudmouth, he might have led Alberto to disaster, but Stefano cared, he paid attention.

On Friday, December 7th, an unsigned letter arrived for Ernesta. It told her to meet a representative from a Swiss bank, in Manhattan, the next Monday. She did so, leaving her children with a neighbor. With a puzzled glance at her, but no hesitation, the bank representative handed over the Colombian's second installment. Ernesta marched right to the Paterson National Bank to add to her account. *Alleluia*, the Colombian was a man of honor.

On Tuesday, December 11th, another letter arrived, official-looking, signed by Attorney General Charles Bonaparte. Ernesta later learned that he was a great-nephew of Napoleon. "This letter is to inform you that your husband, Alberto Agresti, has been imprisoned for life. The location will be unknown to you, and you may not communicate with him. He is in good health, recovering from wounds after proper medical care. If you divulge this information to anyone, agents will deport you and your family."

Alberto, Ernesta knew, could have been shot. Or hanged after a trial. His children might be labeled as the tainted fruit of an assassin. His neighbors might be rounded up and brutalized. Of all the possibilities Ernesta had imagined over the last month, permanent exile had never occurred to her. It would take her time to decide if this outcome was better or worse than what she had feared. No, it would take her forever.

By Frederick Palmer

December 8, 1906, Collier's Magazine

"Hereafter I shall recommend to anyone who wishes to see all America, and truly to get its best spirit in a great endeavor, to go to the Zone. This strip of tropical territory forty miles long and ten miles broad is like a microscopic slide, revealing the blood corpuscles of our national life. North and South and East and West work together. On the same mosquito-screened veranda of Washington pine put up by a New York carpenter, perhaps, you heard the New England twang, the full vowels of the Pacific Coast, the drawl of Missouri, and the soft accents of the South.... There are times when every citizen has differences with Theodore Roosevelt. But when you see him at close range for days in the pouring rain on the battle line, you cannot help being for him. He impressed the Panamanians, who are of an alien way of thinking, as well as his own people. For he understood them as he understood the engineers thinking only of excavation, the doctors thinking only of sanitation, and all the different elements of effort working each in its own groove and overlooking the importance of the others. He brought them together... [That] Congress will leave him to go on with the work with full authority...was the hope of every one of the group, weary and wet, who had followed the bespattered duck suit, after he had gone aboard the Louisiana,

290

whose lights were soon vanishing across the roadstead around which she and her sister battleships draw the circle of defense of the little sister republic and the great work which is one with the honor of the nation."

By Anthony Thompson

Tuesday, July 2, 1963

Dear contest sponsors,

I wish my granddad, Michael Thompson, could write this himself, but he left us for heaven a few months ago, just after we learned about your essay contest for elderly canal workers. He offered to dictate his memories, while he grew weaker and weaker. He died at age seventy-eight, just missing the 50th anniversary of the opening of the canal. He wanted to be part of the festivities since he felt pride at what he and others built.

I didn't need him to dictate because I remembered his stories. He talked about the canal to me, through that funny gap in his teeth, ever since I can remember. I am not talented enough to win the $50 prize you are offering, but I want to write this for my children and their children, not just for the contest money. Thanks to what my granddad accomplished, I received a fine education, even went to college here, and became a teacher. I owe it to him to offer his story for your records.

Michael Thompson grew up on a plantation in Barbados, in Christchurch parish. His father had worked on the Knox family plantation in the sugar fields and mills, as had all his kin going back many generations to the time they were brought over on slave ships from West Africa, probably around 1700. Granddad, too, could find sugar field and millwork, nothing else. On the edge of the Knox plantation, his family and other families lived in wooden shacks, called chattel houses, built on stakes to keep out flood waters and to allow people to move their house from place to place to follow the work or to find drier land. No paved roads led to the shacks, just muddy paths. No beds, just hammocks. No bathrooms or outhouses, just latrine pits. Mr. Knox expected Granddad to do what today we call unskilled labor, but the Knoxes rented their workers little plots of land around the big house. Granddad and grandma could plant vegetables there.

My grandma was named Aletha. Her wandering eye embarrassed her, made her shy, but she was more competent than people realized. Michael and Aletha never married. Few couples married during that time in Barbados. Michael made twenty cents a day, and Aletha grew bananas, limes, and coconuts, and raised some small farm animals.

The family got by until about 1900, when the market for sugar from Barbados dried up. The old-fashioned planters relied on inefficient methods instead of newer technologies. They used windmills to grind cane and open pans to crystallize sugar. I teach about the planters' inertia today, to give my students a sense of the necessity for technological progress. Then the tariff rules changed. Sugar from Barbados got expensive to buy. The final straw was a few years of floods, followed by droughts, followed by floods. Planters declared bankruptcy, including the Knox family. Granddad heard they needed to sell their porcelain and some of their furniture, just to have a chance to keep their grand manor house. They didn't need workers every day, maybe only two or three days a week. Wages fell to ten cents a day. When the workers struggled to find food, they got sicker and sicker. The parish health inspectors didn't do much to help. Michael and Aletha had two children before they immigrated to Panama. One died at birth, and the other died of typhoid early on. Granddad said my dad, Victor, was a miracle. He was born in 1907. Michael's older brother and that brother's wife died in 1904 in Barbados, leaving their daughter Selina with my grandparents.

All the young men struggled. Around 1903 they heard about the call for workers on the Panama Canal. A few men from the parish who went there returned to Barbados, saying that if they stayed in Panama Yellow Fever or malaria would kill them. Two years later, the reports improved. The workers who returned for a visit said disease had ebbed, and they flashed around the money they had earned. To granddad and his buddies, signing up for canal work seemed like the only option. Emigrating would be an adventure. Grandma fretted about granddad's plans, but she didn't have a better idea. He promised he would send for her and his niece Selina after he settled in.

One day he saw a notice in the *Jamaican Gleaner*. Granddad could read, unlike many of his mates. He saved the notice, and we found it when we went through his bureau last month. It was dated January 10, 1905. The ICC, that's the Isthmus Canal Commission, put out a call for 500 laborers. They would work eight hours a day, for ten cents an hour, and be offered return passage after 500 days, free medical care, free quarters for themselves and families, and board for thirty cents a day. This seemed like a fortune.

Granddad and his friends had never left their parish. Wearing the only clothes they owned—field hand clothes—they walked to the recruitment office in Bridgetown. As they got closer, for the first time, they saw sections where white people lived, houses with hibiscus hanging over the walls, giant palms, and bungalows with lovely verandas. Until then, they had seen grand plantation homes but never entire sections for whites.

The young men stood in line for three hours at the recruitment office in Trafalgar Square, the same Trafalgar Square that you can see there today. Then it was just a little park. Granddad knew that recruiting agents had already selected hundreds of workers the previous week, and he saw that the long line at the office snaked around the block. Men he recognized came out of the office shaking their heads, turned away. Granddad was the right age at twenty-two, strong, and healthy. Finally, the agent called in the next group in line. A doctor pulled on Granddad's eyelids, made him pull down his pants, and pressed on him in ways that seemed wrong. Most frightening of all, the doctor vaccinated him against smallpox. Michael thought the needle would kill him.

At the end of the exam, one of the men in charge handed Granddad a contract. He could read enough to know that the terms, shockingly, followed exactly what the newspaper advertisement had promised. The same man who handed him the contract told him to pay attention to the contract number at the top and to report back to the port in two weeks, when he would board the Royal Mail Steam Packet *Solent* for passage to Panama. Michael felt like he had won the Barbadian lottery.

Grandad was one of thousands of Barbadians who went to work in Panama. They say that forty percent of the male workforce emigrated—19,900 laborers. They built that canal. Not everyone realizes that they also changed their native country. I read that in one year alone, in 1907, the Barbadian laborers sent back to their countrymen and women $270,000 in money orders, $50,000 folded into letters, and $25,000 by check or via traveling friends. Barbados would never be the same.

Granddad experienced many successes and failures in the next decades. I can't write about every story he told me because I must honor the length limit for this contest, but I will write about one event I want my family to remember.

The ICC officials gave Grandad a pick and a shovel and sent him to a work site at the Culebra Cut. For two weeks, he just dug and dug. Next, they assigned him to a work crew that handled explosives. He dug holes, then another man loaded sticks of dynamite into those holes. Later I learned that those sticks were made by DuPont. Then Granddad covered the holes with dirt. He didn't understand—even though he was smarter than the white bosses realized—how careful he had to be. The second morning on this job, his shovel struck a cap of the unexploded dynamite charge. He lost three toes on his right foot.

That also changed his future. His gang loaded him into a boxcar they used daily to transport wounded workers to the Ancon Hospital. Granddad went to the ward for West Indians. The doctors and nurses took good care of him and liked him. About that time, the hospital carpenter, a Jamaican named Aaron Blake, needed an assistant. Dr. Peterson, to whom we owe a great deal, doubted that his patient, with one useful foot, could go back to Culebra. By chance, Dr. Peterson, who often helped to recruit hospital staff, knew of the carpenter's needs. The doctor asked grandad if he wanted to stay in the hospital to assist Mr. Blake. The job paid the same as the work crew, but with better conditions.

The explosion changed the Thompson family history. Working in the hospital, grandad learned carpentry, and he also learned the ways of the Americans. He never returned to Bridgetown. We all, my family, my children, we are all Panamanians.

I hope this essay meets your expectations.

Sincerely, Anthony Thompson

Historical Note

As is typical of historical fiction, I based my story on research, then added invented material. Theodore Roosevelt did visit the Panama Canal on the dates recorded in the novel and he was the first president to visit another country while in office. His itinerary on the isthmus, from Colón to Panama City, and back to Colón, is accurate. The assassination plots run the gamut from likely to imagined. A rumor did circulate in 1903 about an assassination plot in Lincoln, Illinois, but details remain unknown. I imagined what might have happened. Chilean Jerome Kehl did in fact threaten the President. I imagined Arthur Sitwell and his plans, as well as Alberto Agresti and his plans, doing so in the context of the history of anarchism.

Although all dialogue and the letters to and from Theodore Roosevelt regarding Elliott Marsh are fictional, a number of documents I quote are part of the historic record. These documents include John Stevens's offensive letter to Theodore Shonts, the *New York Times* quote describing Maurice Latta's role, the refrain of laborers on the steamer *Alliance*, Roosevelt's letter to his son Kermit, Friedrich Engels' view of the health of cutlery grinders, Felix Ehrman's dismissive report on casualties resulting from Colombia's bombardment, the *San Francisco Call's* report on the Chinese Exclusion Laws, Roosevelt's speech in the central plaza, and Fredrick Palmer's article in *Colliers's*.

Most of the officials I name are real people, including Maurice Latta and the three Secret Service agents, but the information available on even some of these historic characters is slim. The two officials not based on actual people are John Connell and Edgar Winston.

The unskilled and skilled laborers who built the canal left minimal written records of their experiences, so I imagined those characters, except for labor activist J.C. Virden. As I created their stories, I have stayed close to the historical record—municipalities functioned as gold or silver towns, laborers from Spain and Greece had a liminal status, workers on the canal experienced constant danger, trains crashed, many of the White women who came to the canal managed servants for the first time, women of color often worked in abusive situations. I invented Michael Thompson's grandson's essay, basing it on similar essays in the historical record.

Journalists Frederick Palmer and Herbert de Lisser are real people who deserve themselves to be topics of books. Wong Kong Yee is most likely the name of the victim of the Colombian battleship shelling in 1903, though this is hard to confirm. I imagined his son, Shing Wong. Gilbert & Bennett, Illinois Central, and Bucyrus all existed as businesses. I imagined Northern Vermont Lumber and Troy Building Supply.

Sally and Sean Miller are fictional, but Katy and Elliott Marsh are based on actual people of different names. In short, Theodore Roosevelt's brother, Elliott Bulloch Roosevelt, did have a child with a woman who worked as a maid in his home and a lawyer for that woman did request funds from TR. The Roosevelt family agreed to pay her an unknown sum, perhaps $10,000, but it is not clear that the sum made it into her hands. According to the historical record, a few years later she wanted to request additional funds, or perhaps the original sum, when Elliott Bulloch Roosevelt died in 1894. She never did so. What is clear is that the Roosevelt family wanted to silence the maid, and that she wanted recompense and money to sustain herself and her child. I have not used the names of the maid and her son because I think their stories are their own to tell and because of contradictions that I cannot resolve in the historical record.

In two cases I made decisions about characters for the sake of clarity more than historical accuracy. Labor leader J.C. Virden worked alongside R.B. Elliott, who may have been more active. But Elliott's name was the same as other characters, so I singled out Virden for attention. James Amos was the name of Theodore Roosevelt's valet, and probably would have been called James, but I called him Amos to avoid confusion with James Sloan.

Similarly, I referred to Maria Roda, a historic character, as Roda, to avoid confusion with Maria Amador.

The ICC built the grand Tivoli Hotel, which stood on Ancon Hill until 1971. I invented the Gomez House, the Linton Hotel, and Mrs. Hunter's Boarding House.

TR did travel on the impressive USS *Louisiana*. I used historical records to guess at accurate names for steamers and other ships.

I dug deeply into the history of the Panama Canal, the history of anarchism, and plots against presidents. Hundreds of scholars, government officials, journalists, and participants have written on these topics. The superb references I consulted are too numerous to list here. They include books, journal articles, and newspaper articles as well as government websites. I am indebted to these authors.

Acknowledgements

My family has helped at every stage. My husband Mark, a historian of the period, let me vent about contradictory accounts and offered countless suggestions. My brother, Robert Parker, served as an extraordinarily astute reader and constant supporter. My sister, Carol McConnell, helped repeatedly with research, proofing, and technological issues. My children, Aaron Wasserman and Danielle Blass, have assisted in too many ways to list.

Verena Rose, Shawn Reilly Simmons, and Harriette Sackler—the powers behind Level Best Books—continue to inspire me with their energy, entrepreneurship, wisdom, and creativity.

About the Author

Marlie Parker Wasserman is the author of *The Murderess Must Die*, a novel based on the life of the first woman in the world executed in the electric chair. Marlie lives with her husband in Chapel Hill, North Carolina, and continues to write historical crime fiction.

SOCIAL MEDIA HANDLES:
  Twitter: @MarlieWasserman
  Facebook: Marlie Wasserman
  Instagram: marliepwasserman

AUTHOR WEBSITE:
  marliewasserman.com

Also by Marlie Parker Wasserman

The Murderess Must Die

CPSIA information can be obtained
at www.ICGtesting.com
Printed in the USA
LVHW041331270123
738013LV00006B/383